Fantastic Tales
of Time and Space

SIGNET DOUBLE SCIENCE FICTION:

TODAY
WE
CHOOSE
FACES

and

BRIDGE
OF
ASHES

D1570655

SIGNET Science Fiction You'll Enjoy

☐ **THE REBEL WORLDS** by Poul Anderson.   (#E9046—$1.75)
☐ **A CIRCUS OF HELLS** by Poul Anderson.   (#E9045—$1.75)
☐ **DANCER FROM ATLANTIS** by Poul Anderson.
(#W7806—$1.50)
☐ **THE DAY OF THEIR RETURN** by Poul Anderson.
(#W7941—$1.50)
☐ **PEOPLE OF THE WIND** by Poul Anderson.   (#W7900—$1.50)
☐ **A TIME OF CHANGES** by Robert Silverberg. (#W7386—$1.50)
☐ **DOWNWARD TO THE EARTH** by Robert Silverberg.
(#W7134—$1.50)
☐ **BIBBLINGS** by Barbara Paul.   (#E8937—$1.75)
☐ **PILLARS OF SALT** by Barbara Paul.   (#E8619—$1.75)*
☐ **GREYBEARD** by Brian Aldiss.   (#E9035—$1.75)†
☐ **A CAT OF SILVERY HUE** (a horseclans novel) by Robert
Adams.   (#E8836—$1.75)*
☐ **THE SAVAGE MOUNTAINS** (a horseclans novel) by Robert
Adams.   (#E9034—$1.75)

* Price slightly higher in Canada
† Not available in Canada

Buy them at your local bookstore or use this convenient coupon for ordering.

THE NEW AMERICAN LIBRARY, INC.,
P.O. Box 999, Bergenfield, New Jersey 07621

Please send me the SIGNET BOOKS I have checked above. I am enclosing
$_____(please add 50¢ to this order to cover postage and
handling). Send check or money order—no cash or C.O.D.'s. Prices and
numbers are subject to change without notice.

Name _____

Address _____

City_____ State_____ Zip Code_____
Allow 4-6 weeks for delivery.
This offer is subject to withdrawal without notice.

TODAY WE CHOOSE FACES

and

BRIDGE OF ASHES

by
Roger Zelazny

A SIGNET BOOK
NEW AMERICAN LIBRARY
TIMES MIRROR

PUBLISHER'S NOTE

These novels are works of fiction. Names, characters, places, and incidents are either the product of the author's imagination or are used fictitiously, and any resemblance to actual persons, living or dead, events, or locales is entirely coincidental.

NAL BOOKS ARE AVAILABLE AT QUANTITY DISCOUNTS WHEN USED TO PROMOTE PRODUCTS OR SERVICES. FOR INFORMATION PLEASE WRITE TO PREMIUM MARKETING DIVISION, THE NEW AMERICAN LIBRARY, INC., 1633 BROADWAY, NEW YORK, NEW YORK 10019.

Today We Choose Faces: COPYRIGHT © 1973 BY ROGER ZELAZNY
Bridge of Ashes: COPYRIGHT © 1976 BY ROGER ZELAZNY

All rights reserved

These books originally appeared in paperback as separate volumes published by The New American Library.

 SIGNET TRADEMARK REG. U.S. PAT. OFF. AND FOREIGN COUNTRIES REGISTERED TRADEMARK—MARCA REGISTRADA HECHO EN CHICAGO, U.S.A.

SIGNET, SIGNET CLASSICS, MENTOR, PLUME, MERIDIAN AND NAL BOOKS *are published by The New American Library, Inc., 1633 Broadway, New York, New York 10019*

FIRST PRINTING (SIGNET DOUBLE SCIENCE FICTION), AUGUST, 1981

1   2   3   4   5   6   7   8   9

PRINTED IN THE UNITED STATES OF AMERICA

TODAY WE CHOOSE FACES

To Philip K. Dick,

electric shepherd

Part I

Drifting . . . Placid, yet relentless. Peaceful, yet merciless. Drifting.

A bolt of lightning, followed by an infinite sigh . . .

Rushing, falling . . .

A slow shower of jigsaw pieces, some of them coming together about me . . .

. . . And I began to know.

It was as if I had known all along, though.

Then the picture was complete, and I beheld it in its entirety as from a timeless vantage.

There was a sequence, of course, like vertebrae or dominoes, and it was not at all difficult to here, here, there it.

Here. For example.

. . . Leaving the club on a cold Saturday night in November. A little after 10:30, I guess. Eddie was with me, and we stood behind the glass doors at the front of the place, buttoning our overcoats and looking out at a damp Manhattan street, gusts of wind sailing bits of paper past us, while we waited for Denny to bring the car around. We said nothing. He knew I was still in a bad temper. I took out a cigarette. He hurried to light it for me.

Finally, the glossy black sedan drew up. I had just pulled one glove on and was holding the other. Eddie moved forward and opened the door, held it for me. I stepped outside and the chill air stung my eyes, bringing tears to them. I paused to get out a handkerchief and wipe them, mainly conscious then of the wind, the idling of the engine and a few distant horn notes.

As I lowered the handkerchief I became immediately aware of another figure which had appeared in the car, in the rear seat, and in the same instant realized that the rear window was down and that Eddie had moved six or seven paces away from me.

I heard some of the gunfire, felt the impact of a couple of the slugs. It was to be a long while before I learned that I had been hit four times.

My only consolation right before the lights went out was, twisting as I fell, seeing the smile vanish from Eddie's face, his hand jerking after, but not making it to his own weapon, and then the slow beginning of his topple.

And that was the last I ever saw of him, falling, an instant before he hit the pavement.

Here. For another.

Listening to Paul talk, I regarded what could have been a lovely view of a bright mountain lake fed by a little stream, a giant willow tree quivering beside it as if chilled by the water it tested with the green and shiny tips of its limbs. It was a fake. That is, it was real, but the picture was relayed from a spot hundreds of miles away. It was more pleasant than looking out a window from his upper-floor apartment, though, when all I could see would be a section—albeit a neat, attractive area—of that urban complex which extended from New York to Washington. The suite was soundproof, air-conditioned and I suppose tastefully decorated in accordance with the best sensibility of the times. I could not judge, since I was not yet familiar with the times. Its brandy was excellent, though.

"... Must have been puzzling as all hell," Paul was saying. "I am amazed at how quickly you have adapted."

I turned and looked at him again, a slim, still-young, dark-haired man with an engaging smile and eyes that really told nothing of what went on behind. He was still a thing of fascination for me. My grandson, with six or seven greats in front of the word. I kept looking for resemblances, finding them where least expected. The jut of the brow, the short upper lip, heavy lower one. The nose was his own, but then he had our way of quirking the left corner of his mouth at moments of pique or amusement.

I sent the smile back.

"Nothing that amazing about it," I replied. "The fact that I made the provisions I did should have indicated I had done some thinking about the future."

"I guess so," he said. "But to tell the truth, my only

thought was that you had been looking for an out on death."

"Of course I was. I was aware of the possibility of my getting it the way that I did, and while body-freezing was still a fairly novel thing back in the 'seventies—"

"The *nineteen*-seventies," he interrupted, with another smile.

"Yes, I do make it sound like just a couple of years ago, don't I? Try it sometime and you will understand the feeling. Anyway, I figured what the hell. If I got shot down, whatever got damaged might be replaceable— someday. Why not set things up to have them freeze me and hope for the best? I had read a few articles on the subject, and it sounded like it might work. So I did. After that, it was funny . . . It got to be kind of an obsession with me. I mean, I got to thinking about it quite a bit, the way a real religious man might think about heaven—like, 'When I die, I'll go to the future.' Then I found myself wondering more and more what it would be like. I did a lot of thinking and a lot of reading, trying to figure different ways that things might work out. It wasn't a bad hobby," I said, taking another drink. "It gave me a lot of fun, and as things turned out it's paying off."

"Yes," he said. "So you were not really surprised to learn that a means of traveling faster than light was developed, and that we have visited worlds beyond the solar system?"

"Of course I was surprised. But I had been hoping for it."

"And the recent successes in teleportation, on an interstellar scale?"

"I was more surprised at that. Pleasantly, though. Hooking the outposts together that way will be a great achievement."

"Then let me ask you what you have found the most surprising."

"Well," I said, finding myself a seat and taking another sip, "outside of the fact that we managed to get this far and still have not found a way to remove the possibility of war—" I raised a hand at this point as he began to interrupt me with something about controls and sanctions. He shut up. I was glad to see that he respected his elders. "Outside of that," I went on, "I suppose that the single

11

most surprising thing to me is that we have gone more or less legitimate."

He grinned.

"What do you mean 'more or less'?"

I shrugged.

"Well?" I said.

"We are as legitimate as anybody," he countered, "or we would never have been able to get listed on the World Stock Exchange."

I said nothing, but found another smile.

"Of course, it is a very well-run organization."

"I would be disappointed if it were not."

"Just so, just so," he said. "But there we are. COSA Inc. All legal, proper and respectable. Been that way for generations. The tendency in that direction had actually begun in your day, with—as feature writers liked to put it—the 'laundering' of funds and their reinvestment in more acceptable enterprises. Why fight the system when you are strong enough to be big in it without fighting? What are a few dollars one way or the other when you can have everything you want and security, too? Without the risks. Just by following the rules."

"All of them?"

"Well, there are so many that it has become, if anything, easier, when you can afford the brainpower."

He finished his drink, fetched us refills.

"There is no stigma," he concluded then. "The image we had in your day is ancient history now."

He leaned forward conspiratorily.

"It must really have been something, though, living in those times," he said, and then he looked at me expectantly.

I did not know whether to be irritated or flattered. From the way they had been treating me since my arousal a couple of weeks earlier, I obviously shared some historical niche with the bedpan and the brontosaurus. On the other hand, Paul seemed to regard me with more than a little pride, rather like a family heirloom which had been entrusted to his keeping. By then, I was aware that his position in the organization's power structure was both secure and potent. He had insisted that I be his houseguest, though I could have been put up elsewhere. He seemed to take a great delight in getting me to talk

12

about my life and times. I learned slowly that his knowledge of these things was largely based on the gaudier writings, films and rumors of the day. Still, I was eating his food, sleeping under his roof, we were relatives and the statutes had long since run. So I obliged him with some reminiscences.

It might have disappointed him that I had spent a couple of years in college before taking over my father's business when he met his sudden, untimely end, but the fact that I spent a chunk of my earliest life in Sicily before he had sent for the family seemed to make up for this. Then I believe I disappointed him again when I told him that to the best of my knowledge there had never been a worldwide criminal conspiracy centered there. I saw the *onorata società* as a local, not unbeneficial, family-centered thing, which had in its time produced such notable *galantuomi* as Don Vito Cascio Ferro and Don Calò Vizzini. I tried to explain that there was a necessary distinction between the *società degli amici* with its own, parochial interests and individuals who migrated, who may or may not have been *amici*, who engaged in illicit activities and preferred doing business with one another rather than with strangers, and who preserved a strong family tradition. Paul was as much a victim of the conspiracy mystique as any tabloid devourer, however, and was convinced I was still preserving some secret tradition or other. I gradually came to see that he was something of a romantic, that he wanted things to have been the other way, that he wanted to be part of the unreal tradition. So I told him some of the things I knew he would enjoy hearing.

I told him how I had dealt with the matter of my father's passing, as well as several other encounters which helped justify my name, Angelo di Negri. Somewhere along the line, the family had later changed it to Nero. Not that that mattered to me. I was who I was. And Paul Nero smiled and nodded and lapped up the details. He had an infinite capacity for secondhand violence.

All of which may sound somewhat contemptuous, but is not, not really. For I came to like him considerably as time went on. Perhaps this was because he reminded me somewhat of myself, in another time and place—a softer, easier-going, more urbane version. Perhaps he was like

13

something that I might have been, or wished that I could have afforded the luxury of trying to be.

But I was pushing forty. My character had long ago hardened. Though the circumstances that shaped me had long since passed, my pleasures in a, to me, almost pressureless society, were infiltrated by notes scored to a different measure, resulting at first in a vague uneasiness, to be followed by a growing dissatisfaction. Life is seldom so pivotally crisis-conditioned a thing as novelists would have us believe. While it is true that we sometimes recover from shocks with a sense of the freshness of reality and the wonder of existence, this state of mind does pass away—and fairly rapidly, at that—leaving both reality and ourselves untransfigured once more. Consciousness of this fact came to me as I sat sentimentalizing past crudities for my descendant, and grew into a major discontent during the weeks that followed. I had not changed much, though everything else had. It was not completely a sense of being superfluous, though there was something of that, nor could it be nostalgia, as my memories were sufficiently recent and substantial to preclude any glossing over of what, to Paul, was the distant past. Perhaps it was a growing sensitivity to the fact that people seemed a trifle gentler, more pacific, that aroused some feelings of inferiority, as though I had just missed out on some necessary step in the process of civilization. I was not ordinarily given to such introspection, but when feelings become sufficiently strong and persistent they force their own exploration.

Still, how does one picture his mental life to anyone, let alone one who seems a distorted image of himself? What I wanted to say was manifold and not the sort of thing that could really be communicated by words.

Paul may have done better than I thought in understanding it, in understanding me, though. For he made two suggestions, one of which I followed immediately, while thinking about the other.

There. For example.

I went back to Sicily. An almost predictable thing, I would say, for a man in my circumstances and state of mind. Aside from the obvious associations it held, reaching back to my childhood, I had learned that it was one of the remaining places in the world which had not yet suffered

14

from overdevelopment. It was then, in a very real way, a means of traveling back through time for me.

I did not stay long in Palermo, but headed almost immediately into the hinterland. I rented an isolated place that had a familiar feeling to it, and spent several hours every day riding one of the two horses that had come with it. Mornings, I would ride down to the rocky shore and watch the surf come creaming and booming toward me, picking my way along the wet shingles it slid from, listening to the squawks of the birds as they arced and dipped above it, breathing the acrid sea-wind, watching the play of dazzle and shade across the graywhitebleak prospect. Afternoons or evenings, as the mood moved me, I would often ride in the hills, where scraggly grass and twisted trees clung desperately to the thin soil and the damp breath of the Mediterranean drifted sultry or cool, as the mood moved it, about me. If I did not stare too long at the several stationary stars, if I did not raise my eyes when a transport vehicle flashed high and fast over head, if I refrained from using the communications unit for anything but music and rode to the nearest small town but once every week or so for perishable supplies, it was almost as though no time at all had passed for me. Not just the intervening century, but my entire adult life seemed to recede and fade into the timeless landscape of my youth. So what happened then was not wholly inexplicable.

Her name was Julia, and I encountered her for the first time in a rocky cul-de-sac that grew lush by comparison with the bruise-colored hills through which I had been riding all that afternoon. She was seated on the ground beneath a tree which resembled a frozen fountain of marmalade to which some pale confetti had adhered, her dark hair drawn back and fastened with a coral clip, sketchpad in her lap, eyes darting and hand shifting, precise, deliberate, as she sketched a small flock of sheep. For a time, I just sat there and watched her, but then a cloud moved on and the emerging sun cast my long shadow down past her.

She turned then, and shaded her eyes. I dismounted, twisted the reins about a nearby shrub's handiest branch and headed down.

"Hello," I said, as I approached.

15

It was ten or fifteen seconds before I reached her, and it took her that long to decide to nod and smile slightly.

"Hello," she said.

"My name's Angelo. I was riding by and saw you, saw this place—thought it might be pleasant to stop and smoke a cigarette, to watch you draw. If that's all right?"

She nodded, bit into the lower half of a new smile, accepted a cigarette.

"I'm Julia," she said. "I work here."

"Artist in residence?"

"Bio-tech. This is just a hobby," she said, tapping the pad and letting her hand remain to cover her work.

"Oh? What are you bioteching?"

She nodded toward the woolly crowd.

"Her," she said.

"Which one is she?"

"All of them."

"I'm afraid I don't follow . . ."

"They are clones," she said, "each one grown from the tissue of a single donor."

"Neat trick, that," I said. "Tell me about clones," and I seated myself on the grass and watched it being eaten.

She seemed to welcome the opportunity to close the pad without letting me see her work. She launched into the story of her flock, and it required only a few questions here and there for me to learn somewhat of herself also.

She was originally from Catania, but she had been to school in France and was presently in the employ of an institute in Switzerland which was doing research in animal husbandry and was employing cloning techniques to field-test promising specimens in various environments simultaneously. She was twenty-six and had just ended a marriage on a very sour note and gotten herself transferred to the field with a test flock. She had been back in Sicily for a little over two months. She told me a lot about clones, really warming to the subject in the face of my obvious ignorance, describing in overabundant detail the processes whereby her sheep had been grown from cellular specimens of a hybrid in Switzerland to replicate her in all details. She even told me of the peculiar and still not understood resonance effect, which involved the fact that all of them would exhibit temporary symptoms of the same illness should one of them be stricken—in-

16

cluding the original in Switzerland and others in other parts of the world. No, to the best of her knowledge, cloning had not yet been attempted at the level of human beings—myriad legal, scientific and religious objections existed—although there were rumors concerning experimentation on one of the outpost worlds. While she apparently knew her business quite well, it struck me after a time that her words were put forth more with a pleasure at having someone to talk to than from any desire too inform. And we had this, too, in common.

But I did not tell her my own story that day. I listened, we sat a time in silence, watching the sheep, watching the lengthening shadows, talked again, in a desultory fashion, of small, neutral matters. As we talked, a mutual assumption gradually became manifest in our speech, that this was but a part of a continuing conversation, that I would be back, the next day or the day after, that we would be seeing one another again, and again. Nor was this assumption incorrect.

Before very long, she became interested in horseback riding. Soon we were riding together every day, mornings or evenings, sometimes both. I told her where I was from, and how, omitting only what I had done there and the exact nature of my passing. I did not realize that I was falling in love until long after we had become lovers. I did not discover the fact until the day I determined to reach a decision on Paul's second suggestion and I realized how much of a factor she had become in my thinking.

I rose, crossed the room to the window, drew back the curtain, stared up through the night. The embers in the grate still glowed cherry and orange. The outer cold had passed through the walls and was pressing now like a spiritual glacier toward our corner of the room.

"I must be leaving soon," I said.

"Where will you go?"

"I may not say."

Silence. Then, "Will you be coming back?"

I had no answer, though I wished I did.

"Would you like me to?"

Silence again. Then, "Yes."

"I will try to," I said.

Why was I going to take the Styler contract? I had

wanted to from the moment Paul had described the situation to me. A high-level sinecure with the company and a big block of expensive stock were but the surface returns on the thing. I had no illusion that my thawing, my treatment, my recovery had been the result of an unsullied desire for my company on the part of my descendants. The necessary techniques had been available for several decades. It is not unpleasant to feel needed, however, no matter what the reasons. My pleasure at their attentiveness was in no way vitiated by the knowledge that I had something they wanted. If anything, it was enhanced. What other hold had I on the day? I was more than just a curiosity. I had a value that went beyond the emotions of the moment, and its realization could restore to me some measure of mastery, could earn me another sort of appreciation. I had been thinking about this, or something like it, earlier when I had drawn rein above the nearest village at a place where the olive terraces rose to scrub and bleakness, and stared down at the light and movement. Shortly, Julia came up beside me.

"What is it?" she had asked.

I was wondering at that moment what it would have been like if I had awakened with no memories of my earlier existence. Would it have made it easier or more difficult to find me some slot in life, to be satisfied with it? Might I then be like the inhabitants of the village below, bringing interest and something of pleasure to simple actions at their ten thousandth repetition?

Standing beside a shallow, sheltered inlet on a warm, bright afternoon, watching the reflected ripple of the water trace trembling lines across her naked breasts as she stopped splashing and the smile went out of her face and she said, "What is it?" I was thinking of the seventeen men I had killed back when they had begun calling me "Angie the Angel," as I had risen through the ranks to secure that earlier existence. Paul had not known about all of the killings, of course. I was surprised that he had known of as many as he did—eight, to be exact, the names spoken with a measure of confidence I did not feel he could have faked. For my part, I found it virtually inconceivable that the legal niceties and organization-chart formalities had become something more than a facade, that in fact there were few reliable professional

18

killers to be had any more. So it seemed that I had indeed brought something of value across the years with me. I had for the most part personally eschewed such activities, however, once I had secured my position at a higher level within the organization. Now, to be offered a contract, in a sedate time of almost total cultural availability, smoothly meshing gears, life prolongation and interstellar travel . . . It seemed more than a little strange, no matter how delicately Paul put it.

As we had eaten oranges in the shade of the water-processing plant, its doubtless onetime sleek and shiny walls softened partly by weather and partly by the intervention of lilac and wisteria to a monastery-like finish, I had stroked her hair and she had plucked the pale-green hellebore, that ancient remedy for madness, tangling those flowers in my own, and my thoughts had strayed beyond the severely drawn diagrams of skull and walls, softened by their froths of blossoms, and into the completely automatic workings of the installation, whose sounds were repeated to us, softly, inevitably, as it took in, purified and spewed through underground conduits I knew not how many thousands of gallons of the sea, and I considered the dual nature of Herbert Styler, field representative for Doxford Industries on the planet called Alvo, so far removed from the pale human star we formed as to be equally inconceivable, but this time she did not notice and say, "What is it?" as I wondered whether the man who had undergone experimental neural abridgment of a kind still illegal on Earth, supposedly permitting him full conscious access to the workings of a great computer complex, whether this man, who, for his company, stood in the way of COSA's expansion on the choicest of the outworlds, could be considered a machine with a human personality or a man with a computer mind, and whether what I had been asked to do was properly homicide or something totally new—say, mechanicide or cybicide— while the muted thudding of the sea and the nearer vibration of the waterworks came into us, along with the fragrances of the blossoms and the touch of salt the breezes bore.

Paul had assured me that I would be given the best training and equipment available for the fulfillment of the contract. He had then recommended that I take a trip.

"Get away for a time," he had said, and, "Think about it."

Staring up through the night, feeling the cold, wondering whether I could kill him, get away, come back and start over, fresh and clean, belonging here, my other life as dead and sealed then . . .

"I will try to," I said, and let the curtain fall.

Here, then.

. . . Seeing her seated beneath that crazy holiday-tree, soft hair fixed with a pale, coral clip, head and hand moving as she transferred her sheep to paper, precise, deliberate; then a brightening of the day, the fall of my shadow, her attention, the turning of her head, the movement of her arm as she raised her hand to shade her eyes, me dismounting, twisting the reins about a branch, starting down toward her, reaching for a word, a face, her nod, her slow smile . . .

Here.

. . . Seeing the fire-flowers unfold all in a row beneath me, the final blossom covering half of the building, its target; my vehicle faltering, diving, burning then, myself ejected, the cabin intact about me and moving with a life of its own, dodging, darting, firing, downward and forward, downward and forward, coming apart then and dropping me gently, gently down, my prosthetic armor making the barest of clicks as my feet touch the ground and the repellors cut off; and then my lasers lancing forward, cutting through the figures who advance upon me, grenades flying from my hands, waves of protoplasm-shattering ultrasonics flowing from me like notes from some rung, invisible bell . . .

How many androids and robots I smashed, mockup buildings I razed, obstacles I destroyed, projectiles I hurled in the two months that followed, there on that barren worldlet where I was taken to be familiarized with all the latest methods of violence, I do not know. Many. My instructors were technicians, not killers, who would later undergo memory-erasure, to protect both the organization and themselves. The discovery that this was possible intrigued me, recalling to me some of my earlier thoughts. The techniques, I learned, were highly sophisticated and could be employed quite selectively. They had been in use for years as a psychotherapeutic tool. The instructors, for

20

their part, were a strange mixture of attitudes and moods, at first exhorting me almost constantly to perfect my techniques with their weapons while scrupulously avoiding any reference to the fact that I would soon be using them to kill someone. Later, however, as the realization gathered that whatever they said or felt or thought would subsequently be removed from their consciousness, they began to joke frequently about death and killing and their feelings toward me seemed to undergo a reversal. From an initial state of undisguised contempt, they came in a matter of weeks to regard me with something approaching reverence, as if I were a sort of priest and they vicarious participants in a sacrifice. This disturbed me, and I took to avoiding them as much as possible on my own time. For me, the job was simply something that I had to do, to find my place in what seemed a better society than the one I had left. It was then that I began to wonder whether people were changing rapidly enough to assure the race's continued existence, if these men could revert so readily, reach so eagerly for a violence-fix. I had few illusions concerning myself, and I was willing to try to live with me for the rest of my life; but I had considered them my moral superiors, and it was their society I was trying to buy into. It was not until near the end of my training, however, that I learned something of the dynamics which underlay their altered attitude. Hanmer, one of the least objectionable of my instructors, came to my quarters one night, bearing a bottle which made him somewhat welcome. He had already done considerable work on its predecessor, and his face, which normally bore the certainty of expression generally found only on ventriloquists' dummies, had grown rather slack, his voice slowed from its usual chatter to a thing of slow puzzlement. It was not long before I learned what was bothering him. The sanctions and controls were not doing so well. It appeared that a limited armed conflict—the situation to which I had alluded when speaking with Paul some time before—had moved several steps nearer actuality, was indeed imminent, as Hanmer saw it. The politics of it bored me, for they were not yet mine, but the possibility of its occurring at all, with the ever-present danger of its growing into something large and terrifying, was ironic as well as

21

alarming. To come all this way, and in the manner that I did, just to arrive in time for a worldwide conflagration ... No! It was absurd. Absolutely. It began to seem that their proximity to an instrument of violence, myself, at a time like this had served to trigger something quite deep-seated and well suppressed within these men. While it had released something violent and irrational within the others, in the case of Hanmer, who, after a time, sat monotonously repeating, "It can't happen," it had broken something.

"It may not," I said, to hearten him, since it was his whisky I was drinking.

He looked at me then. Hope seemed to flicker for a moment, then went away from his eyes.

"What do you care?" he said.

"I care. It's my world, too. Now."

He looked away.

"I don't understand you," he said at last. "Or the others, for that matter ..."

I thought that I did, though it was of small help to anybody. All my emotions at the moment were things based on absence.

I waited. I did not know him well enough to know why his reaction should be different from the others', and I never did find out. He said one other thing that remained with me, though.

"... But I think everybody ought to be locked up till they learn how to behave."

Trite, laughable and quite impossible, of course. At the time.

Mixing the remainder of the booze into two stiff ones, I hastened him on his way to oblivion, partly regretting there was not a bit more around, so that I might follow him.

Here, here, and then: There ...

                          .

[Stars]   . [Out of the tunnel

                         . under the sky & down]

                         .

                         .

[Entry]   .   [Strobe lights
                           .   & thunder]
                           .
                           .
                           .
                           .
                           .   [Song of the air]
[Clouds   .   [Invisible fingers
                           .   of matter]
                           .
                           .
                           .
      clouds   .
                           .
                           .
        cl ou d   s] .
                           .
                           .
[Explosion #1]   .   [Lasciate ogni
        [#2]   [#3]   .   sper-   anza
                           .   voi   ch'
                           .   en-   trate?]
                           .
                           .

     . . . were flashes like scissors of lightning cutting the sky apart. Despite the shielding and my distance from the detonations, I was batted about like a shuttlecock. I was hunched forward in my battle armor, letting the computer deal with these disturbances, but ready to cut in on manual should the need arise. Alvo flashed beneath me in a too-quick pattern of greenbrown-grayblue for me to distinguish features, unless perhaps I had had the time to simply sit and stare down at it. But I was not especially tense as I wound the miles inside me, annihilating the distance, threading its thunder. To do the job as quickly as was deemed necessary now allowed no time for subtlety. Doxford's internal security setup was too strong for anything short of a years-long infiltration campaign. A surprise thrust, a juggernaut attack, had therefore been decided upon as having the best possibility for success. Styler's defense was excellent, but we had expected nothing less.

He must have picked me up almost immediately upon my appearance in the vicinity of Alvo. I spent little time wondering at the technical feat involved in my detection, as I swept along, low now, speeding toward that fortress of an office complex where he made his headquarters, but I wondered what Styler's thoughts and feelings must have been when first he had noted me. How long had he expected this attack? How much might he know concerning it?

For a time then, I dodged or withstood everything he threw at me, my own weapons systems ready to come into play in an instant. I hoped to at least commence my assault from the air.

A crackle of static, a whistle, a sound of heavy breathing. My radio had come to life. I had not expected this. It seemed something of an exercise in futility for anyone to try to threaten or cajole me at this point.

However, "Unidentified vessel and etcetera, you are passing over unauthorized such-and-such. You are ordered to . . ." did not emerge.

Instead, "Angie the Angel," I heard. "Welcome to Alvo. Are you finding your brief visit interesting?"

So he knew who I was. And it was Styler himself speaking. I had heard his voice and viewed his likeness many times in the course of my preparations. I had had to force my instructors to cut a programmed accompaniment of vilification which had been part of the familiarization sessions, as I had found it distracting. They found it difficult to believe that I did not feel it necessary to hate the short, pale-eyed man with the puffy cheeks and the turban about his head that covered the terminals of his permanent implants. "Of course it is propaganda," they said, "but it will help you when the time comes." I shook my head slowly. "I do not need emotions to help me kill," I told them. "They might even get in the way." They had to accept this, but it was plain that they did not understand.

So he knew who I was. It was surprising, but hardly prostrating. Tremendous amounts of current information were regularly dumped into his computer adjunct, and he was supposedly possessed of a sound, somewhat spectacular mind, complete with imagination. So while I felt he was guessing, it was doubtless a very informed guess, and of course an accurate one. I saw no reason to talk with him, though; or, for that matter, not to talk with him. It made no difference at all to me. Words could change nothing.

Still, "It *will* be a brief visit," he insisted. "You will not be leaving here, you know."

A shaft of something like lightning ran through a dark cloud, ahead/beside/behind me. The ship shook, some circuits sputtered, a wave of static took away some of Styler's words.

".. are not the first," he said. "Obviously, none of the others . . ."

Others? He could have tossed that out just hoping to upset me. But it was something I had not considered. Paul had never said that I was the first to attempt this. In fact, thinking about it, it was probable that I was not. While this did not disturb me, I did wonder how many others there might have been.

No matter. Contemporary kids. They had probably required the brainwashing business, had needed to work up a hatred in order to essay the thing. Their business. Their funerals. It was not my way.

"You can still call it off, Angel," he said. "Land your vessel and remain with it. I will send someone to pick you up. You will live. What do you say?"

I chuckled. He must have heard it, because, "At least I know you are there," he said. "Your attack is an exercise in futility in more ways than one. Outside of the fact that you have no chance of succeeding and will doubtless die here, and soon, the reasons for your making the effort at all have been removed."

He paused then, as if waiting for me to say something. That was his exercise in futility.

"Not interested, eh?" he said then. "Any moment now my defensive assault will pierce your screen. COSA had no way of knowing what I have added to the system since their previous effort. Any one of these next might do it."

25

There followed a series of jarring explosions. I emerged from these without mishap, however.

"Still there," he observed. "Good. That still allows you a chance to change your mind. I would like you to live, you know, as I should be very interested in talking with a man like you, from another time, a man with your background. As I began to say, there are other reasons than fatal obstacles for giving the thing up. I do not know what you may or may not have heard, because I know you have been offworld for a time, but it is true that there has been a war—and I suppose, technically, it is still in progress. From all reports I have received, the Earth is in a pretty sorry state just now. Both of our employers have been very hard-hit. In fact, I believe we lack home offices at the moment. This being the case, I see more need for salvaging whatever remains of both organizations than for continuing our conflict. What do you say?"

Of course I said nothing. I had no way to verify any of his talk, and he had no way of proving it to me, unless I were willing to land and take a look at whatever he might have to offer in the way of evidence—which was naturally out of the question. So there was no basis for conversation on that count.

I heard him sigh, across a tiny rivulet of static.

"You are determined that there be more death," he said then. "You think that everything I have told you is purely self-serving in nature . . ."

I almost cut him off then, because I do not like people who tell me what I am thinking, whether or not they are right. Still, it was the best show in town . . .

"Why don't you say something?" he said. "I would like to hear your voice. Tell me why you are about this business. If it is only money, I will pay you more to give it up—whatever they are paying you—and protect you afterward." He paused, waited, then went on, "Of course, with you, there is probably something else involved, too. Family loyalty. Solidarity. The tribal blood-bond. That sort of thing. If that is what it is, I will tell you something. You are probably the only one around who believes in it the old way any more. They do not. I know these men, have known them well for years, whereas you have only known them for a brief while. It is true. Their values are no longer yours. They are capitalizing on your loyalty.

26

They are using you. *Are* you doing it out of family loyalty? Is that what it is?"

His voice had sounded a bit strained near the end there. It was more relaxed when he started in again.

"It is a bit frustrating, talking to you this way," he said, "knowing you are out there, coming closer and closer by the moment—hearing me. Still, I see it your way now. You are determined. Nothing that I can say can change your mind. I can only try to kill you before you kill me. You are moving and I am fixed at this location. It is too late for me to try to flee. You will not succeed, of course. But, as I said, I see it your way now. You have nothing to say to me, and I really have nothing to say to you. This is what irritates me. You are not like the others. They all talked, you know. They threatened me, they cursed me, they died screaming. You are an ignorant barbarian, incapable of understanding what I am, but this does not deter you, does not disturb you. Does it? I was attempting something intended to benefit the entire human race, but this does not bother you. Does it? You simply remain silent and keep coming. Have you ever read Pascal? No. Of course you haven't ... 'Man is but a reed, the most feeble thing in nature,' he said, 'but he is a thinking reed. The entire universe need not arm itself to crush him. A vapor, a drop of water, suffices to kill him. But if the universe were to crush him, man would still be more noble than that which killed him, because he knows that he dies and the advantage which the universe has over him; the universe knows nothing of this.' Do you understand what I am saying? No, of course not. You never think of these matters. You are a vapor, a drop of water ... There comes a time, if there is some sort of fulfillment in life, when one can accept death, I believe, without too much in the way of resentment. I have not yet achieved such a state, but I have been working on it. Let me tell you—"

At that moment, the barrage rose to a sudden pitch of fierceness that lit up the sky, drowned all lesser sounds and hit me with shock waves that came like a maniac surf.

But then my target rocked into view, the Doxford Building, backed against the hills at the far end of a distant valley.

Moments later, I began the attack. Fountains of light

27

erupted from the floor of the valley and on the hillside. The right corner of the building crumbled, there was fire on the roof . . .

I was hit myself, within instants of that small triumph, and immediately began the downward tumble. As I had not been ejected, I realized that the control section must be reasonably intact. A quick survey—physical, and via the warning-board—showed me that this was so. There had been a successful separation, though, and I caught glimpses of the twisted outer framework of the vessel plunging groundward.

Another hit, and while my armor would probably save me, I would be ejected. If I could make it to the ground with the cabin intact, though . . .

"Are you still alive?" I heard Styler saying. "I see a piece—"

There came an explosion that took my attention away from his words, shaking, jolting, tumbling me about. I had the controls on manual by then, for I did not want to slow my descent until the last possible moment.

"Angel? Are you still there?"

I managed to convert all the necessary systems as I fell, braked at the last possible instant, hit at a bad angle, rolled, stabilized, brought the vehicle around intact. I slapped it into gear and rolled forward immediately after that.

I was at the opposite end of the still-smoking, dust-misted valley from the Doxford complex. It was quite rocky, and full of craters and potholes, not all of them recently formed. This seemed to lend some credibility to the assertion that mine was not the first attack on the place. It also made it difficult for the defenders to mine the area, a fact that came in handy as I proceeded through it, looking for potential boobytraps.

I could not help wondering whether he had spoken the truth about the war, though. My few tenuous links with the past and my only important ones with the present were all involved. I could see no reason for anyone bombing Sicily, though. But was she still there? Several months had passed, and people were very mobile these days. And how was Paul? And some of the others I had met? I knew they possessed elaborate shelters. Still . . .

"You *are* alive! I've got you on the screens. Good! This

makes it even easier for you to throw in your hand. No worry about landing on a mine once you are already down. Listen. All you have to do is stop and wait now. I will send someone to pick you up. I will show you evidence to support everything I have said. What do you say?"

I eased my guns forward in their mounts, and swung them, elevated them, lowered them, to test the mountings.

"That, I take it, is your answer?" he said. "Look, it will gain you absolutely nothing to die here—and that is exactly what will happen. Our employers are both out of business by now. Your range is being taken even now, and you will shortly be blown to bits. It is senseless. Life is a precious thing, and so much of it has just vanished recently. The human race has just been more than decimated, and that remainder may well be reduced to a tenth also, from the lingering effects of this thing. Then there are the present difficulties facing the qualified remainder—rounding up the survivors and providing for them, rigging sufficient teleportation gates, transporting them offworld, trying to resettle them. The Earth is barely habitable, and conditions will continue to worsen. Most of the outworlds are not ready for prolonged human habitation, and we are in no position to change them further at the moment. Some sort of shelters have to be set up, communications established and maintained among the worlds. There is no need for more deaths, and I am offering you a chance to live. Can you accept that? Do you believe me?"

I achieved a fairly level run of rock and increased my speed. Through the smoke, the dust, the fumes, I could see that flames flickered behind the hole I had knocked in his fortress. No matter how certain he tried to sound as to his ability to destroy me, he could not gainsay the fact that I had scored a hit.

From somewhere at his end of the valley, the firing began—first short, then long, taking my measure. I varied my speeds, was thankful when I reached an irregular incline and started up it, for the angle seemed to throw them off a bit. I readied my rockets, though I hoped I could get in closer before firing them. I checked the time, sighed. It was past the time for arrival and detonation of the two high-powered missiles that had separated from the flier the same time I had and gone on ahead. He had gotten them, then. Their chances had not really been that good, though.

Then the barrage began, shaking me, jarring me, bouncing me about. The noise became deafening, the flashes near-blinding, the smoke heavy. The ground vibrated, and fragments of rock were blasted against the vehicle, fell upon it in an almost steady hail.

"Hello? Hello?" I heard faintly within the noise. Then whatever followed was drowned out by three that came very close.

I swerved sharply, moved at an angle, straightened, utilizing the cover afforded by several high stands of stone. The firing became more erratic, falling farther and farther away from me. My radio had gone dead once I had gotten in behind the rocky hedge. I kept advancing, spotted a tricky and roundabout way leading off to my left and took it because it seemed somewhat sheltered. It did seem to baffle his detection, because his shots kept landing farther and farther afield.

As I worked my twisted way along, I almost overlooked another complex of buildings, deep in a coomb, still farther to my left. They were very new and seemed completely deserted. They had not been mentioned in my orientation, had not been indicated on any of the maps or photos I had studied. I kept them covered until I had passed, but had no reason to fire.

As I climbed higher, the radio found his voice again, faintly at first, strengthening as I went.

". . . So you see," he was saying, "I am free for the first time in my life, free to use some of these things I have developed as they should be used—noncommercially, for the benefit of the entire race—to help get us through these perilous times. There is a great need for my abilities, my facilities, now. Even the cloning tech—"

I had been spotted. A series of heavy explosions occurred behind me. Moments later, I had rounded my sheltering rocks and was out in the open once more. There was scant cover for hundreds of yards, and the way was entirely uphill. I moved forward with all the speed I possessed, knowing that my luck had just about run and hoping that it would hold a few moments more so that I

30

could fire my rockets. From the position I then occupied, it would be virtually impossible to reach him.

The next ones landed far ahead of me, and I swerved to avoid the blasted area. Moments later, there was another to the rear, very close this time.

But I made it to my shelter, spent a handful of heartbeats working in close and toward the right while the rocks were pounded and splintered ahead of me, then ventured a diagonal dash toward another, nearer refuge.

I did not deserve to make it, and I almost didn't. I was hit seconds after I pulled out, and I spun completely around. I was lifted off the ground, dropped, bounced and given a sudden, unexpected view of the shattered landscape through an eighteen-inch hole in the shielding a little above my left shoulder. But I was able to keep moving, despite a clanking noise and a heavy sway to the left, and I made it to the next sanctuary, a row of explosions trailing like knots in a kite tail behind me.

I had made it around halfway up the valley, which was about as good as could be expected. Maybe even better, all things considered. I nosed in close again, bore to the right. I pulled out at the far end, where I was screened by an overlapping mass of boulders about fifty feet ahead. I made my way up to them and kept bearing right, until I had gone about as far as I could go without exposing myself. This was about two hundred yards beyond my previous shelter, which was then taking quite a pounding. I had no idea what the layout was on the other side, so I decided to investigate on foot.

I left everything running, including the radio, with its faint, importuning, "Are you there, Angel? Are you still there?" and I climbed down onto the rocky ground, feeling its continuing vibrations through my armor, and I smelled burning chemicals and tasted salty dust.

I circled carefully, keeping close to the boulder, dropping to my belly and crawling the final distance as I rounded it. As I did this, I picked up Styler's voice on my suit-radio.

"I'm sorry it had to be this way, Angie," he said. "If you are still alive and can hear me, I hope you believe that. For whatever it is worth, everything that I said was true. I was not lying to you . . ."

Yes! If I brought it around to the right and up that

sharp upswing, I would have a clear line of fire! If I got all the rockets off, there was a sharp downgrade I might be able to reach. It led to what looked like a dried-out streambed . . .

". . . I am just going to keep firing now until nothing remains. You have left me no alternative . . ."

I made my way back to the vehicle and rechecked all systems. The rocks behind me would soon be a gravel pit. Or sand.

Everything was ready. Any second now he might throw something really heavy this way, too. I had to be fast.

I clanked forward and up at a respectable speed. At times, the list almost made it seem as if I were about to topple to the left.

I made it, though, had a momentary, clear view of the Doxford headquarters, flameless now, but emitting a great plume of gray smoke, and then I halted, locked in and fired my rockets, one after the other, each jolt threatening to knock me back down the slope.

I did not wait to see the result, but plunged ahead the moment the last missile had been discharged.

I reached the bottom of the downgrade, swung left and kept going. Very soon thereafter, the rise from which I had fired erupted in flame and was reduced to a smoldering crater. A shower of gravel pelted me moments later.

I continued undisturbed for what seemed a long while. The firing continued, but it fell in a random pattern now and seemed a trifle more sporadic than it had been.

I could not leave the gulley at the rock-shrouded spot I desired. I tried, but the engine was not able to haul me up the slope. Its clanking had grown more ominous, also; and I detected the smell of burning insulation.

When I finally reached the only grade it could take, I pressed on up it and discovered that I was within four hundred yards of Styler's citadel.

The near side of the building had caved in completely, and I could see flames dancing beyond the rubble. There was more smoke than before. The guns—wherever they were, whatever sort they were—went crazy briefly, then fell silent. This lasted for perhaps ten seconds. Then one of them commenced firing again, slowly, regularly, at some imaginary target far off to the right and back. A long line of squat, heavy-treaded robots was drawn up

32

before the building, absolutely still, presumably guarding the place.

"All right, you were lucky," Styler said, and his voice sounded strange after the long silence. "I cannot deny the damage you have done, but you have come about as far as you can. Believe me, it is a lunatic mission. Your vehicle is about ready to break down and the robots will swamp you. Your death will be useless to anyone, damn it!"

The robots began to roll toward me then, raising what were obviously weapons. I opened fire on them.

The sound of his breathing filled the cabin as I advanced, shooting, and the robots did the same.

I destroyed about half of them before the vehicle collapsed and began coming apart around me. One of the guns still worked, though, so I stayed with it, firing, adjusting the devices on my armor the while. I was hit quite a few times personally, but the suit held fairly well against the laser slashes and the projectiles.

"Is there really someone there?" Styler finally said. "Or have I been talking to a machine? I thought I heard you laugh earlier. But hell! That could have been a recording! Are you really there, Angel? Or is something that knows nothing of it in the process of crushing a reed? Say something, will you? Anything. Give me some sign there is an intelligence out there!"

The robots had divided themselves into two groups and flowed toward me in a sort of pincer movement. I hammered away at those on the right until my gun was destroyed. I damaged four of them before this happened, and the grenade that I threw as I leaped from my burning wreck took out three more.

I ducked behind the hulk, hurled a grenade at those to the left, slapped together my laser gun, moved to the right again, began firing at the nearest machine.

It took too long to burn it to a stop, so I slung the gun, threw another grenade, came out running. I might be able to run fast enough to hold a lead on an uphill course. I was not certain.

Three of the dozen or so remaining robots could not be avoided, so I had to stop and grapple with the nearest. It had snagged me with a long cablelike appendage as I tried to get by it.

33

Hoping that the prosthetic strength augmentation would be sufficient, I caught hold of it low and struggled to raise it above my head. I managed this just as the next tried to close with me, so I brought the one down upon the other as hard as I could, stopping them both, pushed the third over onto its side and ran.

I made thirty or forty yards before their fire knocked me over and their beams made the armor more than just uncomfortably warm.

"At least you appear to be human," came Styler's words, on my suit radio. "It would be terrible if there were nothing inside, though, like one of those evil, hollow creatures in Scandinavian legends—an empty presence. God! Maybe you are! Some piece of a nightmare that didn't go away when I woke up . . ."

By then I had a grenade ready, and I threw it back at my pursuers and followed it with my second-to-last one. Then I was on my feet and running toward the heaped rubble that lay before the building. It was about thirty yards and I felt their beams upon me and I was knocked down and got up and staggered on, feeling the burning at all points where my armor contacted my body, smelling my sweat and cooking flesh.

I dove behind a pile of masonry and began tearing at the clasps to my armor. It seemed to take me ages to get out of it, and I bit partway through my lip while holding back a scream. The headpiece addressed me in Styler's voice as it fell to the ground:

"Do you not think the human race is worth saving? Or worth the effort, the attempt, to save it? Do you not feel it deserves the opportunity to exercise its potentials in the full—"

It was smothered then beneath a slide of rubble as I clawed my way forward into a firing position, not bothering to check my burns, bringing the laser to bear on the nearest of the advancing robots. There were three of them still in action, and I held the beam upon the foremost for an intolerably long while before I burned a hole through its turret and it came to a sputtering, smoking halt.

I shifted it to the second one immediately, and it occurred to me then that they had not necessarily been designed for combat purposes. They were not sufficiently specialized. It seemed as if he had marshaled and armed a

34

horde of multi-use machines and sent them against me. They could have been designed to move faster and perform with deadlier efficiency. Their weapons were not really built into them, but borne by them.

"Of course the race is worth saving," I said through the taste of salt. "But whenever circumstances conspire against it, its own irrationality pushes it forward for the kiss. This madness is its doom. If it were mine to do, I would beat it out, breed it out." I laughed then, as the second robot came apart. "Hell! I'd start with myself!"

I could hear the crackling of flames at my back, as well as the swishing of a sprinkler system. I had my beam on the final robot now, and I was beginning to fear I had gotten to it too late. Its own beam was melting and pulverizing my heap of protective junk, and I kept ducking my head and pulling it to the side, blinking dust from my eyes, blowing it from my nose, smelling my burning hair and my charred ear.

It came, it came, it came. My left hand seemed to be on fire, but I knew that I would not move until one of us was extinguished by the blaze.

I kept firing after it had stopped, I guess, because I had my eyes squeezed shut by then and my head turned to the side, and I did not see it happen.

When I realized that too much time had passed for me to be alive if things had not gone right, I stopped firing and raised my head. Then I let it fall again and just lay there, knowing it was all right now, aching, unable to move.

After perhaps half a minute, I knew that I had to get up and go on, or I would just lie there losing the benefit of all that adrenalin, growing weaker and sleepier before my pain and fatigue. I pushed myself upright, reeled back. I almost fell as I stooped to retrieve my final grenade from its place at the hip of my armor. Then I turned and faced the building.

The large metal doors were closed. When I moved to them and tried them, I found that they had been secured. While I had knocked many holes in the building, fires seemed to be burning behind all of them. I backed away, half-expecting an explosion when I tried it, raised my gun and burned away the locking mechanism.

Nothing happened. No hidden charges.

I moved forward, opened one of the doors, entered.

It was a simple lobby, of the sort to be found in office buildings anywhere. Deserted, though. And hot and smoky.

I stalked ahead, ready to fire at the first movement of anything, wondering about concealed guns, bombs, gas nozzles, hoping they were damaged now or powerless, if present, and going over the plans for the place which I held in my mind.

My feelings were that he would be downstairs in the brain room. It was the safest as well as the most sensitive place in the entire installation.

As I worked my way toward the rear of the building in search of a stairwell, Styler's voice came to me over the loudspeaker system:

"I was not mistaken about you," he said. "I was afraid of you from the first. It is a pity that we could only meet under these circumstances. You possess a quality I admire greatly—your determination. I have never seen such a singlemindedness, such a definition of purpose before. Once you made up your mind to take the contract on me, that was it. You closed it to everything else at that moment, and nothing short of death will stop you now . . ."

I dashed through a burning corridor, leaped over a section of fallen wall. Sprinklers soaked me as I went.

". . . We were miscast, you and I, you know? Have you ever considered what would have happened had Othello been faced with Hamlet's problem? He would have dealt with matters as soon as he had spoken with the ghost. There would only have been the one act and no great tragedy. Conversely, the Dane could have resolved the poor Moor's dilemma in a twinkling. It is sad that such things continue to be so. Had I been in your place, I would be in control of COSA by now. They were in terrible shape. Seriously. This assault on Doxford is part of their death throes. Their top management hated one another more than they did their competitors. You could have exploited your ruthless grandfather-image and moved right in, then bullied them into line. You— Oh, hell! It doesn't matter now, I have answers for everybody's problems but my own. If you sat where I sit, knew what I know, you might have been able to stop the war. I didn't, though, so why talk about it? I was still busy weighing

36

alternatives when the bombs were going off. You would have done *something . . .*"

The door to the stairwell was jammed shut. I burned it and kicked my way through. Smoke billowed out, but I held my breath and plunged ahead.

". . . And I am still thinking, considering the possible ways of handling the present situation . . ."

I groped my way about the first landing, continued on down, my eyes stinging and watering.

The door at the foot of the stair was locked. I burnt away the lock plate, my head spinning, blood hammering in my temples. Another flaming corridor confronted me. I ran its length, blasted another door and entered a hot but unfired hallway.

I hurried, cutting my way through several more doorways, expecting an explosion, a round of gunfire, the hiss of gas at any moment. The air grew cooler, cleaner, as I proceeded, finally approaching something I considered normal and comfortable. The lights burned steadily, and though there were communication boxes at regular intervals, the only sounds that emerged were those of heavy breathing and whispers, possibly curses, that I could not quite make out. I wondered—had wondered all along—whether he was alone. I had not yet encountered a single human being, living or dead, on Alvo, and while it seemed likely that any others would have headed for his sheltered area when the attack began, the monologue-like quality of Styler's speech would tend to indicate that he was alone and possibly had been so for some time. Where, then, was everybody else? This was a big place, with a supposedly large staff.

Soon, though, the matter would be resolved. I caught sight of the heavy door that marked the entrance to his sanctuary.

I approached cautiously, found it to be sealed, as I had expected. I raised my gun and began to burn it.

The charge gave out before I had finished, though. The lock still held too well.

I had the grenade, of course. But if I were to use it to blow the door, I would be disposing of my only weapon capable of killing at a distance. The only thing I would have left beside my hands would be a stiletto I had picked up in Sicily. My instructors had laughed when I had

37

insisted on bringing it along. They did not believe in good-luck charms.

I drew it from my boot, casting the gun aside. I located the grenade.

"I imagine you expect to be picked up by your associates after you have completed your mission," Styler said, his voice coming from a speaker above the door. "When they fail to come for you, you may begin to wonder whether you have been abandoned or whether perhaps I spoke the truth concerning the war on Earth. I spoke the truth. Then you will look for some means of departing Alvo on your own. You will find that there seems to be none available. You will begin to suspect that you are the only human being on the planet. This will be correct. Then you will wish that you had believed me, for you will realize that with me you slew the solutions to your various dilemmas."

I backed down the hall, threw the grenade and ducked into a recessed doorway.

"I have sent everyone else away. You see, I saw this coming months ago. Now, with the war, it is doubtful that any will be returning. The refugees are being sent to those worlds where settlement had already be—"

The explosion, in that confined area, sounded enormous. I was out of my niche and running before the echoes had died, the vibrations ceased, before all of the rubble had hit the floor.

If he had indeed sent everyone else offworld, it indicated that there was no one to come pick me up, had I halted at any point in my expedition as he had requested. Therefore, he had simply wanted a stationary target. The hell with him! Any possible beginnings of sympathy quickly vanished.

I plunged across the blasted threshold, my stiletto low and ready.

I did not stop moving once I had entered, but took in my surroundings as I made my dash. No splash of Renaissance splendor, as I had half-anticipated. The far wall was the face of an enormous console, the near one housed a multitude of screens, showing various views of the valley and the building's burning interior. The front of the room was separated from the rear by a decorative screen, was carpeted and furnished for full-time residence.

Styler, looking as he had in the pictures, was seated at a small metal desk, near to the left wall. An elaborate machine, possibly some extension of the behemoth at the rear of the room, jutted from the wall to enclose him on the right. His head was bared, and a mass of leads ran from it to the unit. He was staring at me, and he held a gun in his right hand.

I did not know how many times I was hit until afterward. I believe the first shot missed me. I am not certain about the second one. It was a small-caliber weapon and he managed to fire it three times before I knocked it aside, plunged my blade into his midsection and watched him sag back into the seat from which he had risen.

"You will—" he began, then opened and closed his mouth several times, a look of surprise breaking, for an instant, the grimace he had worn.

His right hand shot out, threw a small switch on the panel at his side. He slumped forward then, across the desk top, twitching.

On the corner of his desk, near to where I was leaning, breathing heavily, there was a telephone. It began ringing.

I stared at the thing, fascinated, unable to move. It was ridiculous, absurd, that it should be ringing. I fought back a wild impulse to laugh, knowing that it would do me no good, that it might take me a long while to stop.

I had to know. I would always wonder, if I did not find out now.

I reached out and raised the receiver.

"—discover possible solace," his voice continued, coming now through the earpiece, "in the building at the other end of this valley."

I controlled a sudden desire to scream, I maintained my grip on the receiver. With my other hand, I reached out and grasped his shoulder. I pushed him back in the chair. He was either dead or so close to it that it made little difference.

"The neurons are still firing," came his voice through the phone, "and with my hookup, I can activate anything here that still functions, even though my own vocal cords are now beyond my control. Everything here goes through the formulator, and its voice is my own.

"You will have to study what you find in the other

building. It will not be easy. You may well fail. The alternative is to spend the rest of your days alone in this place. But there are teaching devices, records, my notes, books. You have nothing but time now, in which you may make the attempt or not, as you choose. So far, I have anticipated everything correctly. I feel that this is about as far as I can go—"

There came a click, followed by a dial tone.

I collapsed.

Here, here, there and again. The years, the clones, the gates . . . I learned.

I studied the materials in what was to become Wing Null. I learned. The alternative was some worse form of madness than the one I already knew. I had to get out of there, try to find Julia, do something.

Jigsaw and evening star . . .

I got out of there. I never located her grave, if she had one, but I was able to establish that she was not one of those who had made it into the House, whose Wings existed on the outworlds which were not quite ready for man.

I got out of there. There was a lot of forgetting that I wanted to do, and having had an abundance of time for introspection I could even be specific about it. I possessed the techniques for pinpointing everything I disliked about myself and erasing it from my mind. I decided to do it. I wished it might be done for the whole human race—what was left of it—and decided there might be a way to do that, too. Only it would take more time, a process of moral evolution, with me there to guide it and evolve along with the others, staying only one step behind, as I saw it, to take care of the dirty work, for which I was well suited. This pleased me. I destroyed a portion of myself and soldered pin one in its place. Later ones might be pulled in an emergency, but I wanted Angelo di Negri to stay dead. I hated him. Then I activated the clones, and we could trust us completely.

We got out.

Part II

1

As I felt the bullet enter my heart, my first reaction was an enormous bewilderment. How—?

Then I was dead.

I do not remember screaming, though Missy Vole said I did, and clawing wildly with my right hand. Then I stiffened, relaxed, was still. She was in the best position to know, poor girl, as it happened in her bed.

A crazy thought ran through my mind just before I died: *Pull pin seven* ... Why, I had no idea.

I remember her face, green eyes mostly hidden behind long lashes, pink lips slightly parted in a smile. Then I felt the pain and the bewilderment, not hearing but seeming to have just heard the shot that killed me.

A doctor was later to tell me that I had sustained no cardiac damage, despite the symptoms I had exhibited, that there was no apparent reason for my experiencing chest pains and blacking out. I was already aware by then that this was the case, and I just wanted to get away from the Dispensary and go direct to Wing 18 of the Library, cubicle 17641, to deal with the aftermath of my passing.

But they detained me for several hours, insisting that I rest. The fools! If there was nothing wrong with me, why should I rest?

And I was unable to rest, of course. How could I? I had just been murdered.

I was quite frightened and very puzzled. How could anyone do such a thing? And, as an afterthought, why should they?

As I lay there, surrounded by antiseptic whiteness, alternately perspiring and shivering, I knew that I had to go, I wanted to go, to see what had been done to me, to cover it over quickly. But I also experienced a tremendous revulsion and physical fear of the sight, the evidence of the act. This occupied me for a long while, and I made no effort to depart. I was sufficiently rational to realize that I would be useless until these initial feelings had eased.

So I rode with them, forced myself to think about them. Murder. It was virtually unheard of these days. I could not recall when last a murder had been committed, anywhere, and I was in a better position than most to be aware of such matters. Early conditioning and plenty of violence-aggression surrogation had a lot to do with it, as well as considerable medical expertise when it came to patching up the victim of a pathological outburst. But a cool, premeditated killing, such as mine had been ... No, it had been an awfully long while. Some more cynical ghost of an earlier self whispered in my ear that it just might be that the real cool, premeditated ones were so well done that they did not even look like murder. I quickly banished him to the oblivion he had earned long ago. Or so I thought. With the quality of information maintained on everyone in the House, it was next to impossible.

It was especially unfortunate that it had to be me. I was now required to do what I had just dismissed as inconceivable in another. That is, find a way of concealing the fact that it had occurred. But after all, I was a special case. I did not really count—

The chuckle unnerved me, coming as it did from my own throat.

"Well said, old mole!" I decided within me. "I suppose there is a certain element of irony involved."

Crap! You have no sense of humor at all, Lange!

"I appreciate the incongruity of my position. But I do not consider murder a laughing matter."

Not when we are the victim, eh?

"You employ the wrong pronoun."

No, but have it your way. You are as red-handed as any.

"I am not a killer! I have never murdered anyone!"

I suppressed the beginnings of another chuckle.

What about suicide? What about me?

"A man has the right to do as he would with himself! You? You are nothing! You do not even exist!"

Then why are you so disturbed? Psychotic, perhaps? No, Lange. I am real. You killed me. You murdered me.

44

But I am real. And there will come a time when I will be resurrected. By your own hand.

"Never!"

It will be because you will need me. Soon!

Choking with fury, I rebanished my sire to his well-deserved limbo.

For several moments I cursed the fact that I was what I was, realizing simultaneously that this, too, was a pathological outburst brought about by the death-trauma. Before very long, it passed. I knew that so long as people remained people, it was necessary that I endure, in whatever form the day required.

We should be waiting for me to move. I knew that, too. Waiting and covering. The longer it took me to act, the more difficult things could become in the normal course of human surveillance. We all knew that, but we appreciated the scope of my feelings and understood that there would have to be a delay before I could function coherently again.

I ground my teeth and clenched my hands. This self-indulgence could be costly. It would simply have to be postponed.

I forced myself to get up and cross the room, to regard the gray-haired, dark-eyed reflection of my fifty-some years in the mirror that hung above the basin. I ran my hands through my hair. I smiled my lopsided smile, but it did not look too convincing.

"You are a hell of a mess," I told myself, and we nodded agreement.

I ran the water cold, sluicing the cracked pavements of my face, washed my hands, felt slightly improved. Then, trying hard not to think of anything but the immediate task, I fetched my clothes from the wall-slot and dressed. Once I had begun moving, there arose a compulsive need to continue. I had to get out of there. I rang for attention and began pacing. I paused several times at the window and looked out at the small, enclosed park, empty now of all but a few patients and visitors. High overhead, the lights had already entered the dimming cycle. I could see three corkscrewing jackpoles and the wide balconies of an arcaded area far to my left, the glint of enclosure-facings in the shadows to their rear. Traffic on the belts and crossovers was light, and there were no special airborne vehicles in sight.

A sudden nurse fetched me the young doctor who had said earlier that there was nothing wrong with me. Since we were now in apparent agreement on this point, he told me that I could go home. I thanked him and departed, discovering that I actually felt better as I walked down the ramp and headed for the nearest beltway.

At first, I did not really care which way I moved. I simply wanted to get away from the Dispensary, with all its smells and reminders of that unfortunate state through which I had so recently journeyed. I slid by enormous medical supply depots, airborne ambulances occasionally passing overhead. Walls, dividers, shelves, pilings, platforms, ramps—all were white and carbolic about me. I edged my way inward and onto the fastest belt. Orderlies, nurses, doctors, patients and relatives of the deceased or ailing slipped by me with increasing speed and good riddance. I hated the place with its caches of medical stores, clinical subdivisions and supervised residences for the recovering and those headed in the other direction. The belt flowed through the corner of a park where such unfortunates waited, on benches and in power chairs, for the day when the black door would open for them. Overhead, birdlike power cranes transported units of people and machinery, to maintain the perpetually recomputed requirements of the shifting people:things:power: space equation, moving with but the faintest clucking amid the great crosshatchery in the sky. I changed belts a dozen or so times, not drawing another easy breath until I was well into the crowded, daylighted Kitchen, with its smells and movements and sounds and colors to remind me that I was a permanent part of this and not that other.

I ate in a small, brightly lit cafeteria. I was very hungry, but after the first minute or so the food became tasteless and its chewing and swallowing mechanical. I kept glancing at the other diners. Unbidden, the thought came into my mind: Could it be one of them? What does a murderer look like?

Anybody. It could be anybody ... anybody with a motive and a capacity for violence, neither of which appears on a person's face. My inability to think of anyone

46

possessing these qualities did not alter the fact that they had been exercised a few hours earlier.

My appetite vanished.

Anybody.

It was a hell of a time to go paranoid, but I felt the sudden need to move again, to get away. Everything about me had assumed a sinister aspect. The casual gestures and glances of the other diners grew menacing. I felt my muscles tense as a fat man with a tray passed behind me. I knew that if he bumped my chair or brushed against me I would leap to my feet, screaming.

As soon as the aisle was clear I got up. It was all I could do to keep from running as I headed back to the beltway. Then I simply rode for a time, mindlessly, not wanting to be in a crowd, but not wanting to be alone either. I heard myself cursing softly.

There was of course a place where there would be people, where I could be unafraid. I felt fairly certain of that. There was an easy way to find out, but my mood might be communicable and I wanted to keep it to myself until it went away. The easiest thing to do was simply to go there—to the scene of the murder.

I decided that I wanted a drink first. But I was not about to order one in this Wing. Why? Again the irrational. I had been discomfitted in my own chambers.

I followed the overheads, belting to the nearest subway station.

Finally, I saw in the distance the towering wall with its changing pattern of lighted numbers and letters. I disembarked at the station and studied the departures. A small number of people trickled through the incoming gates and others stood about or sat in the bleachers, keeping an eye on the board. Studying the thing, I learned that Gate 11 would take me to the Cocktail Lounge of Wing 19 in six minutes. I entered the cage at 11—there was no line—and presented my card for scanning. There came a humming followed by a click, after which the meshed door in the rear opened.

I passed through and headed up the ramp to the waiting area by the Gate. There were three men and a girl there. The girl had on a nurse's uniform. One of the men—an old codger in a power chair—might have been in her care, though she was standing quite a distance from him. He gave me a brief, sharp look and a faint smile, as though he might be interested in striking up a conversation. I glanced away, still feeling antisocial, and moved to a position far to his left and forward. Of the other two men, one stood near the Gate, his face partly hidden by the paper he was reading, and the other paced, briefcase in hand, his eyes on the clock.

When the red active light came on, accompanied by a buzzing sound, I waited for the others to pass through before I moved toward the Gate.

I submitted my card for rescanning and moved through the entranceway. As I entered the subway, I could hear a faint crackling all about me and the smell of ozone came into my nostrils. A hundred or so yards of metal-lined tunnel lay ahead of me, faintly illuminated by dirty overhead glow-plates. A haphazard array of advertisements and graffiti covered the walls, random bits of litter dotted the floor.

Halfway along the tunnel, a short, swart man stood reading a poster, hands clasped behind his back, mouth working around a toothpick. He turned and grinned at me as I approached.

I edged my way over to the left, but he headed toward me then, still grinning. As he drew near, I halted and folded my arms across my chest, the fingertips of my right hand separating the mag-bound seam of my jacket beneath my left armpit and coming into contact with the tiny butt of the tranquilizer pistol I carried there.

His grin became more conspiratorial, and he nodded it, saying, "Pictures."

Before I could respond, he had drawn open his jacket and was reaching inside. I relaxed, for I saw that he was not going for a weapon, but did indeed have a sheaf of photos sticking up out of an inside pocket. He withdrew them and took a step nearer, shuffling them slowly.

Anywhere else, some other time, and I might have arrested him or told him to get lost, depending on my mood. But there, in the territory-less way through subspace, the question of jurisdiction was always tricky. It would be especially complicated if he had been waiting around through several shiftings, as I suspected he had. Also, I was off duty and all out of professional feelings at the moment. I moved to the right, to go around him.

He clutched at my arm and thrust his pictures before me.

"How about that?" he asked.

I glanced down. My mood must have been even more pathological than I had estimated, for I kept looking as he played slowly through his glossies.

For reasons I did not attempt to analyze, I found myself fascinated by the display, though I had seen all of them in some variation or other countless times in the past.

There were three deep-space shots of the Earth, one each of the other planets, perhaps a dozen of planets in other solar systems and a score of star groups. I was strangely moved by them, and slightly irritated with myself for feeling that way.

"Nice, huh?" he said.

I nodded.

"Fifty," he said. "You can have the whole lot for fifty dollars."

"Are you crazy?" I said. "That's too much."

"They are very good pictures."

"Yes, they are," I said. "But they are not worth that much to me. Besides, I don't have fifty."

"You can have any six for twenty-five."

"No."

I could simply have said I never carried cash and ended things right there. Theoretically, there was no need for cash, since my i.d. card was also good for charging anything against my personal account, the balance of which was instantly verifiable. But everyone, of course, carries some cash, for purchases he does not wish recorded. I could also have told him to go to hell and kept walking.

All right, I was stalling for some reason. The reason must be that I was attracted by the photos. In the interest of dealing with my post-death trauma as expeditiously as possible, I decided to humor my neuroses and buy a couple.

I selected a crisp, clean shot of the Earth and one of the black and bright sprawl of the Milky Way. I gave him two dollars apiece for them, tucked them away near my pistol and left him there with his toothpick and his grin.

A few moments later I stepped into the Cocktail Lounge in Wing 19.

I moved down the ramp and out of the station. I mounted the beltway. It was always evening here, and I found it comfortable for that reason. The ceiling was invisible in the darkness, and the little areas of light were like campfires in a vast field. I remained on the slow belt and had it pretty much to myself. The four who had preceded me through the Gate were nowhere in sight. I transferred several times, making my way toward one of the darker areas, far in toward the left. I passed among the carefully contrived nooks and adyts, done up in all manner of motifs, some of them occupied, many of them not. Here and there, I came upon a party and could sometimes hear the strains of music and the sounds of laughter. Occasionally, I glimpsed a couple, fingertips touching, heads close together above a small table on which a tiny light flickered. Once I caught sight of a solitary figure, leaning heavily on his table, drinking in the dark. I must have proceeded for several miles before a satisfactory sense of seclusion enfolded me and I stepped down to seek my own place.

I made my way among darkened tables, turned a corner, crossed over a small bridge and passed through a cluster of fake palm trees, moving quickly to escape the Polynesian decor. Several more turnings, and I came to a surprising little place. Settling myself onto a chair with a cross-stitch seat at the side of a small table, I leaned forward and turned on the imitation oil lamp. Its soft, yellow light showed me armchairs with lace antimacassars on their backs, an upright piano, a pair of expressionless portraits, a shelf of expensively bound books. I had wandered into a Victorian drawing room, and it struck me as just the mood-easer I needed, eminently solid and secure.

I sought the ordering unit, located it beneath the table. Inserting my card, I ordered a gin and tonic. As an afterthought, I requested a cigar. A moment later, they arrived and I lifted the hatch and brought them to the tabletop.

I took my first cool sip and lit the cigar. Both of them tasted fine. I stopped thinking for a short while and simply sat there wrapped in a pleasant feeling. Something finally

50

stirred down at the bottom of my mind, though, and I slipped my hand into my jacket and withdrew the two photos. I placed them side by side on the tabletop and regarded them.

Again, the fascination and something strangely like nostalgia for these unseen things . . .

As I pondered the Earth and that great river of stars, I attempted to analyze these feelings. Failing this, an uneasiness came over me, rising to a near-certainty as to their origin.

Old Lange, my late senior . . . It had something to do with him, the sacrificed part . . .

But there was only one way to find out for certain—an emergency procedure which I could not recall ever having been used. Even though a terrible, frightening thing had happened to me, I did not see that an exploration of my post-traumatic reactions to some pictures warranted its employment. The dead were dead, and they were meant to remain so for very good reasons. While the present situation was quite serious, I could not conceive of any set of circumstances which would justify pulling pin seven—

My God! Like somebody I could not recall and his piece of spongecake, there came a sudden remembrance. My crazy, dying thought, smothered until that moment by the pain, the fear . . . *Pull pin seven* . . .

Why, I still had no idea.

There came no mocking chuckle, no delirious schizophrenic reaction. And I would have welcomed even that right then, for I felt completely alone with a fear so naked I could almost see the bones.

I was afraid of what it stood for, what it meant. Even more than death, I feared pin seven.

Why did I have to be the oldest, be the nexus? Why did the responsibility have to be mine?

I gulped my drink, not allowing myself to say, "It is not fair." There was a quick, easy way to relieve my aloneness, but this would not be fair to the others. No. I had to sweat and figure this part out for myself. It was the only way. I cursed my weakness and my fear, but knew there was no help for me this side of the black door. Damn it!

I ordered another drink, sipping this one slowly, and puffed on my cigar. I gazed at the pictures, trying to

51

penetrate their mystery by sheer eyeball power. Nothing. Attractive and *verboten*, nobody alive remembered what was left of the Earth, and who the hell had ever seen a star? Despite my age, I still felt somewhat guilty and self-conscious to be sitting there staring at a picture of the place we had come from and its galactic backdrop. However, my intentions were not prurient.

I thought that I heard a noise, but with all the partitions and furnishings it was impossible to determine its direction. Not that it really mattered, I suppose. There could be someone seated within a few feet of me, neither of us aware of the other's existence. Though I preferred the actuality, the illusion of solitude would be sufficient, I supposed. I was not yet ready to get up and move on.

I listened to the ticking of the clock in its glass case. I liked this little area. I would have to note down its coordinates so that I could come again. I—

I heard the noise, unmistakable this time, louder. Someone had bumped against a piece of furniture. But there was also a background sound now, an underlying accompaniment that was soft and whirring, mechanical. That was better. It meant that it was probably a robotic cleaner-upper, in which case it would avoid a functioning area.

I took another sip, smiling faintly as I moved my hand away from the photos. I had automatically covered them when I thought that someone might be coming this way.

After several moments, I heard it again, very clear, very near. Then he came into sight, rounding the corner at the far end of the room. It was the old man in the power chair who had preceded me through Gate 11. He nodded and smiled.

"Hello," he said, gliding forward. "My name is Black. I saw you at the subway station—Dispensary, Wing 3."

I nodded.

"I saw you, too."

He chuckled as he drew up beside the table.

"When I saw you get off the belt here I figured you were stopping for a drink." He glanced at my glass.

"I didn't see you on the belt."

"I was fairly far behind you. Anyway, I find myself in a slightly awkward position, and I thought you might be willing to help me."

52

"What is that?"

"I would like to buy a drink."

I gestured at the table.

"Go ahead. The unit is underneath."

He shook his head.

"You don't understand. I can't do it. Directly, that is."

"What do you mean?"

"Doctor's orders. My account is flagged. If I stick my card in that machine and ask for a drink, Central will order it not to sell me one when it runs the automatic credit check."

"I see."

"But I'm not broke. I mean, I have cash. Only, that thing has no use for cash. Now what I had in mind was this: If I could find someone who would buy me a drink on his card, I could reimburse him in cash—hell! I'd even buy him a drink, too!—and there would be no real record of my having done it."

"I don't know," I said. "If your doctor does not want you drinking, I'm not sure that I want to be responsible for something that might not be good for you."

He nodded.

"Oh, the doctor's right," he said. "I'm hardly the picture of health. Just look at me and you can tell that. It's no fun being in the shape I'm in. They keep me alive, but I'd hardly call it living. A little physical discomfort tomorrow is not too high a price for a stiff bourbon on the rocks. It won't kill me." He shrugged. "And even if it would, it would not matter to anyone. What do you say?"

I nodded.

"It's not illegal," I said, "and you are the only real judge of what is important to you."

I inserted my card in the slot.

"Make it a double," he said.

I did, and when I passed it to him he took a long, slow sip and sighed. Then he set the glass down, fumbled inside his jacket and withdrew a pack of cigarettes.

"I'm not supposed to have these either," he said, lighting one.

We sat in silence for perhaps a minute, sorting out our private feelings, I guess. Strangely, I did not resent the intrusion on the solitude I had gone so far to achieve. I felt sorry for the old man, doubtless alone in the world,

53

waiting around to die, finding pretexts to go off from whatever rest facility housed him and cadge an occasional drink, one of his few remaining pleasures. But it went beyond sympathy. There was animation, defiance, strength in his deeply lined face. His dark eyes were clear, his mottled hands steady. There was something comforting, almost familiar, about him. I was certain I had never met the man before, but our meeting here, this way, gave me an odd, irrational feeling that it had been somehow prearranged.

"What have you got there?" he asked, and I saw the direction of his gaze. "Feelthy pictures?"

My face grew warm.

"Well—sort of," I said, and he chuckled.

He reached halfway toward them, then met my eyes.

"May I?" he asked.

I nodded.

He picked them up, leaned back with them. His shaggy brows dropped toward a squint and he cocked his head to one side. He stared for a long while, his lips pursed. Then he smiled and placed them back on the table.

"Very good," he said. "Very good pictures." Then his voice changed. "See Earth and then die."

"I do not understand . . ."

"It is an old saying that I just made up. 'See Venice and die.' 'See Naples and die.' 'May you die in Ireland.' Many places once took such pride in themselves that they considered a visit there to be the greatest thing in anyone's life. At my age, one can be a bit more cosmopolitan. Thanks for letting me see the pictures." His voice hardened. "They brought back many memories. A few of them were even happy ones."

He took a large swallow of his drink and I stared at him, fascinated. He seemed to grow larger, he sat more erect.

It was not possible, though. It simply was not possible. But I had to ask him.

"Just how old are you, Mr. Black?"

Part of his mouth grinned as he snubbed out his cigarette.

"There are too many ways to answer your question," he said. "But I see what you are really asking. Yes, I have

54

seen the Earth—actually, not just in pictures. I remember what things were like, before the House was built."

"No," I said. "That is physically impossible."

He shrugged, then sighed.

"Perhaps you are right, Lange," he said. He raised his glass and drained it. "It does not matter."

I finished my own drink, setting the glass down beside the photos.

"How is it that you know my name?" I asked him.

Reaching into his pocket, he said, "I owe you something."

But it was not money that he withdrew.

"See the Earth," he said, and, *"A rivederci."*

I felt the bullet enter my heart.

2

How—?

The music was swirling all about me, pumping, throbbing, and the lights were changing color faster and faster. Then it was time for me to come in on the clarinet. I managed it. Shakily, but sufficiently.

Before too long there was applause. Weak-kneed, I got through the bows. Then the bandstand darkened and I followed the others down.

As we moved around back, Martin's hand fell on my shoulder. He was the leader, stocky going to fat, three-quarters bald, heavy pouches under his pale, watery eyes. A very good trombone player and a nice guy, too.

"What happened to you up there, Engel?" he asked me.

"Stomach pains," I said. "Must have been something I ate. They were pretty bad for a couple minutes."

"How are you feeling now?"

"A lot better, thanks."

"Hope you're not getting an ulcer. They're no fun. Something been bothering you?"

"Yes. But it will be over soon."

"Well, that's good. Take it easy."

I nodded.

"See you tomorrow."

"Right."

I moved away quickly. Damn! I had to find a collapsing place in a hurry. Every second counted now. Damn! How could I have been so complacent, so blind? So stupid! Damn!

I slapped my instrument into its case, changed clothes in record time and ignored or avoided everyone and everything that might slow me as I made for the beltway. I got over into the fastest lane and began some evasive traveling. I switched belts at nearly every intersection. I jackpoled down three levels and walked until I was fairly certain I was not being followed. Then I took to the belts again and worked my way toward the Living Room.

My sense of urgency was enormous by then, and I knew that I was near to the edge of hysteria. A small, hot core of anger was the only thing that kept my panic in check. Something I did not understand had reached me and struck me, twice. Then, almost without my realizing it, the anger was there, and I could feel it growing. It was strange and it was strong. I could not recall whether I had ever felt so before. I must have, since I recognized it and embraced it so readily. Whatever, it seemed to buoy me a bit. Perhaps it was this, that in its incipience had served to prevent my collapse this time around. I felt the slow beginnings of a desire to reach out and punish my murderers—for purposes of a personal accounting, rather than in the interest of justice. Though I recognized the aberrant nature of the impulse I did not seek to straitjacket it with self-discipline, for I had to have something to sustain me.

... And it was not an altogether unpleasant feeling.

Now the faintest of smiles quirked the corners of my mouth upwards. No, it was not a bad thing to be angry. It was a natural, human feeling. Everybody knew that. It almost seemed a shame to waste it on aggression surrogates ...

I stepped down into the Living Room and walked through section after section. People sat, stood, reclined, talking, reading, napping, listening to music, viewing tapes, and there was always a quiet nook for someone who wanted to be alone. I hurried across the soft carpeting, rounding corner after corner, passing through a great variety of periods and styles, hoping I would not encounter anyone who knew me.

Luck!

A small, deserted alcove, dimly lit ... a fat, green chair that looked as if it might recline ...

Sure enough. It did. I turned the light even lower and leaned far back. There were two entrances to the place and I could keep an eye on both, though I was certain I had not been followed.

The first thing I did was try to relax and decide who I was. It is gratifying that the nexus-mesh occurs so smoothly. You always wonder, I guess, what it will feel like. Then it happens and you still do not know. You only know that it worked.

I knew I was not the same Mark Engel I had been before the old man shot Lange. I was Lange, but Lange was also me. I mean, we were us. We had merged, more or less, with the shifting of the nexus, when his body was destroyed. It did not require a massive adjustment, since we had experienced the same phenomenon on a temporary basis countless times in the past. Now that it was for keeps, there were a number of things I had to do to tailor the arrangement, so to speak. But they would have to wait. We should have acted right away, after the first murder. Lange had dragged his heels, though, and it had proved fatal. I did not approve of his postponing an important action, regardless of his mental condition. I could feel this tendency warring with my own resolve even then. That part would be sacrificed—soon—when I inserted pin eight.

Although the identity situation would ordinarily have precedence, it would have to take second place this time around.

About three centimeters behind my eyes, that is where I seem to live. My mind, my consciousness . . . I tightened and relaxed, tightened and relaxed, there in my home. A mental heartbeat, a mindbeat . . . Then it was all diastole, and thoughts the mindblood flowing uncontrolled . . .

Then we were there and together—Davis, Gene, Serafis, Jenkins, Karab, Winkel and the others. Suddenly, I was all of us and we were all of us me. There was little hesitation as everyone slipped into place, recognizing the new position of the nexus. A good, comfortable, familiar feeling.

I saw through many eyes, heard many sounds, felt the weight of all of our flesh. It was as though we were one body, our various limbs in all of the Wings. All but two, that is. And in a very special sense we were but one body.

In a timeless moment, we were all of us aware of the conscious contents of all of our individual skulls. It was a brief eternity of realization, a plasmic state of being wherein our temporary surrender of individuality caused all of us to grow, instantly, by the sum of the new

58

experiential units which had come to be since our most recent meshing, perhaps a month earlier.

There was fear, and my surprise at the fact that there was so little anger other than that which I had brought to the meshing. My anger was countered by an attitude of mild reproval, tempered by the awareness that I had just received the nexus and had not had time to make the necessary adjustments. Otherwise, the anger might have been washed away, submerged. As it was, I saw that they also feared any reaction that might affect me before my new personality had solidified. Good. I felt the same way about it.

The first death had been that of Hinkley, in the Library, Wing 18. We knew that it had occurred in cubicle 17641, his private living quarters there, as we had all become instantly aware of his terminal impressions. He was with us still, but he was unable to supply any clues as to the motives or identity of his slayer. We had all reacted differently to the death, in keeping with our private temperaments, but none of us had any notion as to the reason for the killing and no one had done anything about it yet. As for Lange's/my body, it still lay in the Victorian drawing room of the Cocktail Lounge of Wing 19, unless the old man had done something with it.

. . . And nobody recognized Mr. Black. No one knew him from anywhere. I assigned myself the task of running the search for him, as I would have access to the necessary equipment very soon.

Davis was in the Library, Wing 18, keeping an eye on cubicle 17641. He had already seen to it that the quarters were shown as vacant and the phone switched to automatic answering. It was decided that he should not enter yet, but continue his watch until Serafis could get there. Serafis was a medic and could file the necessary papers showing death from natural causes. Then the body would be taken to Winkel's funeral home and disposed of quickly.

Lange was a problem, though. It was not only that another natural-causes certification by Serafis would look peculiar, coming from a different Wing and so soon after Hinkley's—but Lange had just had a very thorough checkup and had been found to be in good condition.

It was decided that Winkel would go after the body and

dispose of the evidence while he was at it. He was in a position to make the pickup look legitimate if almost anyone else came upon the scene. The body would then be transported to Wing Null, causing it to vanish from known existence. There it would be frozen, until we decided upon its most suitable disposition. In the meantime, we would have Lange put on leave from his employment and use his card for transportation, meals and occasional small purchases, so that he would continue, officially, to exist.

All available evidence would of course be gathered for our own private investigation of the killings. The fear that we felt was very strong. It had to be more than coincidence that two of us had gotten it as we had, and we were unable to come up with any guesses as to the reason which were not absolutely chilling. The exercise was somewhat futile, so we agreed to break the mesh for the time being and get on with the necessary actions immediately. I was to proceed to Wing Null, to make the adjustments needed for a permanent arrangement between Lange and myself.

I blinked away the shadows of their thoughts and rose quickly. I brightened the light, paced off a few tentative steps, reevaluating myself now that I was me once more. Well, almost me.

As I saw it, someone was out to destroy the entire family. The motive was immaterial. The fact that the only two murders in recent times should be of family members was sufficient. There were not that many of us around. It indicated, to me, that what we had thought the best-kept secret in the House had somehow been found out—at least in part. Mr. Black was doubtless waiting, planning to strike again. I would begin seeking him from Wing Null as soon as I had taken care of my other business there.

And when I found him, what?

I pushed the question aside, still unwilling to consider the answer my anger was offering. Later, later . . .

And again the fear . . . Not only my distress at the thought that death might be waiting for me anywhere now—but the Lange/me fear of the partial suicide we were now constrained to commit. You are not supposed to look at it that way, any more than you consider the removal of a throbbing tooth to be a small death. But there it was, and we had to go do it now.

60

As I left the alcove, thinking along these lines, I do recall it passing through my mind that if we were capable of doing it to ourself ...

I did not retrace my way through the Living Room, but traveled a circuitous route in the other direction, coming at last to a slow, narrow side-belt which I rode for a time. A flat, towering partition lay to my left, covered with an abstract design, dark-toned and seemingly endless. To my right were great, semi-lit sections of the Living Room, resting people haphazardly distributed within.

When I switched to another belt, moving at right angles to the one I had ridden. I glanced back. There was a figure, several hundred yards to the rear, which had not been present when I had mounted the conveyance. I waited perhaps two minutes and looked again. He had switched also, was still there. In fact, he was nearer now, as he was walking on the belt.

I waited several moments and began walking myself. Most likely, he was quite innocent, but I considered no precaution unwarranted at that moment. I changed again at the next intersection, but refrained from looking back. I saw that we were headed toward a somewhat crowded area.

As we passed through that section of the Living Room, I stepped down beside a group of sofas, took a few paces and glanced back again.

Yes, he was on this belt now, and he was looking at me.

I turned, folded my arms across my breast and stared back at him. There were dozens of people about me, talking to one another, reading, munching snacks, playing cards. I felt quite secure in their presence. He must have thought I was, too, if he meant me harm, for he immediately looked away and continued on by. I felt a small satisfaction in watching him pass, a tribute to my alertness and ingenuity. This vanished as soon as I began to uncross my arms, when I realized that I had unconsciously parted the seam of my jacket beneath my left armpit and was fingering the nonmetallic tranquilizer gun we all carried there. Then the fear was there, full force, as I realized it had never, really, left me. Emotionally chastened, and stoking my anger in hope of sparking some courage to flame, I moved forward and remounted the belt.

61

I could still see the man, up ahead. I had gotten a fairly good look at him, what there was to see. He had shoulder-length brown hair and a slightly darker beard. He wore blue mirror-glasses, a matching jacket and white, knee-length trousers.

A flash of blue, as he glanced back . . .

I began walking toward him, my heart pumping heavily. It was suddenly very important to me—more important than my fear, even—that I obtain his reaction.

He turned away, stood still for perhaps half a minute, then looked back again. I had kept walking, continuing to close the distance between us. The second time he looked back, I raised my right hand and slipped it inside my jacket in the fiction-honored fashion of a man reaching after a deadly weapon.

He moved quickly then, stepping down from the belt and darting behind a partition that projected out near to its edge. It was only then that I noticed his limp. I had not detected it when he had been walking straight toward me, but he tended to favor his left leg.

I got off the belt immediately. It would not do to let it carry me right past him if he were armed himself. I hurried to my right, heading toward a different partition. So far as I was concerned at the moment, the fact that he had fled was sufficient to establish that he harbored nasty intentions toward me.

Slipping along the partition, I worked my way back and in, cutting through an empty alcove and moving behind another partition that formed one wall of a corridor that bore off to my left—his direction—and dead-ended into a three-walled section containing four sofas, miscellaneous chairs and tables and a crackling fireplace. I dashed across its width and ventured a quick look around the near corner.

There was no one in sight.

I could see into several deserted sections before my view was blocked by more partitioning perhaps a hundred and fifty feet ahead. There were five or six crannies and chambers into which I could not see, however.

Cautiously, I advanced, drawing my gun and palming it now. In the space of four or five minutes, I had worked my way through, discovering no one. A couple more minutes, and I was into the area where the man had fled, searching it carefully.

He did not seem to be about. He had had time to slip off in any of several directions. I felt quite uncomfortable as I stood there, considering it. He might be circling, slipping up behind me, lying in ambush. The thought occurred to me that there might even be more than one person involved, that perhaps I was supposed to see this fellow while another . . .

The safest thing for me to do, I decided, was to get out of there as quickly as possible, confuse any pursuit and beat it to Wing Null.

I worked my way back to the belt, waited until it bore a group of passengers abreast of me and climbed on, moving immediately to a position in their midst. I received some foul glances and fishy stares from passengers I pushed by and elbowed aside, but that was all I got as we slid on through the area. I was a near-impossible target where I stood.

". . . You are very rude," a husky, redheaded woman with blue eye makeup was saying.

I nodded my agreement and kept watching the furnishings and people we passed. The man was nowhere in sight.

About half a mile farther along, we came to an intersection and I switched over, heading off to the left. The people I had used for shields continued on, sending a few remarks after me. They had all been together, apparently—a party coming or going somewhere.

Traffic was heavier on the new belt, and before too long it bore me to a two-way, multilane beltway. Crowds of people, staler air and an increased sound level enfolded me. I got into its fastest lane and rode for several minutes. Then I began switching again, following signs to the nearest jackpole.

It was a down tube, transparent, echoing, forever screwing itself into the House. A small boy came rushing upward, laughing and looking back over his shoulder. I reached out and seized his arm. He attempted to pull away, then turned and glared at me. A moment later, a woman—presumably his mother—came puffing upward, red-faced and looking even meaner. She slapped him and took hold of his other arm.

"I told you!" she said. "I told you never to do that!"

Then she looked at me.

"Thank you," she said, "for stopping him. I don't know why they like to run up the down ones and down the up ones."

I smiled.

"Neither do I," I said, releasing my grip somewhat reluctantly.

They got off at the next level, Kitchen, and while she was saying, "Wait till I get you home!" the boy turned around and stuck his tongue out at me.

I tried to think what it must be like, to be a child, to have parents.

I continued on down to the next level, the Recreation Room, disembarked there and found a fast belt through the playing area. Every team sport I could think of seemed to be in progress somewhere in the field section. For a time, the beltway was elevated, and I could see for miles in all directions. Balls were hit, kicked, thrown, caught, dribbled, run with, on fields and courts, over nets, against walls, into cages. Banks of spectators cheered and stamped their feet; wide, towering boards flashed scores; overhead speakers emitted decisions and static. The ceiling was light blue, a pleasant, somehow appropriate color. At the moment, I could detect no crane activity upon that peaceful, gridded surface. Swimming pools glimmered, cast dancing ghosts on towers and stands. Air currents bearing smells of sweat and liniment swept by, seeking ventilation units into which they might retreat to cleanse themselves.

The belt was fairly crowded, so it was impossible for me to tell whether I was being followed. I began switching down to smaller and smaller beltlines, heading in the general direction of a dimmed area. Traffic fell off as I came upon long rows of tables featuring more sedentary pastimes. Small groups and solitary players sat at cards and board games. Some competed against themselves, some against machines, their luck, skill, knowledge taxed to whatever degree they desired. Dice fell, wheels spun, cards were shuffled and dealt, counters pushed about; pieces advanced, retreated, jumped, captured, were captured themselves; numbers were called out, bids were made, tricks taken; people bluffed, attacked, sought wins, points, stalemates, proceeded directly to Go without collecting two hundred dollars, some money often changing hands beneath the table. I am not much of a gamester myself.

The blue was beginning to darken overhead, the voices diminishing, when I heard a shrill, ringing sound: a phone in a callbox at the near end of a deserted aisle. A strange feeling, that: hearing it and seeing it there with nobody around to answer.

There was a jackpole deep in the dimmed area, glowing beads marking its crystal spiral. I transferred again, onto an empty, one-lane belt. There was a weak light every hundred yards or so, and maintenance machines bumped and hummed in the gloom on either side of me. I kept looking back over my shoulder to see whether anyone else had come onto the belt. No one had.

A moment or two later, and I came to another intersection, decided to switch again. The juncture-point was completely deserted. Motes of dust, disturbed by the cleaning machines, swirled in the yellowish light of the lamp on the corner tower. As I passed there, I heard the ringing once more. Another phone, in a recess at the tower's base, had commenced to jangle. I could hear its persistent summons for a long way down the line. It was sort of sad, the effort to reach someone who just wasn't there, or the trying in the wrong place—whichever it was.

I passed an empty polo field, the mechanical horses standing like a row of depressed statues. The dark surfaces of pools buckled constantly, like memories. Opened to the floor, gray sacks bulging and swaying above, mouths on rollers moved among lockers and gaming tables, consuming refuse. An ambulance rose from some distant bay or playing field and sped through the twilit air, red cross aglow. I slid by a couple embracing in an alcove. I would not even have noticed them if they had not moved suddenly when they became aware of me. They averted their faces. So did I. Then I passed a partition on which a painted "STARS" had not been completely obliterated. Checking behind me, I saw that I was still alone on the belt.

I switched again, bridged over a series of exposed conduits, got down and walked for two blocks to shortcut my way to a belt that headed straight for the jackpole. The area was very silent and virtually deserted. A few individuals advanced toward the pole from various directions, though none were emerging from it at the moment. Three men loafed about a candy and periodical stand nearby, and I had a feeling that I could replace Lange's photos there—or lay a bet, or make certain other unauthorized purchases.

A draft of warm air struck me as I entered the glowing tube and descended. I was probably all right now, had doubtless been quite safe since I had departed the Living Room. Nevertheless, considering its destination, I was determined to make a thorough job of my flight. To my knowledge, there had never been a question of pursuit when any of us had retreated to Wing Null before.

I emerged at the next level into a section of the Office that was just closing operations. The sight of all those people getting ready to call it a day reminded me just how tired I had grown. For a moment, I debated continuing down to another level to avoid the rush. But mingling with a crowd would help obscure my trail that much more, so I decided to go ahead.

I mounted the main beltway and a few minutes later a whistle blew and waves of humanity came toward me from every direction. I rode the middle lane, which was soon filled to capacity, and I was jostled, crushed, immobilized and borne helplessly along. I was squeezed into anonymity, however, which I kept telling myself made it all worthwhile.

Turning my head, I could see the seeming endless rows of desks from which these people fled, arrangements of phones, blotters, papers softening in the already dimming light. Soon the cleaner-uppers would begin their rounds among them. I speculated as to the work performed there each cycle, then quickly closed my mind. Better not to think about it.

I resolved to follow the path of least resistance, and the press of the crowd bore me from belt to belt for perhaps ten minutes before it eased, died down, left me to make choices on my own once more. Then I followed my previous inclinations and worked my way toward a hinterland.

Soon I was riding feeder-belts and moving near to a completely dimmed area of the Office. I tentatively set my objective as another down-jackpole, this one on the far side of the darkened space.

As I zigged and zagged my way in that direction, I became aware of a possible pursuer. I was not certain, but it seemed that one of the several figures far to my rear had changed belts with me several times. But my nervousness had subsided considerably, as though I only had a limited supply and had already used most of it. I changed again and waited. Eventually, one figure followed. According to my watch and my estimates as to beltspeed and the distance between us, he was in the proper position to be the same individual.

All right, that much resolved, I decided on a course of action: I would make a final attempt to lose him. If that failed, I would wait in ambush.

I headed into the darkness and he followed. Then I changed until I came to a short one and began running. I reached the next intersection and switched before he appeared. I ran again. This belt was longer, and I was feeling all of my forty-six years by the time I came to another intersection. But he was not behind me when I turned then either.

I stood still for a moment, breathing heavily. I could hear no unusual sounds. It was quite quiet, and sufficiently dark for my purposes.

I stepped down from the left side of the belt. Acres of desks lay before me, vanishing beyond the dark frontier of my vision as though extending into infinity. I moved toward them.

The jackpole was still a good distance away. I did not head directly for it, but moved off at a tangent, passing along an endless-seeming aisle through the work area. I ran by desk after shadowy, identical desk, until I was well back into the darkness.

Slowing to a walk when I was unable to run any longer, I found myself taken by an eerie treadmill illusion. The relentlessly recurrent sameness on either hand—small swivel chair, gray desk, green blotter, phone, in-basket, out-basket—all worked to create a sensation of nonmovement. There came a feeling of inescapability, accompanied by that odd intimation of eternity which sometimes occurs along with a monotonous stimulation of the senses, and for that timeless instant it seemed that I always had been and always would be running in place at the center of a universe of desks.

I stopped and leaned against one, to demonstrate its substantiality as well as to catch a moment's rest. Checking back toward the lighted belt trail, I saw no one. If anyone had been following me, I seemed to have given him the slip. There was no movement that I could detect among the dark hundreds of desks that I had passed.

Then, but inches away from my hand, the phone rang.

I screamed and began running. Everything that had been pent up, suppressed, pushed aside, ignored, forgotten, emerged in that awful instant.

I fled, a mindless bundle of perceptions and reactions; and pushing, hammering, driving even these apart, the ringing followed me.

... Pursued me, seemed to keep abreast of me—dying behind and breaking out afresh on each desk that I passed—my black-clad gorgons, wreathed by electric snakes. And this moment, too, seemed timeless and eternal.

I ran—wildly, madly—bumping into things, stumbling, cursing, no longer a man, but a frightened movement in a forest of menace. Some part of me seemed as if it might be aware of what was happening, but that did not benefit me in the least.

It—everything—was too much for me: the deaths, the menace, the pursuit, this assault by the unknown. I was afraid to look back. I might see something. Or, worse yet, see nothing. This was my breaking point, each ringing of the bells a fresh stab at the wound.

My breath came hard and hot into my chest, depositing a bit more of pain on each visit. My eyes and face felt moist; but then, I think my trousers were, too.

Through the wet kaleidoscope of my vision, far ahead, I seemed to see a light, a small, yellow halo—and perhaps that was a man bending within it.

Sobbing, I strove to reach it, whatever it might be— probably because it was warm and bright, so unlike everything else.

Then came the explosion that tore all sound from my ears, the flash of light that ripped the seeing from my eyes and the burning, body-rending shock that tore me to pieces, almost before the desperate words appeared on the screen of my mind: *Pull pin seven!*

Then everything ended.

3

Bone by weary bone, I came together again. I was uncertain as to where I was, what had happened or how long it had taken. I wanted to return to oblivion, rather than face whatever damage had occurred.

But consciousness was a persistent thing. It grew, rather than going away. I was just beginning to realize that I was still me and that I did not seem to hurt anywhere, when my eyes opened without any special planning on my part and began to focus.

"Are you all right?" said the voice from the fuzzy image less than a foot from my face, at once the most asinine and pleasant thing I had heard in a long while.

"I don't know," I said. "I just arrived. Give me a minute."

A great tidal wave of thought passed through my mind. I remembered everything that had happened, and I understood the last of it. Davis and Serafis were dead. Serafis had gone to Wing 18, as planned, and met there with Davis. Together, in the Library, they had entered cubicle 17641, Hinkley's residence. They tripped something that caused an explosion, killing them. I experienced their deaths.

I was surprised that I was still rational. I would not have believed that I could have remained so after going through the dying business four times in one day with extreme prejudice. Either I had grown emotionally numb, or I possessed greater resiliency than I had realized. Whichever it was, I was grateful that I was considerably less upset this time than I had been on the previous two occasions. Disturbed, naturally; concerned, of course. And very irritated.

I was lying on the floor, an arm about my head and shoulders, raising them. I was staring into a face that was near to my own, a girl's—and she looked more frightened than I felt, actually. I would not have called her pretty, although she had possibilities along that line—of the dark-haired, pale-eyed, high-cheekboned variety—but she was a doubly welcome sight when I considered the possible alternative. Her glasses were thick, colorless ovals and she wore no makeup. Whether it was concern or the glasses that so enlarged her eyes, I was uncertain.

"How are you feeling?" she said.

I nodded my head several times and struggled into a sitting position. I massaged my eyes, ran my hands through my hair and took a couple of deep breaths.

"All right now, thanks," I said. "It's all right."

She was kneeling beside me in the aisle. She had on black trousers and a gray shirt. She did not release her hold on my shoulders.

"What happened?" she said.

"I was just going to ask you that," I said. "What did you see?"

"You came running up the aisle. You screamed and fell."

"Did you see anyone else? Behind me? Near me? In the distance?"

"No." She shook her head slowly. "Was there someone with you?"

"No," I said, "I guess not. I thought I heard someone. It must have been you."

"Why were you running?"

"The telephones," I said. "It startled me when they all began ringing. Do you know why they acted that way?"

"No. They stopped about the same time I saw you fall. Some sort of electrical mixup, I guess."

I climbed to my feet, leaned against a desk.

"Would you care for a drink of water?"

I did not, but it would give me a chance to make up some lies, so, "Yes," I said, "that would be good."

"Sit down. I'll be right back."

She indicated the chair at the lighted desk. I went and sat in it while she hurried off somewhere to my left. I glanced down at the work spread out on the blotter. Pages of statistics and a pad full of longhand notes, which she seemed to be turning into some sort of report.

I searched in my pockets until I located a tiny pillbox

70

containing some capsules I sometimes used to keep me bright, alert and cheerful when playing a late stand. One could not hurt any and might do me some good, though I really wanted it as a prop.

When she returned with a cup of water, I said, "Thanks, I should have taken this earlier," and tossed off the capsule.

"How serious is it?" she said. "I can call—"

I shook my head and finished swallowing, satisfied that I had established my condition as fitting into some neat medical category.

"It is not as bad as it looked," I said. "I have these spells sometimes. I forgot to take my medication earlier. That's all."

"You're sure it's all over?"

"Yes. Everything is fine now. I guess I'll be moving along."

I started to rise.

"No," she said, placing her hands on my shoulders and pressing firmly downward. "You wait. Rest awhile."

"All right," I said, sinking back. "Tell me, why are you working here all alone?"

She glanced at the materials on the desk, blushed and looked away.

"I got behind," she said softly.

"Oh. Overtime, huh?"

"No, I'm doing it on my own."

"Sounds like real dedication."

Her lips tightened, her eyes narrowed.

"No," she said, "just the opposite." Then, "You don't work around here, do you?"

I shook my head.

"Well," she said, sighing, "I don't like what I do at all, and I am not very good at it. I got all confused, and I am way behind on everything. I came in on my own to see if I could get caught up."

"Oh. Sorry I interrupted you."

She shrugged.

"It's all right," she said. "I was just getting ready to quit when you came along."

"All finished?"

She smiled, faintly.

"You might put it that way."

71

"Oh?"

"Yes," she said. "In a few days they will find out, and my employment here will be terminated."

"I'm sorry."

She shrugged again.

"Don't be. I will go back to the unemployed labor pool, and maybe I will like the next job they find me better."

"How many have you had?"

"I forget. A couple dozen, I guess."

I studied her more closely. She only looked to be about twenty.

"Sounds pretty bad, doesn't it?" she said. "I'm not very good at anything. I'm accident-prone, too."

"Perhaps there is an error in your aptitude-profile," I said. "Maybe you should be doing a different sort of work altogether."

"Oh, they've tried me at damn near everything," she said. "They just sort of shake their heads now when they see me coming back." She chuckled. "What do you do?"

"I'm a musician."

"That is something I've never tried. Maybe I will sometime. What is your name?"

"Engel. Mark Engel. What's yours?"

"Glenda. Glenda Glynn. Mind if I ask you why you were walking through the Office in the dark?"

"Just felt like taking a walk," I said.

"You are in some sort of trouble."

I felt it strange that she had not at least put it as a question.

"What makes you say that?" I asked.

"I don't know," she said. "It is just a feeling that I have. Are you?"

"If I said yes, what would you do?"

"Try to help you if I could."

"Why?"

"I don't like to see people in trouble. I seem to be in it all the time myself and I don't like it. I'm a sympathetic person."

I could not tell whether she was joking or being serious, so I smiled.

"Sorry to disappoint you," I said, "but I am not in any trouble."

She frowned.

"Then you will be," she said. "Pretty soon, I'd say."

I was a trifle irritated by the amount of certainty she put into the pronouncement. Since I was just about to depart and doubtless never see her again, it should not have mattered. Somehow, though, it did.

"Just for curiosity's sake," I said, "would you mind telling me how you know this?"

"My mother told me it is because I am Welsh."

"That's crazy!"

"Uh-huh. But I'll bet you were thinking of going to the Basement when you leave here. You shouldn't, you know."

She must have read my bewilderment on my face, because she smiled. At least, I hoped she only read it on my face. I *had* been thinking of cutting through the Basement in my effort to rid myself of pursuit. She made me feel uncomfortable about it. She also cinched my decision to do it.

I snorted.

"That's silly. You couldn't know—"

"I told you."

"Well," I said, climbing to my feet, "thanks for your help. I am going to leave now." I could feel the pill starting to work, and it was the best I had felt in a long while. "I hope your next job is a better one."

She opened the desk's top drawer, swept all the papers into it and pushed it closed. I glimpsed an amazing entanglement of personal and business effects. Then she removed a sleeveless black jacket from the back of the chair, slipped it on and extinguished the desk light.

"I'm going with you," she said.

"I beg your pardon?"

"Maybe I can help," she said. "I feel sort of responsible for you now."

"That is ridiculous! You are not going anywhere with me!"

"Why not?"

I bit my lip. I could hardly admit that it might be dangerous when I had just been insisting on my trouble-free state.

"I appreciate your concern," I said, "but I'm all right now. I really am. There is no need for you to go out of your way—"

"No trouble," she said, taking my arm and turning me back toward the beltway.

It was only then that I realized she was just a little under six feet—just a few inches shorter than me—and very strong, despite a certain willowiness.

Suppressing several possible reactions, I considered the situation. It was possible that she had saved my life just by being where she was when she was. If it had been my pursuer's intent to panic me, he had succeeded admirably. Had he intended to administer the *coup* when I slipped over the edge of rationality, then Glenda's presence was probably what had stopped him. This being the possible case, I might be safer having her with me for a while. While I did not want to place her in jeopardy, I could not see, just off hand, any easy way to get rid of her yet. I would keep her with me for a few perambulations calculated to discourage pursuit, then leave her at the first opportunity and cut for Wing Null. Yes, that seemed best for all parties involved.

It troubled me that my adversary seemed to know me so well. It was not just that he was able to follow me so easily, but that he seemed to know precisely what sort of pressure to apply and when to apply it, to break me as readily as he had. I was beginning to wonder what it would take to stop him. Something extraordinary, I was afraid. Well, that could be arranged . . .

They seem to be getting closer.

"The sooner we get them in range, the better," I said within myself.

You are a better incarnation than Lange was.

"I know that."

But still not good enough, I fear.

"What do you mean?"

You are learning, but not fast enough. I think they will get you, too.

"Maybe. Maybe not."

It might not be a complete loss, though. You may learn something from the experience.

"Such as?"

Forget the dead and stop running. Get your enemy, then clean house.

"I have already established my own priorities."

A lot of good they are doing you.

74

"I will take your advice on forgetting the dead, though, beginning with you—"

Wait! You need me, you fool! If you want to live—

"Go!"

—pull pin seven ...

I completed the expulsion and sighed, "Some help I can do without."

"What did you say?" Glenda asked.

"Nothing," I said. "I was mumbling to myself."

"For a moment it seemed there was someone beside you."

"That is your Celtic imagination trying to justify its existence."

"No," she said, "that is what I pay it for."

I glanced at her then and she laughed. Peculiar sense of humor, that.

I was wary as we neared the beltway, but there was no one in sight this time either. We mounted it and were borne on through the gloom, side by side. Her presence seemed to have a stabilizing effect on me, a human anchor against my neurotic storms.

"How are you feeling now?"

"Better yet."

"Good."

After several minutes, we came to a crossway and switched to a larger belt. Our route was then better lighted and there were other travelers about. One more changeover and we would be headed toward the jackpole.

Pull pin seven ... It was an intriguing—if heretical—thought, to release whatever beasts Lange had enchained in the dark night of his soul. For a moment, I wanted to laugh, then felt offended, hurt and mildly amused in rapid succession. That part of me which had been plain old Engel found it very funny to think of prissy old Lange in such romantic terms. Because of his appearance, he often got the assignment of cruising about as an aging queen, picking up young men in need of rehabilitation. To think of him as wrestling nameless demons and then going through with a more than symbolic act of suicide in order to establish the nexus, was close to inconceivable to plain old Engel. That part of me which now was Lange had been hurt and offended. But already the divisions were beginning to blur, and I—whoever I was—reacted finally

75

with only a mild amusement. It was good that the merger was proceeding so smoothly on the surface, though I wondered what conflicts might be raging in the greater, unconscious portion of my mind.

... To pull pin seven would be to undo Lange's greatest work in our continuing effort to direct the moral evolution of human consciousness. I did feel a certain tension as that which was Lange within me resisted my even thinking along these lines. That which was not, however, continued to speculate as to the nature of the sacrificed portion. It became a moth-and-candle thing. I had inherited Lange's personal demon, and he of course would like nothing better than to hear my shouted *Zazas, Zazas, Nasatanada, Zazas*, the words which fling wide the Gates of Hell ...

Where had I picked that up? Either from that portion of Hinkley which was mine, from Lange or from beyond pin seven, I decided. As if in answer, I could almost hear Hinkley's voice reciting something from Blake:

But when they find the frowning Babe,
Terror strikes thro' the region wide:
They cry "The Babe! the Babe is Born!"
And flee away on Every side.

I took it to be his answer to the diabolical metaphor for pulling pin seven. Since he had been the librarian, he had a good deal from which to choose. Upon reflection, though, did it represent approval or disapproval of the notion? There was no accompanying feeling to help me judge it. Ambiguity, I decided, was the trouble with literary types. I—

Damn! I pulled myself back from the distraction. Was the whole thing Lange's doing, an attempt to direct my thoughts away from my initial considerations?

Or was it he-who-had-been, attempting to whip up some enthusiasm for a resurrection?

What would I be like when my turn came?

I would play the clarinet to them, I decided—sweetly, yet with infinite pathos ...

I bit my lip. I stared out beyond the belt and marked our movement. I studied the curling of Glenda's hair behind her right ear and at the nape of her neck. I tapped my foot. It was time, I could tell, to shift my attention to externals. It had become too, too apparent that the conflicts within me were indeed stronger than they had seemed several jagged moments earlier.

"How far do you propose to accompany me?" I said.

"As far as is necessary."

"Necessary for what?"

"To see you safe," she said.

"That may be a bigger job than you think."

"What do you mean?"

"You were correct a while back when you said that I was in trouble."

"I know that."

"All right. What I am trying to say is that while you were right as to the condition, its degree is another matter. My trouble is serious and dangerous. You have already helped me more than you realize. Now that I am back on my feet and on my way again, I can best repay you by saying goodbye. There is really nothing more that you could do to help me along now, but if you were to remain with me the trouble could become contagious. So I thank you again, Glenda, and I will be leaving you at the jackpole."

"No," she said.

"What do you mean 'no'? I was not asking you. I was telling you. We have to separate. And very soon. You helped me. Now I am returning the favor."

"I have a feeling you will require additional assistance. Soon."

"It will be available."

"Yes. Because I will be there."

I rejected several possible retorts as we swept along, then, "Why?" I said. "Mind telling me why?"

"Because," she said, without hesitation, "I have never been involved in anything exciting before. All my life I have wanted to, but nothing ever happened. I was beginning to believe that nothing ever would. Then you appeared while I was sitting there knowing I was going to lose another stupid job. As soon as I heard the phones ringing and saw you running, I knew this was going to be something different. It almost seemed fated. The peculiar way the bells seemed to pursue you . . . your dramatic collapse—almost at my feet . . . It was very exciting. I have to know how it all turns out, you see."

"I'll call you when it's all over and let you know."

"I am afraid that will not be sufficient," she said.

"It will have to do."

She simply shook her head and turned away.

"We have to change at this intersection," she said, after a few moments, "if we are going to the jackpole."

"I know."

We transferred to the other belt, and the traffic was somewhat heavier. I was unable to tell whether we were being followed at that time.

"I imagine you are now trying to figure the best way to get rid of me."

"That is correct."

"Give up," she said. "I am not going to go away."

"You have no knowledge of the situation into which you are trying to force your way," I said, "and I am not about to enlighten you. I have already told you that it is dangerous. Anyone who rushes toward an unknown peril simply to satisfy a desire for excitement is a fool. I begin to understand why you cannot hold a job."

"You cannot insult me into going away."

"You *are* a fool!"

"Have it your way," she said, "but I have a right to use public transportation the same as anyone else. I have already decided where I am going, so you might as well be graceful about it."

"It strikes me as in a category with accident-watching."

"My intention is to do more than watch, if necessary."

"I shan't argue with you any further," I said. "But how do you know I am not depraved, psychotic, criminal or any of a number of other undesirable things?"

"It does not matter," she said, "since I have already chosen sides."

"That says something about your own stability."

"I suppose it does. But why should it matter to you, if I don't mind your being all those things?"

"Never mind. Forget it."

I watched the jackpole for a time. Overhead, a crane ground by, bearing a massive load of office furniture. In a pit to our right, the darkness was smeared away by the bright tongue of a welder, repairing or replacing a conduit. Faintly, very faintly, and but briefly, I heard some strains of music. Far ahead now, a geometrically disciplined parklike area came into view at the base of the jackpole. It was not overly lit, there was a statue of somebody or other at the near end and benches here and there along the walks. As we drew nearer, I saw that the trees were natural, not artificial, and there seemed to be a fountain toward the rear.

"It reminds me of something out of Wolfe," Glenda said, looking in the same direction, and I became more Hinkley than anything else, almost without realizing it.

"Yes," I found myself saying. "He got a lot of mileage out of the town square, didn't he?"

"This one could use a city hall and a courthouse with a big clock on it."

"There is a clock above the entrance to the jackpole."

"Yes, but it is silent and always has the right time."

"That's true. No bird droppings either."

"Could use a stonemason's shop, too."

"But not the tombstones."

"True."

I wondered then about real squares back on the Earth. Did the strange Mr. Black really remember such things, or had he simply been killing time before he killed me? Since I had no such recollections on which to base any nostalgia, I could only blame my feelings on Hinkley's preoccupations: he was a romantic, an armchair time-traveler, a naturalist in a place that was all out of nature. Sad. And that was how I felt for several moments. About Hinkley, squares, everything.

"You read a lot," I said.

She nodded.

We disembarked at the park and walked into it. Periodically, hidden speakers released recorded bird-notes from within the bushes and trees. The peculiar smell of moist earth came to our nostrils. I directed our route around the jackpole, where we passed beside the small, sparkling fountain. Glenda dipped her fingers.

"What are we doing?" she asked, as we completed our circuit of the pole and headed back in the direction from which we had come.

"Biding a bit," I said, as I eased myself onto a bench and stared back along the walk toward the beltway.

She settled herself beside me, followed the direction of my gaze.

79

"I see," she said.

"While we are biding, you might tell me something about yourself," I said.

"What do you want to know?"

"Anything. Free-associate for me."

"Will you return the favor?"

"Maybe. Why? Is that a condition?"

"It would be nice."

"I will see what I can think of to say while you are talking."

"I am twenty-two years old," she said. "I was born in this Wing. I grew up in the Classroom. My father was a teacher and my mother was an artist—a painter. They are both dead now, and I live in the Library. I—"

I gripped her arm.

"That's him?" she said, studying the figure which had just come into view on the beltway. "The enemy you flee?"

"I cannot be sure," I said. "But I am going to operate under the assumption that it is. Come on."

We returned to the far side of the pole and entered there.

"You could just be doing this to keep from talking about yourself," she said.

"I could, but I am not."

We began the descent, augmenting our speed by walking rapidly down the gyre. Running to get away, then waiting for the pursuit to catch up could prove self-defeating if I continued the practice any further. It was not my intention, however. I had wanted to establish something, and I believed that I just had.

If it were the same man, it seemed to me that he would have been following at too great a distance to maintain visual contact for the whole junket from the Living Room. While he might be good at anticipating me, the ability was hardly a thing in which to invest complete confidence. Since his hand had already been exposed and it seemed fairly certain that he was out for blood, it would seem to follow that he had some means of tracking me which I had not so far considered.

How could he have planted a transmitter on me?

The answer was not long in coming, although it was of no immediate use. My present clothing had hung in a locker, unattended, while I was on the bandstand. It would not have been overly difficult to get to it and insert something that would broadcast my whereabouts when I left.

It could be microscopic, though, and situated anywhere. Locating it could be quite an undertaking. Unfortunately, the alternative of discarding my garments would not serve to make me less conspicuous in this Wing.

I was glad that I had taken the time to test him though. If I had not, I would be leading him toward my jumping-off place, even if I appeared to lose him. That would never do.

We rode all the way down, to the Basement, and my plan was already in pretty good focus by the time we reached it.

Save for maintenance people, the Basement was pretty much unfrequented. But it was a wilderness of machinery—reactors, generators, circulators, conditioners, pumps, computers, transformers, indicator panels—half-hidden in a jungle of pipes and cables, service belts every few yards, metal stairways that seemed to lead nowhere, flimsy platforms that vibrated when you mounted them, a maze of catwalks at every level, gantries, cranes, the smells of grease and burnt insulation, an unremitting hum, rush, whirr and crackle arising from it and the blue presence of electricity everywhere.

... All of which offered plenty of physical cover, as well as possible interference for whatever broadcast device I might be wearing.

I stood for a moment and took my bearings. Although I could make out a couple of distant jackpoles, it was a subway exchange that I wanted. I located signs indicating the way to the nearest and headed toward the belt leading in that direction. My intention was to skip from Wing to Wing until I hit a station offering immediate transport to the Room I wanted, whatever the Wing, and then move directly to Go, without stopping, without collecting two hundred dollars, cursing the whole damned game the while. If my man could track me through interstellar space perhaps he deserved to win. I had strong doubts concerning his capability along these lines, however.

... And somewhere, before I reached the Gate, I would have to dispose of Glenda. I could not very well take her along to the place where I was going, and I saw no real

81

danger to her should I leave her behind. A quick shot of trank as soon as I was certain we were alone, and she could sleep this one out on some workman's bench. It would be safer for her than keeping her with me much longer, I decided.

It was a wide belt and it was slow, but it had us out of sight of the jackpole within a minute, so packed were the environs with the equipment that maintained the Wing. Once we were in the midst of it, we felt rather than heard the throb of the place. Two quick changeovers and we were on a narrower, faster belt, the course of which roughly paralleled the first. We were actually only a few hundred feet away from it, but it was completely hidden to us. So far, we had encountered no other people.

Anyone descending the jackpole might still catch sight of us without our seeing him, though, because of the way the lights played on the surface of the thing. If someone was, he might have seen me shrug at the thought, because that was about all I was able to do for the moment.

I wondered about the others—what they were thinking, doing, whether they had guessed my present situation correctly. This seemed likely, since they knew I was alive and therefore doubtless aware of the most recent killings, yet had no new orders for them. They must have guessed that I was still running and would contact them as soon as I could, that attempts to contact me could only distract me from my immediate problems. I wondered how much initiative they possessed. We would have to confer again as soon as I reached Wing Null.

We walked quickly, adding our own speed to that of the belt. The light was very bright, almost glaring, for it was always full day here. Cranes moved constantly overhead, dipping, rising, sidling. The machinery hissed, chattered, hummed, hissed, chattered, hummed. I felt an irrational relief when we passed a callbox and the phone within it did not jangle.

"Will you tell me now why you are fleeing, and from whom?" Glenda said.

"No."

"It might be helpful if I knew."

"You invited yourself on this trip," I said. "It is not a conducted tour."

"The danger I felt earlier . . . it is very near now."

"I hope that you are wrong."

But I felt that she was right. My paranoid tendencies were easily stimulated, but they had had a lot of practice recently. I took the next sidebelt to my right, not knowing where it headed. Dutifully, she followed. We were squeezed between towering cliffs of metal. The temperature soared, quickly became oppressive. About twenty feet overhead, two workmen on a metal scaffold stared down at us with something of surprise on their faces.

We took several more turnings, even spending a couple of minutes on a maintenance belt so narrow we had to stand sideways. After a time, we found our way to another, more normal belt, heading in the proper direction. The only other people we passed were schoolchildren on a tour of the ventilation complex. They were far off to our left, and quickly lost to sight.

I began looking about for a safe nook or cranny in which to leave Glenda. I drew my gun and palmed it. I did feel a certain uneasiness at the thought. I do not like leaving loose ends about, I guess that was it. I was curious about her. A strange girl, who could not hold a job, who had helped me . . . I would check back on her as soon as possible. I would attend to her welfare as soon as I had assured my own.

". . . Don't look suddenly," I heard her saying, "but I think we *are* being followed. Not on the belt. Up above. To the left. Back."

I turned my head, trying to be casual about it. One brief glance was sufficient, and I looked away again.

He was up on the catwalks, moving at a brisk pace, shortcutting us, gaining.

. . . And those bright, bright lights shone upon the blue of his glasses.

I saved my curses. I had more than half expected him. For a pathological instant, I wished that I were bearing something more potent than a tranquilizer gun. I pushed the thought aside. I took two paces forward, and Glenda immediately followed.

"Damn it! Don't stand so close to me!" I said.

"It may be to your advantage that I do."

"And your disadvantage. Stay away!"

"In a word: No."

83

"All right. I have warned you. That is all I can do. Enjoy your excitement."

"I am."

My mind raced ahead. I had been faster than Lange, but perhaps still not fast enough. If not, so be it. Maybe I deserved to die. The fact that I was stronger than Lange had been by himself was no assurance that I was fit enough to survive the present situation. I had at least learned a few things about my pursuer and I intended to learn a few more.

I checked ahead, seeking some hunk of machinery with crawlspaces, slots, overhangs—a place where I would be a difficult target, but could get off some clear shots myself. Several possibles presented themselves. Then I looked back, trying to estimate his rate of progress.

"What are you going to do?" Glenda asked me.

I was beginning to have a funny feeling which I could not quite explain, but I had no time to analyze it.

"Bleed all over you," I said, "unless you do exactly what I tell you."

"I am listening."

"Ahead. To the right. About three hundred yards ... The big gray machine with the black cowl on the near end. See it?"

"Yes. It's a Langton generator."

"I am going to head to the left in about a minute. When I do, you remain on the belt for a few more seconds. He will be watching me. Then you will be almost abreast of that thing. Run for it and get in behind it. As soon as I occupy that man overhead, back off and lose yourself in the complex to the rear. Keep an eye on what happens and gauge your actions accordingly. Good luck."

"No. I'm coming with you."

Turning my body so that it could not be seen from behind and above, I twisted my hand and pointed the gun.

"If you try it, I'll trank you and let the belt take you out of here. Don't argue. Do as I say."

Then I jumped down and dashed for the refuge I had chosen, catching sight of the figure overhead as he hurried toward me, his right arm rising.

I heard the shot. With him running like that and all, I was not surprised that he missed. I was out of his line of sight before he got off another. I scrambled around the corner of the unit and moved into the channel I had seen, which cut partway through its middle, was interrupted by a three-foot-high hedge of metal and some hanging cables, then seemed to continue unobstructed to its farther end. There appeared to be eight service adits along its way, and a possible side channel. I could see upward through the gaps among struts and cables, and it pleased me that I had guessed correctly: He would have to get awfully close in order to fire successfully through that mess.

I was only a few paces into it when I heard her.

"Damn!" I said, turning. "I told you to head for the generator!"

"I decided not to," she said. "I knew you would not look back once you began running."

I shrugged, turned away and continued forward. I heard her following. I could see several sections of the catwalk, including a branch that passed above the far end of the machine. According to my calculations, he could be coming into sight any moment now.

"What should I do to help?" I heard Glenda say.

"Whatever strikes your fancy," I said. "I resign all responsibility for your welfare. Your death is on your own head."

I heard a sharp intake of breath and she bit off the beginning of something she had begun to say. I continued to edge forward.

He could have descended one of the ladders or walkways to the floor and be working his way toward us through the mazes of hardware. Or he could be halted or proceeding along another overhead route. He might be very near. It was futile to listen for footfalls, because of the background noise, because of the vibrations of the machine within which we stood.

As I drew near the possible side channel, however, a sharp sound did succeed in penetrating everything. It was the ringing of a telephone in some service niche nearby.

Cursing under my breath and flattening myself against the wall, I resolved to introduce the thing into his alimentary canal from one end or the other at my first opportunity. This time, however, I remained steady. The sound played hell with my nerves, but I succeeded in maintaining control.

A moment later, I heard the crash of his boots and realized what he had done.

Somehow aware of the manner in which the ringing would affect me, he obviously carried a repairman's service unit capable of locating and activating phones. He had worked his way to a position above my shelter, buzzed the nearest call box in hope of disconcerting me, and dropped down atop the machine. Only this time I was not biting. Pressing against the housing, I could feel rather than hear his quick steps. He was seeking an opening, looking for a clear shot. Hoping to find me a quivering mass of jelly, I presumed.

Suddenly, a head, arm and shoulder flashed into view, high up, to my right, about thirty feet down the channel, from behind a juncture of beams.

Even as I whipped my own weapon upward and squeezed, I heard the sound of his shot and the sound of its ricochet. Then he was gone.

I backed up. I bumped into Glenda. Without looking, I pushed her toward the niche, snarling something unintelligible and backing in myself. As I crowded back against her, I heard the thud of his boots again and realized that he had leaped across the right-hand channel. I moved my gun to cover what I guessed to be his new position and felt a sudden, insane pleasure at the thought that the phone had stopped ringing.

Then he appeared, fired again, missed. I got off another shot, too. The next time, I felt, would decide it. He knew my position now.

I leaned back and aimed upward. It was going to be over the top of the niche this time, I felt it.

My chances, as I saw them, were not good. Even if I nailed him perfectly, he was going to get off a shot. My concern, along with protecting the girl, centered upon the seriousness of the injuries I would sustain, should I survive. I was going to get him—I knew it, I felt it, I swore it. Even if he put that bullet right through my heart again, my reflexes would snap off a shot and he would be out for a while, up there. I wanted to live, to drag him back to Wing Null with me, to turn his mind inside out and dump its contents on the floor. It would be so wasteful, to die, to leave him vulnerable and not be able to do anything about it.

"... If I die," I heard myself saying to Glenda, "and leave him unconscious up there," and it was not me that was saying the terrible thing I overheard, I realized, even though the words were coming from my own mouth, "would you be willing to go up and finish him off with his own gun? A bullet through the brain? The heart?"

"No! I couldn't! I wouldn't!"

"It would save me a lot of trouble later."

"Later?" She giggled, half-hysterically. "If you're dead—" Then she shut up, but I could feel her heavy breathing, her tenseness.

What was he waiting for? Damn him!

"Come on!" I cried. "This is the last time! Even if you get me, you're dead!"

Nothing. Still nothing.

Then I heard Glenda whispering, rapidly, urgently.

"You are the one. I was right. Listen. It is important. Take me with you to the secret place. I have something for you. It is important—"

It was also too late. There were three more footfalls and a thud, as he leaped across our channel and fired downward. I felt a searing pain down my chest and ribcage. I fired back, felt that I had hit him.

White pants, blue jacket, long brown hair, blue mirror-glasses, he had turned as he jumped, landed in a half-crouched position, left arm thrown high for balance, right extended downward, weapon pointed, clenched teeth showing through a tight, humorless smile.

"Mr. Black! No!" I heard Glenda scream, as another shot caught me in the shoulder, slamming me back against her.

The trank gun fell from my hand as my whole right arm became useless. I had hit him, though, I knew that.

And it was Mr. Black. It was the same man with whom I had sat in the Cocktail Lounge—how long ago? Eliminating the color and length of hair, the different outfit, the glasses, I saw the same jawline, the same ridges and creases ...

I raised my left hand as he tried to steady his weapon for another shot. Glenda was still screaming as I bit my thumb and glared at him and heard and felt his final shot tear into my guts.

87

He fell backward then as I toppled forward, a cloud of ink seeming to rise from my middle and rush to my head.

The ringing echo of the shot faded, was gone, though I still felt the vibrations of the machine through the wetness, forming and re-forming the words *Pull pin seven*, and Glenda was crying, "Library! Cubicle 18237! Important! Library! Cubicle 18237 ..."

Then soft nothing.

4

I picked myself up and started running again. Crazy, but I could not help it.

Good thing that nobody I could see was in any condition to notice.

Then a knot of live ones appeared, and it was either slow down or become conspicuous—the last thing I wanted to do. I bit my lip, looked in all directions, came to a halt, took several deep breaths.

Then something of Engel began to take hold, and it was better . . .

Tough. Who would have thought Engel able to acquit himself as well as he had? An aging clarinetist—a quiet, peaceable guy. Now only I/he/we knew what had been inside him, and I already different, never to be quite the same again, still changing, aware of the process like mercury within me, impossible to pin down, heavy, flashing, flowing, providing strength, steadiness . . .

Tough, we were tougher than I had thought. It was just that the engine had had to cough a few times before it began to function smoothly. We were almost to our goal now and I, Paul Karab, was nexus . . .

My flight had begun as a thing unrecommended and perhaps slightly ignoble, but now it had become a mission. I had done the proper thing for the wrong reasons.

. . . Paul Karab, reasonably healthy, thirty-five-year-old Living Room Representative, Wing 1, youngest member of the Household Staff, running scared.

Now the fright-factor had diminished considerably—just now—now that Engel/Lange was here. Better and better by the moment.

All of the killings had panicked me, each more than the previous. I had passed out on each occasion and come around in worse shape than before. I had been ready to start running at the time of the meshing, but it had served to stabilize me. Then when Serafis and Davis got it, reason had gone up in smoke. I felt that even my position, with all its safeguards, was not proof against this sort of an attack, an attack that was obviously a well-planned attempt to destroy the entire family. I had not possessed curiosity such as Lange had known, nor anger like Engel's. These would have come later, I was certain, but my panic had submerged these important survival factors. I was ashamed of it, but only for a moment. It had served a useful purpose, and I was no longer the person it had overwhelmed.

I watched the slow progress of the mourners following the box on the belt. The preacher walked at their head, pacing the coffin, reading the final prayers. From where I stood, I could see the area where the service had been conducted, but various partitions and furnishings prevented my viewing the black door toward which they were headed. The obvious analogy came and nested in my mind with small clucking sounds, dark feathers and haste: The Paul Karab I had known all my life was dead, half the family was dead, our whole way of life might well be sucking its final breaths.

No.

I would not permit it.

My determination surprised me, but there it was. I knew what I was going to do, had to do. Without having made a conscious decision, I just knew. The others might not approve. But then again, considering the circumstances, they might. Anyway, it was my choice to make.

The Chapel was, as always, a checkerboard of light and darkness. I moved diagonally to my left, passing to the entrance-point to a darkened section. Glancing about, I dropped to the floor and crawled in, not wanting to break the warning beam that would turn on gentle illumination, the odor of incense, relaxing music and lights on the altar. I slipped into a pew and sat sideways, so that I could look back out and keep an eye on the funeral procession. I wanted a cigarette but felt kind of funny about lighting one in there, so I didn't.

From where I was seated, I could see the black door—gateway to eternity, the underworld, the afterlife, whatever. The belt terminated right before the door, feeding back down around its rollers there. As the mourners advanced, tight-faced, dark-clad, slow, a representative of the funeral director moved forward and pressed out an opening sequence on the plate set into that dark frame.

Silently, the door swung inward and the casket passed through it, followed by considerable remembrances of artificial flowers—of course I could not be certain of this from where I sat, but that many real flowers would have cost a fortune, a circumstance denied by the smallness of the cortege—and since the track then inclined at an appropriate downward angle and was equipped with rollers, the entire display vanished smoothly from sight. Then the door closed, there were some final words from the clerical-type and the people turned and slowly moved away, talking among themselves or silent, as things had it.

I watched them go, waited perhaps ten minutes until the area went dim, waited ten more. Then I rose, crossed over, crawled out again.

Still, silent . . . Even the pall-belt had been turned off. The nearest illuminated area was a good distance away, far enough so that I could not even hear the music.

I advanced, moved up to the belt. For some reason, I reached out and touched it, trailing my hand along it as I walked beside it toward the wall. Tactile person? I thought of Glenda. What was she doing right now? Where was she? Had she contacted the police, or simply fled? Steady finally, my thoughts moved back to those final moments which they had, till now, but skirted. What had she been saying right there at the end? Not the usual hysterical nonsense one would expect from a young woman in the presence of sudden, violent death. No, it had not seemed that way. She had been repeating an address and telling me how important it was. If this were not a form of hysteria, though, the alternative was disconcerting. What use could a dying man have for the information, unless he happened to be me?

But she could not have known. There was no way I could think of for her to have known.

. . . Or anyone else, for that matter. Say, Mr. Black.

. . . Whom she apparently recognized.

Going back a bit further, it was somewhat unusual, our meeting the way that we had . . .

I would have to find out, of course. Anything that might have some bearing on the present unpleasantness was vital.

... And her seeming irrational insistence on accompanying me.

Yes, I would have to pursue the matter. Quite soon.

I crossed over the belt, moved parallel to it, approached the black door. I had to be on the right side in order to reach the plate.

I halted when I came to the black door, the route by which the dead depart the House, the only way anyone leaves the House. It was of a light alloy, was about six feet by eight and in the dim light seemed more a blot or a hole than an object. I manipulated the plate and it swung silently inward. More blackness. Even standing where I was, it was difficult to tell that it was now open. Which suited me fine.

I mounted the belt and stepped through, leaning to the rear to maintain my balance and keeping one hand on the smooth wall. I caught hold of the door then and drew it toward me, pivoting about its advancing edge, and pushed it closed. It would not snap true until I activated the mechanism, but it would do if someone came along during the next few minutes.

I got down on all fours again and crawled backward down the tunnel. It only runs about forty feet. When I reached the rear wall, I rose, leaning against it, and slid my fingers along its surface, seeking the maintenance box.

It took only a moment to locate it and slide its coverplate open. When I did, its small interior light came on and I could see what I was doing once again. The unit seldom, if ever, required servicing, and what I did to it then was definitely not in the service manual. There was no reason, anyway, for anyone to fool with the broadcast coordinates that sent the dead on their one-way subway ride among the stars.

No one but one of us, that is.

I finished, slid the panel shut and waited. There would be a lapse of fifteen seconds before it functioned. After that, it would reset itself to its old coordinates.

Somewhere behind and above me, I heard the door click faintly. All right. There was something I was supposed to remember ...

I was suddenly pitched to the ground. I caught myself with my hands, slipped onto my side and rose to my feet again. Yes, I was supposed to remember that while I was standing on an incline in the tunnel, the surface to which I was transferring was not so canted.

Then there was light all about me. It was a brief, bright corridor, the walls so brilliant and dazzling that they hurt my eyes. As I shielded my gaze and moved along it, my person was being analyzed at hundreds—perhaps thousands—of levels, by hidden devices which would only permit one person to pass through the door at its end.

As I neared it, the door slid upward, and I echoed its sigh as I passed through and into Wing Null.

The feeling of relief, of release, was intense and immediate. I had come home. I was safe. The enemy could not reach me here.

I followed the curving of the red-carpeted hallway to the left, moving about the hub of the fortress, passing the great sealed vaults of Lab, Comp, Storage and Files. I wondered as I walked concerning the state of mind that had moved some earlier version of myself to give them such prosaic names, considering what they really held. Sardonic, I guess.

I continued on by them all and entered the study or lounge that eventually occurred on my right. The lights came on as I did so and I extinguished them with a slap, the illumination from the hallway being sufficient. It was a small room, light-walled, dark-carpeted, containing a desk, two easy chairs, a couch with end tables, a glassed-in bookcase. Everything was just as I remembered it.

I crossed over to the far, blank wall, switched on the control in the chair rail and transpared it.

It was night outside, and a fat, orange moon hung above the white, stone hills about half a mile to my left, giving them the appearance of half a jawbone filled with fractured teeth. Near to hand, the rocks were dark and slick, giving the appearance of having been rained upon recently. There was a flock of pale, retreating clouds in the distance and a bright profusion of stars overhead. An indicator off to my right showed me that the temperature out there was a little over 13° C. I backed away, turned an easy chair to face the panorama and seated myself.

Still staring, I located a cigarette, lit it, smoked.

No matter how urgent the situation was, I had to have this moment, this cigarette, this view of the outside, before I took the next step. I had to be in a tranquil state of mind before I could proceed. It would make a difference.

What it came down to was that I was going to have to violate several directives in order to follow another one. It was a matter of judgment. If we were to mesh now, I believed there would be considerable disagreement, but I was the nexus, the sole heir to Engel's final experiences and the only one in a position to take action. The decision was mine to make and I had made it. •

Bravo! We finally have someone with some sense in the driver's seat!

"It was none of it your doing, old-timer," I said.

Of course it was! All the way!

"Well, I am not about to argue with you over it. It makes little difference now, and will make none whatsoever in a short while."

Perhaps.

"What do you mean 'perhaps'?"

Let us wait and see—in a short while.

"You have no better idea of what will happen than I do. Well, not much better."

I suppose you are right. Shall we go and find out?

"You have waited this long. You can damned well wait until I finish my cigarette."

All right. Enjoy your brooding. You don't even understand what you are looking at.

"I suppose you do?"

Better than you.

"We'll see."

We will.

The night was sufficiently illuminated for me to make out several large craters in the distance, their outlines softened by a low growth of dark vegetation. Staring hard, I could also discern the outlines of the great, ruined, fortresslike building at the foot of the hills. The prospect fascinated me. Maybe I was going to learn some more about it . . .

Enough! There were so many things! That ruin . . . How many hundreds of times had I seen it? Through how many eyes?

Rising, I mashed out my cigarette in a nearby tray, turned, and left the room.

My excitement was high by the time I reached the Files vault. I commenced the delicate, complicated and potentially fatal manipulations of its lock mechanism.

A quarter of an hour later, I had it open. I entered and the lights came on. Several moments later, the door closed and relocked itself behind me.

The room ran back about forty feet at the middle and was around sixty across. Its rear wall was concave, curving about the operating area, which was raised a foot or so above the floor. A lap-level countertop ran along the entire wall, extending out for perhaps thirty inches. Mounted above it were bank upon bank of control assemblies, sweeping outward like wings from the central board and its console. The massive control chair was swiveled in my direction, as if waiting.

I took off my jacket as I walked forward, folded it, placed it on a shelf. Then I seated myself, turned to the console and began warming the thing up. It took about ten minutes to ready it, what with checking out systems and activating subunits in their proper sequence. I was glad of this, for the activity fully occupied my attention for a time.

Finally, though, the lights were arrayed in the proper order, and it was time to begin.

I opened the cabinet to my left, swung out the hood on its long, heavy arm. I ran several quick checks on it, also. Perfect.

I fitted it over my head, lowering it until it rested upon my shoulders. There was an opening about the eyes which permitted me to see what I was doing. I activated the mechanism which caused it to check me out.

There was a vibration as its innards rotated to align themselves with whatever they deemed salient portions of my cranial anatomy. Then there came a tightening as pads moved into place against my skull. There followed a small jolt and a few traces of moisture. The anesthetic. As it was vibrated through the skin, some of it was blocked by my hair. That was all right, though. I did not want to shave or wear a wig. I could stand a little runoff down my neck.

I do not suppose that anyone enjoys contemplating the

violation of his innards, least of all the interior of his skull. Whatever one's knowledge and experience, thinking about feelings gives rise to emotions. It need not even be necessary that the feelings actually occur. Within a very brief span, however, the blue indicator flashed before me and I realized that all of the necessary filaments had succeeded in painlessly penetrating my scalp, skull, dura, arachnoid and pia mater, worked their ways into appropriate areas of my brain and formed themselves into a network capable of performing the work they had to do. And I was still gnawing my lower lip. Thus are we hoist by our own forebrain.

The machinery was ready. Now was the time for the standard procedure employed by each new nexus. Now was the time for me to go back through my/our/the mind and systematically erase all those portions of Lange and Engel which I felt to be in conflict with my own personality and to excise their memories dealing with things before my own time. Now was the time for the sacrifice, the partial suicide, the jettisoning of the excess baggage, of the things which served only to clutter the mind, create conflicts, make life less tolerable. As no one knows how much the human mind can hold, somewhere along the line we decided not to tamper with its limits. I believed that to be the reason. Somewhere, back in the dreamtime, the decision was made. To the best of my knowledge, we had always proceeded on the basis of this rationale, and since the family was still around, it had always proved effective. Until now, of course. Now was the time for Lange and Engel to depart—to become, perhaps, autonomous complexes, or personal demons in the underworld of my subconscious.

Now, however, the threat to our existence was foremost in my mind, and I wanted to be larger, not smaller, to know more things, not fewer. Preserved in memory and ringed round with a directive not to erase, was the notion that, as an emergency procedure in a time of great peril, the dead might be resurrected. I did not believe it had ever been employed, and of course had no idea what the result might be. That it would be more than memory, though, was obvious. Still, I felt myself a very definite and very real me, despite being partly Lange and partly Engel. The situation warranted drastic action.

I became very conscious of my heartbeat as I turned my attention to the patchboard with its seven pins and spaces for many more.

Each pin, the life of a nexus; each, a generation of our kind skewered there like an invisible butterfly . . .

My palm was moist as I reached forward.

A pin was inserted in the master board each time the process of erasure was completed. To draw one would be to undo the work of a predecessor, to cause *his* predecessor to live again within me.

What was I doing? I was supposed to be here to insert pin eight . . .

My hand began to shake.

This was wrong! It was ridiculous even to consider . . .

My hand grew steady, continued to move forward. I tried, but was unable to halt it.

I watched with a peculiar fascination, as it moved across the board, settled upon its target and withdrew pin seven.

5

I was not at all certain what it was I had expected. A clash of cymbals? A mind-riving jolt, followed by unconsciousness? Something dramatic, I guess.

It was, however, more than anything else, like waking up in the morning, memories of the previous day gradually hefting themselves above the horizon. A mere clearing of the head, revealing what had been there all along. A gallery of familiar pictures.

Old Lange . . .

Of course. It had been an instance where we had posed as being our own son. It was only chance that the nexus passed from one Lange-identity to another. And there had been others in the mesh, long forgotten, but with me once again, as if they had never been away.

I was now the demon who had been addressing us. I was Engel, Lange, Lange Senior and those things the older Lange had retained of his predecessor, a strange mind I would almost have called alien minutes earlier: Winton. But regarding him as his successor had seen fit to preserve him, he did not seem all that different. What was it? What was happening? My accumulated memories now ran back for over a century, but it was more than a matter of timespan and quantity. The sense of differentness that accompanied the reavailability of all this experience was . . . qualitative. Yes, that was it. And what was the quality?

That is something you cannot truly appreciate in your present state.

Powerful. There. Him. Winton. For a moment, I was too dumbstruck to reply. The knowledge had always been present, but I had not taken the time to consider it—that in releasing Lange's demon and absorbing him, I would come up against the older, earlier interface, with the demon of whom I had previously known nothing capable of addressing me from behind it.

You needed what you have now, he was saying, *as a point of departure. You are smarter and somewhat stronger for what you have obtained, but it is not sufficient against Mr. Black. To understand, and to possess the ability to do something about it will require the pulling of pin six. Do it now.*

Determined. And strong. He was. In his insistence. That was what made the decision for me. I wanted that determination, that strength.

That is why, before I could marshal the arguments against it, I moved my hand several inches upward on a diagonal and pulled pin six.

Yes! Yes, as the fogs rolled away and my memory reached back for perhaps a century and a half, it was not only the recalling of vast quantities of experience that moved me. The memories themselves, still, were dreamlike and not especially charged with emotion. It was a tightening, a toughening of attitude that came into me, that reassured me as to my own ability to deal with the present situation. And more, more than that . . .

I had hardly begun sorting out my reactions, let alone considering the matter which had elicited them, when Birnam Wood began to shuffle its feet, so to speak.

The feeling. God, the feeling . . . It was like flood waters suddenly welling behind an ancient dam. I felt the gathering might, I was uncertain as to the fortifications.

Yes, you were weak and you have been strengthened. But now is not the time to stop. Reach out and take it all. You need every weapon you can get your hands on right now. You will face an enemy who is also strong. For this reason you must be more fully yourself. Pull pin five and restore me within you. I will show you how to deal with Mr. Black.

"No," I said. "Wait," I said. "Wait . . ."

There is no time. Black's position grows stronger with every moment you delay. Do not discard the tool that may cut the diamond, throw away the stone that may be key to the arch. You will need me. Pull pin five!

My hand moved toward it, but I feared I might have gone too far already. There was no way to gauge the strength of the entity that would then urge me to pull pin four, and then three—and all the way back, to the beginning, unbuilding the painfully erected edifice, undoing centuries of collective effort to achieve moral evolution.

I share your sentiments, I agree with your principles. They are all of them useless, however, if you are no longer available to further them. You require my knowledge of specifics in order to defend yourself properly. Therefore, as the day the night . . . Pull pin five! Now!

The muscles in my arm began to ache. My fingers were curved and stiff, clawlike.

"No!" I said. "Damn it! No!"

You must!

My hand jerked, my fingertips touched the pin.

I had gone too far too fast. I was way off balance in every department of my mind. He might be right, Jordan—I suddenly knew that to be his name. He might be right. But I was not going to have him pressure me into it. I was not even certain what I had just become. To release another unknown within myself was tantamount to lunacy.

Of course you are uncertain. But you must also realize that your hesitancy jeopardizes the others, as well as the girl . . .

"Wait!"

Then the anger came, deadly. I, James Winton, had blotted him out, sacrificed him, broken him with my will. Now this pitiful ragtag, tail-end self was trying to order me about!

Slowly, I clenched my right hand into a fist. Then I slammed it down against the countertop.

"No!" I said. "I have what I need."

You are a fool!

I raised my hand, very deliberately, and pressed my thumb against pin five.

Silence.

Trying not to think of anything, not to sort out any thoughts or feelings, I shifted to a motor level of activity and began the process of disengaging myself from the equipment.

Finally, the pressure let up on my head and the lights indicated that the hood might be removed. I did this, returning it to its cabinet, then shut down all units and departed Files, sealing the place carefully behind me. I moved along the hallway to Comp and began the unlocking procedure there. Then I returned to my den, for the time-lock mechanism on Comp had a little over ten minutes to go.

I flopped into the chair, lit another cigarette and stared out into the night. The moon had traveled a detectable distance in the brief while I had been away. The shadow patterns had shifted across the landscape, revealing more evidence of ancient devastation as well as additional vegetation. The prospect was considerably more familiar to me now than it had been earlier, though I still did not understand the nature of the carnage. A war, perhaps? There was something even more intriguing and disturbing about the ruins at the foot of those stark hills now . . .

My ruminations were cut short as I stared at that wreckage. It seemed as though there had been a movement.

I rose and crossed to the window.

Again, something. A glint . . . Yes, there was a flicker of light back within the collapsed walls. I continued to watch, and it came again, several times. I tried timing the flashes, but there did not seem to be any special pattern to them.

Then there was a blaze, as though a beacon had been swung quickly across the wracked landscape and fallen directly upon me, where it stopped.

I raised my arm to shield my eyes against its brilliance, and with my other hand I felt for the control and darkened the window once more.

I sank back into the chair then, some small part of me surprised that I was not especially disconcerted by the phenomenon. The feeling quickly passed. Nothing that strange about the light, really. It had undergone periodic bursts of such activity for generations. I had just forgotten—or, rather, just remembered—about it. Yes, it seemed something mechanical that was occasionally disturbed, underwent a brief spasm of activity, lapsed into quiescence again. One of the *so what?* facts of existence.

Or was it? Oh, hell! I had more pressing matters demanding my attention.

Like, who was I? I realized I was no longer the same individual who had come to Wing Null. And it was not a loss, but a gain. That was the way I felt about it. But what was the gain?

101

I felt more Winton than Karab, to be truthful about it. But it was as if this had always, really, been so, and the other was but a temporary phase, a life-laboratory I had employed for the conduct of certain experiments. And the necessity was now upon me to abandon this research for a time, in order to deal with larger matters which had arisen to trouble me.

Lord! how naive I had allowed myself to become! I smiled at my prissy latterday selves. Their fears. Their qualms.

On whose shoulders did they think they stood? Who had bought them the right to indulge their precious squeamishness? Who had provided the opportunity for them to exercise their higher instincts, as a band of anonymous humanitarians and benefactors of the House? Within the present generation, the time of Lange, they had stopped a plague, prevented several large-scale disasters from being far worse than they were, promoted several productive lines of medical research, discouraged three programs of scientific inquiry which could have led in an undesirable direction, guided the computers and politicians toward several sound decisions concerning population control, aggression-surrogation and areas of emphasis in education, aided in the development of new amusements, saw the crime rate decline even further and assisted numerous groups and individuals in times of distress. But why had they had this opportunity to indulge in what, to some, might seem officious intermeddling, to others, altruism? Their way had been paved with thought, sweat, sacrifice and more than a little blood.

On the other hand, it had all been worth it. Strange, to think of myself simultaneously from two temporal perspectives. But they were merging, merging even as I thought them, and I felt considerably enriched therefor. Jordan's perspective would be even broader, I knew. I had some of his memories, and I knew that he went back a long while. Perhaps I had been hasty in dealing with him—

No! The line had to be drawn somewhere. What I now possessed seemed sufficient. There was a solid, important reason for everything that we did, I knew that. I did not need all of the specifics. Based on my present knowledge of myself, I had faith in all my earlier decisions. I believed

102

that I had never suppressed arbitrarily, that there was a reason for each partial suicide. To undo everything as an exercise in academic curiosity would be an act of madness.

My scalp began to tingle, bringing my thoughts back to more immediate considerations.

I got to my feet. The lock on Comp should be about ready for further manipulation. I massaged my head lightly as I headed back down the hall. I wondered about Gene, Jenkins and Winkel. They were still alive, which was all that really mattered. They should not be in any immediate jeopardy, since I had left Mr. Black somewhat distraught; and they had all had what seemed sufficient time in which to prime their senses of survival and throw up a few defenses. I saw no point in contacting them until I had something to tell them, which would not be for a little while yet.

I had a brief wait remaining before I could get into Comp, which time I spent puzzling over Glenda. It was fairly apparent from her parting comments that she knew something about me. What she knew was not nearly so important to me as how she had come to learn it. And she knew something about my old enemy, who was calling himself Mr. Black these days. If for no other reason than this, she would be high on my schedule of priorities.

The mechanism came to its final activation point, I completed the sequence, opened the door and entered. The layout of the room was similar to that of Files, only cast on a somewhat larger scale. Here, too, equipment— though of a different variety—filled the far wall and the control chair, while situated farther to the left, was of the same comfortable order as the other. I locked the door behind me and moved toward it.

I activated the Bandit. Funny, my nickname for the thing had been dropped somewhere along the line, to be replaced by the simple, bland understatement: Comp. It was more than a computing device, however. It was also a data embezzler. The fact that its operations had never been detected was some sort of tribute to the skill of its nameless creator, who had provided it surreptitious access to the master data banks of Wing 1. And more, even more than this. Should necessity require, it could monitor, compute the best points of violation and introduce new materials. Comp, indeed!

So I set it to looking for Mr. Black. My hopes were not great in this department, but I had to try. He might have slipped up somewhere this time around. I had a fairly extensive file on him, already digested within the Bandit's gleaming guts, and it drew on this in its search. A mistake had been made—albeit an understandable one—in eradicating this portion of our memory. The erasure had probably occurred because the whole affair did seem to have been concluded satisfactorily and conscious recall of the violence was an undesirable thing to my carefully civilized scions. That made it my mistake, by proxy, anyway. So I had to be understanding and forgiving, damn it!

I set the Bandit to finding me a history for Glenda, as well as her most recently recorded movements. I also ran vital-statistics searches for Hinkley, Lange, Davis, Serafis and Engel, to see whether any of the deaths had been reported yet.

Then the klaxon began squawking and I was full of adrenalin and on my feet in an instant.

I moved to a sideboard to my left, flicked on a viewscreen and activated an arsenal after switching the many deadlies from automatic to manual control.

I was disappointed when I saw that the arrivals were Winkel and a coffin. A scan showed the mass and indicated the nonliving status of the coffin's contents—so presumably the box contained what was left of Lange. I smiled at my disappointment. I should have been happy that Winkel, of all of us, had proved successful in what he had set out to do. Instead, I was a little irritated that it was not Mr. Black, trying again. He would soon discover that I lacked a few of my brethren's qualms. Among other things, those two pins had represented over a century's inhibitions. So far, he had only had clay pigeons to shoot at. It was about time he encountered a rabid vampire bat. I only hoped that I would have time to tell him it was Winton, again, before the end.

I turned off the klaxon and switched on a speaker.

"Good show, Winkel," I said. "I'll be there to help you in a minute. I'm in Comp."

"Karab," he said, facing the screen, a fairer, thirty-year-old version of myself. "I was worried. When you didn't mesh—"

"Relax. The situation is improving."

I turned off the screen and the speaker, opened a drawer, removed a small pistol, checked it over and loaded it, jammed it into my pocket. Why, I am not certain. Something about the hardiness of old habits, I guess, for it was certainly not that I was unable to trust anyone, even—and I chuckled at the thought—myself.

I departed then, there being no delay in opening the door from the inside, and I felt a small twinge of conscience at not locking it behind me, so deep-dug was the routine's rut. Damn Mr. Black, anyway! He was the reason for the whole procedure, that time he had actually made it to Wing Null and only been surprised by accident. If I had nailed him then, life would be so much simpler.

I moved on up the hall, passed through the entrance defenses and nodded at Winkel, who stood looking tense beside the coffin.

"All right," I said, "let's lug the guts over to Storage. We have a lot of things to do."

He nodded back, and we caught hold of the thing and carried it out.

"I was worried you hadn't made it here," he said as we went.

"Your fears were obviously groundless."

"Yes," he said, and moments later as we deposited the container outside the storage vault and I was turning my attention to the lock, "That looks like a gun in your pocket."

"It is."

"It doesn't look like a trank gun. It looks like one of the other kind."

"That's right."

"What is it for?"

"Think about it for a minute," I said, as I manipulated the locking mechanism.

I worked it to the point where the time device took over, then straightened and jerked my head to the right.

"Come on over to Comp. I have some things to check while we wait."

He followed me, but halted abruptly as we neared the door.

"It isn't locked!" he said.

"True. Time is more than a little essential just now," I replied, pushing it open.

He followed me inside, saying nothing as I crossed to the Bandit to learn the results of my inquiries. As I had suspected, Mr. Black had covered himself well. There was nothing on him, yet. The Bandit would continue its search, of course, looking farther and farther afield for indications of the man.

None of our deaths had been recorded yet, I noted. Probably Hinkley's place was such a mess that they still had not determined who all was involved. And it was kind of soon to have anything in on Engel, even supposing the body had been found—which may not have been the case.

... No indeed, I decided, as I began skimming the data on Glenda. Mr. Black was not about to report it, and the more I learned about Glenda the less predictable she seemed.

"Did you have any trouble getting Lange's body here?" I asked.

"No, no difficulty. No one had come across—"

The klaxon sounded once more. I switched the screen on again and saw that it was Jenkins.

I killed the klaxon, activated the speaker and said, "Hello. Winkel and I are in the Comp Room. Come on over. Don't trip on Lange."

I broke the circuit before he could reply, another nervous youngster of our size and build.

I felt Winkel's gaze and I turned to face him.

"You have changed," he said. "Tremendously. I do not understand what has happened, what is happening. Why didn't you mesh with us after you got here? Why not do it now?"

"Patience," I said. "Right now time is a very expensive commodity and I have to budget it carefully. I will explain everything before too long. Trust me."

He smiled weakly and nodded.

"You do know what to do, then?"

I returned the nod.

"I know what to do."

Moments later, Jenkins arrived. He was breathing heavily and his face was flushed.

"What's happening?" he yelled, and he sounded more than a little hysterical. "What's happening?"

Winkel moved to him, seized his shoulder and said, "Take it easy, take it easy. Karab's going to explain everything. He knows how to handle it."

Jenkins shuddered once, then seemed to shrink a little. He turned his head and stared at me.

"I hope so, I really hope you do," he said, regaining control of his voice and softening it, slowing it. "Maybe you can start by telling me what happened to Wing 5."

"What do you mean?" I asked. "What's wrong with it?"

"It's gone," he said.

6

So Kendall Glynn, the poor bastard, had been her father. Interesting, as well as sad, strange and uncomfortable. The latter, both because I distrust coincidences and because I suddenly realized a feeling of guilt over the way Lange had handled things. Funny, he had not. He had felt it the most civilized way of dealing with the situation because he abhorred violence, whereas I would simply have waited for the proper moment and shot the fellow myself. Not that I would not have felt guilty about that, but it would have been a different kind of guilt—a bit cleaner, to my way of thinking.

I thought about him as I worked the lock on the door to the Supplies vault. Jenkins and Winkel were far up the hall, in Storage, wrestling Lange's body onto ice. It seemed a good thing, not just to give them something to do until Gene arrived and I could address them all together as an alternative to meshing, but to have them actually touch the dead reality as well. It might make it a little easier for them to accept what had to be done.

It had been around sixteen years ago, so Glenda was too young to remember it well. Though of course she knew about it—too much and not enough. I/we/it/the nexus had occupied Lange's now cold form in those days, and Kendall Glynn had had to be stopped. He had been sufficiently vocal concerning his ideas to keep me both aware and wary for several years. In a lesser man, I would not have been so concerned. But Glynn was more than a master of engineering. He was one of those scientist-artists who comes along every few centuries to justify the existence of that overworked word "genius." His colleagues respected, envied, admired him; his name was known to the man on the belt as well as the man in the lab. Though it was not until his late forties that he married and fathered Glenda, there was nothing especially

108

misanthropic about him, as is often the case with brilliant men who spend their first thirty or so years being misunderstood. He was engaging, rather than belligerent, for a man who was out to destroy most of the orderly traditions of society and fill the cart with a new species of apple. He was the last real revolutionary I had known, and I respected him. As Lange, though, my main feeling was one of apprehension.

When I learned that things had gotten beyond the talking stage, that he was actually preparing a presentation for the Council and had apparently obtained sufficient support from several representatives to have his request for a pilot project put to a vote, I paid him a visit in my Jess Borgen persona, an old Fellow of the Academy of Sciences. I remembered that day and that body well, as my prostate was giving me a good deal of trouble and I had had to stop off several times on the way over to his place . . .

Kendall was not the lean, scholarly type. He was somewhat short and stocky, with rather rugged features and a thick mane of black hair only slightly frosted above the ears. His most striking feature was his eyes; they were magnified enormously by corrective lenses, especially the left one, and gave the impression that they had looked upon just about everything, could see through just about anything. Considering my own situation, I found this somewhat disconcerting. In fact, it was not for completely urological reasons that after only a few minutes' conversation I had to excuse myself from his welter of globes, star charts, work tables, drawing boards, eco-injection module-mockups and his computer-access station. It was because I had realized that here was a man who just might be able to pull it off, the thing that others had only mumbled about occasionally over the years.

"But the eighteen worlds of the House are already grossly terratype," he had said, "or we would not have located the Wings on them," in response to my, "But each one represents a radically unique environment."

"And you want to thrust people out into them before they are ready?"

"The people or the worlds?" and he had smiled.

"Both."

"Yes," he said. "They can reside in the modules while conducting the planoforming."

"Granting for a moment that it would be to our advantage to adapt the exo-environments, why bother with the intermediary stage? Why not do the work from the House itself, and when things are ready those who want can move out and take advantage of it?"

"No," he said. "I'm afraid," and his voice was very soft and he was no longer looking at me, but at the array of globes on the table to his right. "I consider the House an evolutionary dead end for the human race," he went on. "We have created a static, unyielding environment, to which man must either adapt or go under. Being the durable, adaptable creature that he is, he has not gone under. In the span of only a few centuries, he has changed considerably."

"Yes, he has worn off a lot of rough edges, has become a more rational, more controlled being."

"I do not like that last adjective at all."

"I meant self-controlled."

He made a noise halfway between a chuckle and a couple of snorts, and I excused myself to visit his washroom.

We talked for close to two hours, but that was the real point of contention right there. I did not question the physical feasibility of his proposals. I was certain that all of the worlds in question could indeed be made habitable for man. I was also reasonably satisfied that the various life-support systems he had worked out for those planets which would require them would adequately serve to shelter their inhabitants while the terraforming was going on. I also had no doubt that his other pet project, a new program of interstellar exploration in faster-than-light vehicles, would result in the discovery of new worlds, some of which might be eminently suitable for human use. Whether these were to be pursued simultaneously, as he desired, or only in part, any part, was immaterial to me.

My real concern was over the threat it represented to the House. I was not afraid of what was Out There, but rather of what the availability of Out There would do to what was In Here. It was obvious that his programs were on a collision course with my own.

"What is it that you have against the House?" I asked him, half-joking, at one point.

"It has already succeeded in conditioning much of what is left of the human race," he said, "to behave at the reaction level of a herd of cows. Someday a bull is going to come along and that is the position in which he is going to find us."

"I have to take issue with that," I said. "The House is the first place in the history of the human race where people have succeeded in living together peacefully. They are finally learning to cooperate rather than compete. I see this as a strength, not a weakness."

His eyes narrowed within their pools, staring at me as if seeing me for the first time. Then, "No," he said. "They are beaten over the head if they do not cooperate. Their brains are scrambled, they are shot full of drugs and subjected to therapy to adjust them to an unnatural norm if they are not peaceable in terms of that norm. They become well-programmed claustrophiles. But in learning to live together in the House and love it, I fear that we are sacrificing our ability to live anywhere else. The House cannot endure forever. Its end may also be the end of the human race."

"Ridiculous!" I said. I might have argued over the durability of the House. I might have argued that the dispersion of the race over eighteen separate worlds was a pretty strong factor in favor of its continuance. But both of these arguments would have been specious. My real disagreement with him lay in the interpretation of what the House was doing to people. I could not argue this point fully, however, without explaining my part in matters and giving him an idea as to my overall plan. So I settled back into my Establishment role and said, "Ridiculous!"

With a small smile that was mostly upper lip and malicious, he turned my comment and nodded.

"Yes, I suppose so," he said. "It is ridiculous that the situation managed to reach the point that it did. It would be a little more encouraging in terms of racial sanity if there were some valid devil theory of history, if some person or group could be singled out as sponsor of this madness." He sighed. "However, I am hoping that we can learn from our mistakes, in time."

111

I felt uncomfortable at this, and was able to switch the conversation over to the details of several of his accommodation systems. They were all of them, unfortunately, very well designed. I was determined that they, at least, would not be wasted, eventually.

If only I could have spotted some technical flaws in his work or some major defect in his concepts . . . But no. He had been too thorough. He was just too good. If only he had, I could have had him discredited on those grounds, could have stopped the project that way. If only . . .

There was enough interest in his work to worry me. I was already whipping up an opposition among the conservatives on the Council and in the Academy, but I was not at all that certain that I could see the thing soundly defeated—and it would require a good trouncing to keep it from rising again to plague me.

So, my Lange-incarnation reasoned, there is an alternative to attacking a man's ideas.

A comprehensive check by the Bandit failed to turn up anything juicy and exploitable on the man. Dull or discreet, it did not matter. I could not find my weapon in his past.

I winced as I reviewed my latter ego's thinking, his decision, his action upon it. I had certainly changed a lot in a few generations.

During the next week, we removed five girls from the neighborhood, ranging in age from about five to around seven, at unobtrusive and coverable times during their daily schedules. They were subjected to hypnotics and viewed movies of Kendall while they received suggestions as to what he had said and done during the past few months. It was decided that two of the girls should actually have been molested, and the hymen was surgically broken by Serafis and minor vaginal infections instigated. One would come forth with the revelation, the accusation, the other would duplicate it, the remaining three would provide stories about the dirty old man with the pocket full of candy bars. The girls would of course be treated later by proper medical authorities and made to forget what they believed to have actually occurred. Thus did we salve our collective conscience over the girls.

It happened exactly as we had desired. Once the news got out, Kendall was ruined, the project was ruined and,

112

by association, stars became an even dirtier word. Once he was sent up for his brainwash, it was definitely all over.

I recalled his abhorrence of adjustive techniques, but it never occurred to us that he might be a genuine violence-prone patho, by Lange's definitions, a real throwback. I guess we should have recalled his reply to our casual question, as we headed toward the washroom for the last time, "What will you do if you lose out, badly?" He had stared down at his slippers, bunched and unbunched his toes a couple times within them, then said, "It's all over for us if it doesn't pass." That's all.

About four weeks later, he hanged himself in his quarters in the Dispensary. Glenda must have been about five or six at the time.

While we deplored violence, we did not feel especially guilty about it. We tended to look upon what had occurred as one of those unfortunate, unforeseen things that sometimes happen when you are just doing your job. Also, it was then impossible for us to entertain the possibility of any sort of connection between Kendall and Mr. Black. Black had been deemed dead in my day, and memories of the man were duly erased when Old Lange sacrificed me. Now that I was back, however, the entire Kendall Glynn incident took on a different, more sinister appearance. Unlike my successors, though, I felt rotten about the way things had been handled. I realized that a debt of honor existed toward Glenda.

I thought about this as the clock ticked its way toward opening and Lange's remains were stashed in the cooler. This, and a lot of other things. Of course, I was going to go after Glenda. She knew something—possibly quite important—that she wanted to tell me. Even if she did not, however, I would have gone because she had asked me to, and because of the very strong possibility that she was in danger.

When the vault finally opened, I entered and removed a variety of things I might be needing. I hauled them all off to the little lounge, leaving this vault open behind me, also.

"Library! Cubicle 18237!" Glenda had kept repeating. Since she had not added a Wing designation, this indicated that she meant Library, Cubicle 18237 of the Wing we then occupied.

... Wing 5, of which the Bandit had verified Jenkins' bit of news. As of but a brief while ago, the subways had stopped running and all communications had terminated. It was as if Wing 5 had suddenly ceased to exist.

After I had deposited my gear, I returned to Comp, where I ran another check with the Bandit. It reconfirmed the initial report I had received, with no new developments. A survey of my private subway system to Wing 5 showed all lines to be operational, however. This was as I had expected. Their power source for my uses was located here, not there. Even if it had not been, I had a funny feeling that they might still be working. There seemed to be a pattern emerging, and I had a part in it.

It was not very long before Winkel and Jenkins reentered.

"All set?" I asked.

"Yes," Winkel replied. "Listen, we have a right to know what's going on—"

"Of course," I said. "You will."

"When?"

"We will wait awhile longer to see whether Gene is coming."

"Why not just mesh with him and find out?"

"I'll be talking about that, too."

I turned and walked toward the door.

"What should we do now?" Jenkins asked me.

"I think it would be a good idea for you to wait here for Gene, to turn off the klaxon when he arrives."

"Why not just turn it off now?"

I returned to the control panel and switched our defense system from manual back to automatic. I also removed the pistol from my pocket and set it on the countertop.

"Because it just may be that someone else will come through," I said, turning on the screen and the speaker.

"Who?" said Jenkins.

"I'll tell you about that later, too."

"What should we do if it is someone else?"

"If the equipment doesn't get him, you'd better."

"Even if it means using that gun?"

"Even if it means using your teeth and fingernails. I'm going up to the lounge now. I have some things to do."

I could hear them talking as I headed on up the hall,

but I could not make out what they were saying. Just as well, I suppose.

I entered the lounge, crossed it and activated the window. The temperature had dropped slightly and the moon had traveled a considerable distance, shifting the shadow patterns about. The light from the ruin was no longer visible. I stared for perhaps a minute, still puzzling over its earlier occurrence, then turned my attention to the equipment I had fetched.

Stripping to my undergarments, I donned lightweight body armor that protected me from groin to neckline. I put on full-length black trousers then, because I wanted to wear some explosives taped along the inside of my left calf. A heavy-caliber revolver went into a belt holster to be covered by a white, short-sleeved shirt. Something from outside disturbed me as I was taping the stiletto to my left forearm. A movement?

I lit a cigarette and spent a few minutes staring out the window.

The flicker. Yes. It came again. Once, twice . . .

My observations were interrupted by the sound of the klaxon. I departed the lounge immediately and headed down the hall. The alarm ceased before I had gone twenty feet, so I slowed to a walk. I continued on far enough to see that it was Gene, our youngest member, then waved to him and turned back.

"Wait!" I heard him call out, followed by the sounds of rapid footfalls.

"I'll be with you in a few minutes," I called back. "Go on into the Comp room. Jenkins and Winkel are there."

The running continued and I decided the hell with him. I had already told him where I was going, and I was not about to stand there and justify myself.

He caught up with me just as I was about to reenter the lounge. Whatever he was about to say was forgotten, however, as we made the turn together and the burst of light hit us. He gripped my arm and we stood there for a moment, unmoving.

Then I stepped into the room and he released his hold and followed me across it. We moved to the window and stood there squinting into the light. Yes, it was coming from the ruin all right.

115

From behind us, I heard Winkel make a brief noise, like, "Wha—?"

Then the light was gone, and everything out there was as it had been before.

I reached out and opaqued the thing again. I moved toward the nearer chair, where I had been standing earlier, and arrived there just as Jenkins burst into the room.

"What is going on?" he inquired, searching our faces.

"Nothing," I said, picking up a light-gray jacket and pulling it on, "now."

I dropped a handful of extra ammo and two gas grenades into my left side pocket. Three small fragmentation bombs went into my right.

"We are going back to Comp, right now," I announced. "Someone must be on duty there at all times, until this thing is over. There must be no unauthorized visitors."

"Have there ever been?" Jenkins asked.

"Yes."

"Who?"

"I'll tell you about it in Comp. Come on."

They followed me into the hall. As we headed down it, Gene said, "What was that light?"

"I don't know."

"It could be something important."

"I am certain that it is."

We entered Comp and I moved to adjust the subway equipment to take me to Wing 5. Before I could set the circuits, however, Winkel stepped in front of me and stood there, hands on his hips.

"All right," he said. "What's the story? Why didn't you mesh?"

"Because," I said, "you would have been radically changed by the process, and I want you just the way you are until I have decided what I am going to do about my condition."

"What condition? What is the matter?"

I sighed, lit a cigarette, moved to his right and seated myself on the countertop, facing the three of them.

"I pulled pins seven and six," I said.

"You *what*?"

"You heard me."

116

There was silence. I had expected a blizzard of questions, but they just stared.

"It had to be done," I said. "We were being killed left and right, and there was no apparent reason, no way of stopping it. By unlocking generations of experience, I hoped to find something—information, a weapon. I was scared, too."

Winkel dropped his eyes and nodded.

"I would have done the same thing," he said.

"So would I," said Gene.

"I guess I would have, too," Jenkins said, joining in the effort to make me feel better. "Did you find something?"

"Yes, I believe I did. But it is rather complicated, and I only have time to hit some of the highlights now."

"Before you do," Winkel said, "tell us one thing: Who are you now, really?"

"I am the same person I was before," I said, feeling that I was lying and feeling, too, their need for reassurance that everything was not coming apart at the same moment. "The only difference is that now I have access to all the memories of old Lange and Winton, as well as those of Jordan which Winton did not choose to sacrifice."

But he saw, I think, and persisted.

"Of them all, who do you most feel like?" he said.

"Myself! Damn it!" I said. I was half-minded to mesh then and there and remove all cause for argument and explanation both. But I held to my conviction that this might not be wise in terms of whatever personal editing I might eventually be required to undertake. Also, from the look on his face, I believed that Winkel might be prepared to resist the mesh at this time. So, "There was some influence, of course," I said. "That was unavoidable. Fortunately, it is of benefit in the present situation. I am still basically me, though."

He still looked unconvinced, but further insistence was not going to strengthen my statement—just the opposite, perhaps—so I decided to let it rest at that and get down to essentials.

"It appears that, several generations ago, an individual became aware of our existence," I began. "How he learned of us remains a mystery. But he demonstrated his knowledge of the personal identities of all the members of the family at that time. He did this in a manner that bore

117

a close resemblance to our present plight. He attempted to murder all of us. He was obviously unsuccessful, possibly because the tendency was still strong within us to strike back instantly. We did not, however, succeed in obtaining his destruction, rehabilitation or even—for that matter—knowledge of his identity. He did succeed in killing three of us before we increased our wariness and the variety of our defenses to the point where several further attempts on his part were frustrated and he became the hunted. We came close to capturing him on two occasions, but he managed to escape us both times. Then he vanished. The attacks ceased. Years passed. Nothing.

"While we did not forget what had occurred," I went on, "the absence of the peril allowed for a gradual return of some feelings of security. Perhaps he was dead, we felt. Or had given up on his vendetta for reasons as inscrutable as those which had caused him to embark upon it. Whatever his disposition, he apparently took his knowledge of our affairs with him, for there was never any indication, anywhere else, of an awareness of our existence.

"Then, almost nine years later, he struck again, as suddenly as before. His planning and his coordination were very good. He got five of us at that time. He might have done even better, had not Benton been able to shoot him before he died himself. He was apparently pretty badly wounded, but he managed to get away before we reached the scene. Then, again, nothing. For several years. We assumed he had died as a result of his wounds."

"How do you know it was the same man?" Gene asked me.

"An assumption," I replied, "based primarily upon the similar pattern of attack. We also have a gross physical description, from the terminal impressions of several of his victims. And we have other data, such as his blood type—"

"Was it the same man who shot you?" Winkel asked.

"In light of what I know now, yes. I believe that it was."

"Where there any other attacks besides the two you have described?"

"Yes. Many years after the passing of Jordan, during the time when Winton was nexus, he came here, to Wing

118

Null. The nature of his intentions was never clear to us. We have no idea what he would have done had the place been unoccupied, as it is so much of the time. As it was, Winton just happened to be here—here in Comp, as a matter of fact—when he arrived. The klaxon sounded and Winton picked him up on the screen. Interestingly, he had succeeded in avoiding the automatic defenses. How he achieved this remains a mystery. Winton headed for the hall and startled him there, opening fire immediately. He fled, returning the fire, and although he was wounded he succeeded in throwing himself across the grid and making an exit. Winton returned here and traced him, discovering he had gone to the Chapel on Wing 7. He immediately meshed with the others, and we attempted an intercept there. But beyond a few gory traces, he was not to be found."

"That was the last such occurrence—until recently, that is?"

"Yes. Old Lange retained the memory as a precaution. Lange erased it as a useless violence-reminder when he became nexus, though. So much time had passed that it seemed a safe assumption that our enemy was dead."

"A mistake."

"Obviously."

"He left no clues?"

"A few here and there. Dead ends, all. For instance, he dropped a tool kit when I—Winton shot him. It proved to have been stolen from a maintenance locker in the Cellar of Wing 11. The trail ended there."

"No prints, no traces of any sort on the tools or their container?"

"None. He always wore gloves at the proper time. Careful sort. We spent a long while checking on everybody even remotely associated with the maintenance locker. Again, nothing. But the nature of the tools themselves gave rise to some interesting speculations."

"Of what sort?"

"The tools were of the type a person might choose to work on the locks we had on the vaults then. Does that remind you of anything?"

"The missing clone!"

"Exactly. Our big, unsolved mystery, over a century old

119

now. One day a clone is gone from its locker, never to be seen again. Where? How? Why? No answers. Absolutely useless to anyone but the family. Supposedly inaccessible to anyone but us. Gone. That was why we installed fancier locks on the vaults and built the defense system. We changed our subway setup, too. Despite these precautions, though, someone reached us again and it was only by chance that we were able to stop him. The connection seems unavoidable, though the motive is anybody's guess. We revamped the whole security framework, achieving what we have today. As the years went by, we relaxed again. Eventually, so much time passed that we felt safe in allowing ourselves to forget, piece by piece, everything but the nagging fact of the missing clone, which for some reason no one felt quite up to erasing. I feel our Mr. Black is involved with the whole thing.

"Therefore," I concluded, "I want a man on this panel at all times, monitoring the arrival station. If we should receive an unwelcome visitor and he is able to avoid the automatic defenses, you must be ready to switch over to manual immediately. Also, I want you to break out something heavier than trank guns and carry them until this thing is settled."

Their faces were blank, puzzled, irritated, going from left to right.

"What exactly are we supposed to do with Mr. Black?" Winkel said.

"Well, I would like to have the contents of his head intact," I told him. "But if they happen to get in the way of a bullet, that's all right, too."

I moved to a panel and set my course for Wing 5.

"You haven't told us everything yet, have you?" he asked.

"Just essentials. Time is important. You are next in line for the nexus, though. If anything happens to me, you will wind up knowing more than I do now. That is one of the advantages of serial immortality."

"I may not want to have it all."

". . . and you need not keep it. That is one of the advantages of partial suicide."

I turned away and headed toward the door.

"Do you intend to bring him here for interrogation?"

I paused and shook my head.

"My goal is a more modest one," I said, "I just want to kill the son of a bitch."

A minute later I was in a dark, silent place on Wing 5.

7

I emerged cautiously, but no one seemed to be about. Fine. I closed the black door behind me and moved away quickly.

Something was wrong, and it took me several seconds to sort out my impressions.

It was the stillness. It was eerie, hearing nothing beyond the echoes of my own footsteps. There were no machine sounds, no humming, whirring background noises; even the beltways had been muted. The air seemed much warmer than usual and hung motionless about me. The dimness was much heavier than normal, though I could see an area of illumination, faint, far off to my right.

I suppressed my curiosity as to the light source and continued on in the direction I had chosen. That way lay the nearest jackpole, a jet tower rooted in a wilderness of broken outlines and vanishing into infinity. I would have to walk its spiral, I feared.

Was Mr. Black waiting for me somewhere between here and there, I wondered? Possibly, knowing our use of the black doors, knowing that I would come to Wing 5.

Was this a mad extreme to which he had gone in his effort to destroy us, or was it the other way around? Was this some part of a thing long in the planning, to which our removal was but an ancillary provision?

Either way, it mattered little now. I was as ready as possible, under the circumstances.

I walked on through the blackout. Had there been a breakdown in the cellar, or was the power being diverted elsewhere to meet some emergency?

And what of Glenda? What did she know? What was her part in this thing?

Then I froze in my tracks and had my hand on my gun, half-drawing it from the holster. What—?

A chord. Then another. Then angry, throbbing music. Violent. Jerkily played. It was an organ, suddenly come to life in a recess not too far to my left. Moments later, I recognized the music, strange sounds for a place of worship and meditation: the *Damnation of Faust*.

I followed it, of course. There are circumstances under which the anomalous should be courted. Ignorance is one of them.

As I moved diagonally toward the entrance to the area, I caught a glimpse of a weird tableau within. A somewhat disheveled man in clerical garb was seated at the keyboard. A small candelabra gave him light from atop the instrument, and two wine bottles kept it company.

I advanced, entered. He smiled at me, closed his eyes and continued playing. As I moved nearer, he opened them again and his smile vanished, to be replaced by a loose-jawed look of horror. His fingers stumbled into a final discord and he slumped forward, shaking.

I stood there for a few moments, undecided as to what I should do. He resolved the matter, however, by raising his head and lowering his hands from his face. He stared at me, panting, then said, "Don't keep me in suspense. What is the verdict?"

"What do you mean?" I said.

"Has my petition been granted?" he asked, his eyes dropping to regard my feet, then turning toward the altar.

I followed his glance and saw that the altar was in disarray, with the crucifix inverted above it.

I gave a small shrug. So the local preacher had decided to switch sides. Was it worth the time it would take to find out what had prompted it?

Possibly, I decided, since something recent and traumatic was doubtless involved.

"Well?" he said.

"Who do you think I am?" I asked.

He smiled slyly and bowed his head.

"I saw where you came from," he said. "I have been watching the black door since I made my offering. When I saw you emerge, I played propitious music."

"I see. And what do you seek to gain by this?"

"You have heard me, you have come. You know what I would have."

123

"Do not try my patience!" I said. "I want to hear you say it! Now!"

His eyes widened and he threw himself prostrate before me.

"I meant no offense!" he said. "I seek only to please you!"

"What prompts this sudden appreciation of that which is most fitting and proper?"

"When it happened, and people began to come to me, with stories, of the terror . . . I held services. People kept coming. Finally, I was granted a glimpse. Before the power failed. Before the evacuation order. I saw that we had been forsaken. I knew then that we had been given over to destruction, and I thought, 'Make to yourselves friends of the mammon of unrighteousness; that, when ye fail, they may receive you into everlasting habitations.' "

"Why do you feel you have been forsaken?"

"For our presumption, our resentments, our secret desires—"

"I mean, what happened?"

He raised his head, looked up at me.

"You mean the explosions and all?"

"Yes. And get up off the floor."

He scrambled to his feet and backed away. When he came up against the bench, I nodded and said, "Sit down."

He did, and, "The explosions, just a few hours ago," he said, "when they tore through the wall, they showed us—the stars . . . Oh God!" He looked comically startled, then added, "I'm sorry."

"Which level?"

"Living Room," he said, glancing at his bottle atop the organ.

I sighed. Good. That was down four, whereas the Library was only two levels below me. All the way through the wall . . . It must have been quite an explosive, that.

"What happened after the explosions?" I said.

"There was a rush to get away," he said. "Then when everybody realized what had happened, there was a rush to go and look out." He licked his lips, looked at the bottle again. "Then another rush to get away," he finished.

"Go ahead and drink some," I said.

He seized the bottle, put it to his lips and threw his

124

head back. I watched his Adam's apple do pushups off his collar.

Wing 5. At least, he had picked a fairly congenial planet for his catastrophe—the atmosphere was breathable, though somewhat irritating, and the temperature was bearable at night.

"And you went and looked?" I asked.

He lowered the bottle, nodded and began to cough. Then, after a few moments, he pointed at the altar.

"I saw eternity," he said. "The sky just goes on and on forever. And I saw the lights in the heavens. I smelled the fumes of the Pit. People were screaming and fainting. Others were pushing forward. Some were running. Some went out into it, I think, and were lost. They herded us back finally, and off that level. They may have sealed it off by now. Many people came to the Chapel. There were services going on all over. I held three myself. I felt stranger and stranger all the while. I knew that it was Judgment Day. I knew that we were all unworthy. It is the end. The House is falling and the heavens have been opened. Man is insignificant, worthless. I knew that when I looked on eternity." He paused to take another drink, then continued, "After my last service, I knew that I could not go on. I could not go on praying for deliverance from that which I knew we deserved. Better to embrace it, I decided. So I came to this section which was not in use. All of the others are over that way." He gestured in the direction of the illumination—candles, doubtless. "Here I did what I thought most fitting," he concluded. "Take me, master," and he hiccuped.

"I am not he whom you have summoned," I said, and I turned to go.

"No!" I heard him cry; and I heard the bottle fall, and I heard him curse and scramble after it. Then, "I saw where you came from!" he shrieked. "You came through the black door!"

"You are mistaken," I said.

"No! I know what I saw! Who are you?"

His plight must have moved me a little further up the philosophical alley than I had realized, for I actually considered his question for a moment and answered it honestly.

"I don't really know," I said, and I kept moving.

125

"Liar!" he called out. "Father of Lies!"

Then he began to weep.

"So *this* is Hell . . ." I heard him saying as I departed.

I moved away quickly, thinking about the reactions of others. I wondered whether he could be typical. I thought not. I hoped not. He was an aberrant, that was all. His was not the direction in which we had been steering them.

I walked at a brisk clip, paralleling the still beltway that led off toward the jackpole. Small knots of figures moved along it, passing in both directions through the gloom. What light there was came from those appliances and signs equipped with their own power units, from candlelit sections of the Chapel, luminous trouble-plates and handbeams borne by the pedestrians. And during the next five or ten minutes, I passed two slow processions where everyone bore a lighted candle. I saw no one who was not part of some group.

I thought again of the power loss. This sort of emergency would hardly call for an action that would require most of the electrical output, even for one level. No. There had to have been a bit of simultaneous mischief in the Cellar. Which indicated a time bomb rather than teamwork, as Black had always impressed me as playing a completely solitary hand. The timing, of everything, was very important. The attack on the family, the hole in the wall, the loss of power. I could feel the pattern there, although I could not understand it. It was quite possible that I never would. I would probably have to kill him before he could tell me. And the alternative made no provision for our enlightenment either. Pity. All that planning, timing, coordination—with success entailing the destruction of the only ones capable of appreciating your work. Kind of sad, any way you looked at it, whatever happened.

Before too long, I reached the jackpole and entered there. It was dark and still. I began walking down its spiral. I hurried past the next level—the Bedroom—for I could see clearly there because of several fires, one near at hand. People were rushing about in their vicinities, and at first I thought that they had either panicked or become irrational and started the things themselves. But no. Most of them seemed to be beating at them or soaking them. Something appeared to be wrong with the sprinkler system. There were fire vehicles all about and more on the way—both in the air and on the ground. Groups of cranes hung frozen above them in a variety of attitudes.

As I reached the next level, my destination, I was pleased not to observe any disasters in progress. There were numerous small lights in motion below me. Personal handbeams, it seemed. I was glad that Mr. Black had not seen fit to indulge in incendiarism in the Library, too.

Quite a few people seemed to be entering at the base of the jackpole, but so far I had encountered no one. Which indicated that they were all heading downward. In the direction of the damaged Living Room. I wondered at their purpose.

Going over my mental map, I recalled an emergency-vehicle hatch about a quarter-mile in the direction of the far wall. I resolved to appropriate whatever might be available for flight, as the number Glenda had given me was a good distance away.

When I reached floor level, I stood aside as people hurried in past me and headed for the downward winding. They spoke excitedly, some near-hysterically, and many of them carried parcels.

"Where are you going?" I asked a man who had come running, and then paused to catch his breath.

"Out," he said.

I could not believe that he meant what he seemed to mean.

"You mean outside?" I said. "Out of the House?"

"Where else? It's coming apart around us, the House."

"But you can't—I mean, it's sealed off, it's quarantined down there, isn't it?"

He laughed.

"Take my advice and come along," he said. "You wouldn't believe what it is like out there."

"What is it like?"

"It's beautiful!"

"But—"

He hurried away then and was quickly out of sight.

I was of course disturbed. Overheard snatches of conversation indicated a variety of motives for this small-scale exodus, ranging from a fear of the imminent collapse of the House to a desire for adventure, a morbid fascination with the effects of disaster, religious fervor, scientific interest

127

and just plain primate curiosity. Whatever the reasons, the results of the action would be around for a long while. I did not relish the introduction of unpredictables into my closed, controlled system.

There was nothing to be done about it just then, however. I pushed my way out the door and hurried in the direction of the vehicles bay.

I sprinted the final hundred yards or so to the bay, the doors of which stood open. I shone the beam I had appropriated from the man who had bumped against me and begun cursing me on the way out. There appeared to be two vehicles down to my left. I climbed over the edge, hung for a moment at arms' length and dropped to the landing stage.

One of the fliers was blocked up for maintenance work and the other was secured in a parking area. I checked the fuel level of the second one, unchocked its wheels and with considerable effort managed to roll it out onto the stage.

It started quickly, and within three minutes I was airborne. I moved carefully, fairly near to the ceiling, my forward and side lights switched to their brightest, avoiding cranes and pillars as I went. Below, it was like a photographic negative of moths about a flame, all those little lights flitting toward the black tower.

Cubicle 18237. That was quite a distance across the room. Periodically, I dropped lower, to shine my light on coordinate markers. Another flier passed me, going in the opposite direction, but I received no signals from it.

I withdrew my mind from thoughts of people's reactions and turned my attention to my own affairs. My enemy had planned things carefully, and I doubted he was about to slack off at this point. I thought of Glenda once again, and of the possibility that I was heading for some sort of trap. She had helped me earlier—a good sign—and she was Kendall's daughter—which was sufficient, to my way of thinking, to justify any action she cared to take against me, were she aware of my part in things. What moved her, and what were her intentions? Was Black using her? If so, how? Though I pushed my mind through a series of mazes, I could come up with no approach other than the direct. There were simply too many variables. Any attempt to be especially devious could boomerang on me.

Most of the effects of Black's trank would have worn off by now, I knew.

When I came into her section, I located an open space near to considerable cover in the form of tables, partitions and machines, landed the flier, killed its lights and engine, and disembarked. It was quite dark, but I had swept the area with my spotlight before coming down. It had seemed to be empty of people.

I rushed for cover, nevertheless, and began a circuitous route that would take me into the area of the cubicle I sought.

I spent several minutes working my way toward the door of 18237 and investigating the vicinity. There were no ambushers that I could detect. But while the glow of candlelight emerged from the windows of the adjacent quarters, Glenda's were dark.

I approached with the pistol in my hand, rapped upon her door with its barrel, waited.

As I stood there, I wondered whether she had been caught up in the general confusion, or whether any of a number of other things had worked to keep her from returning. If she were not present, I resolved to enter and wait for her.

As I moved to knock again, however, I heard a noise from within and the door was unlatched and opened partway. Glenda stood there in the faint light, and her eyes moved from my face to the gun and back again quickly.

"Yes?" she said. "What do you want?"

"We parted rather abruptly a little while ago," I said. "But you invited me to drop by."

Her features constricted and relaxed in the space of an instant. Her voice was normal, even cheerful, as she then said, "Of course! Come in! Come in!" But she raised her right hand as if to bar my way as she said it. Then as I hesitated, puzzled, she hurled herself against me.

As I stumbled back to retain my footing and she slipped to the floor, I heard the sound of a shot from within. She had succeeded in thrusting me far enough to the side to be out of the line of fire, however. I immediately put two rounds through the door, just to let him know I was not standing there doing nothing, waiting to be shot at again, the while shouting to Glenda to get the hell out of sight.

She did not really need the encouragement, though, as she vanished quickly and soundlessly in the direction from which I had come.

I threw myself sprawling and slid up against the wall, as I had been in line of sight from both windows and had no idea where he was inside. My foresight was repaid as the nearest window was shattered by another shot. I fetched out one of my two gas grenades, activated it and lobbed it through the window. Moments later, I followed it with the second one.

Hugging the wall, I crawled backward, the better to cover the near windows as well as the door and the window on its far side.

I waited. I heard the things go off, with soft popping sounds, and after a time ghostly tendrils drifted out through the shattered window and the still-gaping door.

While I was wondering what was going to happen next, it happened.

There came an explosion and fragments of the wall fell all over me. I was engulfed in a cloud of dust and gas. I fought to keep from coughing, my eyes watered and I could see nothing but a blurred haze. I felt as if I had been kicked in several dozen places along my back and side. I jerked my pistol free of the mess and kept blinking my eyes to clear them.

I barely caught sight of the figure leaping through the rubble, right on the heels of the explosion. It was somewhere in the vicinity just vacated by the door. He passed to the right, running, and I fired after him. I missed, of course, and he kept going.

Shaking off debris, I struggled to my feet and plunged after him, staggering through my first several steps. He was still in sight, and I had no intention of losing him this time.

Coming to a partition, he whirled suddenly and fired back at me before passing behind it, not waiting to see the effect of his shot. I felt a stinging sensation along my left forearm, and I raised my weapon and put three rounds through the partition. I veered to reach an alcove then, and reloaded quickly once I had achieved it.

I dropped to all fours before I looked around the corner, and I pulled back quickly when I saw him, leaning around the edge of his partition and pointing a weapon in my direction. The shot followed a moment later, fairly high and wide.

I fired back before I withdrew to prime an explosive grenade. When I exposed myself to hurl it, he fired again. I drew back immediately, primed another grenade and sent it after the first.

The first one exploded while the second was still in the air. By the time the second explosion came, my weapon was back in my right hand. I rounded the corner and raced toward what was left of the partition.

There was no one about when I reached the wrecked area. I halted, casting about in all directions, and then I caught sight of a fleeing shadow, far off to the left. I plunged after him.

He was crossing an open area, heading toward a warren of narrow aisles and reading booths. I ran as fast as I could, and the distance between us narrowed. I fired a shot and he jerked, stumbled, recovered and kept going.

When he reached a post at the edge of the area, he threw himself against it, turned suddenly and began shooting. I was out in the open with nothing to duck behind, so I kept going, raising my own weapon and firing back at him.

The only reason I could see for his missing me under those conditions was the fact that he was injured. He emptied his weapon at me, realized that he did not have time to reload it, turned and lurched off up the nearest aisle. Mine had been emptied also by then, and I refused to allow him the time it would take me to reload. I pursued him up the aisle.

Ahead, he turned left into a side passage or booth, and I slowed. While it was still sufficiently dark to confuse my sense of perspective somewhat, I realized with a start that the overhead lights were glowing faintly now and could easily have been doing so for the past several minutes. A bad sign, the power coming back so quickly, when I wanted to get him and clear out before any measure of order returned to the place.

I jammed my pistol back within my shirt and tore the stiletto loose from where it rode my forearm. It was moist and slightly bent, and it occurred to me that it had been grazed by a bullet and driven to break my skin—the stinging I had felt earlier.

I swung wide at the corner where he had turned, dropping into a crouch, blade low.

He sprang at me. He had a blade of some sort—I saw its faint gleam as it came toward me—but he held it awkwardly and his first strike, which I was able to push aside, was faster than anything that followed. He blocked mine with his forearm and slashed at my abdomen. My armor deflected this, and after a few feints I was able to sink my blade up to the hilt in his stomach. He made a bubbling noise, stiffened and sagged against me. I caught him and lowered him to the floor.

I struck a light to better study his face. I tugged at his hair and it came away; it was a dark wig. Beneath, his own hair was white. Yes, it was indeed the same man who had occupied the power chair, who had gotten Lange to order him a drink and then shot him. Mr. Black.

And he stared at me and smiled.

"Jordan . . . ?" he said.

"Winton," I replied.

"Close, close . . . It couldn't have been anyone later. Those creampuffs . . ."

"Why?" I said. "Why did you do it?"

He shook his head.

"You'll find out. Soon," he said. "Oh, very soon!"

"What?"

He grimaced, then forced the smile once more.

"I could have taken you—with the knife—if I had wanted . . ." he said. "Think about it—"

He died then, grinning at me, and suddenly I realized what he had meant.

8

Mesh—No!

He was old, and somewhere along the line he had changed the facial structure a bit more radically than the rest of us, but as I felt his death within my own being and fought to block an abrupt mesh-effect, I realized that Mr. Black was the missing clone.

Gritting my teeth, squeezing my temples, I built walls of resistance about my mind. There is always a meshing when one of us dies, and its effects vary. It does not matter too much, though, since we are all of us contained within one another, "nexus" only being the term by which we refer to the oldest among us, who is automatically head of the family.

Black was indeed one of us, since the terminal mesh-effect was occurring. For all of his life he must have been blocking the ordinary meshings each time that they occurred. Still, as a silent party to our telepathic bond, I could understand his uncanny ability when it came to pursuing us, knowing our whereabouts.

Having dwelled apart from us all of his life, he was totally unfamiliar. The effects of his personality on our own could be catastrophic. They would of course vary in each instance. I had a strong feeling that he would tend to dominate, however.

I held him off. The impulse that had been beating against my mind died down, faded, was gone.

For an instant, Winkel, Gene and Jenkins would think it was me that had died.

Then it would be too late.

Which of them would break first? I wondered. And what would he do when he did?

Damn!

I twisted the blade out of his belly and wiped it on his

jacket. Our wayward brother had certainly stacked the deck. I had to get back to Wing Null immediately to try to deal with whatever catastrophe was about to break loose there. And I was taken by the feeling that I might not be able to.

I dropped the blade into an inside pocket and turned away. Glenda was standing about ten feet up the corridor, digging at her cheek with her fingertips.

"He's dead," she said. "Isn't he?"

"I'm afraid not," I said, going to her and taking her hand away from her face.

I did not release her arm, but used it to turn her gently, back in the direction from which we had come.

"Come with me," I said. "There are things we must talk about, later."

She did not resist as I led her away from the smiling figure and back toward the flier. The lights continued to brighten as we went.

It was not until we were airborne and on our way to the jackpole that she spoke again:

"Where are we going?"

"To a place called Wing Null," I said.

"Where is that?"

"It is too complicated to explain just now."

She nodded.

"I understand about your secret place—that you have one, I mean."

"How is it that you do? Mr. Black?"

"Yes," she said. "What did you mean when you said that he was not dead? I saw you—kill him."

"Only a body died. *He* still exists."

"Where?"

"Wing Null, I fear."

"How? The same way as you—do it?"

"Perhaps. What do you know about it?"

"I am sure that you are somehow Mr. Engel, the man I was with earlier, the man I saw die. You transmigrated some way, and you came to the address I gave you then. I have no idea as to the mechanism involved."

"Mr. Black again? That is where you heard of this?"

"Yes."

"What is he to you?"

"He was my guardian, after my father died and my

134

mother had to be sent away, for treatments. He volunteered and the plat council appointed him. He had been a friend of my father."

"What did he do? What was his occupation?"

"He was a teacher. Classics. He used the name Eibon then. Henry Eibon."

"Why?"

"Originally, he had told me it was a game. You see, I had known him as Mr. Black when he used to visit us. He began using the other name when he became my guardian. Later, of course, I realized that it was more than a game, but I kept my mouth shut because I loved him. He was very good to me. —You say there is a chance that I will see him again soon?"

"I am afraid so."

"Suppose you tell me what he is to you?"

"We have been enemies for a long while. He started the vendetta. I have no idea why."

She was silent as we traveled the remaining distance and I located a deserted area not too far from the jackpole and landed the flier in a three-walled reading lounge. As I helped her out, I said, "Do you?"

"What if I were to say 'yes'?"

I seized her by the shoulders and spun her, so that her face was about eight inches from my own.

"Talk!" I said. "Tell me why!"

"Let me go! I didn't say that I knew!"

I tightened my grip, then relaxed it. I slid my hand down her arm and turned her by the elbow.

"Come on," I said. "We have to go up a couple levels."

If she did not want to talk, I did not have the time to shake the answers out of her. I had wanted to reach her for two reasons: to protect her and to obtain the information it seemed she possessed. Now she seemed to be in no need of protection and unwilling to part with information. But now that I was aware of her special relationship with Black, I felt myself automatically begin thinking of her as something of a hostage. I was not pleased with the discovery of this reaction, but I was not about to abandon it either.

"Basically," she said, as we headed toward the jackpole through the growing light, "you want to keep people in the House, don't you?"

"Well," I said, "to be basic and general about it, yes. I think it is a good idea."

"Why?"

"It is the best way I know for people to learn to really live together."

"By forcing them?"

"Of course. When the alternatives to proximity have been removed and aggressive energies are rechanneled, people tend to cooperate rather than compete. Some measure of coercion is needed, though, to set up such a state of affairs."

"Then what happens?"

"What do you mean?"

"Have people changed much, from living in the House?"

"I think they have."

"Will they continue to change?"

"I believe so."

"They will be allowed to go outside when they have reached some ideal point of adaptation?"

"Of course."

"Why 'of course'? Why not right now? Why do you want to see them prisoners until they have changed?"

"They are not prisoners. They can come and go as they please."

"In the House!"

"In the House."

"Why not outside, too?"

My head began to hurt and I became acutely aware of all my other aches and pains. I did not feel like answering her.

Do you want me to?

"Why not?" I decided. "Go ahead, Jordan. Say whatever you want."

Give me your mouth, your throat, your breathing. Relax.

I did this, and moments later he began to speak.

"Turn them loose?" he said. "To diversify, accentuate their differences, to stimulate competition, aggression, violence toward one another? They very nearly succeeded in destroying themselves that way once. Given similar circumstances, they might succeed the next time. To prevent this, man himself needs to be changed. He is not yet what he will be, but he is better than he was. When he has learned to live with himself, peacefully, here in the House, then he will be ready to go outside it."

"But will he still be human?" she said.

"Whatever he is will be human, for that will then be the measure of humanity."

"What gives you the right to make all these judgments?"

"Someone must. Anyone who wants can."

"Mr. Black did. And he disagreed with you. To make the House safe for your nonaggressive, nonviolent ideals, you killed him."

"I shall exist only for so long as I am needed to promote tranquillity, then I, too, shall pass."

"Who is to decide when this time has arrived?"

"I am."

She laughed.

"Can we count on it?" she said.

"I see no reason not to. I have done it many times before."

She shook her head, turned to stare at me. She tried to halt, but I still had hold of her arm and I continued to propel her toward the pole.

"I get the feeling we are talking two different languages or something," she said. "One moment you sound rational, and the next you go off on a tangent. Are you one entity, or is your name Legion?"

I tightened my will like a vise, and "Get thee behind me, Jordan," I said within myself.

All right, I'm going, and he was gone.

"I am myself," I said.

"Should I call you Engel?"

"Why not? It is as good as anything. Tell me why Black wants to get people out of the House."

"He felt it was lobotomizing the race, turning people into vegetables—and that if they finally did make it outside, they would be in no condition to survive."

"Our disagreement then is too basic for argument, since it centers on a matter of interpretation. What has he told you about me?"

"He told me there is a multibodied enemy of the people who feels as you say you feel about things."

"Did he tell you how he came to be aware of this state of affairs?"

"No."

"What did he tell you concerning his own—background?"

"Nothing at all."

"You are lying."

She shrugged.

"What are you going to do about it?"

"Nothing, just now."

We entered the jackpole. People kept hurrying past us, all of them heading downward.

"What if I were to scream?" she said. "What if I were to refuse to accompany you any farther?"

"You will not. You will come without causing any difficulties."

"What makes you think so?"

"I have totally engaged your curiosity, and yours is one of the most active minds in the House."

"What do you know about my mind?"

"I know just about everything there is to know about you."

"Now you are lying."

This time I shrugged, and smiled. We made our way around and upward, upward and around.

". . . You would have tranked me," she said after a time, "and acted as if I had been taken ill."

"Perhaps."

Moments later, I collapsed against the wall, an involuntary cry escaping my lips. She caught my left arm as it flailed the air, and helped to support me as I was taken by spasm after spasm, the world advancing, receding, coming apart, being reassembled about me and within me.

"What is it?" she said.

But I could only gasp, "Wait. Wait . . ."

Finally, things fell together, the center held. I regained my balance, sucked a couple of deep draughts of stale air and began to move once again. Glenda kept hold of my arm and repeated her question several times.

"Good old Mr. Black just murdered two more people," I said, hurrying. "He thinks he has the upper hand now, and if it is any consolation to you, he may be right."

She did not respond, but hurried along with me. A few people rushed past us, heading downward. They ignored us completely. I wondered what had become of the little boy who liked to run in the wrong direction. In my mind's eye, I saw him standing before an enormous hole in the wall, turning to stick out his tongue, then racing on through and out across a starlit field.

When we reached the level of the Chapel things were brighter than they had been, though still not much better than twilight. The soft glow of candlelight came from several new directions. The belts remained dead. I aimed us in the direction from which I had come, wondering if the apostate preacher had passed out yet.

It was Gene and Jenkins who had died, Winkel who had yielded to Black's personality assault. A moment's work with the handiest weapon and he held Wing Null. What now?

Me, of course.

I was the last one left. Once I was out of the way, he could get on with his plans, whatever they might be. I regretted that, if he won, I would probably never understand the exact nature of our relationship, would never know what it was that he had had in mind all along. Finding out would almost be worth the ultimate risk. . . . I shelved that thought for the time being, however.

I wanted to run. I wanted to reach the black door as soon as possible, plunge through it and get things settled, finally. But I was hurting enough as it was and I knew that my reactions had been slowed. There was no sense in arriving all out of breath, too.

I also wanted to say things to Glenda. I wanted to say, "All right, what was it you wanted to tell me when you invited me to your place as I lay dying?" I wanted to tell her that I knew her story about having lost a pack of jobs was a lie, that I knew she held a professorship in engineering. I wanted to ask her why, since she had set me up for an ambush, she had pushed me out of the line of fire at the last moment. I wanted to ask her why she was being so cooperative in accompanying me now. And I was curious whether she was carrying a weapon.

But of course I said none of these things.

We hurried along, passing a few people, ignoring them and being ignored. All of them seemed headed for one or another of the services. In due course, we neared the area of my arrival. There was, unfortunately, a service in progress too near for me to utilize the facility I desired. It took me close to ten minutes to locate another one in a deserted area. I sprang the door and swung it open, climbed up, turned, held out my hand and helped Glenda inside. She did not balk or question this, but followed me down the incline, her hand on my shoulder.

At the rear, I opened the box and fiddled with it, knowing she was watching everything that I did. Well, I could fiddle with her memories, too, later, if there was a later.

The door closed above and behind us. I snapped the box shut and I took up a position in front of Glenda, a primed grenade in my left hand, the pistol in my right. If the defense system was set on automatic, it would not fire when it scanned me, though. If he had it on manual, I was hoping that Glenda's presence would make him hesitate to push buttons. If he did not, we still had my body armor between us and a host of deadlies. Maybe I could knock them out in time.

"I take it this is not a standard procedure," I heard Glenda say.

"Shift your weight backward. We'll be landing on a level surface," I said.

By the time I finished saying it, we already had.

9

<hr />

I lurched slightly forward despite my stance, I heard the klaxon begin its warning and I hurled my grenade at the weapons bank.

I pushed Glenda against the far wall and shielded her from the explosion that followed. Before the echoes had died, I turned and dashed through the opening portal.

There was no one in sight. The klaxon kept wailing. I raced ahead.

Rounding the curved corridor's first big blind spot, I saw that the door to the Comp vault was still open. I swung around the massive metal frame and entered low, weapon extended.

But there was no need for such an entry. Only Gene and Jenkins were present, and I already knew that they were both dead. The manner of their passing was not especially important to me, though I noticed that Gene had been shot in the left temple and Jenkins had blood on his chest and abdomen. Faint memories of the attack came into my mind as I looked upon the scene. It is strange how a terminal mesh works. Had things been the other way around, they would know my final moments with a terrible clarity. It always seems to pass with more clarity from older members of the family to the younger, painfully enforcing a kind of seniority system in the descent of the nexus. Why this should be so, I do not know. Not that it really matters, I guess.

I crossed the room and killed the klaxon. Glenda entered as I was turning away from it, then halted and turned pale. I went to her, turned her about and pushed her back outside.

"This way," I said, and I led her on up the corridor.

The door to the Files vault was open also. I halted

when I saw this and proceeded toward it on my own. I edged close, went in quickly.

It was empty. But before I could relax, sigh, straighten, my eyes automatically moved to the most important part of the room, and there they remained.

Pins five, four, three and two had been pulled. The chair had been swiveled to the right. The helmet hung at a lopsided angle above it.

It was the ache in my shoulders that made me realize how tense my muscles had become. I took a deep breath, mopped my brow, turned.

For a little while, I refused to accept it. Whoever—whatever—he was inside, Black had added to it four of my own demons, three of whom I did not know. As one of the clones, there was no reason why he could not. But the thought that he might had not occurred to me, until then. Unprepared as I was, it came to me as a greater shock than anything that had happened recently, including my deaths and the disruption at Wing 5.

I leaned against the doorframe, keeping an eye on the corridor. Automatically, I found a cigarette and lit it. I had to think clearly and act very quickly now.

Locate him. That came first.

All right. He could be anywhere. He could still be around, or he could have returned to the House. The first thing, then, was to check with the Bandit, to see whether he had done anything recordable yet as Winkel. A negative there, and the second thing would be to commence searching Wing Null for him.

Dimly aware of Glenda's troubled presence, I returned to Comp. I did not note her reactions to the bodies this time, but she remained at my side.

But I did not query the Bandit. When I crossed over to it, my gaze was drawn downward to a red light that winked within the map of Wing Null that was laid beneath the clear surface of the countertop. It indicated that a hatch had been opened. If this was not a trick meant to distract me, then it meant that my quarry could have gone outside, onto the surface of the planet itself. The chronometer showed me that the hatch had only been opened about four minutes earlier.

"Damn him! What does he want?" I said, my mind racing.

Then I made my decision and seized Glenda by the hand.

"Come on! We are going back next door again. I have to show you something. It is urgent."

I took her back to the central console in Files. Fetching out my stiletto, I used it to chip away the blob of solder at the base of pin one. Then I turned to Glenda and realized that I was still holding her hand. Her eyes moved from the machinery to the blade to my face. I put the weapon away and lowered her hand, released it.

"I want to ask a favor," I said. "It is extremely important and I do not have time to explain what it represents."

"Go ahead and ask," she said.

"I am about to leave this place and go outside. I have no idea how long I will be out there, though I only intend it to be a brief while. When I return I might be confused, incoherent, injured. That would be the point at which I would need your assistance." I slapped the chair. "Should this occur, I want you to get me into this chair, even if you have to trank me to do it."

"With what?" she said.

"I'll give you a trank gun in a minute. If I seem in any way disturbed or—altered—get me into the chair and lower this hood over my head." I pushed it with my hand. "Then throw these switches—the entire row beginning at the left and taking them in order to the end. Everything else is properly set. Then all you have to do is wait until this blue light comes on. When that happens, pull this pin all the way out of the board. That's all."

"Then what happens?"

"I do not know—specifically, that is. But it is the only treatment I can think of for what might occur. I have to go now. Will you do it if it seems necessary—if I am dazed, bewildered?"

"Yes. If you will promise to answer my questions afterward."

"Fair enough. Please repeat the procedure back to me."

She did, and I hurried her outside once more.

"I will take you to a comfortable place near to the hatch," I said, "where you can wait, and view the surface outside. You will be able to see me depart and return."

I wondered about that light, though, and decided to

143

show her how to opaque the window if it became necessary.

"... One other thing," I added. "I may not be me when I come back."

She halted.

"I beg your pardon," she said.

"My appearance could be different. Well, I could be another person."

"What you are saying then is that I force the next person I see under that machine, whether he likes the idea or not."

"Only if he seems confused, disturbed . . ."

"I'd think anybody would be if you tried to force him under that thing."

"It won't be just anybody. It will be me, in one form or another."

"All right. It will be done. But there is one other thing."

"What?"

"What if nobody comes back?"

"Then it is all over," I said. "Go home and forget all about this."

"How? I have no idea where we are, let alone how to get back."

"In the room of the dead men," I said, "low, and to the left of center on the far wall, there is a small green panel which controls the transport system. It is fairly simple. You would be able to figure it out if you had to."

I steered her into the lounge then, and she drew back against me, uttering a small cry. The window had been transpared. The moon was out of sight now, but a pale light suffused the landscape, indicating that the second moon—slower, larger, brighter—was already up, but blocked from our view for the moment.

"That is not just a picture. That is a real window, isn't it?" she said.

"Yes," I said, pushing her gently forward, passing around and fetching her a trank gun. "Do you know how to use one of these?"

She was advancing toward the window. She glanced at the gun, murmured, "Yes," and kept going, as if mesmerized. I crossed over, picked up her hand, placed it on her palm and closed her fingers over it.

"I have never seen the outside before—really," she said.

"Well, look all you want. I have to go now. There is a simple on-off switch to the left there, under the frame. That's right. That will opaque it for you, if you want."

"Why would I want to? It is beautiful."

"There is an optical phenomenon—a blinding light—which comes and goes. You will want to opaque it if it comes."

"Well, until that happens, I am just going to look. I—"

"Then goodbye for now. See you again soon."

"Wait!"

"I've waited too long already."

"But I saw something move out there. It could have been a man."

"Where?"

She pointed in the direction of the ruins.

"Over that way."

I did not see anything moving and she said, "Gone now," and I said, "Thanks," and left her standing there, looking out, wondering whether she was conscious of my departure.

I made my way on up the corridor to the recess that held the hatch. It was actually a series of three doors, offering various degrees of resistance and forms of protection. All three were undogged, and I passed through quickly, pausing only to check out the pistol.

It was cool, and the smells of the night came into my nostrils—damp, and tinged with the faint halations of growing things. In a moment, the feeling of novelty faded. I had been outside a few times before—long ago—and the impressions were not unfamiliar.

I quickly adjusted to movement across the irregular surface and struck off in the direction of the ruin. The silence was occasionally interrupted by little chirping noises, whether by bird or insect I could not tell. I passed through small pockets of fog whenever the ground dipped appreciably. The stones were moist and slippery. In clear spaces I had a shadow, so strong had the moonlight become. Turning, I could see the huge, white orb in its entirety, fat above my fortress now. A few wisps of cloud fled before it, but the sky was otherwise clear and blazing with countless stars. I was taken then by a series of peculiar feelings that began, I suppose, with something of doubt and apprehension.

The stellar panorama had something to do with it—those stars we had tried to make somehow obscene—as well as the still, stark landscape through which I moved, alone now for the first time in ages, outside the House, pursuing the most enigmatic individual of whom I had knowledge, in the direction of those puzzling ruins. It was unusual that I should think along these lines. The ruins had not been puzzling to me up until then. They were simply there, and that was it, a fact which also contributed to this odd moment's introspection. The possibility then occurred to me that peculiar things which did not normally strike me as puzzling were probably things about which I had once known something, and like a sword in a stone the edge of my curiosity was blunted at a subconscious level.

How many things had I known and forgotten? Would any of them be of value to me now? Was I rushing to my destruction by pursuing a man who knew almost everything that I knew, plus several lifetimes' experience of which I knew nothing? Possibly. But I thought I had this encounter worked out. The thing that bothered me was that he should be able to see it, too.

And why choose this place as our battlefield? It had to do with the ruins, I knew. I realized then that I was somewhat afraid of them. Why?

If only I had pulled more pins . . .

I moved ahead, ready for an ambush but doubting one would come, yet.

Not a sparkle, not a glimmer emerged from the ruins. They were still, their shadows only just now beginning to retreat from the moonlight.

My footfalls came soft, muffled. My breathing seemed the loudest thing about me . . .

The ground rose, then dipped again, and for a moment I had a very clear view for a good distance. He was nowhere in sight, though. There came a breeze, cool, light, and the fogs diminished, were gone, as I made my way onto higher ground.

I was aiming to kill a man in the name of pacificism, harmony, fraternity, and to maintain the integrity of the House. That his intentions toward me were also lethal was fairly obvious by now. While I was uncertain as to the principles involved, it was apparent that he disagreed with me on the question of cloistering humanity. This was sufficient reason to remove him, so far as I was concerned. However, while with anyone else I would simply have dismissed him as misguided, his persistence and occasional ingenuity had aroused my curiosity as to his reasons.

I had no doubts as to the correctness of my own beliefs, that human nature could be altered, that man could be forced to evolve morally. As I made my way about a small, scummy pool at the center of a crater, I did, for a moment, wonder why. It was not a questioning of the notions, simply a sudden curiosity as to where I had obtained them. It seemed that they had always been a part of my mental equipment. This being so, it struck me that with all those pulled pins Black and I now shared an ancestry with which he should be by far the more conversant. Such being the case, it would seem he should have acquired the proper philosophical attitude. There were several possibilities . . .

Either he possessed an overriding imperative to the contrary, he *had* been changed, or our early past was sufficiently ambiguous for him to live without altering his attitudes.

It may have been that all three were to some extent correct. The nature of the former was presently as unknowable to me as the ultimate source of my own sentiments. I mean, I was aware that my own notions were rational without necessarily being logical, that is to say, deductive. They were a part of my mental—"tradition" I guess is the best word. Say his feelings were as strong, and I suppose it was possible that the accumulations of four lifetimes dumped upon him by the pulling of the pins might not have swayed him over to my way of thinking. Still, there had to be some effect . . . It was like guessing at the results of a test wherein two virtually unknown chemicals were to be mixed and heated, though.

The third thought was what troubled me, as it touched on something of a sore spot I had but recently developed . . .

Namely, the possibility that my past was not so firm a thing as my present. Supposing there was actually something there to comfort and abet him? The reason for the partial suicide by means of the pin with each succession of the nexus was more than personality adjustment for a permanent meshing. It was also intended as a progressively civilizing act, a further paring away on each occasion of those elements best classified as antisocial, in keeping with the evolving temper of the times. My present state of being was evidence of the effectiveness of the system. I was capable of things which I knew would have caused Lange or Engel to writhe, to recoil with revulsion, possibly to pass out. For the moment I was glad of this, because of the man I pursued. But although I felt myself a necessary evil, I regretted the necessity. The means were vindicated only because Black was an anachronism.

But what things lay behind the other pins? That was what troubled me. I knew what I had been until very recently, and I knew what I had become. The return had been a comfortable and natural thing, and I absorbed and dominated my later selves quite easily—as if they had been but brief moods. All the unsacrificed portions of Jordan were part of my memory; the rest I knew through the interface darkly when, at times of crisis, he became my personal demon. Offhand, I would say that he was a trifle meaner and more unprincipled than I. By extension, then, might not the even earlier versions of myself lend support rather than contradiction to whatever made Black run? I had been lifting myself by my own bootstraps, step by painful step. But what if I had not? What if there had been no overpowering will to improve my condition, and no effort? Black and I were of the same flesh. I did not understand how or why, but we were. And this was what made me apprehensive. The only real difference between us was an idea, or an ideal. And, as facets of the same person, we were still willing, in a completely literal sense, to kill ourself over it. The feeling that gripped me at that moment was not unlike the one that had taken Engel as he fled by ranks of jangling phones. Only I knew that if I answered, the voice on the other end would be my own.

Peering ahead, I picked my way among haphazard heaps of shattered stone. I contained my feelings, partly suppressed them, kept alert. He could be waiting in ambush at any point.

I passed a small crater within and about which the rocks had been fused. Almost immediately after that, the ground took a turn upward and I picked a broken course up the long incline, shards and splinters of some mineral glittering underfoot. Abruptly, I came to a high point beyond a stand of boulders, from which I could see the ruins about three-quarters of a mile distant.

I sought cover immediately and studied the prospect. It was still and clear in the moonlight, with no apparent movement anywhere, except for a few small flying things that dipped and darted quickly by. There was no light from within the ruins. I watched for a brief while, glanced back at the dark bulk of the Wing with its one small square of illumination, turned my eyes ahead once more.

Then I saw him.

Advancing quickly, he had just emerged from a jagged declivity that lay like a broken lightning bolt halfway across the plain. Dodging among rocks, he continued on toward the ruins.

I was after him immediately, racing down the slope, skidding and slipping, dislodging gravel. No need for stealth now I knew where he was. I broke into a run at the first opportunity. It appeared that he was indeed making his way toward that smashed fortress, and I felt a sudden need to reach him before he got there. I felt more troubled that he was heading for it than if he had been laying a simple ambush. His knowledge of the past being greater than mine, I feared that he knew to seek something within that might give him the edge in our coming conflict.

Down, then up again. There were no more major dips the rest of the way. It was all uphill, pocked, fused, cracked, strewn with rubble. Running became impossible before very long, but I pushed myself to my limits and gained on him. How long before he became aware of me?

Minutes later, it did not matter. I was closer to him than he was to the ruins. And the first couple of times he looked back he missed me somehow. I was gasping by then and very conscious of the rushing of blood in my temples. I slowed. I had to.

He caught sight of me shortly after that, stared a moment, turned and broke into a run. Cursing, I followed at the best pace I could manage. We were still too far apart to bother shooting at each other.

For a little while then, it was a question of hoping for him to tire quickly while I tried hard not to myself. If I could just hold up a little longer, he might become convinced that this was the way it was going to work. I wanted him to decide that running was not going to get him where he was headed in time, so that he might as well turn and fight and get things over with, one way or the other.

He looked back again, and although it pained me I put on a burst of speed. We were almost within hailing distance. He faltered slightly, hurried again.

Slowly, things cleared a bit, steadied. It seemed my second wind was on its way. I began to feel that I would hold up. When he looked back about a minute later that was apparently his conclusion, too.

He veered to the right, making for an area of large stones and small rubble. Great! I did the same. I was not about to play it slow and careful when I was wearing body armor.

I had my pistol ready before he disappeared behind the nearest boulder. I swung wide as I passed it, but he was not there. He had kept going, and the first shot came at me from a stand of stone about a hundred feet away.

I held my own fire as I charged his position, waiting for him to show himself again, as he pulled back that first time. I was not going to waste a shot on that skimpy a target at that distance.

He did, at about fifty feet, and we both fired. I felt the impact on my chest armor, and my own shot ricocheted off the stone.

I kept running and we both kept firing. This time he did not retreat. My armor stopped two more of his shots, I believe. Then he jerked with one of mine. For a moment, my hopes rose.

We each got off one more shot, though.

It came as a blinding pain in the left side of my head, and I stumbled. My pistol fell from my numbed fingers.

I could not permit it to end that way. I thought that I heard a metallic click near to my head. Turning, I saw the tops of his shoes. My right arm was completely useless, but I could not let him simply stand there, reload and pull the trigger again.

I grabbed at his ankles with my left hand, and I caught one. The left, I think. He tried to pull free, but I was able to maintain my grip. Then he tried to kick me with his

150

free foot, just as I jerked at his ankle and rolled myself toward him.

He went down.

I let go, and with my left hand I managed to get the bent stiletto out of my jacket.

It was too far to his heart or throat, though, and he was already moving again. The only thing I could see was to try severing the artery in his leg nearest me with the one slash I might be able to make. I might be able to throw myself on him and hold him down while he bled to death. Then only one ordeal would remain.

I made the thrust and he blocked it. He caught my wrist.

I tried to twist it away, but it was no use. He was weakened—I could even see the blood on his garment, but he still had the advantage. He brought his other hand across and began to pry my fingers loose from the weapon.

I was at the rearmost edge of consciousness by then, but even so I realized that this was it, that there was nothing left I could do.

He wrenched the blade free and reversed it. Ironic. My own weapon ... I had intended to kill him, block the mesh and so be rid of him forever. Now, though ...

The last thing that I saw before I felt the sting of the blade was his face. His expression was not one of triumph, however—only fatigue, and something of fear.

10

Silence, light, blood. Pain—
Too late. Too late . . .
Block . . . No! Through . . . Yes! Dizzy . . .
. . . And the light. The light!

I kept blinking. I kept blinking my eyes. I felt wet all over. Perspiration, blood, saliva . . .

My head was full of whirlwinds, catching thoughts, twisting them, juxtaposing images, driving my awareness in circles . . .

To stop thinking, to hold down my cerebration as much as possible, to confine my consciousness to the level of observing and reacting—this seemed the only way to maintain a measure of stability.

Pain. I hurt in many places, but the pain in my right hand was particularly intense. I had been staring at it all along, but now I forced my attention to cover this area of existence.

My hand had grown white from the strain of gripping the hilt of the blade which protruded from the throat of the man lying across my legs. There was a bullet wound above his left eye, and blood on his forehead and cheek as well as his neck.

Yes, yes, I understood, but I pushed that out of my mind as soon as it occurred and considered the problem of my hand. I squeezed it and tugged at my fingers, bringing back another memory I immediately suppressed. Gradually, they relaxed, and I cried out involuntarily at the untying of the knots in my muscles. Once free, though, I let the hand fall immediately and squeezed my eyes tightly shut.

The light—

It hurt, directed as the beam was, full in my face. I turned my head away, opened my eyes again. It was still too bright, off to the side now. I decided to go away from it. For that matter, I wanted to get away from the corpse, too.

Slowly, I pulled myself free, keeping my head averted from the body and the light. I immediately became very aware of my other pains, particularly the moist area at my waist, on the right side. I got to my feet, though, and leaned back against the boulder beside which I had lain, breathing heavily and dizzy again for several moments.

I felt as if I stood in the middle of a nightmare, afraid to think of what had just happened, afraid of what might be coming. As soon as the world stood still, I pushed myself forward and began walking. I followed the big white moon downhill.

. . . To get away from that blazing light. But it followed me.

I veered to the right, then to the left. I quickened my pace. It remained with me, though.

I fought back a flash of frenzy.

"No! Don't think! For God's sake, don't think!" I said aloud, surprising myself with my own voice.

Don't think. That way lay panic, confusion, chaos. Entertain only one notion at a time and concentrate on it to the exclusion of all else.

I fixed my attention on my movements, counting my steps, staring at my surroundings, thinking about my feet, my legs.

But I was going in the wrong direction.

Wasn't I?

Yes.

Yes, I was supposed to be heading toward the ruin. I—

"Don't think!" I reminded myself. "Get away! Get away!"

Yes. It was more important that I get away from that light than do anything else just then. Good thought. Hold that.

But—

Hold it! Get away!

I moved quickly. Fifty paces. A hundred. Go right. Fifty paces. Angle left. Fifty . . .

The brightness followed, casting my changing shadows far before me, illuminating my way. It was an eerie thing

153

to behold, and I ran, seeking some barrier that could be interposed between myself and the source of the light.

I saw a suitable formation a few hundred yards away and raced toward it, moved around to its far side, rested there panting. Automatically, I reached for a cigarette.

Cigarette? There were none. But that was right. Winkel did not smoke. Rather— Wait! Black— No!

Don't think. I chewed my lip. The light could not reach me. It was dark, and I was alone in a quiet place. I sighed. I tried to relax, and felt my breathing begin to slow. My heartbeat followed its example. The throbbing pain in my side changed to a dull ache. It still bled, though not so profusely. I kept the palm of my hand pressed against it.

I had to go back, to get to the ruin. But that damned light— If it would just go out, I could be on my way.

But why? Why the ruin? What I really wanted was to get away and— No! Wait! Wait . . .

I had destroyed the last of them. It was all over now.

No.

I had finally gotten Mr. Black.

No.

No?

No!

Then Hell's lid was lifted. I/he had been too weak to resist the final meshing. The most horrible result of this realization was a desire to laugh and to scream simultaneously. Realizing what had occurred was not tantamount to accepting it—or being able to do anything about it. Helplessly, I regarded what I had become: namely, literally, looking at it from both directions at once, I was my own worst enemy. I believe I did laugh, or snort, momentarily. I was haled through corridors of memory where all the actions recalled were driven by sentiments and desires which now encountered their opposites at every hand. I began to choke. It was too much. Much too much. It was pulling me apart.

I was completely unable to help myself at that point. Whatever I thought or felt, there came an immediate reaction, a countersurge of guilt, anger, fear. The thing that saved me, that slammed the lid on all of this once more, came from the only place that it could—the outside world. I was distracted.

It was a noise, not loud and quite distant, but completely out of place. Metallic. Recurrent.

Suddenly, my existence was concentrated in my senses, and the residue of the past moments' emotions consolidated into an overall wariness.

I listened, moved to my right, dropped low, peered around the edge of my rocky shield. The light still bathed the other side of the stone, though for a moment or so it did not shine directly into my eyes. It did catch me more squarely very soon after that, as it played back and forth upon the stone, but not before I had caught sight of the source of the noise.

It was a squat robot of some sort, with four cablelike extensors and photoelectric eyes, rolling toward my position on dark treads.

I turned immediately and raced away. That it was coming for me, I had no doubt.

Down. Then up. Then down again. The light followed for a time, but the angle of the slope quickly took me below its reach. I slowed, puffing, pressing my hand to my side. I had to ration my energies carefully. The fact that much of the remaining course was downhill would be of help.

I looked back, but the machine was out of sight beyond the ridge. Ahead, the moon silvered the face of the fortress of Wing Null. I could make out the solitary, lighted window. I could trace the trails I had followed. The ground-clinging mists, the pockets of fogs, of vapors, were touched with phosphorescence. The moist rocks glistened like black glass. I felt that I had an even chance of making it ahead of my mechanical pursuer.

I could still hear the thing periodically, scattering pebbles, scraping stones, coming along my trail at a good clip. Whether, ultimately, I would owe it thanks or blame, I did not know. While I had been tormented by that light, I had also been attracted by it. Now that I knew, to some extent, who I was, it made understanding a little easier. We really had been trying to reach the ruins—just why, I was uncertain. It was not just part of an elaborate ploy to get the last of them/us. No. And the desire to go there was still strong within me. That light was several things, I felt, and one of them was a beacon, a call, to me. Only the me that it reached was no longer the me for whom it had been intended. Part of me had been startled by it, frightened, had drawn away. Its call persisted, however, and even as I fled I had been attracted by the summons. This ambivalence was resolved in favor of continued flight, though, with the appearance of the robot. There had to be some sort of intelligence behind the thing. Not understanding what it represented was sufficient reason to flee it.

It was not very long, though, before the sounds grew louder. The thing seemed to be moving faster now. I kept glancing back as I went.

I dodged among jagged stone formations, rifts, ravines, craters, getting down near to the misted area once more. I had small hope of losing the robot there, however, as I realized that the level attitude of the area would soon see me back within range of that light. Staring then, I thought I caught glimpses of it sweeping the prospect far ahead.

Forcing myself to hurry, I stumbled, almost panicked at my slowness in regaining my feet, pulled myself together, proceeded more deliberately.

The robot continued to pick up speed, was moving faster than I was moving. It was not precise and undeviating in its course, however, as it did take blind turns, halt, back up, alter direction, circle objects. Seeing this, I dodged behind a rock and altered my course to keep as many obstructions as possible between myself and the thing. Still, it seemed cognizant of my general direction. I began to have second thoughts concerning my ability to outdistance it once I was out in the open and on level ground. What the devil was I to do?

Knock it blind, you fool!

The jolt lasted only a moment, for it was but a part of me that was unfamiliar with my demons.

"How?" I asked.

Turn your head farther to the right. —Stop! See that scarp? Get to it and climb it!

"I will be spotted."

That is the idea. Go!

I went. He had a plan, which was more than I did. If you can't trust your demon, whom can you trust?

The idea splashed in as I moved toward the escarpment. Nothing very complicated about it—which, considering the circumstances, was good.

The sounds of increased activity upslope warned me

that I had been detected. When I looked back, the machine was racing toward me. I quickened my pace, and when I looked ahead again I realized what a steep slope it was that lay before me.

I began to climb immediately, however, not even bothering to look back.

Thus doth fear make athletes of us all.

"You're right," I said, my blood pounding, the sounds of pursuit coming louder.

I wondered as I went whether the thing would essay this slope or just try to wait me out. I did not believe that it could make it all the way to the top, because I was not even certain that I could. It kept steepening, and I had to seek handholds as well as footholds, finally. My grip was weak, and my side kept aching and oozing. When I achieved a height where I felt safe from the machine my greatest fear came to be that I would pass out and fall.

Gasping, I was able to pull myself up onto the broad shelf we had spied, about forty-five feet above the ground, where I collapsed. I believe that I was unconscious then for a brief while.

It was the sounds from below that aroused me. But not quickly. My limbs felt weighted, my head ready to explode. Tag ends of thoughts and images, like bits of dream, coalesced and fell away before I could scrutinize them closely.

I propped myself on my elbows, raised my head and turned to look over the edge and down.

The robot was attempting to mount the slope. It had attained a height of about fifteen feet. The angle of the incline increased at that point, and it was grinding its way very slowly, forward and upward, its extensors flailing after rocky projections.

Get to it! Get to it!

"All right! Damn it!" I muttered. "All right!"

I cast about, looking for ammunition. Most of the stones seemed either too large or too small. I cataloged them quickly. Should I try to roll down a big one or hurl some of the smaller stones? My muscles answered that one.

I got to my knees, then rose, collected a dozen or so of the fist-sized ones into a heap near the edge. By then the machine had advanced another yard and had succeeded in catching hold of a solid projection. It continued its advance.

I threw three of the stones. Two missed completely and one struck the chassis, low. Double damn! I threw two more, and only one passed near the receptors.

It found another hold, drew itself four or five feet nearer, reached forward again.

My next rock smashed a receptor. It was a lucky cast, but it raised my hopes. I bounced all my remaining stones off its chassis, though, without noticeable effect.

By then it was around twenty-five feet up and still moving. Its angle seemed quite precarious, but its whiplike appendages were of a heavy, shiny cable that looked more than adequate to support it so.

I sought out more ammunition. I located a cabbage-sized stone which I pitched at it underhanded, using both hands.

It crashed against the robot with considerable force. To my surprise, the thing halted for several moments, just hanging there. Slowly, however, it resumed its upward course.

I struggled with another rock, about three times the size of the previous one, and managed to repeat the performance. This time the machine emitted a brief burst of clicking noises before it began to move again.

But I had just about depleted my arsenal. Of readily manageable stones, that is. There were some that were quite sizable, but I all but despaired of moving one. However . . .

There was one farther back and somewhat higher up. Certainly large enough to produce the havoc I desired. If I could dislodge it, it would roll. If it would roll, it might make it to the edge and over. If it did that and went over at the right spot, my immediate worries would be over.

. . . Unfortunately, it was irregularly shaped, and I could not be certain as to the precise course it would follow.

As I stood there thinking about it, the robot suddenly jerked forward another three or four feet and immediately began casting upward after anchoring positions. I turned hurriedly and headed for the stone. The machine had already passed the halfway mark.

At first, I was unable to budge it. I must have thrown

my full weight against it six or eight times before it moved slightly. By then, my arms felt almost useless and the combination of my headache and dizziness with the pain in my side were about to prostrate me. But the fact that it had moved at all strengthened me a little more. I shoved twice again and it stirred on both occasions. By then the sounds of the robot were frighteningly near.

I tried bracing my back against the slant of the shelf and pushing with my legs. It increased the pain in my side, but it moved it some more. Turning my head, I saw the extensors whipping up over the edge of my aerie, seeking holds, falling back, coming again. I renewed my efforts.

The stone shuddered, swayed forward, rocked back. Again.

Again.

It almost toppled. But I felt drained. Unable to push another time. Hardly able to move . . .

Two of the extensors caught onto something. A labored humming sound followed, to be joined moments later by a screeching from the treads. But I still had not recovered my strength. I lay there aching and hearing.

There came a glint of light, another as it backtracked and overshot, and then the beam was upon me once again. Cursing, I turned my head away. In that instant, I found the extra strength that I needed.

I tensed my legs, almost convulsively, and began to push. My teeth were clenched so tightly I thought they would all crack. Fresh perspiration broke out upon my brow and ran into my eyes. My side throbbed in time with my heart.

Then, slowly, slowly, the stone moved forward. It moved several inches, I would judge, before it stuck. I relaxed and let it rock back. Then I tensed again and shoved.

This time it kept going beyond the point where it had halted before. It slowed but kept moving, and I continued the pressure until I thought that I would explode.

It slowed, began to bind, felt as if it were about to stop. Then it went forward and I went supine.

I would have missed seeing what happened next except for the fact that my head rolled to the left and the light struck me in the eyes again. I twisted away and by that movement obtained a view of the stone's progress.

The forward section of the robot was in sight—ten or twelve inches' worth. The stone seemed to be going wide, and I feared that it might miss.

But it did not. It caught the left corner of the thing with a magnificent crash. Then both were gone. I heard the sounds of its impact below just as I was passing out again.

Just how long I lay there then, I do not know. I think that I dreamed, of stars, without number, drifting like bright isles in a dark lake, of men, going to and fro among them, peaceful, serene, wise, noble. I seemed to be pleased by this, for conflicting reasons: either the work I had set out to accomplish had been finished, and finished properly, or this had occurred in spite of what had been done, and because of its speedy termination. Either way, it was a pretty, if unframed, picture and I regretted being drawn away from it. I guess it was the light that roused me. When I finally came around, I could not be certain whether I had actually been dreaming or simply staring up at the stars in a kind of reverie. Not that it really mattered.

I turned over and managed to get onto my hands and knees, keeping my face averted from the light. Slowly, I crawled to the edge.

The robot lay, broken, twisted, on its back, all the way down and perhaps thirty feet out. The stone was nowhere in sight.

I lowered myself to my stomach and lay there staring at it, feeling at first elated, then depressed. What was I but some sort of broken mechanism myself? Preserving only what I deemed essential, I had streamlined myself at each accession, wound me up and run until I stopped. Then again.

Or, rather, he had.

Damn it! No! *I* had.

We had?

All right. I was beginning to accept what had occurred. Things had been sorting themselves out unconsciously ever since that most recent meshing. All of the pin-pulling, with its resultant restoration of memories I had previously stripped away, produced psychic shocks of varying intensity, but the material revealed was ultimately assimilable because it was mine, it was familiar, it had fit and

160

belonged. Then came the alien nexus, through which other portions of my original self had been filtered.

Alien, though? Not any longer.

No.

For, in an instant, I was on the other side of the mirror, regarding the detestable baggage I had acquired by the pulling of the pins and the killing of Winton. Even so, I had not obtained what I wanted—an understanding of the ultimate motivation of that gang of meddlers.

Meddlers? I was, too, of course. But it was in reaction to them.

Them?

Us. Now.

Funny.

. . . For none of us knew why we kept winding ourselves up in a certain way—whichever the way—or who we really were. I had indeed been the missing clone, a theft made necessary at that time by virtue of my advanced age and declining powers. It had taken a carefully controlled suicide to effect the transfer without allowing the others to become aware of my true nature. Before that, I had been around for generations, almost from the beginning. But there things grew murky. I had always known that I was of one blood with the enemy; and we had always been enemies, for I had disagreed from the first with their dispositions in the setting up of the House. I had been powerless, though, and had bided my time, disapproving. I knew them both from their actions and as an occasional silent party to their meshings. It was a long while before my distrust of their policy of confinement and progressive control reached the point where I began to consider their removal.

The House had only been intended as a temporary measure—the linking and consolidation of all the outposts as a common shelter for humanity following the disaster that had engulfed the Earth—a place to pause for a second breath, as it were. The family had decided to make it more permanent, however, holding that the same thing would happen again, wherever we went, unless something was done to change man himself. They were for making the human race a prisoner and a patient, as I saw it. My own feelings were that simple dispersal would be sufficient to guarantee human continuity, by virtue of divergence,

divergence and the multiplicity of opportunities for development that would lie available. I had been back to Earth in its last days, working with the evacuation teams, and I believed it had all been an accident, a misunderstanding, a mistake, the war, the disaster. And even if this were not so, the same thing need not occur over and over again. I wanted man out of the House and on his way once more.

I lacked the organization and capability of the family. All that I shared was the anonymity. I decided to take advantage of it to the fullest and plan carefully, strike quickly and be thorough. I failed the first time, but they still did not know who or why it was. The authorities were useless, unaware of the family's existence and subject to its influence. I studied their methods, emulated them in concealing myself and, yes, learned something of their early ruthlessness. It was not that difficult.

They changed, though. I knew why. That notion of moral evolution they entertained and practiced, even on a personal level. That finally undid them. This time they were too weak and I had won—in a Pyrrhic sort of way.

I did not know who I really was either. My earliest memories involved wandering in the Cellar of Wing 1, where I eventually came to work, for a time, as a maintenance man. It was only gradually, by observation and telepathy, that I learned of the family and their grand experiment. I resolved to thwart them and I set out to educate myself.

I knew that by destroying them I might be throwing away the key to my own origin. I was willing to make this sacrifice, however . . .

The pins I was able to pull did not bring me this knowledge. If I had responded to the light sooner, I might have . . .

What was it about that light? As soon as it fell upon me back in the lounge I had been drawn to it. If I had not paused to seek knowledge of the pins, I would have reached it. I would have avoided . . .

No good.

I would have avoided a conflict that was really necessary for the successful completion of my work. Now it was just a matter of maintaining stability, of keeping the upper hand within my own being. I . . .

But I no longer wanted to follow the light. Now I was repelled by it. I—

We . . .

Yes. We.

No. I.

We are I.

I stared at the broken machine, sharing its wreckage.

Time ticked by.

The light spilled over my head from the back, casting me in Rorschachs of shadow.

My head continued to throb.

A small breeze herded sheep of mist past the robot.

Something dark and quick darted through the air.

Something tiny and not too near croaked and buzzed, briefly.

In the corner of my seeing, the moon was a wheel of ice, rolling.

My teeth began to chatter. My fingertips felt icy where they touched against the stone.

Get up!

"I—"

You have to climb down now and go back. Get up.

"I am tired."

Get up. Now.

"I don't know whether I can."

You can. Get up.

"I don't know whether I want to."

What you want is immaterial. Get up.

"Why?"

Because I said so. Now!

"All right! All right!"

I pushed myself up, slowly. I rested a moment on my hands and knees, then sat back on my haunches.

"Better?"

Yes. Now stand up.

I did. After a few seconds' vertigo had passed, I knew that I could hold it. I kept my back to the light, which had me facing Wing Null.

That is where you are headed. Get going.

I lowered my head, took several deep breaths and set about it.

Climbing down, I discovered, was not as difficult as

163

climbing up. Especially when I slipped and slid the last eight feet or so.

Rise. Go on. Go on.

"Am I never to rest?" I asked. But I found my footing once more and began to walk, bent partly forward, clutching my side. My descent had put me out of range of the light again, and that helped some. I passed the robot without granting it a second look. I climbed, I descended, I staggered. I stumbled and rose again, went on.

The exertion warmed me somewhat. After a time, I sighted the dark bulk of my Wing once more. The lighted window reminded me of Glenda, which in turn made me think of her father. He had been my friend, and I had destroyed him. Not the same I. Not then. Not now. I tried to regard it in this fashion and felt the beginnings of acceptance. It was not that I was beyond remorse, but that I was no longer the same person I had been—then, or even a few days or hours earlier. Perhaps the shattering and restructuring of my ego was less debilitating than it might have been because I had had so much practice at it. I understood now who I had been—up to a point. That was a beginning, anyway, of finding out who I was currently.

I had encouraged Glynn, seeing in him a hope for the future, a means of breaking out of the House. I had come to like him personally, however, and when they destroyed him I had taken the child. I had had no special plans for her then. I had done it solely because of my friendship with her father. Later, though, when I saw that her intellectual endowments were quite formidable, I saw to it that along with an extensive education she was also aware of her father's hopes and plans, down to the level of details. She embraced them with enthusiasm. By then though, I had almost come to consider her more mine than his. So it was only natural that I eventually made her privy to some of my own hopes and plans as well. She was completely sympathetic, which is why I had enlisted her aid. I wished now that I could have done without her. She did not know I was going to kill Engel or force Winton to kill me. Still, it had worked. I could see no other way. I had won . . .

But it had worked and I had won, then why was I headed for Wing Null rather than the ruin?

Because . . .

Keep walking.

There had to be a reason. I just could not recall it. My head was as foggy as the night about me. It still throbbed like a sore tooth.

Do not try to think. Just keep walking.

Glenda. That was it. She was waiting for me. I was going back to see Glenda, to tell her it was all over now.

Get up!

Strange. I did not remember having fallen. I struggled to my feet and almost immediately collapsed again.

It is not very much farther. You must continue. Get up.

I wanted to. I wanted to cooperate. This spirit was quite willing . . .

. . . Only my legs kept getting tangled, doing the wrong things. Damned uncooperative, this body . . .

Pendulumlike, I could feel my mind doing strange things again, too. It was all right, though, if it would just make me go.

Another try, then down again.

A little thing like that should not bother me, though. It was not necessary that I stand in order to proceed. I had driven bodies beyond this point before. It was all a matter of attitude. Singlemindedness, determination—these were what mattered. Perhaps stubbornness was a better word.

I crawled forward. Time ceased to have meaning. My hands were cold.

Up a slope. I hardly noticed when the light hit me again after a time. When I did realize it, it brought me the passing illusion of being onstage, performing before an invisible audience, utterly silent, so taken were they by my performance.

Just before my arms gave way for the third time, I saw the Wing again, I saw the window.

It was near now, much nearer. Slowly, very slowly, I pulled myself along, like a half-crushed insect. It would be ridiculous to fail at this point. Absurd . . .

It was an effort to open my eyes partway and raise my head. How long had I been lying there?

No good.

One can lash the body, drive it, push it. But the comings and goings of the mind follow a different set of rules.

This one was a going. . . .

165

Part **III**

From a timeless vantage, I saw it all.

The family had picked me up, loaded me and pointed me at Styler. Styler had taken me, manipulating circumstances in a pattern that programmed me to play Othello to his Hamlet, and turned me loose to condition humanity along pacifistic lines he deemed propitious. I could only guess, but it seemed fairly obvious that he had obtained a specimen of my tissues at some point in my early experiments with cloning. He had robots capable of managing that much for him—still had robots—and he had designed Wing Null. The means was not really that material. Somewhere, he had used that sample to clone the original Mr. Black, implanted suggestions that made him something of an anti-me and sent him into the House with amnesia and his survival instinct going for him. He was placed there to check me and balance my efforts when the time came, operating like some sort of sociological time bomb. The time had come and this had happened. A wall was down, Glenda was ready with the Glynn formulations and I had been neutralized. I could almost hear Styler's voice saying, ". . . Now add 8 cc's of Black base to the di Negri acid."

I glared back at the colored lights. Finally, I reached out and began throwing switches.

I heard a startled noise from my right and a hand came forward and fell upon my arm. I could not turn my head to see her because of the hood. I had a vision from long ago of peasants plowing a small field, its boundary marked by an animal skull mounted on a low post.

"It's all right," I said.

The hand slipped away.

"Who—?" she finally said.

How the hell was I supposed to answer that?

"I was Legion," I said finally, haltingly, "a whole gallery of faces. I was Black, I was Engel, I was Lange, I was Winton, I was Karab, I was Winkel. And Jordan and Hinkley and Old Lange. And a horde of others of whom you have never heard. I should say that it does not matter, but it does, for I am me. I suppose that I should choose a face. Very well. Just call me Angelo. That is how it all began."

"I am afraid that I do not understand. Are you—?"

I raised the hood from my head and turned to regard her.

"Yes," I said, "I am really all right. Thank you for doing as I asked. Did I make it all the way back, or did you have to drag me?"

"I helped," she said. "I saw you fall."

"You mean you went outside?"

Her face brightened.

"Yes. I was hoping for an excuse. Not that kind, I mean. But—it was so fine!"

I rubbed my side.

"You patched me up some, I see."

"You were bleeding."

"Yes, I guess I was, wasn't I?"

I got to my feet, steadied myself for a moment against the back of the chair, moved to the counter and began searching the shelf beneath it.

"What are you looking for?"

"Cigarettes. I want to smoke."

"There were some in the other room, where I was waiting."

"Let's go there then."

I refused her arm. We walked into the hallway and up it.

"How long since you brought me in?" I asked.

"About an hour and a quarter."

I nodded.

"What has that light been doing recently?"

"I don't know. I haven't looked since I brought you in."

We came to the room, entered it. She indicated the cigarettes, declined one herself. I moved to the window and looked out as I lit up. A puddle of tawny light, spilled at the far edge of things, was seeping across the sky. I inhaled deeply, sighed smoke.

"You really liked it out there?" I said.

"Yes—and it is so beautiful now, with the sun starting to come up."

"Good. I want you to come take a walk with me outside."

"You're not in such great shape."

"All the more reason to have someone with me then. Besides, I'll need a secretary."

She cocked her head to one side and narrowed her eyes. I smiled.

"Come on. We'll take it slow and easy. The walk will do us good."

She nodded and followed me out to the locks. We passed through them and entered the cool morning.

"I can't get over the smells," she said, drawing a deep breath. "The air is so different from that in the House!" Then, "Where are we going?" she asked.

I turned my head and raised it.

"Up there."

"To the ruin? That is pretty far . . ."

"Slow and easy. No hurry," I said. "We have all the time in the world."

We started in that direction, and I was irritated by my need to stop and rest frequently. We had to go out of our way, also, for I directed our course in such a fashion that we did not pass near to the body I had left. Although I tried to conceal the pull in my side, she noted it and moved around and took my arm. This time I allowed it.

I chuckled.

"Remember when I gave you those skates for your seventh birthday?" I said. "And you slipped and twisted your ankle the very next day? I thought it was sprained, but it was really broken. You wouldn't let me carry you, though. You leaned on me like this. You didn't want to cry, but your face was all wet and you kept biting your lip. You tore that little blue dress you liked so much when you fell. The one with the yellow stitching on the front."

Her fingers had tightened to an almost painful grip upon my arm. A light breeze came out of the east. I reached over and patted her hand, "It *is* all right now," I said, and she nodded quickly and I turned away.

Before I saw it, I felt the glint from that light in the ruins. It flickered by, returned, stayed with us. It was not

171

quite so overpowering when the air was filling with day-light.

We worked our way among the stones, about the craters, up the hill, down, then up again.

"A bird!" she cried.

"Yes. Pretty. Yellow."

It was a pleasant morning that was being fetched into the world, softening the tones of the landscape where my nightmare had been enacted. Some piled cumulus to the left promised a later rain, as did a cool breeze from that direction, but the east was still clear in its brightening and there was more greenery about than I had thought.

The light he had used to hunt me was finally blocked by the upper edge of that portion of the building's front which still stood, blackened and cracked, doors gaping, as we approached.

"Are we going in there?" she asked.

"Yes."

We moved forward and entered the caved-in, burnt-out lobby, skylighted by the collapsed roof, filled with the detritus of centuries.

"What are we going to do here?" she asked, as we picked our way through the litter in the direction of the more sheltered southwest corner of the room.

"In a minute. I think you will know in a minute or so," I said. "That's why I wanted a secretary."

The rear hallway I had taken so many years before was completely blocked by a cave-in that appeared to have been augmented by a landslide from the high hills to the rear. I led her into a relatively clear waiting alcove where the shapes of furniture persisted within piles of dust. Yes, I had remembered correctly. The dark instrument crouched, tarantula-like, in its recess in the wall. I withdrew my handkerchief.

While I was wiping it off, the telephone rang.

Glenda uttered a brief, incoherent noise that might have been part question.

"There," I said, stepping back, "I have it reasonably clean now. Answer the phone for me, will you?"

She nodded, and with a mixture of great puzzlement and some trepidation, moved forward and lifted the receiver.

"—Hello?"

She listened a moment, then covered the mouthpiece and looked at me.

"He wants to know who I am."

"So tell him," I said.

She did, listened again, covered it and sought me once more.

"He wants to know if Mr. Angelo di Negri is here."

"You are Mr. Negri's secretary. Ask him what he wants."

Again, and, "He wants to talk to you about your work," she said.

"I am busy just now," I said, as I began dusting a chair. "Tell him that you will fill him in a bit and describe to him the structure of the House, with its Wing setup and its internal organization. Answer any questions he has about it."

This took a long while. I had finished cleaning the filth of ages from the chair, doing a very thorough job, and had seated myself in it before she turned to me again.

"He wants to know whether he can speak with you now."

I shook my head. I lit a cigarette.

"Tell him that the wall is down on Wing V, and that people are going outside. Tell him that you are going back to provide a program for sheltering the exodus that is to come."

"I am?"

"You want to, don't you?"

"Yes, but—"

"You possess knowledge of the necessary equipment? Of its fabrication and employment?"

"I think so."

"Then tell him about that, too."

I finished smoking. After a long while, I lit another one.

"He wants to know what you think has been learned from all this," she said finally.

"How the hell should I know?" I said. "I am not even certain what I have learned myself, except that I now appreciate what it feels like to have been assumed into the workings of a great machine."

She spoke with him briefly, then said, "He says he would like to hear your voice. He says he would like you to say something to him. Anything."

I rose to my feet and stretched.

"Tell him the debt of honer is canceled between us," I said. "Tell him you are sorry, but Mr. Negri is not receiving any calls at this time. Then hang up."

She did this, and I accepted her arm once more and allowed her to help me back out of the ruin. The sun was up and the clouds were nearer. I thought we might be able to beat the rain. Then again, maybe not, but what the hell.

BRIDGE OF ASHES

For Sally Turner
and
Sally Albaugh

Part I

I—

Day was the—

It—

. . . Saw the man, is—

. . . Man is moving through the woods. With him a band of others, hunters all. They are clad in the skins of animals. They bear sharpened sticks, fire-hardened. Mine is tipped with stone and decorated with a tracery of lines, inscribed with the point of the flint knife which hangs from the strip of leather about my—his waist. He wears leaves in his hair, and a shining object hangs from a thong about his throat. It is a thing of power which he had brought with him from the land of spirits beneath the sea. He leads the men in the hunt, raven-haired father's father of them all. His dark eyes describe the circuit of the beast. Silent, nostrils flaring, the others walk in his track. The air bears a sometime hint of the salt and the wrack, of the not-too-distant shores of that great water, mother of us all. He raises his hand and the men come to a halt.

He gestures again and they draw up on either side of him, crouching, spreading into a forward-curving arc. Then, once again, they halt.

He moves. He adjusts his grip on the haft of his weapon. Then, suddenly, his hands are empty. There comes a roar of pain from the glade before him. At this, the others rush forward, their spears held ready. The man draws his knife and follows.

He reaches the wounded beast—fallen and panting now, three of their shafts protruding from its side—in time to cut its throat. A cry goes up about him as the quick slashing movement is executed. The weapons are withdrawn from the carcass. The stealth of the hunt is gone, replaced by words and laughter. The man moves to dress their prize, dividing most of the flesh for transport, retaining some for the victory meal which is now at hand.

The firemaker gathers tinder. Another fetches him dead limbs for fuel. Someone begins a nonmelodic song, a recitation with a lilt. The sun pushes its way toward the treetops. Small flowers unfold among the roots, the rocks, the fallen timber. There comes another whiff of the sea.

As the man skewers chunks of the flesh and passes these to the firemaker, he pauses for a moment in mid-gesture and rests his fingertips upon the shining object he wears. It seems a trifle warm to his touch. The moment passes. He shrugs. He hands the meat to the other. He moves to cut more.

There comes a sound—a deep, drawn-out hooting, breaking into a long, rising note which grows into a whistle, passes then beyond the audible, cuts a wake of vibration, showing that somewhere, strongly, it persists.

After a time, this subsides and the hooting begins once more—louder, nearer. It is accompanied by a distant crashing and crackling, as of the passage of a heavy body amid the shrubs, the trees.

The man places his hands on the ground and feels the vibrations within it. He rises to his feet.

"Go!" he says to the others, and he takes up his spear. "Now! Leave the food! Hurry!"

They obey him, fleeing the kill, the fire, leaving the man there alone.

When they have departed, the man begins his retreat from the wood. The notes of the challenge have run through yet another cycle and the forest still echoes with the sound of their passage.

When the hooting comes again, it is with such force and volume that it is felt as much as heard. The man hurries toward the meadow his party had crossed earlier. There had been a rocky knoll in its midst. . . .

He breaks into the open, running toward the hillock.

4

From the thunder at his back, he is already aware that he will be unable to attain a sufficient vantage in time to roll rocks down upon his pursuer.

He races toward a stony cleft, slips within it and turns, crouching.

The reflected sunlight dazzles his eyes, bouncing and dancing on the countless scales of its long, lithe body, flat tail, crooked limbs, horned head. It plows deep furrows in the meadow as, belly low, legs splaying, it propels itself with an awful power directly toward him. Neither sapling nor boulder causes it to swerve from its course. The tree is splintered, goes down, vanishes beneath it. Its head turns from side to side as its horns encounter the stone. The boulder begins to move, almost imperceptibly at first; the stone is rocking, more and more of its damp underside exposed at each teetering shift; it is cast, rolling off to the left, with a final toss of that sea-wet thick neck, sun-rich and throbbing with a great new hooting shriek, blasting dust and gravel before it, continuing the sidewise swimming strokes which bury each limb in the earth as they drive it on.

The man braces the butt of his spear against the stone. He searches that blazing body for some flaw, some imperfection, some weakness. He makes his decision and aligns the point of his weapon. He squints against the blown dust. His ears ache from that high-pitched cry. He waits.

Moments later, his spear is shattered and the rocks about him are shaken by the impact. He flattens himself against the rear of the crevice as a horn drives toward him. The horn stops inches short of his belly.

Now, it begins to throw its weight from side to side, spatulate legs continuing their paddlelike movement, body ringing like a great bell each time that it strikes against the stone. The man smells the dried brine upon its armored hide. He is nearly deafened by the new cry it emits. He stabs at its tossing head, but his flint blade is broken in his hand. He feels the rocks shudder again. He clutches at his amulet, now burning hot upon his breast.

5

The next thrust penetrates his side, and we scream as we are impaled and lifted—thrown. . . .

Pain and breaking. Blackness and pain. Blackness. Light. Has the sun moved higher? We are wet with our own bright blood. The beast is gone. We are going. Here, alone, among the grasses . . . Insects circle us, walk upon us, drink of us. A jagged mount of bone has risen from the continent of my body, snow-capped. . . . I—

Blackness.

The man awakens to the sound of their wailing. They have returned to him, his children. They have brought her with them, and she cradles his head in her lap, weeping. She has strewn him with herbs and flowers and wrapped him in a bright garment. He smiles to her and she touches his brow. His amulet has grown cold. His awareness begins to fade once more. He closes his eyes, and above him she begins to sing the long lament. At this, the others turn and move away, leaving them there alone. There is love. We—

I—

There is a flash of blue, a circle of white. . . .

The beast has returned to its place.

And of self the—

—to old be. Was the—

. . . Man by the seaside. See—

. . . Drawing is the man in the damp sand. Power. His eye the binder of angles. His I— Opposite and adjacent, of course. Where the line cuts them. At hand, the sea forms green steps and trellises, gentle, beneath the warm blue sky; gentle and unnoticed, as he scribes the circle. For seventy-some years has he known the sea near Syracuse, here in Sicily. He had never been far from this sea, even in the days of his studies in Alexandria. It is not surprising then that he can ignore its wash, splash, spray, its plays of light and color. Clean sea, living sea, a touch of deafness and a totality of concentration, and the sea is as distant and abstract as all the grains of sand he reckoned to fill the universe, displaced about all bodies within it in accordance

6

with the law he had determined in the matter of the purity of the King's crown, that day he ran naked from his bath shouting he had found it. . . . The sea and the sigh of the sea at the side of the sea . . . Now, now very few things matter but the relationships between forms. The pulleys, the pumps, the levers, all of them clever and useful in their time. But Syracuse has fallen. Too many Romans this time even for the mirror-trick. And does it really matter? The ideas outlive their embodiments. The ingenious devices were only toys, really, flitting shadows of the principles he had cast for with nets of thought. Now, now . . . This one . . . If a relationship between things, between events, could be expressed in a great number of small steps . . . How many? Many . . . ? Few . . . ? Any. Any number desired. And if there were a boundary of some sort . . . Yes. A . . . A limit. Yes. Then up to that point, any number of steps . . . As we had done with π and the polygons. Only now let us take it a step further. . . .

He does not see the shadow of the man on the sand to his left. The thoughts, the deafness, the promise of the Roman commander Marcellus that he would not be harmed . . . He does not see, he does not hear the question. Again. Look up, old man! We must answer! The blade comes out of the scabbard, and again there are words. Respond! Respond! He traces another circle, idly, thinking the steps of change within limits, groping for the new vocabulary its expression will require—

The stroke!

We are pierced. We fall forward. . . . Why? Let me—

My eyes fall upon that final circle. There is a soft blue all about it. Not of the sea, the sky . . . There is—

Now, now, now . . . The pain, the waste of it all . . .

I, Flavius Claudius Julianus, he thinks, pacifier of Gaul, Emperor of Rome, last defender of the old gods, pass now as they have passed. Pity, Lord of the lightnings, and thou, shaker of the earth and tamer of horses, and thou, lady of the grain fields, and thou,

thou . . . all ye other lords and ladies of high Olympus . . . pity, pity, pity that I could not have served you better, oh lovers and holders of the world and its trees and grasses and wet holy places, and all things fleet and crawling, flying and burrowing, all that move, breathe, touch, sing and cry. . . . I could have served you better had I stayed at Ctesiphon, laying siege to that great city, than cross the Tigris to seek King Sapor in this waste. For here I die. This wounding's mortal, and all the Persian army rings us round. Hot, dry, desolate land . . . Fitting. A place like this perhaps, where the Galilean went to be tempted . . . Is this irony necessary, new Lord? You have wrested the earth from its keepers to throw it away. . . . It is another world you claim to lead them to. . . . You care no more for the green, the brown, the gold, the glades, the glens, than this dry, hot place of rock and sand . . . and of death. What is death to you? A gateway . . . To me it is more than my end, for I have failed. . . . You slay me as the children of Constantine took my kin. . . . For yours this may be a gateway, for me it is the end. . . . I see where my blood pools. . . . I give it to the Earth— Gaea, old mother. . . . I have fought and I have finished. . . . Old ones, I am thine—

The blood's red ring is bleached. About it, for an instant, a blueness. A roaring seems to begin. He. He. He . . . I—

Tell me if anything is ever done. . . . This then, I—

He stares from the window, sorting the motions of the birds. Spring has come to Rome. But the sun is falling and the shadows lengthen. He sorts the colors, the shades, the textures. Had I this city to build, I would have done differently. . . . He regards the clouds. But then it might never have been done. . . . He leans his head back against the wall, runs his fingers through his beard, tugs at his lower lip. There were so many things. . . . To fly, to go beneath the seas, to build palaces and marvelous devices, to channel rivers, to plumb all the laws of nature, to merge the scientific and the esthetic, striving perpetually within me, getting in each

8

other's ways ... Yet there were many things done for Ludovico, only all of them trifles. ... The Great Horse ... He would have liked to have seen that carried to completion. Sad, how the opportunities invariably arose at the wrong times. Or if things did seem to be going right, that something always came to cancel them. So many things that might be of use. It is as if the world resists. ... And now ... The Magnificent Giuliano de' Medici dead this March past ... There is little to hold me here now, and this new French king has spoken of the manor of Cloux, near Amboise, a pleasant place—and no duties. ... Perhaps the rest would be good, to think, to pursue my studies. I may even paint a little. ...

He turns from the window, retreats. There is a white circle on that field of blue, though the moon is not yet risen. He might— I—

Tell me if anything is ever done. ...

... And she sings the lament as he lies bleeding.

The beast is returned to the sea. She brushes away insects. She cradles his head in her lap. There is no movement. He does not seem to breathe.

Yet some warmth is in him still. ...

She finds more words. ... Trees and mountains, streams and plains, how can this thing be? He whose sons and sons' sons have hunted among you since before the hills were made ... He who has spoken with the powers beneath the sea ... How can he pass as men have passed into the land of dreams? Rend yourselves, hide yourselves, spill yourselves over, weep ... if the son of the land can walk it no more.

Her voice carries across the meadow, is lost among the trees. ... Pain, pain, pain ... I—

Drunk again. Who cares? Perhaps I am as worthless as they say, a dirty Swiss madman. ... I saw and I spoke. It is they who are mad, who do not listen. ... Yet ... Nothing I have said has been taken right. Suppose it is always to be so? Suppose ... Damn Voltaire! He knew what I meant. He knew I never intended that

9

we all go live in the woods! Out to show his wit at the price of an idea ... Natural, within society, is what I said—over and again.... Only in society can man have knowledge of good and evil. In nature he is merely innocent. He knew! I'll swear he knew, damned mocker! And damn all popularizers of a man's work! The perversity of costumed dandies playing at the simple ... Thérèse! I miss you tonight.... Where is that bottle? There ... Seek goodness and God and order in nature and in the heart ... and in the bottle, I should have added. The room swims well tonight. There are times—damn these moments—when it all seems worthless, all, all that I have done and all else in this mad world. Who cares? At times, I seem to see so clearly. ... But ... The faith of a Savoyard Vicar is not mine tonight.... There have been times when I feared that I was truly mad, times else when I doubted some thought or other.... Now I fear that it does not matter whether I am mad or sane, right or wrong. Does not matter in the least. My words are cast into the Föhn, strewn, effectless, gone. ... The wind blows on, the world goes as it will, coursing the same route it would have taken had I never been at all. ... *Bacche, benevenies gratus et optatus, per quem noster animus fit letificatus.* ... It does not matter that I saw and spoke. It does not matter that those who scorned me may be right. It does not matter. ...

Head resting on outflung arm, he regards the bottom of the bottle. We see it go white in the flickering light, and all around it blue. ... We spin. We—

I—

Aiee! she cries, shaking, the lament done, the blood drying, the body still and pale. And again, as she throws herself upon him and clings to the once-warm form. Air rushes from my lungs with a noise like a sob. The pain!

The pain ...

... But there is nothing left. My hopes—the dreams of a fool ... I welcomed this thing when it came.

The old order, into which I, Marie Jean Antoine Nicholas Caritat, was born Marquis de Condorcet, had had its day and darkened it Long ago had I seen that, and I welcomed the Revolution. But three years past was I seated in the Legislative Assembly. And the terror . . . But one year past, because I favored Gironde, did I fall from grace and flee the Jacobins. . . . Laughable. Here I sit, their prisoner. I know what must come next, and they shall not have it of me. Laughable—for still do I believe. . . . Everything I said in the *Sketch* . . . That man may one day be free from want and war, that the increase and the spread of knowledge, the discovery of the laws of social behavior, may bring man toward perfection . . . Laughable—to believe this and plot to cheat the guillotine this way . . . Yet, moderation is not the way of revolution, a thing we humanists who get involved often learn too late. . . . I still believe, yet these things seem farther off than once they did. . . . Let us hope that that is all there is to it. . . . I am weary. The entire business tedious . . . I find that I am of no further use here. . . . It is time to write an ending and close the book. . . .

We make the final preparations. At the moment of pain, I—he . . . We see through a blue haze dimly a pale circle upon the wall. . . .

Now, now again, ever and always . . . The pain and the broken body she clutches, breathing into the mouth, beating upon my breast, rubbing his hands and neck . . . As if by this to call back, as if by this to share her spirit in her breath . . .

The ground is sharp beneath our shoulders, and there is pain as the breath rattles forth. . . . The blood will flow if I move again. He must stay very still. . . . The sun drops spears upon our eyelids. . . .

. . . Gilbert Van Duyn cast a final glance over his speech. A crutch, he thought. I already know what I am going to say, know exactly where I might depart from the text, and how. . . . Not really that important. The thing is already distributed. All I have to do is get

11

up and say the words. Still . . . Addressing the General Assembly of the United Nations is hardly the same as talking to a classroom full of students. I was less nervous in Stockholm, that day, eight years ago. . . . Strange, that the Prize means so much. . . . Without it, someone else would be reading this—or something very like it. . . . And it probably would not have made that much difference. . . . The main thing is to get it said. . . . He ran his hand through what remained of his hair. How *will* the voting go, I wonder? They all say it should be close. . . . I just hope the ones we are concerned about can take a longer view, be willing to see beyond the surface inequities. . . . God! I really hope so. . . .

The speaker was nearing the end of his introduction. A soft undercurrent of murmurs the texture of half a hundred tongues still flowed across the hall, fading as the moments ticked by. Soon, soon now . . . He glanced at the speaker, the clock on the wall, his own hands. . . .

The speaker concluded, turned his head, gestured. Gilbert Van Duyn rose and moved to the microphone. He smiled as he placed the papers before him. A momentary pause . . . He began to speak. . . .

Dead silence.

Not only the murmuring, but every small sound within the hall had ceased. Not a cough nor the scraping of a chair, not the rattle of a briefcase nor the scratch of a match; not a rustle of paper, the clink of a water tumbler, the closing of a door nor the sound of a footstep. Nothing.

Gilbert Van Duyn paused and looked up.

Nor was there any movement.

Total stillness, as in a snapshot . . . Not a body stirred. Cigarette smoke hung motionless in the air.

He turned his head, seeking some small activity—anything—within the assembly.

His eyes passed over the figure within the tableau several times before the expression and the stance registered, before the object clasped in both hands and thrust forward came suddenly to his notice.

12

Then he froze.

The man, in the delegation from one of the smaller, warmer nations, had obviously sprung to his feet but a moment before—his chair still tilted backward, an upset folder still hanging at an impossible angle before him, spilling still papers into the air.

The man held a pistol, pointed directly at him, a thin wisp of unmoving smoke twisted to the left of its muzzle.

Slowly then, Gilbert Van Duyn moved. He left his notes, drew away from the microphone, stepped down, crossed back, made his way toward the place where the man stood with the pistol, eyes narrowed, teeth bared, brows tightened.

When he came up beside him, he stood for a moment, then reached out cautiously, touched the man's arm.

. . . Stiff, unyielding, statuelike. It did not feel like flesh beneath his fingers, but some substance much denser, more rigid. But then, even the cloth of the sleeve felt stiffer than it should have.

Turning, he touched the next nearest man. The sensations were the same. Even the shirtfront behaved as if it were of a coarse, heavily starched material.

Gilbert Van Duyn regarded the papers, still unnaturally suspended before the gunman. He touched one. The same rigidity . . . He tugged at it. It cracked soundlessly.

He extracted an automatic pencil from a delegate's pocket, held it before him, released it. It hung in the air, motionless.

He glanced at his watch. The second hand was not moving. He shook it, put it to his ear. Nothing.

Returning to the gunman, he sighted along the barrel of the pistol. There could be no doubt. It was aimed directly at the spot he had recently vacated.

. . . And what was that up ahead?

He straightened, made his way forward, regarded the pellet about six feet out from the muzzle. It was the bullet, almost hanging there, creeping forward at a barely perceptible velocity.

13

He shook his head, stepped back.

Suddenly, it became necessary that he know the extent of the phenomenon. He turned and headed for the door, his pace increasing as he went. Passing through, he moved to the nearest window and regarded the world beyond.

Traffic stood silent and still, birds hovered in midflight, not a flag rippled. There was no motion to the clouds. . . .

"Spooky, isn't it?" something like a voice seemed to say. "Necessary, though. I realized at—you might say, the last minute—that I had to talk with you."

Van Duyn turned.

A dark man, clad in green slacks and a pale sport shirt, was leaning against the wall, left foot resting on a large black satchel. Stockily built, wide forehead, dark eyes, heavy brows, flaring nostrils . . . He was uncertain as to the swarthy man's race or nationality.

"Yes," Van Duyn answered, "it is spooky. You know what's happened?"

The other nodded.

"As I said, I wanted to talk with you."

"So you stopped time?"

Something like laughter. Then, "Just the opposite. I've speeded you up. You may grow extremely hungry in what seems like the next few minutes. Just tell me when you do. I have food with me." He hefted the satchel. "Come this way, please."

"You are not really talking," Van Duyn said. "I just realized that. Your words are coming directly into my head."

The man nodded again.

"It's this or write notes. Listen! You can't even hear your footsteps. Sound is a trifle slow at the moment—or rather, we are too fast for it Come on. Time is a dear commodity."

He turned, and Van Duyn followed him out of the building. He took what seemed an unnecessarily long time to open the door.

Then he seized Van Duyn's hand and did something with the satchel. They rose into the air.

Moments later, they had come to rest atop the building. The man turned then and gestured at the East River, a piece of muddy glass, and at the hazed and grainy sky where strands of smoke lay like bloated things on a beach.

"There is that," he said. "And here ..." He took him by the arm and led him to the other end of the roof. ". . . the city."

Van Duyn looked out, across the silent city where the still cars lay at the bottom of the sea of their exhausts—pedestrians, storefronts, flagpoles, hydrants, shrubbery, benches, signs, tangles of wire, lightpoles, grass, a few trees and a stray cat all embedded within it. He looked up at dark clouds, down at the play of light and shade on dingy surfaces.

"What is it that you want me to see?" he asked.

"There is pollution," said the other.

"I am well aware of that—particularly today."

". . . and power, and beauty."

"I can't deny it."

"The resolution you were about to urge be passed ... What do you think its chances really are?"

"Everyone feels the voting will be close."

The dark man nodded.

"Yet what is it basically?" he said. "A thing which would put some pressure on those nations not party to them to become signatory to several already existing treaties dealing with contamination of the seas and the atmosphere. Everyone agrees in principle that the world should be kept clean, yet there is strong resistance to the measures proposed."

"But understandable," Van Duyn said. "The wealthy, powerful nations owe their power, their wealth, their standards of existence, to the sort of exploitation the others are now being called upon to forgo—and the call comes just at the point when those others are approaching a position where they can indulge in the same sorts of enterprise and reap similar benefits. It is only human for them to feel cheated, see it as a neo-colonial conspiracy, resist it."

"Only human," said the other. "That, unfortunately,

is the problem—and it is a much larger problem than you could possibly realize. I respect you, enormously, Dr. Van Duyn, and because of this I have decided to take this time to tell you exactly what that word means. Human. Do you think Leakey and the others were right, that it was East Africa where some hominid first took his thumb and got a grip on the humanity business?"

"It is quite possible. We may never know for certain, but there is evidence—"

"I will spare you the trouble. The answer is yes. That is where they did it. But they were not entirely unassisted in the matter—at that point, and at many other points far earlier in time."

"I do not understand. . . ."

"Of course not. Your education was based on admirable presumptions of regularity and an unavoidable eschewal of the teleological. You are a victim of your own sound thinking. There is no way you could have arrived at the proper conclusions, short of being told. Yet the answer is teleological: the human race was designed to serve a particular end, and that end is now in sight."

"Mad! Ridiculous!" Van Duyn said, and the dark man gestured toward the city.

"Can you make things move again?" he asked.

Van Duyn lowered his head.

"Then hear me out. Suspend judgment until I have finished the story. Are you hungry?"

"Yes."

The other reached into his satchel.

"Sandwiches, wine, lemonade, chocolate, coffee . . ." He unfolded a cloth and spread the food upon it. "Eat, and listen."

"Ages ago," he began, "a particular creature was selected to develop into the dominant life form on this planet. It was given certain breaks and certain challenges, all of which, when utilized or overcome, marked it indelibly with particular traits as it moved along the road to a higher sentience. Its course was directed through many of the situations recently deter-

16

mined by archaeologists and anthropologists to lead up to the hominids and beyond, to bring about the dominance of this planet by the gregarious killer ape. It was necessary to produce a life form of this sort which would achieve a communal existence and acquire the ability to manipulate its environment in such a fashion as to give eventual rise to an urban life style and an inevitable state of high industrial development."

Van Duyn shook his head, but his mouth was full and he had no choice but to listen as the other went on:

"This was desirable solely because of the physical alteration of the world which would come about as a by-product of such a civilization's normal functioning. The agents of mankind's development sought the evolution of an environment characterized by the presence of such compounds as sulfur dioxide, nitrogen oxide, methyl mercury, fluorocarbons 11 and 12, tetrachloroethylene, carbon tet, carbon monoxide, polychlorinated biphenyls, organic phosphates and numerous other industrial effluents and discharges which characterize the modern world. In short, they devised the human race as a planoforming agent, designed and programmed so perfectly that it would not only do this job for them, but would self-destruct when it was completed."

"But why?" asked Van Duyn. "What purpose would this serve?"

"The human race," said the other, "was so designed by beings from another world. I do not know what events finally destroyed their own planet, though I can make some obvious guesses. A few of them escaped and came here. The Earth apparently filled the bill as a suitable world, if certain changes could be effected. There were too few of them to set about the massive job, so they assured the development of the human species to do it for them. They have been sleeping all this while, in stasis chambers aboard their vessels. Periodically, one of them is awakened to monitor the human race's progress and to make whatever adjustments may be required to keep things moving along the proper track."

"Toward our destruction?"

"Yes. They have calculated things pretty closely— possibly having had experience with this sort of situation before—so that the planet becomes suitable for them at just about the point where it becomes uninhabitable for humanity. Your purpose is to do the job for them and expire at its completion."

"How could such a type of being have evolved? I cannot understand the natural development of a creature adapted to a planet despoiled in such a sophisticated fashion. Unless—"

The other shrugged. "—unless they are some secondary species evolved on an already ruined world? Or the primary one, struck by a fortuitous run of mutations? Or perhaps they were far enough along in the life sciences to induce the changes to save themselves after they had already wrecked their world? I do not know. I only know that they seek a particular sort of post-ecological-catastrophe environment and that they are well on their way to achieving it here."

"You said that they keep us under surveillance, and make—adjustments?"

"Yes."

"This would seem to indicate that our programming to achieve their ends is not perfect."

"True. For the past several thousand years they have been keeping a much closer watch over human society than they had previously. They have always been wary of prodigies, prophets, possible mutations, who might redirect the course of events in undesirable directions. Their impact could be greater now than, say, ten thousand years ago. Also, statistically, the possibility of their occurrence has increased. Consequently, they were much more alert during this time to stifle premature technological developments which might have slowed or thwarted their program, and to discourage philosophical tendencies which could have had similar effects. On the other hand, they encouraged the opposite. For an example, they saw an advantage in promoting the otherworldly aspects of Christianity, Buddhism and Islam for purposes of minimizing the importance of the Earth itself. They have dealt with hundreds of philosophers, scientific thinkers—"

"Dealt with?"

"Killed or ruined, or backed and assisted—as the case may be."

"It is a terrible picture that you paint," said Van Duyn. "Why have you told me all these things?"

The dark man looked away, out over the city, fingering a medallion he wore about his neck.

"I have fought them," he finally said, "for ages. At best, I might have succeeded in slowing things a bit. Now, though, our struggle is rushing to a conclusion—the conclusion toward which they directed the race so long ago. I am not certain how much of a chance remains. It would almost seem necessary to effect some change in the nature of man in order to defeat them. What or how, I do not know. What I am attempting now is to buy time, to slow things as much as possible, while I continue to search for an answer. The passage of the resolution now before the General Assembly would help in this—considerably. I was aware that the voting would run very close. This is why I arranged for a spectacle—your assassination. I felt that with the endorsement of a martyr, its chances of passage would be considerably improved. At the last moment, however, I realized that my respect, my fondness for you, would not permit me to proceed quite so coldbloodedly. I owed you this much of explanation. By then, though, it was too late to stop the assassin. And unnecessary. While no one has ever succeeded in controlling time, that bridge of ashes man leaves behind him, I possess the ability to manipulate a person's physiology to the point where the effect is the same as a time-stoppage. So I did this, to give you this explanation, to give you a choice."

"A choice?"

The other nodded.

"I am capable of using almost anyone. Almost . . ."

"I see," said Van Duyn. "I also see that my death could make the difference. . . . Who are you, anyway?"

The dark man shook his head.

"There is simply no time to tell you my story, as it is longer than all of history. As for names . . . I have lost count of them. You might say I am an early experiment of theirs that went bad. And I managed to steal a few things from them before they caught up with me. They make periodic attempts to destroy me and my woman, but they have never been able to recall our lives entirely. They were handicapped in many ways by the uncongenial environment—and over the ages we have acquired many defenses. I am . . . their adversary. That is all. That is enough."

"All right," said Van Duyn, straightening. He glanced out over the city once more, turned, crossed the roof and regarded the dark river. "All right."

After a time, he turned away and looked at the dark man.

"Take me back down."

The other reached into his satchel. Moments later, he took his hand. They left the roof.

Below, they entered the building. Van Duyn headed toward the assembly hall. He looked back once, to say something to the dark man, and discovered that the other was no longer with him.

He continued on, entering the hall, moving back along the aisle he had previously followed. He paused beside the man with the pistol, studying his contorted face. He checked the position of the bullet, which had advanced considerably in his absence. Then he remounted the podium, returned to the lectern.

He reached for his notes, took them into his hand. He glanced up then at the United Nations flag, blue, with the white circle of the world at its center. From the corner of his eye, he seemed to detect a movement. Then something struck and we— He— I—

Slumped across the lectern now, he— We regard the white circle on the field of blue as everything else grows dim and—

He— I—

I . . . I am— I.
I!
I am! I *am!* *I* am!

. . . He lies there, breathing gently. The bleeding
has stopped. It is night, and she has built a fire and
covered him over with the skins of animals. He has
been very cold. She has brought him water in a large
shell. I begin to understand.

Part II

Richard Guise walked in the hills, beheading flowers with a stick. Northern New Mexico is an extraordinary bump on the Earth and summer brings it to its clement best. But Richard Guise had no eye for scenery that day. His vision was turned in upon himself.

He descended into an arroyo, followed it to a place where it branched, then stood undecided. Finally, he sighed and seated himself on a stone in the shade of the farther wall, sat tracing patterns in the dust.

"Damn!" he said, after a time, and again, "Damn!"

Richard Guise resembled the countryside in some ways, though he had been born forty-some years before in urban New Jersey: heavy-set, well-tanned; hair a mix of sand and gray, darker across the backs of the big-knuckled hands that guided his stick; dark eyes wide of a once-broken nose.

But he was not fond of the mountains, the piñons, the rocks, the cacti, the cottonwoods. He was President of the International Telepathic Operators Union, and despite the enormous efficiencies of twenty-first-century communication, of which he was a significant part, he would have felt far more comfortable in a large urban environment, preferably Eastern. He maintained offices in such locations, true, but his was the same problem which had caused all telepaths with young children to seek residence in remote areas. Only, with Dennis, something had gone wrong. . . .

He reached with his special sense, down into the infra-awareness of a stinkbug picking its way among pebbles.

. . . A world of coarse texture and massive forms, of striking odors and peculiar kinesthetic sensations . . .

He swung his stick and observed the sensations dwindle to nothing, the kinesthetics fading last. It was not at all true that empathy bred sympathy. Sometimes the best thing about a channel of experience was the ability to cut it off.

These walks had become more frequent in recent weeks, as it became increasingly apparent that something was still wrong with their son. Beyond the fatigue factor and the possibility of broadcasting his feelings near the child, he simply did not like shielding his thoughts around Vicki. He had to get off somewhere to think them, though.

"Damn!"

He stirred the mashed beetle into the sand, smoothed it over, glanced at his watch. Perhaps the doctor would have something good to say this time.

Victoria Guise tended her plants. She watered, misted, cultivated; she plucked off dead leaves, added nutriments, shifted pots from courtyard to patio, windowsill to bench, sunlight to shade and vice versa; she fondled them with her thoughts. Blue shorts, white halter, red bandana, leather sandals, hung, clung, wrapped her thin, pepper-haired, five-and-a-half-foot, randomly mole-flecked person. Whenever she was particularly troubled the plants received more than usual attention. Green eyes squinted, she sought and dealt with burn, droop, dryness, mold, wither and insect depredation. She was aware that this was a piece of emotional misdirection. Even so, it was generally effective.

For now, she did not have to shield her thoughts and feelings. Except— It was taking much longer than she had anticipated. The doctor was still in with Dennis, and Dick would probably be returning before much longer. If only— She decided that the impatiens could use a little more light, and the navy petunias still looked thirsty. She returned to the tap.

As she was pinching back the asparagus fern, a faint, inquiring thought reached her: *Is it all right?* She felt Dick's presence, sensed the landscape through which he moved, dry, rocky, house up on the hill ahead. He was passing along the small arroyo to the north.

I do not know, she replied. *He is still in there with him.*

Oh.

She felt him slow his pace, caught a whisper of his feelings.

It cannot be too much longer, she added.

I would not think so.

Several minutes later, she heard a door close inside the house.

Hurry, she sent suddenly.

What is it?

I—I think he is finished.

All right. A sense of their house, nearer.

She passed through the gate, closing it behind her, walked around to the south wall. Only marigolds here. They never seemed to need anything special. She inspected them.

"Mrs. Guise?"—faintly, Dr. Winchell's voice from within the house.

She paused, studying the flowers. Another moment or so . . .

"Mrs. Guise—Oh!"

Voices then from the courtyard. Conversation. Dick had returned. She sighed and moved back in that direction.

Entering, she glanced at her husband and the doctor, who had just seated themselves on the chairs near the geraniums. Dr. Winchell was a young, big man, florid, overweight. His straw-colored hair was already thinning, and he ran his fingers through it several times as they spoke.

"Mrs. Guise," he said, nodding, and he made as if to rise as she approached.

She seated herself on the bench across from them, and he eased back into his seat.

"I was just telling your husband," he said, "that it is simply too early to venture a prognosis, but—"

Let us have the bad of it straight, Dick interrupted.

Winchell nodded, glanced at Vicki. She inclined her head slightly, her eyes never leaving his own.

"All right," he said, declining the opportunity to switch away from the purely verbal. "It is not the most encouraging situation, but you must bear in mind that he is still a child—a very adaptable creature—and the fact that this relocation was to a spot as isolated—"

"Has he been permanently damaged?" Richard asked.

"I— It is impossible to answer that at this point. You have only been here a short while and—"

"How long until you can tell for certain?"

"Again, I can't answer you—"

"Is there anything you *can* tell me?"

"Richard," Vickie said. "Please . . ."

"It's all right," Winchell said. "Yes, as a matter of fact I can tell you more about what caused it."

"Go ahead."

"When I first saw Dennis, you lived over twenty miles from the nearest city—a good safety margin, based on accepted range figures for telepathic phenomena. At that distance, a telepathic child should have been sufficiently removed from the urban thought bombardment that he would remain unaffected. Dennis, however, exhibited all the signs of early reception reaction and retreated into catatonia. Neither of you were undergoing anxieties of the sort which might have induced this. At that time, it was suggested that some physical anomaly of the locale might have enhanced reception, or some nearer habitation be housing a broadcaster of thoughts exceptionally distressful to the child. So we recommended you relocate to an even remoter site and see whether the condition would clear up of its own accord."

Richard Guise nodded. "Six times now we've moved. For the same so-called reasons. The kid is thirteen years old. He doesn't talk, he doesn't walk. The nurse still changes his pants and bathes him. Everyone says an institution would be the worst thing, and I am still able to agree. But we have just moved again and nothing is different."

"Yes," Winchell said, "his condition has remained virtually unchanged. He is still suffering the effects of that initial trauma."

"Then the move was of no benefit whatever," Richard said.

"That is not what I said. Simple relocation could not alter what had already occurred. The purpose of the move was to avoid further exposure to adverse stimuli and to give the child's natural recuperative powers an opportunity to effect his return to some sort of equilibrium. It is apparently too early to see evidence of such recovery—"

"Or too late," Richard said.

"—but the move was certainly well advised," Winchell continued. "Just because our study of the few thousand known telepaths has provided certain norms, we should not accept them as gospel—not with a brand-new mutation in human stock. Not this early, not when so much still remains to be learned."

"Are you trying to say he was abnormal—even for a telepath—from the very beginning?"

Winchell nodded.

"Yes," he replied. "I have tried some recently developed tests, including an experiment in which two other telepaths were involved. I entered Dennis' mind and used his receptive abilities to reach them. The nearer is thirty miles from here, the second forty."

"Dennis picked up thoughts from forty miles away?"

"Yes, which explains his initial reception reaction. You were never that far removed from sources of trouble at your previous addresses. Here, though . . . Here, even with a forty-mile range, you have room to spare—plenty of it. His condition appears to be purely functional, and we do have numerous case histories from which to draw encouragement, dating from the days before the mutation was recognized."

"True, there is that," Richard said. "So . . . What do you recommend now?"

"I think we should have one of the new TP thera-

29

pists come out and work with him—every day, for a while—to reorient him."

"I've read a bit about those early cases," Vicki said. "Sometimes the trauma was too strong and they never developed personalities of their own. . . . They just remained schizoid collections of the bits and pieces with which they had been imprinted. Others withdrew from everything and never—"

"There is no point in dwelling on the worst," Dr. Winchell said. "A good number recovered too, you know. You have already done a beneficial thing in bringing him here. Also, remember that the therapists know a lot more about the condition now than anyone did a generation ago—or even ten years back. Or five. Let's give it a chance. Try to think about the positive aspects. Remember how easily your attitudes, your feelings can be communicated."

Vicki nodded.

"Can you recommend a therapist?"

"Actually, I have several possibles in mind. I will have to check their availability. The best course of treatment would probably involve a therapist who could live in and work with him every day—at least for a while. I will investigate as soon as I get back and let you know—sometime tomorrow."

"All right," Richard said. "Tell them we have a nice guest room."

Winchell began to rise.

"We would like you to stay to dinner," Vicki said.

Winchell eased himself back down.

"I thank you."

Richard Guise smiled for the first time that day, rose to his feet.

"What are you drinking?"

"Scotch and soda."

He nodded and swung off toward the house.

"Forty miles . . ." he muttered.

Lydia Dimanche came to stay at the Guise house, a small, graceful woman with a musical voice and eyes which almost matched the black twists of her hair. They guessed that she might be Polynesian.

Lydia saw Dennis every day, feeding, channeling, directing, organizing sensory and extrasensory input. When she was not with Dennis she kept to herself, back in her room, down in town, up in the hills. She took her meals with the Guises, but never volunteered information concerning her patient. When asked directly, she normally replied that it was still too early to see clearly, to say anything for certain.

Months later, when Richard Guise departed on a lengthy business trip, Dennis' condition still seemed unchanged. The daily sessions went on. Vicki spent more and more time with her plants. The few minutes, mornings and afternoons, grew into hours. Evenings, she began reading gardening books; she obtained more plants, had a small greenhouse constructed.

One morning, Lydia emerged from Dennis' room to find the taller woman leaning against the wall.

"Victoria," she said, a beginning smile falling toward its opposite.

"I want to read him, Lydia. All this time . . . I have to see what he is like now "

"I have to advise against it. I have been controlling him quite strictly, and any intrusive thoughts or feelings might upset the balances I am trying to—"

"I am not going to broadcast. I just want to look."

"There is not really that much to see at this point. He will seem as he always has—"

"I have to see. I insist."

"You give me no choice," Lydia said, stepping aside. "But I wish you would think about it for a minute before you go in."

"I have already thought about it."

Vicki entered the room, moved to the side of the bed. Dennis lay on his side, staring past her at the far wall. His eyes did not move, not even when she passed directly before him.

She opened her mind and reached, very carefully, toward him.

Her eyes were dry when she emerged. She walked

31

past Lydia, through the front rooms and out into the courtyard. She seated herself on the bench and stared at the geraniums. She did not move when Lydia came and sat beside her.

For a long while, neither spoke.

Then, finally, Vicki said, "It's like giving isometrics to a corpse."

Lydia shook her head.

"It only seems that way," she said. "The fact that there are no obvious changes cannot be held as too important right now. At any time during the months to come, the exercises in which we are engaged could suddenly become crucial, making all the difference between stability and continued dysfunction. This is another reason I did not want you to check on him now. Your own morale is an important part of his environment."

"I had to see," Vicki said.

"I understand. But please do not do it again."

"I won't. I do not want to."

After a time, *I do not know about the morale part, though,* Vicki indicated. *I do not see how I can manage it. I do not know how to change responses, reactions—here, inside. I was afraid of things so much of the time. . . . When I was a child it was my sister Eileen. She was not TP; I could read her thoughts of me. Later there were teachers. Then the whole world . . . Going to hell in a handbasket . . . Then my first husband . . . Paul . . . Life was a lousy place till I met Dick. I wanted someone like him—older, stronger, who knew how to do all the things I could not do—to keep things safe, together. And he did, too. Before I met him, it always seemed as if the world was on the verge of falling apart all about me. He made the feeling go away—or kept it a good distance off. The same thing, I guess. I had felt there was nothing he could not do, that things would always be good with him. The world would work the way that it should. I would not be hurt. Then—this—happened—with Dennis. Now, I am afraid again. . . . It has been growing and growing ever since it happened. I watch the news and I remem-*

ber only the stories of breakdown, disaster, malfunction, pollution. I read, and I am impressed only by the bad parts of life. . . . Is it the world, or is it me? Or could it be both of us? Now Dick is gone away again and Dennis stays the same. . . . I do not know. I just do not know. . . .

Lydia put her arm about her shoulders.

You have looked and seen and you are afraid, she told her. *Fear is often a good thing. Despair is not. Fear can increase your awareness, strengthen your will to fight. Despair is withdrawal—*

But what is there to fight? And how do I fight it?

There is hope for Dennis. I would not persist in my efforts if I did not believe this. I could as easily be working on other cases where the results are more readily apparent. Yet, somewhere along the way, a therapist develops a feeling about a patient, about his chances for recovery. I have such a feeling here. I do not believe that it will be easy, or that it will occur soon. It may even take years, and it will be extremely difficult. But remember, I know him better than anyone else—even yourself—and I feel there is reason for you to have hope. You have had only a brief glimpse of that which is within him. I have seen more. As to your other fears, perhaps it is that there is some correspondence. At some level within yourself, it may be that the fragmentation of his developing personality is analogous to all the things which affected you so strongly until you met Richard. Perhaps Dennis seems the image of a schizoid world. The fact that Richard can do nothing to help him may have stirred up these other matters with the arousal of this anxiety. It is easy to see how Dennis' condition might symbolize for you the spirit of the times. He is not a single person, but pieces of the many he has touched. And these pieces do not fit together. They clash. Still, he is there, somewhere, just like humanity. —What is there to fight, and how do you fight it? You hold with the hope, which is not unwarranted. You do not let your fear slide over into despair. You do not withdraw. You feed your fear to the hope. Burn it. Transform it into a patient expectancy.

You counsel a hard course, Lydia. . . .

I know. I know, too, that you will do it.

I will—try. . . .

A cold wind from the mountains came and rustled the geraniums. Vicki leaned back and felt it on her face, her eyes looking past the adobe wall, up to the place where the shadow-clad mountain seemed suddenly poised above them.

"He is a child of a special time," she said then. "I will learn to wait for him."

Lydia studied her profile, nodded finally, rose.

"I wish to be with him again for a time," she said.

"Yes. Go."

Vicki sat until night with its stars came above her. At length, she realized it was cold and withdrew.

Autumn, winter, spring . . .

Summer.

The evening before, I had had a drink in the bar of La Fonda, the old hotel at the end of the Santa Fe Trail. Now, I regarded the front of the building and waited. Hot up here, atop the row of buildings across San Francisco. I looked past the low screening wall and up the street to my right. All the buildings were low. Very few things in this town over three stories. La Fonda itself is an exception. Adobe, stucco. Varying shades of brown, set off here and there with brick and tile. No problem, getting to this spot before daybreak, coming across rooftops as I had. But now, the sun . . . God! It blazed down on the plaza, on my back. Should have worn a long-sleeved shirt. Then I would only be roasting now. This way, I would shortly be a sunburnt corpse or a living lobster. Depending on how things went . . . Life is more a process of what happens to you while you are waiting for things than it is the collection of things themselves.

The weapon lay at my feet, a .30/06. It was covered by the dark jacket I had worn last night. I had spent a day with it up in the hills, and even slept with it for several nights running. Yesterday, I had stripped it down, cleaned it, oiled it. Now it was loaded, ready. No need to touch it again until it was time to use it. Another might pick it up, fondle it, fool with it, replace it, return to it. Since the bulk of life is waiting, my feelings have always been that one should learn to do it well. The world comes at you through the senses. There is no way to prevent this wholly, short of death, nor should I desire to. It forces a model of itself upon your inner being. So, willing or not, I have it inside me here. Its will is therefore stronger than my own, and I am part of everything it has shown me. Truly, the highest form of activity in which I might engage is its contemplation. But who can be continuously comfortable with ultimates? I would not have minded smoking as I waited, a thing I did in earlier days before I saw how things worked. The other Children of the Earth would say that it is bad for the health and an incidental air pollutant. For me, the air pollution is enough. Too much, actually. Though the world is greater than I am, I know that it can be hurt. I wish to refrain from doing so in as many areas as possible. Even if the results are negligible, I would see them entered into the image of the world within me with an awareness of myself as their agent. This would disturb me at times of waiting and contemplation; that is to say, much of the time. As to its effects on my health, this would trouble me not at all. I do not much care what becomes of me. A man is born, lives, dies. Given infinity, I will be dead as long as anyone else. Unless there is something to reincarnation, as some of them say ... In that case, though, it does not matter either. All that does matter is to build the image and enjoy it, to keep from disturbing its balances, to refrain from harming it. ... Or, as I am going to do now, some positive thing to improve it or protect it. That is virtue, the only virtue I can see. If I die bearing with me a better image than would have existed but for my efforts, then I will have passed fulfilled, having rendered the Earth my mother some payment for my keep, some token of gratitude for the time of my existence. As for what becomes of me in the process, let them write: Roderick Leishman. He didn't much care what became of him.

Two State cars purred up the street and hissed to a halt before the entrance of La Fonda. I leaned forward as a State trooper emerged from the building and went to speak with the drivers. Soon, soon now . . . I'd helped blow two dams during the past year. That makes six for the COE, and two nuclear power plants. The Children have been busy. Today, though, we might accomplish a lot more. Stop the damage before it begins. Wheeler and McCormack, governors of Wyoming and Colorado, here to meet with the governor of New Mexico to discuss large-scale energy projects—large-scale exploitation, pollution, corruption, destruction. I bear them no personal malice, though. Shouldn't have read as much about them as I did. Not all that bad, as individuals. But the Earth is more important. Their deaths will mean more than *their* deaths. . . .

I watched the trooper turn and head back into La Fonda. Slowly—no real hurry necessary—I leaned and uncovered my weapon. I raised it then and held it across my knees. I had already chalked the sign of the Children of the Earth on the wall beside me.

Not too much longer now, I'd say. . . .

Two troopers emerged and held the doors, one of them the man who had been out to speak with the chauffeurs. They did not even look up and down the street. I shifted my weapon, pulled the stock back up to my shoulder, curled my finger about the trigger.

Four men passed out through the doors, talking among themselves. I had no trouble with identification, at this distance. My first shot, a clean and easy one, dropped Wheeler. I twitched the barrel to the side and hit McCormack twice, as I was not sure where my first one took him. Then I lowered myself, wiped the weapon quickly but carefully as planned, leaned it against the wall, turned, crouching, and began my retreat along the rooftops. I heard shots at my back, but nothing came close.

Now, if only *my* chauffeur was in the proper place, I

36

could begin the car-switching routine that would get me out and away. . . . While I do not much care what becomes of me, I make the effort to prolong the waiting, Mother Earth, that I might serve you as you deserve. I—

Summer.

Vicki dropped her trowel at the mental equivalent of a shriek.

Lydia—? she began, but by then she was aware of the cause.

She left the greenhouse, ran through the courtyard, entered the house.

Partway across the living room, she felt Lydia's thoughts, soothing, surprisingly controlled: *It is all right. You have not been hurt. You must not get excited.*

Then, the voice she had never heard before: "My shoulder—I think it's broken! I have to get down!"

She rushed forward, pushed past Lydia.

Dennis had gotten off the bed. He was standing at its side, leaning against it. He clutched his right shoulder with his left hand and cast his eyes wildly about the room.

"There!" he cried, and then he stumbled forward and fell.

She hurried to him.

"Victoria! Get out of here!" Lydia called.

She raised him in her arms.

"He's hurt," Vicki replied.

"He is not hurt. Children fall all the time. I will have to ask you to leave."

"But he's never gotten out before—or talked. I have to—"

"Leave! I mean it! Give him to me and get out! I know what I am doing!"

Vicki kissed him and surrendered the shaking boy.

". . . And stay out of his mind, too. That is very important. I cannot be responsible if you intervene at crucial times."

37

"All right. I'm going. Come tell me about it as soon as you can."

She rose and departed.

As she crossed the living room, Dennis began to shout again. She looked at all the chairs, then realized she did not want to sit down. She moved to the kitchen and set some water to boil.

Later—she did not know how much later—she found herself seated at the breakfast bar, staring into a cup of tea. When Lydia came in and took a cup, she waited for the other to speak.

Lydia shook her head and sat down beside her.

"I do not know," she said, "exactly what happened. It was more than a hallucination. He had hold of a genuine personality structure—an adult one. Since he lacks one of his own to override it, it occupied him completely. I was able to stimulate his sleep centers and he is now resting. When he awakens, this may have vanished entirely."

"Do you think I should call Dr. Winchell?"

"No, this is in no way out of line with the diagnosis. It is simply more spectacular than the early effects. Basically, Dennis has no personality, no self, of his own. He is a traumatized collection of fragments of other people whose minds he encountered before you moved here. Somehow, he has encountered another and the same thing has occurred, on a larger scale. The individual was undergoing some stressful experience, and Dennis—who is more developed neurologically now—seized hold of a larger chunk of that person's psyche. As to who and where, I did not take the time to probe at length. If there is a recurrence, I will have to. In the meantime, it may even work to Dennis' benefit. I may be able to utilize some of the new material in the structuring of his own personality. It is too early to say, of course, but it is a possibility."

"Then he was not hurt?"

"No. The person with whom he was in contact had been hurt. He was reacting to that."

"I had better call Dick and let him know what has happened."

"You may be disturbing him unduly. I think it would be better to wait and see what the situation is tomorrow. You would have a more complete story to tell him then."

"That is true. He is gone so much of the time now, Lydia. . . . Do you think he is running away from—this?"

"Perhaps to some extent. But the nature of his work—the new union negotiations . . . You know that this is a bona fide business trip. The feeling that he is running away may be a projection of your own desires. It has been a while since you have been away, has it not?"

"God! Yes!"

"Perhaps when this small crisis is past you ought to consider taking a vacation. I could manage things here in your absence."

"You may be right. I will think about it, Lydia. Thanks."

When Vicki rose, late the following morning, Lydia was already in Dennis' room. It was a warm, sunny day, and she worked in the greenhouse till lunchtime. When Lydia did not join her as usual she approached the closed door and stood there a long while before returning to the kitchen. Gentle feelers of thought had detected intense mental activity within. She pressed the general button on the news unit, cut out the viewer, pressed for a repro copy. One by one, sheets slid into the tray. She stopped it at two dozen, gathered the stack, took it with her to the table.

Later, she went to sit in the courtyard, and after a time she slept.

For long moments, she did not know whether she had been dreaming. . . .

She lay there, blinking up at the light. The shadows had lengthened. Somewhere a jay was calling.

Then, *Victoria, where are you?*

She sat up.

What is it?

The news . . . Dennis' fixe . . . The story is right

here! Governor Wheeler dead, and McCormack seriously injured . . . "Assassin fled . . . believed wounded . . ." Dennis was in that man's mind, was still there today. I could not sever the connection. I finally put him to sleep again. I thought he had contacted someone who was fantasizing vividly—a psychotic, perhaps—but I was wrong. This is real—and it was in Santa Fe.

Santa Fe is over a hundred miles from here!

I know! Dennis' ability has apparently increased. Or else Dr. Winchell's tests were faulty.

I had better call the doctor—and Dick.

We had better call the authorities, too. I know the man's name—Roderick Leishman. He is a member of that radical eco group, the Children of the Earth. I had the impression he was heading north.

I am coming. Will you make the calls? Except to Dick.

Of course.

We made it to a COE farm in Colorado that evening. I had lain in the rear of vehicle after vehicle—four, to be exact—clutching my shoulder much of the time. The second driver had gotten some gauze and tape and bandaged it. He had also gotten me aspirins and a fifth of bourbon. These helped quite a bit.

Jerry's and Betty's place is sort of a communal farm. Everyone on it is COE, but only Jerry and Betty and a guy called Quick Smith knew what I had been about and knew that I might show up in need of help. The fewer in on it the better, like always. They took me right to a bedroom they had had ready in the main building, where Jerry dug out the .38 long under a local, cleaned the wound and sewed it up, ground some bones together, plastered me up, shot me full of antibiotics and fitted me with a sling. He was a veterinarian. We did not have a reliable M.D. in the area.

"How many of those damn aspirins did you take?" he asked me.

"Maybe a dozen. Maybe more."

Jerry was a tall, gaunt man, who could have been anywhere between thirty and fifty. He had sweated away everything but sinews and calluses, leaving behind a lot of facial creases. He wore steel-rimmed spectacles, and his lips grew thinner whenever he was angry.

"Don't you know what they do to the clotting factor?"

"No."

"They screw it up. You bleed more. You lost a lot of blood. You should probably have a transfusion."

"I'll live," I said. "I made it this far without going into shock."

He nodded and his glasses flashed.

"Give me a horse any time," he said. "Booze and aspirin. And nothing to eat all day."

I started a shrug, reconsidered immediately.

"I'd have chosen a better menu under other circumstances—and if I were a horse, you might have shot me."

He chuckled, then sobered.

"You did pull it off, though. I wasn't sure you'd make it away afterward."

"We figured it pretty carefully."

He nodded.

"How do you feel about it—now?"

"It had to be done."

"I guess so."

"You see any alternatives? We've got to try and stop them. We're making ourselves felt. They will be treading a lot more carefully after today."

"I see it," he said. "It is just that I wish there was another way. I am still something of a lay preacher, you know? But it is not just that. It is mainly that I don't like to see things killed or hurt. One of the reasons I'm a vet. It's my feeling, not my thinking, that goes against it."

"I know," I told him. "Don't you think I thought about it for a long time? Maybe too much, even."

"I guess so. I think you ought to reconsider moving on, and spend the night here. You need the rest."

I shook my head.

"I know I do. I wish I could. I have to keep moving, though. I am still too close to where it happened to

41

rest easy. Besides, the new vehicle is a van. It has a mattress in the back. I can stretch out there. Anyway, it's better for you if I move along as quickly as possible."

"If I was worried about my own safety, I would never have gotten involved in the first place. No. That's not it. It goes back to my feeling about not liking to see things hurt or dead."

"Well, I stand a better chance of avoiding both if I cloud the trail as much as I can."

He moved to the window, looked out.

"That may be your ride coming along the road now. What color is it?"

"Red."

"Yep. It could be. Listen, I don't want you taking any more aspirins."

"Okay. I'll stick with the booze."

"Polluting your system."

"Better than polluting the Earth," I said. "It's going to be around a lot longer. Care to join me?"

He gave a brief chuckle, followed by a skeletal grin.

"One for the road? Well, why not?"

I fetched my bottle while he got a pair of glasses from the cupboard. I let him pour.

"Safe journey," he said.

"Thanks. Good harvest."

I heard the van draw up. I crossed to the window and looked out. Quick Smith, lithe and prematurely white-haired, who, but for the flip of a coin, would have been in my place, moved to check it out. I recognized the driver, though. So I finished my drink without haste, returned the glass to the counter, retrieved my bottle.

I clasped Jerry's hand.

"Go light on that stuff just the same, hear?"

I nodded vaguely, just as Quick came in to announce the arrival.

"So long."

I followed him outside, got into the back of the thing. The driver, a beefy lad named Fred, came around to see how I was and to show me where things were. There was food, a water jug, a bottle of wine, a .38 revolver and a box of cartridges. I wasn't sure what use the last might prove—if someone caught up with me, I would go willingly enough—and I was not in a position to load it too quickly anyhow. Seeing this, Fred loaded it for me and stashed it under the mattress.

"Ready?" he said.

I nodded and he locked me in. I lay down and closed my eyes.

Dr. Winchell had been unable to persuade Lieutenant Martinez, but during a ten-minute phone call he had been able to convince Richard Guise. Dick had required only a five-minute call across Washington to arouse federal interest to the extent that Special Agent Robertson was at the Guise home that evening. Robertson, thirty, clean, kempt, blue-eyed, gray-garbed and unsmiling, came to sit in the living room across from Vicki and Lydia.

"There is no file on anyone named Roderick Leishman," he said.

"I cannot help that," Lydia told him. "That is his name."

Vicki looked in her direction, surprised by the tone of her voice. Lydia's chin was somewhat raised, her mouth tight.

"Sorry," Robertson said. "No offense. They are still checking. He might have used a different name in the past. You were right about the COE connection. He did leave their sign."

She nodded.

"Tell me," she said. "What will become of him?"

Robertson began a smile, suppressed it.

"The usual. Trial, conviction, sentencing—if your information is correct. As to the details, they will depend on his attorney, the jury, the judge. You know."

"That was not what I meant," she said.

He cocked his head.

"I am afraid I do not understand."

"I was thinking of my patient," she said. "His telepathic fixation on the fugitive amounts to total absorption. I want some sort of assurance that if we assist you the man will be brought in alive. I have no idea what effect his death would have on Dennis. I do not wish to find out."

"I cannot give you any assurance—"

"Then I may not be able to give you any assistance."

"Withholding evidence is a serious matter. Especially in a case like this."

"My first duty, as I see it, is to my patient. For that matter, though, I am not even certain this comes under the heading of evidence. I do not believe there has ever been a case involving anything of this sort."

Robertson sighed.

"Let's not quibble over the legalities," he said. "The man has shot two governors. One is dead and the other may not make it through the night. He is a member of a radical eco group which includes violence as part of its program. He is running around loose now and you admit Dennis can follow him. If you refuse to cooperate, we can bring in a telepath of our own to monitor Dennis. You are not at all that necess—"

"Mr. Robertson, there are very clear legal precedents in that area. You would be invading his privacy in the highest sense—"

"He is a minor. Parental consent is all that is required, and you are not his parent."

He looked at Vicki, who clasped her hands very tightly and turned toward Lydia.

"Dennis would be hurt if they hurt the man?" she said.

"I think so."

"Then I do *not* give my consent," she said. "I am sorry, Mr. Robertson."

"Inasmuch as your husband started this, it is possible that he will give us the release."

Vicki's hands suddenly relaxed.

"If he does," she said, "I will never speak to him again. I will leave and take Dennis with me."

Robertson bowed his head.

"I am not trying to be unreasonable," he said. "Can you tell me how I could possibly guarantee what you are asking? We want him alive. We want to question him. We want to learn as much about his group as we can. We are going to try to take him alive. But men will shoot in self-defense. Even then, they would try not to kill him. But it is possible. He could be killed. *You* try to be reasonable. If you give us exact information concerning him, it will up our chances of landing him whole. What else can I offer you?"

"Very well," said Lydia. "You make some sense. What you can do then is communicate all this to whatever field agents get involved in the pursuit."

"Done," he said. "I will personally talk with them at whatever office gets involved. You can listen to what I say. Fair enough?"

Lydia looked at Vicki.

Go ahead, Vicki indicated.

"All right," Lydia began. "He is in Colorado. . . ."

It was still dark when I awoke. I was very thirsty, and my shoulder was throbbing. It took me several moments to recall what had happened. I leaned forward then and located the water bottle. I rubbed my eyes, ran my hands through my hair, took another drink.

I pushed the curtain aside and looked out the window. Rocks, fenceposts, sandy soil . . .

I checked my watch: 4:35.

"Would you pull over somewhere?" I called out. "My bladder's busting."

He stopped and let me out. I went over to the ditch.

"How much longer till the next switchpoint?" I asked him.

"Half an hour. Maybe less. We're supposed to meet around five."

I grunted.

"How are you holding up?" he asked.

"I'll be okay," I said. "Any trouble while I was sleeping?"

"No trouble. Nothing new on the news either."

I climbed back inside.

It was chilly, so I sat with the blanket around my shoulders. I took a drink of the bourbon. It would seem that we had to be free of pursuit after all this time. I ran my hand over my chin. I would stop shaving, I decided, grow a beard. Let my hair get longer, too. Lay up till the shoulder was better, then get some simple job. Stay at it three, four months ... Drift west. Seattle, Portland ...

I felt the bump in the mattress. Did I want to take the pistol with me? Trouble to be found with it. Good to have, though. I considered concealing it in the sling. Good place for it. Probably ought to keep it till I recovered. Ditch it then. Wish they had picked a smaller piece, though.

I withdrew the weapon, tried it in different positions in the sling. It was least apparent toward the back. Snug enough. Easy to reach. Almost a shame to pass up such a neat means of concealment.

I removed it and returned it to the place beneath the mattress. Something to think about, anyway ...

Still chilled. I took a long pull at the bottle. Better, that. Better than aspirin. No reason not to be a little high.

After a time, we slowed, turned off the road and ground along a rocky surface. Moments later, we halted and he came around and opened the back.

"Okay, we're here," he told me.

"Where's here?"

"McKinley, Wyoming."

I whistled.

"We've come a good distance."

He gave me his hand, helped me down. Then he climbed inside. He gathered the blanket, the pillow, the water bottle, the fifth, placing them within easy reach on the floor behind him. He groped beneath the mattress and drew out the pistol. He glanced at me, glanced at the weapon, then back at me.

"You taking this, too?"

"Why not?" I said, and I accepted the piece and thrust it into my sling.

46

A glister of sleekshifting starlight, low, to my right . . .

"What lake is that?"

"Glendo Reservoir."

He stepped down, turned, picked up the stuff.

He rounded the van and I followed him, becoming aware of a parked vehicle beneath some trees, perhaps a hundred feet away. The damp air was still, the night empty of sound except for that of our own progress. As we neared, I saw that it was a long green sedan. The driver sat smoking, watching us approach. I greeted him, did not recognize him. No names were exchanged.

My driver nodded to him, loaded my things into the back, clasped my good shoulder.

"Good luck," he said.

"Thanks."

I got in, made myself comfortable.

"How are you holding up?" said the new driver.

"Pretty well. Considering."

I heard the engine chuckle and whisper. An arc, a spatter of fire as the driver disposed of his weed. The headlights came on. We moved forward.

A little later the driver said, "It's in all the news. What was it like?"

"It's mostly waiting," I said. "Doing it just takes a few seconds. A mechanical action. Then you are thinking about getting away."

Those few seconds went through my mind again. I saw them fall. I had already made the mark. I wiped the weapon and leaned it . . . so. Then I was crouched, running. I heard the noises behind me, below. The shot . . . my shoulder . . . I had left blood. They had probably typed it by now.

"Nothing special," I said. "It's all over."

"McCormack is still hanging on, last I heard."

"It doesn't matter. The gesture is enough. Hope he makes it."

"Him?"

"A lot of people have learned something. That's enough. I want to stop thinking about it now."

"You think it will really do some good?"

"Who can say? I hope so. I tried."

"It might take a few more incidents like this to really get the point across."

"Incidents, hell! It was a killing. Someone else can do the next one, if it's got to be. I'm retired."

"You deserve a rest."

My shoulder was throbbing again. I opened the bottle.

"Want a drink?"

"Yeah, thanks."

He took it, took a slug, passed it back.

I thought of the waiting, of the image of the Earth in my mind and how I hoped I had changed it. . . . I looked out the window at the shadow shapes of rock and scrub, plain and hill. I wished for a little rain, to rinse things over, for some wind, to blow them dry and clean. But the land lay still and rugged. So be it. I may dislike it this way, yet it pleases me also that the grasses are dry and the animals in their burrows. The pleasure and the pride of humanity are best enjoyed against the heedlessness, the slumbering power of the Earth. Even when it moves to crush, it adds something. To isolate oneself too much from it detracts from both our achievements and our failures. We must feel the forces we live with. . . .

I opened the window and breathed deeply.

Yes. The world was still breathing life into my lungs, and I was grateful to give it back. . . .

"I really do not like keeping him awake this long," Lydia said, staring down at her empty coffee cup.

Robertson clamped his jaws, loosened them.

"I don't think it will be too much longer," he said, "now that the office in Casper has been alerted. He may make it out of Wyoming before they reach him, though. But with the Rapid City people heading out, too, a flier should reach him before he is too far into South Dakota. A green vehicle heading east at this hour . . . Shouldn't be too hard to spot. Another half-hour, I'd say."

Lydia glanced over at Vicki, asleep on the sofa.

"Care for some more coffee?" she asked Robertson.

"All right."

As she poured, he asked her, "Dennis' condition . . . Isn't it rather unusual for a telepath to be able to operate at this distance? Leishman is well over five hundred miles from here."

"Yes, it is," Lydia said.

"How does he do it?"

She smiled.

"We are not even certain why it works at *any* distance," she said. "But you are correct about the range. It is unprecedented to sustain contact for this long at this distance."

Robertson drained his cup.

"Then Dennis has never gone out this far before—even for short periods?"

"No. Frankly, I had thought we would just be giving you a lead, and that Dennis would have lost contact long before this."

"It must be hard on the kid. I *am* sorry."

"Actually, I feel no signs of strain in him, other than normal fatigue at being up this late past his bedtime. You know that is not my main concern—"

"I know, I know. I don't want to damage the kid's mind either. Listen, I've been thinking. Since Dennis is in such good contact, couldn't he transmit as well as receive? Try to talk Leishman into giving himself up?"

"No. Dennis would not know how to go about it."

"What about you, then? Could you operate through Dennis, get a message to Leishman that way? Tell him to stop and wait, to hand over that gun?"

"I do not know," she said. "I have never tried anything like that."

"Will you?"

She took a sip of coffee, then leaned back and closed her eyes.

"I will tell you in a few moments whether it can be done."

I placed the empty bottle on the floor, rearranged

the blanket for the dozenth time. Beyond the window, the world swam pleasantly. Perhaps I would sleep now. . . .

A misty, gray, humming thing of indefinite duration . . .

Roderick Leishman.

I shuddered, I rubbed my eyes and looked about. Nothing had changed.

Roderick Leishman.

"What?"

"I didn't say anything," said the driver.

"I thought someone did."

"You were asleep. Must have been dreaming."

"Must have."

I sighed and settled back again.

No, you were not dreaming, Roderick. I addressed you.

. . . The Earth Mother is aloof, heedless. She speaks to no man. I felt the bottle against my foot and chuckled. I had never heard voices before. I did not feel that drunk, but then the participant is seldom the best judge. When I awoke it would seem a dream. I closed my eyes.

. . . *Neither drunk nor dreaming, Roderick. I am with you now.*

"Who are you?" I whispered.

You have named me.

"What I did today could not have been that important."

There are other considerations.

"What is it that you want?"

Your life.

"Take it. It is yours."

I wish to preserve it, not take it.

"What do you mean?"

At this moment, you are being pursued by federal agents. They are aware of your location. They will reach you before too long.

I drew my slung arm tight, feeling the pistol against my ribs.

No. You must surrender, not fight.

"I might be worth more as a martyr."

A trial would be much better. Your motive would be detailed at great length.

"What do you want me to do now?"

Park the car and wait. Surrender yourself. Do not give your pursuers an excuse to harm you.

"I see. Will you stay with me—through it all?"

I am always with you.

I pushed back the blanket, let it fall. I leaned forward.

"Pull over for a minute, will you?" I said.

"Sure."

He braked and turned off the road. When we were halted, I said, "Do you have a gun?"

"Yes. In the glove compartment."

"Get it out."

"What's the matter?"

"Just do it, damn it!"

"Okay! Okay!"

He leaned over, opened the compartment, reached inside.

When he began to swing it in my direction, I was ready. Mine was pointed.

"Not that way," I said. "Put it down on the seat."

"What is this?"

"Do it!"

He hesitated a moment too long, and, "I've already shot two men today," I said.

He put it down.

"Now reach over with your left hand and pick it up by the barrel."

He did this.

"Pass it over. Drop it on the floor back here."

"What's going on?" he asked.

"I am trying to keep us from getting killed. Do you mind?"

"I'm all for it," he said. "I think it's a great idea. But I don't understand how disarming me will do it."

"I want to avoid a shootout. I think we are about to be arrested."

He chuckled. He opened his door.

51

"Don't get out!"

"I'm not." He gestured outward. "Look, though. We're all alone. No one coming, either way. Listen, I know you're very tired, you've had a lot to drink and your nerves have to be shot after everything that's happened. I understand. With all due respect, I think you're a bit delirious. Why don't you—"

"Don't move! Both hands on the wheel!"

"Look, we are going to seem suspicious if anyone comes by and sees us this way."

"Better than the alternative."

"Getting away?"

"Getting dead. We can't get away."

"Mind if I ask what makes you think so?"

"You do not have to know," I said.

He was silent for a long while. Then, "Is this some sort of setup?" he said. "A part of the plan I'm not in on? Or is it just your own idea?"

"It is not just my own idea."

He sighed.

"Oh. Why didn't you tell me sooner? I would have gone along with it, so long as you know what you're doing."

"Better you don't know."

"You can put the gun away. I—"

"I'm tired of talking. Just sit there."

Richard Guise approached his son, who rested on the courtyard bench.

"How do you do," he said.

"Hello."

"My name's Dick Guise."

Dennis rose, extended his left hand upward, turning the palm out. He held his right across his chest. His dark eyes met his father's.

"Rod Leishman," he said, as Dick clasped it and released it.

"Mind if I sit down?"

"Sit," Dennis said, seating himself.

"How are you—feeling?"

"Shoulder's still giving me some trouble." He reached across and rubbed it. "You a lawyer?"

"Friend of the court," Dick said, seating himself. "They treating you all right?"

"Can't complain. Listen, I am not sure I should be talking with you without Mr. Palmer—my regular attorney—around. Just my ignorance. Nothing personal. Okay?"

"Sure. May I ask you something not connected with the case?"

The green eyes, like Vicki's, fixed him once again.

"Go ahead."

"What do the Children of the Earth really hope to accomplish with all their violence?"

"Our only desire is to preserve the Earth and maintain it as a suitable habitation for mankind."

"By killing people? By blowing up power plants and dams?"

"It seems the only way to convince those in authority that we are serious."

"Let me put it this way. If you were actually to succeed in removing the large sources of energy, you would probably defeat your own aim of maintaining the Earth as a suitable habitation for mankind. Wait! Let me finish. I do not know whether you have ever read Robert Heilbroner's *The Future as History,* written back in the middle of the last century, but he makes a good case for the premise that the major outlines of the future were already history in that they followed ineluctably from the forces already in operation, that they were so powerful we could barely oppose the general course they were determining for us. Technology, for example, would have to advance. This, in turn, would lead to an increasingly bureaucratic state. Abundant production would make living sufficiently easy that economic pressure would not, in itself, be enough to keep people in the less attractive occupations. He proved right on these matters, and on the lesser developed countries springing for whatever political system promised the most rapid industrialization. From there, their futures will follow as ours did—"

"Heilbroner was a shrewd man," Dennis said, "but you cannot project a curve like that forever. The system breaks down before—"

"Technology is proving capable of finding answers to the problems it has created."

"But not enough and not fast enough. The world keeps growing, complicating, overproducing the wrong things. The standard of living is too high when people exist for the sake of industry instead of the other way around. Thoreau—"

"Thoreau and Rousseau and that whole crowd would like to see us all living in the woods again."

"Rousseau has generally been misunderstood, and Thoreau never said that. What they were all getting at, I think, was something like a science of the optimum, an understanding of just how large, how complex, how mechanized, how populous a society should be so as to provide the best life for its people—a science to determine these things and a will to be guided by them. They did not want to go back to the woods, but to find the most suitable middle ground between the basic and the complex. That is what the Children really want."

Dick was silent a moment, then said, "That sounds very noble, and it seems that you are sincere. I am certainly not against idealism. We need ideals. But I feel Heilbroner was correct. We write the history of the future a long time in advance. I hope, and believe, that it will go your way one day. But we have to lose a lot of momentum first, rechannel a lot of energies. Something like that takes generations. It cannot be accomplished overnight. Least of all, it cannot be accomplished by random acts of violence against what has already been built up."

"We haven't got that kind of time," Dennis said. "And I believe Heilbroner can be made wrong about the way we write the history of the future, if we are sufficiently determined to learn from the errors of the past."

"And if we do not, I still do not see chaos waiting around the next corner."

"Then I hope yours is the right corner, but I doubt it."

Dick rose.

"I have to go inside now. I'll see you around."

Dennis nodded.

"Be seeing you."

He hurried away from the small form on the bench without looking back. Entering the house, he passed through the living room without speaking to Vicki and Lydia, who were seated on the sofa. In the kitchen, he poured himself a stiff drink, downed it, poured another, turned, walked slowly back to the front room.

"I still do not believe it," he said, lowering himself into an armchair. "A few weeks ago he was a vegetable. Now ... Lydia, you told me he was in contact with the guy, not that he had assumed his entire personality."

"This is a new development," Lydia explained. "It occurred after we spoke with you, before you returned."

"He is not even acting out the man's predicament. He is responding to new stimuli as if he *were* Leishman."

"Yes."

"How long is this going to last?"

"There is no way of telling."

"Is it a good sign or a bad one?"

"Good, I would say. No matter what happens now, there should be some residue, some remnant of the synaptic processes that have been taking place."

"But is he going to grow up thinking he *is* Leishman?"

"Not if we intervene—which we will, if the effect continues too long. The important thing now is that there is something there, some activity within his skull. His brain needs the workout it is getting. It has been idle too long."

"But those aren't kid thoughts going through it. They are adult thoughts. Mightn't the premature exposure warp him for whatever is to come later?"

Vicki chuckled, and Dick seemed to notice her for the first time.

55

"You seem to be forgetting that a bombardment of adult thoughts is what caused his problem in the first place. Now, at least, he has learned to filter them and focus on one mind at a time. So what if he is doing it exclusively with Leishman? I have spoken with him at length since this occurred. This Leishman is not all that bad a chap. In fact, I rather like him. He is an idealist and—"

"—a murderer," Dick finished. "Yeah, a great guy our son picked. Lydia, is this going to hurt him later on?"

"Did it hurt you?" she asked. "Or you, Victoria? You were both exposed to adult thoughts at an early age. Were either of you permanently damaged by the experience?"

" 'Exposed,' not totally absorbed," Dick said. "There is a big difference."

Lydia nodded.

"All right," she said. "Of course there is the possibility of long-term influence. I am convinced, however, that therapy can correct it if it does occur. But I would rather wait until there is more to work with before I tackle the problem of identity."

"How dependent is Dennis on Leishman? I mean, supposing the man were to drop dead right now? What would happen to Dennis? Would he go on thinking he is Leishman, or would he fall apart again?"

"That is one of those questions which simply cannot be answered from the facts that we have. There is still a connection. He is apparently aware of everything that happens to the man. Yet he also acts independently in terms of the other's identity. I do not know where the line is drawn."

"I think we had better find out. You will need to know that when it comes time to straighten him out."

"I will deal with the problem when it comes due."

"Something suggests itself," Dick said. "What is Dennis' range, anyway? He is keeping tabs on Leishman at over a hundred miles, now that he has been returned, but he followed him for over five hundred miles. What might his upper limit be?"

Lydia shook her head.

"Again, not enough data."

"Exactly," Dick said. "I would like to find out, though. Once he has his mind in shape and has reached maturity, he might well be the greatest telepath the race has yet produced."

"He probably is," Vicki said. "That is what caused his problem."

"Supposing I take him to Europe with me next month? He will have had plenty of time to play with his new synapses. We will pull him out of range of Leishman and see whether he is still dependent on the guy or whether he has absorbed enough to keep functioning as he is."

"I would advise against it," Lydia said. "Supposing he simply retreats into catatonia?"

"Then we bring him back and let him be Leishman again for a while."

"But we do not know that he would pick up on Leishman again. He might simply remain withdrawn."

"Then your theory is wrong, and the sooner we know it the better."

"I can see you have already decided."

"Yes. Even given the worst, the situation would simply revert to one you have already assured us holds hope. What is the difference, really?"

Lydia lowered her head.

"I cannot honestly say."

Dick finished his drink.

"So there," he said. "We'll do it."

"Very well. But either I accompany him—with the understanding that I bring him home immediately if there are any problems—or I leave the case."

"Lydia, you can't!" Vicki said.

"It is the only way."

"All right," Dick said, "I agree. It is something I have to find out, though."

"Lydia," Vicki said. "Could this really hurt Dennis' chances?"

"I think so."

"Then I forbid it. Dick, you are not going to ruin

57

what is left of my son just to determine his TP range. If you insist on this, I'm leaving. I will get a court order if necessary to prevent your moving him."

Dick reddened.

"Vicki. I—"

"You heard me. What will it be?"

"I think you are being silly."

"I do not really care what you think. What are you going to do?"

"You give me no choice. I won't take him. I thought it was a good idea. I still do. Lydia, what about next spring? I am going over again then. Would that be more propitious?"

"Possibly. Probably, even. There would have been more time for him to adjust to functioning."

"Okay, let's talk about it again then. Vicki, I am sorry. I did not realize . . ."

"I know. But now you do."

"Now I do."

Dick took his glass back to the kitchen and rinsed it.

"I think I am going to change and take a walk," he called out.

Vicki rose, headed for the courtyard.

Lydia crossed the room and stared out the window, fingering her pendant as she watched the mountains and the clouds.

Dick was in the East that autumn, when Roderick Leishman's case was heard. Therefore, it was from Winchell's calls following his weekly examinations of Dennis that he learned of the boy's alternate elation and depression as the trial progressed. The news media were unaware of Dennis' connection with the case, and only two other medical consultants knew of his condition.

Dick regarded Winchell in the viewer.

"He still bathes himself and dresses himself . . . ?" Dick said.

"Yes."

"He still feeds himself, and he responds intelligently when people talk to him?"

58

"In the character of Leishman . . . yes."

"He still seems aware of everything that Leishman thinks or does?"

"We have checked periodically on the factual aspect of it, and this does seem to be the case."

"I find it difficult to understand how he manages to respond to two separate environments and not grow confused, not become aware of the contradictions in the situation."

"Well, it is similar to the classic paranoid reaction where the patient can function relatively well in his normal environment yet still believe he is someone else, somewhere else."

"I think I see, sort of. How long do you figure this will go on?"

"No way of telling yet, as I've said before. But I agree with Lydia that it is a situation worth exploiting. Let it sink in. She can take care of personality tailoring later."

"What about the trip I mentioned?"

"The way that I see it is that if he really is going to benefit from this exposure, he should have had enough of it by spring. I don't see why the cord can't be cut at that time, and let the adjustment begin."

"Good," Dick said. "About Lydia . . ."

"Yes?"

"I was just wondering. With all these new developments, is she still the best therapist for Dennis?"

"Is there something about her you don't like?"

"No, not that. I just wanted to be sure Dennis had the best."

"He does. Lydia knows Dennis better than anyone else. It would take months for another therapist to catch up on something like this—and then there is the matter of her rapport with him. It could prove disastrous to pull her off the case and bring in someone else at this point."

"I see. Just wanted to be sure."

"Is something bothering you—about her?"

"Not at all. How do you feel the verdict on the Leishman case will affect him? The man is bound to be convicted."

"Some depression, most likely. Still, Leishman seems something of a stoic, according to the psychiatrists who examined him. Dennis will simply take it the same way he does."

"It shouldn't be too far off."

"No. This week, I'd guess."

"Well, keep me posted."

"I will."

Dick decided to take his secretary to lunch and think about other things. And he was not surprised some time later when Leishman was found guilty. It was the sentencing that troubled him.

"I did not think they would take the psychiatric angle that seriously," he said to Winchell as soon as he heard of it.

"I did. There was always a possibility of this. Basically, it was his attorney's doing. I would not take it all that seriously."

"Well, they have him up at the State Hospital in Las Vegas, so he is still too close to Dennis—and now, if they start giving him therapy ... What will happen if they put him on drugs or fool with his brain? I don't like it."

Winchell was silent for a time. Then, "I see the point. I had wanted to keep Dennis—and us—out of the whole thing. Now, though, we had better find a way of keeping posted as to what course of treatment they plan for Leishman. Perhaps we can still keep it quiet. I will see whether I can work out something with the hospital. If not, we may have to go through the court."

"Well, we had better do something, quickly. The kid is screwed up enough as it is."

"Right. I will call them now and let you know."

"I still think we ought to move out of range and let it go at that."

Winchell gnawed his lip.

"Let's save that for last," he said.

I thought I had caught glimpses of him earlier in the day, but I was not certain until late afternoon, when he came by the reading room where I sat alone, turning pages. He parked the cart he had been pushing, blocking the doorway with it, stepped in, gave a low whistle and winked when I looked up.

"Quick!" I said. "What—?"

He raised a finger to his lips, turned and fetched in a carton from the lower shelf of the carryall. He brought it over and placed it on the opposite side of my chair, out of sight from the hall.

"No problem," he whispered. "I've worked in these places before. My record is clean. Got in here almost two weeks ago. How have they been treating you?"

"Observation and tests all month," I said. "What are you up to?"

He stroked the side of his sharp nose and smiled a yellow smile.

"We're getting you out of here, now. It's all set up. I have the schedule down pat. The car is waiting."

"It's still daylight. Wouldn't it be better if—"

"No. Trust me. I know where everyone is."

I regarded his slight figure, his dark, dancing eyes, pale hair, nimble fingers.

"You're shifty enough," I said. "Okay. What do I do?"

"Get into the clothes in that bundle while I go stand outside by my cart. If anyone comes, I'll whistle and you start taking them off again fast. I will come back inside with the box and you toss them back into it. Okay?"

I nodded and began unbuttoning my shirt.

"No," he said. "Put them on over your things. It's just an orderly uniform."

He moved back to the door.

"How is the shoulder?"

"Fine now. How are Jerry and Betty?"

"Well. You never got traced to them."

He stood fooling with his cart, blocking the door.

"Hey! There's a gun in here!"

"Sh! Stick it in your belt, under the coat. You never can tell."

I checked it. It was loaded. I stowed it. I dressed.

"All right," I said.

"Come on out then. Help me push this cart."

I stepped into the hall, got behind the cart at his side nearest the wall. We began pushing.

"Where to?" I asked.

"Service elevator, through those doors at the end. I have the key here."

We passed along the hall. He unlocked the doors. No one in sight. He unlocked the elevator. We took the cart inside and he pressed the button for the basement.

"I'll stand in front," he said. "If anyone comes by, bend over the cart real quick."

"Right."

I listened to the hum, the occasional creaking of the elevator about us. A wave of cool air passed from the left. I felt myself in a kind of daze. It was difficult to believe things were happening this quickly, with no advance warning. Just as well, too, probably. If I had had time to think it over, I might not be moving this casually. I probably would not have slept last night.

The elevator ground to a halt. Quick drew open the gate, looked outside, nodded to me, tugged on the cart.

I followed him out, pushing. We were in a half-lit hallway, but things looked to be brighter around the corner to the left. We moved in that direction, and he gestured for me to change places with him. I got over to his left before we turned the corner, left again. There was a ramp leading up to an open area—a loading dock where two workmen sat on crates, drinking coffee and smoking. The nearer man glanced in our direction as we moved upward, wheels rattling. Quick pretty much blocked his view of me.

"Damn it!" he muttered. "They don't usually take their break right on the dock."

A white van with the words "Simpson's Foods" stenciled in red on its side was backed against the dock, rear gate lowered. The door on the driver's side was open, and a man in a green uniform sat sideways, legs dangling, checking over some papers on a clipboard, a steaming cup balanced on the dash to his right. Quick waved to him and he waved back. Moments later, he swiveled forward and slammed the door. Shortly after that, he dumped the coffee out the window.

Quick slowed.

"I was simply going to close you in back and let him drive off with you," he whispered. "No good now. Those guys would know something was up." He jerked his head toward the laborers. "I am going to have to go along now—and so are they, I'm afraid."

"Guess we don't have much choice."

He shook his head.

"We stop the cart when we're abreast of them," he said, looking out past the truck and back down the ramp. "Then we stroll over. Get your gun out then and get them aboard the truck."

"Okay."

We halted the cart when we were near, turned and moved in their direction. I grinned and rested my hand on the butt of the pistol.

"Hi," Quick said, "I was just wondering . . ."

The nearer man was squinting at me. I drew the weapon and pointed it at them.

". . . wondering whether you wanted to try and be heroes, or just live and let live."

"It's Leishman," he said to the other.

"God!" the other replied.

"What'll it be?" Quick asked.

"Whatever you want," the second man said.

"Then get in the truck, both of you."

They got to their feet. The first man raised his arms.

"Put your hands down," I said. "Don't do anything conspicuous like that again."

"Sorry."

He lowered them, they headed for the truck, got in. Quick climbed down from the dock, went forward and was talking with the driver, who kept glancing back, an unhappy look on his face.

I followed the men inside.

"All the way back," I said, "and sit on the floor."

I seated myself across from them. Seconds later, the engine spun and caught. There was a scrambling noise from outside, and Quick rounded the corner and climbed in.

"He'll be around to shut it in a second," he said, taking up a position to my right, legs stretched out before him.

A light came on overhead.

The man across from me on the left, a young, slight, dark-haired guy, said, "What are you going to do with us?"

"Nothing," I said, "if you don't make any trouble. You know you would report someone leaving in the truck. We can't have that. Be good, don't make any noises as we leave, and we'll drop you in the boondocks as soon as we're out a ways. Okay?"

"Anything you say," he said. "I've got a family."

"So do I," said the older man beside him. "I'll do what you say."

"Then sit back and enjoy the ride," I said.

The driver came around and Quick went back and whispered with him before he closed us in. Moments later, I heard his door slam. Then the engine started. Presently, we were moving.

Quick leaned over and whispered to me, "We are going to drop them before we switch vehicles. The less they know, the better."

"Good idea. How long will that be?"

"Around twenty minutes, I figure. We ditch them in fifteen."

"Good enough."

The situation finally reached me at an animal level, and I felt a profound desire to pace. My palms began to perspire and I wiped them on my trousers. Ridiculous. I had had no particular reactions when I had done the shooting in Santa Fe. It was probably that I had worked them all off in advance, contemplating the event. This time, however, without preparation, I was easy prey to the uncertainties involved.

We halted. Outer gate. I heard voices but could not distinguish the words. Shortly, we were moving again.

"Mind if I smoke?" the man across from me asked.

"Go ahead," I said.

I watched him light up.

"Could I have one of those?" I asked.

"Sure." He extended the pack.

I got up, crossed over and took one.

"May I have a light?"

He passed me his matches.

"Thanks," I said, handing them back.

I returned to my place across from him and reseated myself.

"That was stupid," said Quick. "You could have had one of mine."

"Didn't know you smoked."

"Haven't had a chance to," he said, producing one and lighting it. "I didn't know you smoked."

"I haven't, for years. I just decided to balance an ecological loss against a psychological gain. My chances are better if I'm relaxed. Anything I can do to improve my chances right now is worth it. If I get away, I may be able to carry off some more big ones for the Children. Ah! that's good!"

"You're a weird guy," Quick said. "I sometimes get the feeling the whole movement is more of a religious thing for you than it is anything else."

"That's fair," I said. "I guess it is."

"You think you'll get pie in the sky for whatever you do?"

"Satisfaction right here is more than enough. The Earth is my reward as well as my concern."

"They said at the trial that you used to be with the Forest Service. I never knew that."

I nodded.

"What the lawyer said was true. It does all go back to that, for me—seeing the land and everything on it constantly taking second place to commercial interests. I talked with COE people on and off for a couple years. Finally, one day, I decided hell! if we are as brutal to them as they are to the land, maybe then some of the exploiters will get the point, think twice. . . . I don't know. I had to do something besides writing protest

65

letters. I get this kind of—mystical—feeling sometimes, when I am out in the country. I feel there is something—some force—I am serving. It does not matter what it is. It does not even matter whether it is really there. I am sometimes comforted by a sense of presence that seems kindly disposed toward me. That is enough."

"You've lived out of doors a lot then?"

"Yes, I have."

Quick glanced at the guys across from us, lowered his voice:

"You could live off the land, then?"

"Yes."

"Maybe that wouldn't be a bad idea, till things cool down. Lots of places, say, in Canada where they would never find you."

"I've thought of it. —What about yourself? Why are you in the movement?"

"Nothing as fancy as your reasons. I envy them, but nothing's ever seen fit to give me the mystic high-sign. No, I suppose I'm just a troublemaker, a professional malcontent. I hate the system for lots of reasons— some of them big, a lot of them probably petty. No profit in citing chapter and verse. If I weren't with the Children, I would be throwing bombs with someone else. This seems a somewhat cleaner cause, that's all. You know, you are probably saner than I am, pantheism or not. I have worked in enough of those places like the one we just left that I picked up some of the jargon, some of the ideas, seen a lot of the cases. I sometimes think a lot of it applies to me." He laughed. "Then on even-numbered days," he went on, "I am sure it is the world that is mad and all that therapy would ever do is make me as batty as the rest of them."

I chuckled. We finished our cigarettes. I listened for sounds from outside the truck and tried to estimate where we might be. I heard nothing but the vehicle's own noises, though, and I had given up counting turns too long ago.

"We never figured out how they managed to locate you as fast as they did," Quick said. "Any ideas?"

"No."

"Well, this time we are being even more careful. If they do not catch up with us during the first hour or so we should be clear."

I thought back to that day, to the voice I thought I had heard. *Are you there now? Is it your will?* I wondered. But there was no answer.

After a time, we slowed and began to jounce about. I assumed we had left the road. We continued in this fashion for several minutes, then came to a halt.

I heard the cab door. A little later, the driver opened the rear of the truck. Looking out, I saw that we were on a dirt road, drawn up beside an arroyo.

I gestured with the pistol.

"All right, you two," I said. "Time to say goodbye."

The men got to their feet, moved back. I followed them and watched as they climbed down.

The older man looked back. For a moment, I thought he was going to say something, but he turned away and headed down the arroyo with the other.

The driver grinned after them.

"There go a couple scared hombres," he said.

"How much longer till we change over?"

He glanced at his watch.

"Five minutes," he said, and he closed the door.

I guess it was that. It seemed only about that long when we had drawn up again, gotten out and were climbing into a passenger vehicle drawn up at the side of the road. Quick and I got into the back. The truck's driver left his vehicle and climbed into the front with the new driver.

We were back on the road in a matter of seconds, with nothing else in sight. It was open country all around us, and I was not certain exactly where we were, not that it mattered. We moved fast.

I was beginning to feel safe when we passed Cornudo Hills and took a turn to the northwest. I judged it had been about an hour since we had left the hospital. I felt some of the tension go out of me even

67

as I wondered whether my absence had yet been noted. Even if it had, the trail was already beginning to cloud. More miles, more time . . .

Another half-hour and I was beginning to think we could make it. It was then that the driver spotted the police.

"Cops back of us," he announced. "They are not coming fast or blinking, though. Might just be a normal patrol."

"Might not, too," Quick said, leaning to the side and looking up. "Nothing in the sky, though," he added. "Of course, that doesn't prove anything, not when the terrain's this irregular. A flier could be circling anywhere, waiting for a car to call it in. If they are onto the break, cars will be alert all over the area and the fliers making regular passes."

"He's picked up a little speed," the driver said. "Gaining on us. Should I try to run for it?"

"No," I said. "That will draw attention. It may be nothing."

I rolled down the window.

"If they stop us and find that gun," Quick said, "they will take a closer look and they'll be bound to recognize you. So you might as well be ready to use it."

"I know," I said.

"Getting closer," the driver said.

"Any weapons in sight?" I asked.

"No. Not that that proves anything. There is a gun under my seat, too. Anybody want it?"

"Pass it here," Quick said. "Between the seats, not up where they can see it."

The driver leaned forward, straightened. Quick took the pistol from his hand.

"They are moving out to pass now. Maybe they will just go by."

Seconds later, I heard the siren.

I turned. They were right alongside us. Nothing to lose now. I fired twice at the right front tire and hit it.

"Go!" I shouted.

We did. There was gunfire behind us and the rear

window was broken, but Quick and I were already crouched. None of us was hurt.

When I looked back shortly thereafter, the patrol car was drawn up by the side of the road. A dip, a curve, and they were out of sight.

"They're on the radio by now," our former driver said.

"Sure," the present driver said. "It shouldn't be too long now and they'll be on us from the air. Any suggestions?"

"We don't know how far away the nearest flier is," Quick said. "It could be several minutes off."

"So? Catch us now or catch us in a couple minutes—what difference does it make?"

"So, we keep going. No sense trying to get out of sight if they know we're here. They would just block off the roads, bring in a lot of men and start beating the bushes. Keep going till we actually see a flier."

"By then it's too late."

"Maybe not. There are four of us in here. They can't tell who's who from the air. When we see the thing, you pull over. One of us gets out and takes off. The rest keep going. What'll they do?"

"I don't know. Chase the man and call for another flier maybe."

"Great. There can't be another one too close by. We gain a lot of distance. They close again, we drop another. That might be enough for you and Rod to make it. If not, you drop him and keep going. For all they know, he's driving. —Rod, it looks as if you might get that chance to live off the land pretty soon."

"Maybe so," I said.

"Who goes first?" the other driver asked.

"I don't care," Quick said. "Is there more ammo for this piece?"

"Yeah, almost a full box."

"Pass it back."

It came.

"Wait a minute," our previous driver said. "I'll go first. If you are figuring on shooting it out with them, I don't want to be second—armed or unarmed. I wouldn't have a chance. Drop me first and I'll give them a good run for it. Then if you get a turn at it, do whatever you want."

"Okay, fair enough."

"Those .38 longs?" I asked him.

"Yep."

"Then give me a dozen or so," I said.

"Check."

He pulled a handful and passed them over. I dropped them in my pocket.

Quick continued his survey of the sky.

"Nothing yet," he said. "Wonder how they found us so fast? Think they picked up those two dockhands? Or just luck?"

I shrugged.

"Doesn't much matter now," I said.

"No."

It was several miles—and again, I was almost beginning to believe we might make it—when Quick caught sight of the flier, topping a range of hills, dropping, coming in low.

"Okay, this is it," he said. "Pull over."

We did, and the other driver scrambled out.

"Luck," I said.

"Thanks."

He took off, sliding and running down the hillside off the road's shoulder.

"What was his name, anyway?" I asked as we moved forward again.

"Bob," Quick said. "That's all I know."

The pilot of the flier could not seem to make up his mind at first. He took the craft up higher and began circling. I suppose he could see Bob and us both at his new altitude.

"Keeping an eye on us while he calls for instructions," Quick said. "Bet they tell him to chase Bob."

"I don't suppose our next changeover is any too soon," I said.

"Sorry," said the driver. "I wish it were, too. Listen, they know where we are right now. If we stay on this drag, they'll box us in. What say I try a side road? I am not familiar with them around here, though. Are either of you?"

"No."

"No."

"What do you think?" he asked.

"Go ahead," I told him. "Pick a good one."

But there were no decent turnoffs for the next five or six miles. The flier, true to Quick's prediction, had finally dropped and vanished. I imagined that cars from Taos would be heading down the road toward us now.

"Better make it the first one that comes up," I said.

He nodded.

"I think I see it now."

He slowed as we approached it. It led down to the right. It was surfaced, but years overdue for maintenance.

It slowed us, but I heard myself sigh after the first mile or so. It did not peter out, did not worsen. There was no one in sight, anywhere.

The sun still had a long way to go. On foot, after dark, my chances might be better, I decided.

"I don't suppose there's a canteen of water aboard?" I asked.

The driver chuckled.

"Afraid not," he said. "I wasn't figuring on anything but taxi service."

"Next time you'll know better," I said. "Pull over by those trees up ahead and drop me off."

"Okay."

"That is not the plan," Quick said.

"No, but it's a better one," I said. "If I can stay out of sight till after dark I can do a lot of hiking before morning."

We reached the trees, came to a halt.

"See you around," I said.

I got out and headed away. The driver called something after me. It sounded like "Good luck."

It was minutes later and some distance from there that I heard the flier. I was under the trees, on the ground, motionless, in a moment. I did not even look up. I just waited for it to pass.

71

But it did not.

The sounds of its engines reached a maximum and held there. Finally, I looked up. It was circling.

Damn! Why? It had not been in sight when I had gotten out. It should be looking for the car. Unless . . . I spat out some dust. Unless they had a personnel detector of some sort—infrared, a heat spotter—and were scanning the area, had picked up my outline.

Yes, that had to be it. The flier was beginning to descend.

The thing was dropping toward a clearing several hundred meters off to my right. As soon as it had dropped below treetop level, I was on my feet and heading off into the trees in the opposite direction. It was not a large stand of wood, but when I emerged I saw where another began across a rock-strewn slope of Russian thistle and chamisa, about a quarter-mile away. I began running toward it. I grew short of breath sooner than I had thought I might. Despite daily calisthenics, my months of confinement had softened me.

I forced myself, breathing heavily, and did not look back. Before I reached the trees, I heard a voice on a bullhorn: "Halt! This is the police!"

I kept running.

"You are covered! We will shoot! Halt!"

The first one would be a warning shot, I figured, and the next would not be all that accurate. I was dizzy and my thighs were beginning to hurt, but I was not about to halt.

I heard the first shot.

"That was a warning! Halt!"

There followed several more and I heard them ricocheting nearby. I was not going to make it to the trees, I realized. I felt on the verge of passing out. There were some rocks ahead, though. . . .

More gunfire . . .

I dove for the rocks, collapsed behind them, lay there panting.

I expected another challenge, but none came. The gunfire rattled on, but none of it seemed to be coming anywhere near me. I peered around the side of the rock.

There were four police, three of them in prone firing positions shooting back into the trees I had departed, the fourth sprawled on his back, his limbs positioned unnaturally.

I panted until my head cleared, studying the situation before me. Shortly, I realized that their fire was being returned. Who . . . ?

Of course. It was Quick. It had to be. He had waited till I was out of sight and followed me, the stupid ass. Now he was trying to delay them, in order to buy me time. Only he was likely to get himself killed with such damnfoolery. My escape was not worth his life. I would as soon go back and do some time as see him get shot over it. I would still be alive. I would get out one day. . . .

It seemed from the fire pattern that he was moving around in the wood. As I watched, trying to figure where he was, another of the figures before me jerked and lay still.

Two remaining . . . They would never take him back alive after this. The fight would go on to a finish, and it could only end one way. Pretty soon now, too. He could not have much more ammo.

I found the pistol in my hand. Neither of them was looking my way. They must have assumed that I had kept going when the diversion began. I got to my feet. Crouched, I began jogging toward them, ready to throw myself flat the moment one turned. I kept telling myself it was not that bad a risk. There were more rocks up near where they lay. If I could make it that far we would have them in a crossfire and it would not take that long to finish things.

As I neared, the firing from the trees ceased. Quick had seen me, did not want to risk catching me with a stray shot. All right. I had covered half the distance back. . . .

I suppose that at first the police thought they had hit him. The thought even crossed my mind. Still, the coincidence of my approach made my first guess seem more likely. They did not move. They retained their positions and held their fire, perhaps also expecting a ruse to get them to expose themselves. I kept running. I was almost within range.

It was this silence, I suppose, that undid me. The man on my right must have caught some sound of my approach. He turned his head, looked back.

Automatically, I dove forward, fixed both elbows, propped my right hand with my left and began firing.

He had turned by then and swung his rifle about. If I did not nail him quickly . . .

On my third shot he slumped, getting off one round, wildly, into the air.

Then I felt a searing pain in my chest and I slumped forward, triggering one unaimed shot in the direction of the second man just before my head hit the ground and I tasted blood and dirt.

Then there was more gunfire. It had a distant sound to it. Everything seemed distant. I struggled to raise my head, propped it on a tower of fists. As through a shrinking tunnel, I saw that a man had emerged from the trees, shooting. It was Quick. The final officer, who had risen to one knee, had swiveled from my direction to that of the wood and was returning the fire. Even as I watched, he toppled and Quick kept coming.

I slumped again, blackness beating about my head. Was it for this? The extra few months I had gained— what end had they served? I could as soon have bought it that morning in Santa Fe. . . . But the trial, the publicity— Yes. That voice I once had heard . . . half-drunk, so late. . . . Real? No difference, I suppose, old Mother. . . . Unto thee . . . Sorry about that last cigarette. I— Are you there? Is it truly . . . ?"

I have never left you.

It is well. . . .

Come to me.

I—

Dennis Guise was catatonic once again. He lay on his bed staring at nothing. He soiled himself and had to be changed like a baby. When Lydia placed food in his

74

mouth, he chewed and swallowed mechanically, giving no indication that he was aware of the process. He no longer spoke, beyond an occasional muttering late at night as he slept. He did not walk about.

Yet Lydia claimed there had been progress, that he had benefited from his association with the slain assassin Roderick Leishman, that locked now within his subconscious were the necessary ingredients for the personality he would one day develop, driven deep by the trauma of the death he had witnessed.

A month passed. And a week.

One cool Tuesday morning when Vicki rose and went to the kitchen, she found the coffee already made. A cup of it steamed on the breakfast bar at the left hand of her son, who, fully dressed, sat smoking and reading the paper.

". . . Goddamn pollutocrats," he muttered, "at it again!"

He glanced up at her. He slapped the paper against the counter, raised it and waved it at her.

"Look what that damn crowd down south is up to," he said. "Fouling the ocean! You'd think they'd want their own fishing industry to—"

Vicki uttered a short shriek, turned and fled.

Shortly thereafter, Lydia, in a green and orange flower-print robe, came to the kitchen and took coffee with him. That evening, having directed soothing impulses through his sleep centers, she left him snoring in his room and went and looked at the stars for a time.

Vicki felt after her mind, but there was nothing there for several minutes. Finally, Lydia came into the house, darkness beneath her eyes.

"I was just going to have a drink," Vicki said. "Would you care for one?"

"Please. Some of your husband's scotch, over ice."

Lydia drank slowly, her eyes on nothing in the room.

"He has, obviously, done it again," she began. "He has located a new personality and occupied it completely. This time it is a man known as Smith,

Quick Smith, an associate of Leishman's who was apparently with him fairly near the end—"

"Should we notify the authorities again?"

"No. It would serve no useful purpose. The case is closed. Leishman and four police found dead in a field, the result of a gun battle. It is over now. True, this man knew him. What of it? That is no crime. Let it go at that. Besides, I have no real idea where he is anyhow. His mind is much harder to get into via this route than Leishman's ever was. A touch of the psychotic there, but that is all right. He is far from here, that much I know, and not up to any harm. Dennis must have picked him up through their association, near to the end, and only recently recovered sufficiently to pursue the connection."

"What will this one lead to?"

"A dead end, I fear. I believe there is already sufficient material stored within him for me to continue the structuring we spoke of. But this blocks it. So long as there is a fresh personality intervening I cannot get at it. Nor do I wish to try it with this new personality, so long as the rapport exists."

"What then are we to do?"

Lydia raised her glass, took a drink, lowered it.

"I spent the entire day seeking the key to this thing," she said, "and when I finally located it, I was too tired to turn it. I believe that I can break this new connection."

"How?"

"Mainly by blocking him for a while. I believe that if I frustrate him here, he will withdraw again."

"Mightn't that hurt him?"

"No. It will just put him back where he was, so that I can continue working with him. The only reason I did not do it today is that it will call for more stamina than I could muster by the time I figured how to go about it. He is extremely strong. I have never encountered a telepath with that kind of power before."

"But might he not just reach out and reestablish the connection after you take the pressure off?"

"I do not think so. Not right away, anyhow. Look

how long he remained withdrawn after Leishman's death."

"True. When are you going to try?"

"Tomorrow, if I am up to it. I feel that I will be."

"Do you want to talk with Dr. Winchell first?"

"Not really. This is my area of specialization, not his. He would leave the decision to me, and since I have already made it a consultation would be redundant."

"All right. Shall we tell Dick?"

"Not yet. This is not really so crucial a point as it may seem. It is just a repetition of the earlier business. Why disturb him when we have nothing significant to report? Wait until there is some real progress."

Vicki nodded. They finished their drinks and talked of other things.

The following day, with some difficulty, Lydia succeeded in breaking Dennis' contact with the man called Smith. As she had anticipated, he returned once more to his catatonic state. But now, his tendency to mutter in his sleep was greater, and he began having occasional spells of somnambulism. Vicki once saw him move past her door and followed, to find him seated in the courtyard staring at the moon. When she led him back to his bed he did not awaken, though she thought he whispered "Mother" as they went.

After two weeks, he was a truck driver named Ingalls, on the road, heading toward El Paso. Lydia broke the contact immediately and continued therapy. He now occasionally muttered unconnected phrases while in a waking state. His sleepwalking became an almost nightly affair, though he never went beyond the courtyard.

A week later, he was a pilot en route to Los Angeles. Lydia broke the contact and attempted to direct his attention to things about him.

Four days later, he was a mining engineer in Montana. Lydia broke the contact and began taking him on walks, as she could now stimulate motor areas of his brain which had apparently undergone some development in the course of his various contacts. Still, it

77

seemed close to his somnambulism, as his mind remained vague throughout the course of the strolling.

Three days later, he was a crewman aboard a cargo vessel somewhere south of Hawaii. Lydia broke the contact and began playing music in his presence.

Two days after that, he was a freshman listening to a guest speaker at a large Eastern university. Lydia broke the contact and put him to sleep.

The following day, he was an Austrian mountain climber somewhere in the Alps. Lydia broke the contact and took him for a walk. As they walked along a ridge to the east, he began speaking to her in Russian. She answered him in that language, then broke the contact and took him home.

Later that evening, he was the son of a farmer in northern India, and he went to the kitchen and began to eat. Lydia spoke with him softly for a time, in a speech full of labial consonants, and then gently broke the contact. She took him to his room then and caused him to sleep.

Lydia accepted more of Dick's scotch and went to sit on the floor before the corner fireplace, shoes off, hair loose, eyes turning liquid in the flamelight.

"What is happening?" Vicki said, coming up behind her, touching her.

"He is just beginning to feel what he can do," Lydia said, "such as reach anywhere in the world, regard anyone's thoughts with total absorption—a vicarious pleasure, and easier than developing his own personality. So long as he is about this, this—vampirism— therapy remains at a standstill."

"What are you going to do?"

"Keep blocking him. Try to implant a suggestion against this sort of behavior. Keep directing his attention to local stimuli."

"Will that be sufficient?"

Lydia sipped her drink, turned and stared into the flames. At length, she spoke, "I do not know. You see, it gets more difficult each time, now that he is growing aware of his power. I have succeeded in blocking him each time by means of technique, not strength. Just today, for the first time, he resisted me slightly. I do not know how much longer it will be before this becomes an active thing. If it should, I will not be able to block him."

"What then?"

"It may not come to that. The suggestion may work. If it does not ... Then I suppose I would have to try another technique. Say, render him unconscious and apply the block immediately as he begins to come out of it. That may work. ..."

"And if it does not ... ?"

"We should know fairly soon," Lydia said.

That night, Dennis made his way to the courtyard and began singing in Italian. Lydia spoke to him in Italian, led him back to his room, returned him to sleep and reinforced the suggestion she had implanted earlier. In the morning, she took him for a walk while the chill still lay on the land. She showed him the sunrise and spoke with him at length. He mumbled inappropriate responses. They returned to the house, where she fed him and played more music.

That afternoon, Dennis assumed the personality of a Japanese policeman. She chatted with him in a singsong fashion for some twenty minutes before gently applying the block that was to break the contact. This time, Dennis resisted more actively. She succeeded in breaking the contact, attempted another reinforcement of the suggestion, went and called Vicki to join her for tea.

"It is not working," she said, "and his resistance to the blocking has increased. It will not be too long before I am unable to contain him. He does not seem to be accepting the suggestions. I will try the sleep approach next time. I feel, though, that he will learn to resist it also."

"Would it help to have Dr. Winchell prescribe some drug? A tranquilizer, perhaps? Something to slow him down, make him easier to control?"

Lydia shook her head.

"It would interfere with the therapy to have him doped up."

"But what else is there to do?"

"I do not know. I had not anticipated this development."

"If we were to move again, someplace out of range . . . ?"

"He is able to reach all around the world now. There is no escape that way."

"I had better see if I can reach Dick—and then Dr. Winchell."

Lydia nodded.

"Go ahead."

Now it happened that Dick's current mistress was a public information officer for Moonbase II. That evening, as Dick sat drinking in her apartment overlooking the Potomac, he told her of the latest report on his son's condition.

"Is there a pattern?" she asked him. "Some common trait shared by all the minds he has occupied?"

"Yes," he said. "I thought to ask Lydia about that, and she told me that all of them were, in some way, eco nuts. Not necessarily COE, but environmentalists and reformers, active or passive."

"Interesting," she said. "If there were none of them available, I wonder what he would do?"

Dick shrugged.

"Who can say, Sue? Withdraw completely, once more? Or find someone else to focus on? No way of telling."

She came over and rubbed his shoulders.

"Then you've got to get him out of range," she said, "to someplace where there are very few people, and where those there are have little time to think of these problems with the same immediacy of concern."

Dick chuckled.

"You do not understand," he said. "He can reach anywhere in the world. Here he is, the greatest telepath alive, and it is his ability that is screwing him. Here I am, the father of the greatest telepath alive, and I can get him anything—anything except the switch that will turn him off long enough for them to straighten him out."

"The moon," she said, "is around a quarter of a million miles away."

He turned and looked into her eyes. He began to smile, then he shook his head.

"It wouldn't work," he said. "There is no way. . . ."

"There are two hospitals there," she said. "I know all the people involved. You carry a lot of weight. I could tell you which strings to pull."

"How do we know it will do any good?"

"What is the alternative? Your therapist admits that she cannot control him any longer. Send him to the moon where there is very little interference. Let their psych teams have a try."

Dick took a large swallow and closed his eyes.

"I'm thinking," he said.

She moved around, seated herself in the chair across from him. He reached out and took her hand.

"Are you reading my mind?" she finally said.

"No. Should I?"

"I don't think you have to."

He smiled and stood. She rose to meet him.

"You're full of good ideas," he said. "I think I'll try both of them."

Part III

The facility lay within a small crater in the southern lunar hemisphere. Cleaned-out, built-up, domed-over, air-conditioned, nuclear-powered, fountained, ponded, treed, painted, furnished and filled with the small noises of life, it was home to a great number of wealthy geriatric patients whose conditions precluded their ever returning to the bluegreen ball in the dark sky, save to dwell within it. It was not noted as a psychiatric facility save in the areas of senile dementia and arteriosclerotic brain disease.

The new patient, a teenage boy, sat on a bench near a fountain, as he did every day at the same time. A therapist, Alec Stern, sat beside him reading a book, as he did every day at the same time. If Alec were to reach out and move the boy's arm into a new position, it would remain there. If he were to ask him a question, more often than not it would be met with silence. Occasionally, though, it would be answered with an inappropriate muttering. As today:

"Pretty, isn't it—the way the colors dance on the water?" Alec asked, lowering his book for a moment.

The boy, whose head was turned in that direction, said, "Flowers . . ."

"It reminds you of the colors of flowers? Yes, that is true. Any special kind?"

Silence.

Alec withdrew a notebook from his pocket and scribbled in it.

"Would you like to walk with me and look at some flowers?"

Silence.

"Come on, then."

He placed the book on the bench and took the boy's arm. There was no resistance as he drew him to his feet. Once he started him moving he kept walking, mechanically. He steered him around the fountain and up a walkway, coming quickly to the area of controlled lighting where the flowerbeds lay.

"See. Tulips," he said, "and daffodils. Reds, yellows, oranges. You like them?"

Nothing.

"You want to touch one?"

He took the boy's hand, pushed him forward, brushed his fingertips against the red petals of a huge tulip.

"Soft," he said, "isn't it? Do you like it?"

The boy remained bent forward. He helped him to straighten.

"Come on. Let's go back."

He took hold of his arm once again and led him down the walkway.

Later, after the boy had been fed and put to rest in his room, Alec spoke with Dr. Chalmers.

"The boy," Dr. Chalmers said, "Dennis?"

"No change. Moves only with assistance. An occasional word."

"But inside? What is his mind doing? What are his reactions to the new environment?"

"Nothing special. He is barely aware of the change. He is a collection of pieces, most of them submerged, surfacing in a random fashion, sinking again—flashes here and there, occasional interactions. Most of them a matter of personal preoccupation."

"Do you feel we ought to shift to brain stimulation?"

Alec shook his head.

"No. I would like to continue along the lines suggested by his former therapist. She was getting results near the end. Things just developed too suddenly for her to keep control in the saturation environment down there." He gestured vaguely overhead. "She foresaw a dormant period such as this following his transfer. But she also felt that the experiences he has undergone would then cause him to come out of it and seek new stimulation after a time."

"Well, it has been almost a month."

"Her guess was a month to six weeks."

"And you buy that?"

"She was good. I can see the results of her work whenever I am with him. I do not understand everything that she did. But there is some sort of effect, almost a kind of cyclical sequencing in the recurrence of imprinted personality aspects. I think we are safest in sticking with her program for now. I still do not know as much about the boy as she did. Too bad she could not have stayed on."

"Something about a divorce and her not wanting to take sides. She was in favor of the boy's transfer up here, though."

"Yeah, a certain amount of it is in Dennis' mind. Very low-key, though. And I've always been an admirer of his old man, so I am prejudiced. Whatever, it is not really material to Dennis' problem."

"I have to send Mr. Guise a report this week. I wish you would stop around the office after lunch and give me a hand with it. He wants one every month."

"Okay. By next time, we may have something more positive to say."

It was almost two weeks later that Alec went to fetch him in the morning and found Dennis crouched on the floor, tracing geometric designs with a forefinger moistened with saliva. Dennis did not seem aware of Alec's entry into the cell, so Alec stood by the door, watching. After a time, he extended his awareness, slowly, carefully. But he was unable to get beyond the most intense concentration he had ever encountered, a concentration focused entirely on the properties of triangles.

For the better part of an hour he stood there, fascinated by the action, the concentration, hoping to be noticed. Finally, he moved forward.

When he stood behind him, he reached out and touched Dennis' shoulder.

The boy turned suddenly and looked up at him. It

was the first time he had seen those eyes focus, the first time he had witnessed anything resembling intelligence in the way that they moved, in the expression which accompanied their regard.

Then Dennis screamed—a sentence or two. And then he collapsed, falling forward across his moist diagrams.

Alec raised him in his arms and carried him to the bed. He deposited him upon it and checked his heartbeat, his pulse. Both were rapid. He drew up the chair and seated himself at the bedside.

As he waited for Dennis to regain consciousness, the sounds of that scream still echoed within his awareness. He had shouted in a foreign language—he was sure of that. The sounds were too regular, too organized, to be random gibberish. Alec had not recognized the tongue, but he was certain it was a bona fide patterned utterance. Everything else about the boy's attitude—his actions, his concentration, his expression—had been informed with too much purposefulness for the picture to fall apart when it came to the vocalization. When Dennis awakened, it should not be too difficult to determine what lunar mind he had invaded. . . .

But it was a long while before Dennis awakened, and when he did his eyes regarded nothing in particular and his mind was almost as it had been the day before. Only the faintest hint of some recent contact remained, a tone, a touch of mood, indefinable, which had not been present previously. Nothing more, nothing of sufficient substantiality to permit an identification.

Alec led him out, for a walk about the compound, attempting to apply neural emphasis to various sensory effects, with the usual results. He finally led him back to the bench by the fountain. It was there that he decided to attempt an exercise based on the recent phenomenon he had witnessed.

Opening his notebook to a blank page, he sketched a triangle, a circle, a square. Then he thrust the notebook before Dennis and held it there.

After a time, Dennis lowered his head. His eyes focused, moved. He reached out and took the notebook in his hands. He moved it to his lap and bent above it. He traced the figures' outlines with his forefinger.

"What are they?" Alex said. "Can you tell me what they are?"

Dennis' lips moved. He whispered, "Circle, square, triangle . . ."

"Excellent! Here." Alec thrust his pencil into his hand. "Can you draw more?"

Dennis stared at the pencil, then handed it back. He shook his head. He leaned forward again, outlined the figures once more with his finger, then looked away. The notebook slid from his lap and fell to the ground. He did not seem to notice.

"What are they?" Alec said. "Can you tell me again?"

Dennis did not reply. His thoughts were shifting in random patterns once more.

Alec retrieved the notebook and began writing.

Dennis' condition remained unchanged for most of a week following this. Attempts were made to interest him in various of the recreative and rehabilitative classes available, and though he began paying attention to music he had no apparent desire to learn to play an instrument. Entered in an art class, he confined himself to the drawing of circles, triangles and squares. His skill in reproducing these figures freehanded soon reached a state of near-mechanical perfection. His conversational abilities were restricted to a word or two— three at most—in response to numerous and simply phrased repetitions of simple questions. He never initiated a conversation.

All of this, however, could be taken as considerable improvement, and was. The next report sent to his parents indicated progress in manual, verbal and ideational skills. What it did not include was the French episode and its aftermath.

When Alec went to fetch him one morning, he found Dennis pacing back and forth in his room, muttering in French. On attempting to speak with him, he received replies only in French. Probing telepathically, he discovered a new identity pattern. He left Dennis pacing and went in search of a young French physician recently assigned to the facility.

Marcel spent the entire afternoon with Dennis and came away with a sheaf of notes.

"He believes he is the Marquis de Condorcet," he announced later that evening, arranging the notes on his desk and looking up at Alec. "In fact, he almost convinced me of it."

"What do you mean?" Alec said.

"He possesses incredible amounts of information about the Marquis' life—and the times."

"It could be something like an idiot savant function," Alec offered. "Something he heard, something he absorbed long ago from some mind he touched, just now surfacing."

"But it is fully consistent, Alec, and he did more than repeat facts. He engaged in intelligent—extremely intelligent—conversation. He was talking about his—rather, the Marquis'—*Sketch for a Historical Picture of the Progress of the Human Mind*. He did not just recite the points. He answered questions and he expanded on the thoughts which exist in the essay itself. It is more than fanciful utopianism, you know. He went on about the perfection of man as a consequence of the diffusion of knowledge, about science as a way of mind which would raise the material level of mankind as well as enhance the intellect of the individual, about—"

"A moment," Alec said, raising his hand. "We have already established that he is not oriented with respect to person and time. What about place, though? How did he justify being on the moon and in late-eighteenth-century France simultaneously?"

Marcel smiled.

"A cell is a cell," he said. "The Marquis spent his last days in prison. That is where he thought he was."

"Victim of the Revolution, wasn't he?"

"Yes. Though it is still a debatable point whether he was executed or took his own life rather than—"

Alec stiffened.

"What—?" Marcel began.

90

"I don't know. But that bothers me. Whatever the source of his information, that might be there."

"Surely you do not think . . . ?"

Alec stood.

"I am going to check on him. It troubles me."

"I'll come with you."

They strode across the compound.

"He has never exhibited any—tendencies—in that direction, has he?"

"Not since he has been here," Alec said, "and there is nothing in the record to that effect. But the way his personality reshuffles itself, it is difficult to guess what he might be like at any given time. My God!"

"What?"

"I'm reading him!"

Alec broke into a run.

They reached Dennis' room to find him on the floor. Using his belt, he had attempted to hang himself from a light fixture. The fixture, however, had given way. Unconscious, he lay beside the chair on which he had stood to make the arrangements.

Marcel checked him quickly.

"His neck does not seem broken," he said, "but I want X-rays. Go get something to transport him. I will stay here."

"Right."

A thorough examination showed that Dennis had sustained no major injuries. It did not show why he had entered a coma, in which he remained for over two days. During this time, he remained in the clinic being fed from a dripping bottle, monitored by observers human and mechanical.

When on the third day he awakened, Dennis clutched at his side and moaned. A nurse appeared, observed his distress and sent for a doctor. A gross examination showed nothing amiss, and more elaborate test were undertaken. While their results were being considered, Marcel and Alec arrived at the bedside and determined that Dennis was no longer the Marquis de Condorcet. A telepathic examination revealed that he believed himself lying in a meadow near a rocky outcrop, bleeding from a wound inflicted by the horn of a fabulous beast from the sea. He also felt that his former therapist Lydia Dimanche was with him and frequently addressed the attending nurse by her name.

"All the tests are negative," said an older doctor who had come into the room during the TP scan.

"It is another of his—delusions," Alec said. "There are instructions in his file for breaking something like this. I think it would help if he had a sedative."

"I don't know," the older doctor said. "He has been out for quite some time. He is weak. . . . What about a simple relaxant?"

"All right. Let's try that."

The doctor sent for the necessary drug, administered an injection. The nurse held Dennis' hand. After a few minutes, a certain tension seemed to go out of him. His moans grew weaker, ceased. Alec moved then, carefully, firmly, to break a hypothetical connection. The mind he regarded suddenly swam, then drifted. Dennis closed his eyes and his breathing grew regular. The doctor moved to take his pulse.

"A normal sleep, I'd say," he announced half a minute later. "You found a way to separate him from the anxiety source?"

"I guess that is as good a way to put it as any. Yes. Unless he comes up with something new awfully fast he should be his old self when he awakens—if he sticks to what seems the pattern he has been following."

"Then the best thing we can do is let him sleep right now—and keep the monitors on." He regarded the flashboard. "His functions are well above the previous coma level."

Alec nodded.

"It seems best. Have them call me right away, though, if there are any changes in his condition."

"Of course," the doctor said.

They went away and left him sleeping.

On awakening, Dennis seemed returned to his more innocuous, earlier self. He walked with Alec about the facility, regarding with slightly enhanced attention those objects presented to him. He considered the flowers in the gardens and the stars beyond the dome, the Earth far away. His communicative abilities grew slowly during the weeks that followed, though he still did not initiate conversations, did not ask questions.

Dennis returned to his art class. He continued to draw geometric figures, but now he began embellishing them, and surrounding them with curlicues and elaborate filigree work. The hard, decisive lines he had originally drawn were softened in the basic figures and more of an element of freehand became apparent in the elaborations.

Alec then decided it was time to ask him, "What is your name?"

Dennis did not answer him, but continued staring at the atmosphere regulation plant across the way from where they were seated.

Alec rested his hand on his shoulder.

"Your name?" he repeated softly. "Would you tell me your name?"

"Name—" Dennis whispered. "Name—"

"*Your* name. What is it?"

Dennis' eyes narrowed, his brows lowered, tightened. He began to breathe rapidly.

Alec squeezed his shoulder.

"It is all right. It is all right," he said. "I will just tell you. Your name is Dennis. Dennis Guise."

The signs of tension vanished. Dennis sighed.

"Can you say it? Can you say Dennis Guise?"

"Dennis," Dennis said. "Dennis Guise."

"Good! Very good," Alec told him. "If you can remember that you will be doing well."

They walked on.

About fifteen minutes later, Alec asked him, "Now, what is your name?"

Dennis' face took on a look of anguish. Again, his breathing increased.

"We talked about it just a little while ago," Alec said. "Try to remember."

Dennis began to cry.

"It is all right," Alec said, taking his arm. "It is Dennis Guise. Dennis Guise. That is all."

Dennis gasped, sighed. He said nothing.

The next day he did not recall it, and Alec abandoned the problem of identity establishment for the time being. Dennis showed no ill effects from the small trauma.

Several days passed, and then the instructor of the art class noticed a totally incongruous sketch on Dennis' pad. His pencil was moving to the completion of an amazing caricature of one of the other students.

"That is extremely good," she remarked. "I was not aware that you did faces."

Dennis glanced up at her and smiled. It was the first time she had ever seen him smile.

"When did you begin using your left hand?"

He performed a palms-up gesture with both hands and shrugged.

Later, the instructor showed some of the new drawings to Alec.

Alec whistled.

"Was there anything leading up to this sort of work?" he asked.

"No. It happened quite suddenly, along with his switching hands."

"He's a southpaw now?"

"Yes. I thought you would be interested in that—as an indication of some neurological development, perhaps—a possible shifting of control from one brain hemisphere to the other—"

"Yes, thanks," he said. "I'll have Jefferson, over in neuropsych, check him over again. Were there any behavioral shifts accompanying this?"

She nodded.

"But it is hard to put a finger on it," she said. "It is just that he seems more—more animated—now, and there is an alert look, something about the way he moves his eyes, that was not there before."

"I had better go see him right now," Alec said. "Thanks again."

He made his way to Dennis' quarters, knocked and reached to open the door.

"Yes?" said a voice from within.

"It's me—Alec," he said. "May I come in?"

"Come in," said the voice, without inflection.

Dennis was seated by the window, sketchpad open on his lap. He looked up and smiled as Alec entered.

Alec approached, glanced down at the pad. It was filled with sketches of nearby buildings.

"Very good," he said. "I am glad to see that you are moving on to other subject matter."

Dennis smiled again.

"You seem to be in good spirits today. I am glad about that, too. Any special reason?"

Dennis shrugged.

"Say," Alec said, almost casually. "I didn't mean to trouble you the other day with that business about your name."

"No—trouble," Dennis said.

"*Do* you recall it, though?"

"Say—it—again."

"Dennis. Dennis Guise."

"Yes. Dennis Guise. Yes."

"Care for a little exercise?"

"Exer—cise?"

"Would you like to go for your walk now?"

"Oh. Yes. Yes. A walk. Exercise . . ."

Dennis closed the pad. He rose and crossed the room. He opened the door, held it for Alec.

Alec led him along their usual route toward the fountain.

"Anything special you would like to talk about?" he asked.

"Yes," Dennis immediately replied. "Talk about talk."

"I—I don't quite understand."

"Talk—ing. Parts."

"Words?"

"Yes. Words."

"Oh. You want to review your vocabulary. All right. Sure."

Alec began naming everything they passed. Suppressing excitement, he reviewed the parts of the body,

95

pronouns, basic verbs. Dennis' speech blossomed as they strolled.

Later, standing beside the fountain, Dennis asked, "How does it work, the fountain?"

"Oh, just a simple pump," Alex said.

"What sort of pump? I would like to see it."

"I am not certain exactly what kind of pump it is. I can speak with someone in maintenance later and probably get you a look at it. Maybe tomorrow."

"All right. Sure. Alec?"

"What?"

"I— Where are we?"

"This is the Luna Medical Facility II."

"Luna!"

"Yes, the moon. You are only just beginning to realize . . . ?"

Dennis had sagged back against the side of the fountain. Suddenly, he looked up.

"No overhead views from this section," Alec said. "If you would like, I can take you to an observation deck."

Dennis nodded vigorously.

"Please."

Alec took his arm.

"I guess that it would come as a shock—if you had not realized it, had not thought about it, all along. I should apologize. I am taking too many things for granted, because of the way you suddenly began communicating since you—since you . . ."

". . . became less mad?" Dennis finished, recovering his composure and smiling.

"No, no. That is the wrong word. Listen, do you have any understanding, of what has been happening to you, of what things have been like for you until today?"

Dennis shook his head.

"Not really," he said. "I wish that I did."

Alec tried a quick mental probe, but as on two earlier occasions during their walk that day, he could not get beyond the surface thoughts, forcused as they were on present circumstances with such force of concentration as to preclude access to anything beyond them.

"I see no reason not to tell you something about it," Alec said. "You have been ill much of your life with a condition brought on by your telepathic faculty. You were exposed to adult thoughts too soon—from birth—and they interfered with your own thinking, until now. Bringing you to the moon got you away from much of the interference. This has finally allowed you to achieve some stability, to sort things out, to begin to think for yourself, to become aware of who you are. Do you understand? You are just now beginning to come into your own as a rational being."

"I—think I see. The past is so cloudy . . ."

"Of course. The elevator is this way."

"What is a telepathic faculty?"

"Well . . . An ability to tell directly what other people are thinking."

"Oh."

"It was too much for a child to cope with."

"Yes."

"Do you have any idea what brought you out of it? Do you recall when your thoughts first came to include a measure of self-awareness?"

Dennis grinned.

"No. It is sort of like waking up," he said. "You are never certain when it begins, but there comes a time when it has occurred. I think it is still going on."

"Good."

Alec thumbed open a door, led Dennis within, pressed a button on the wall.

"I am—quite—ignorant," Dennis said. "Do not take it as a—relapse—if I ask about the obvious—or lack certain words."

"Lord, no! You are making progress right before my eyes. In fact, I find it difficult to believe this is really happening."

The elevator hummed about them. Dennis touched the wall and chuckled.

"So do I, so do I. Tell me, do you possess this—telepathic faculty—yourself?"

"Yes."

"Do many people?"

"No, we are a distinct minority."

"I see. Are you using yours on me?"

"No. I feel we are better off talking this way. The practice is good for you. Do you want to try the other?"

"Not just now. No."

"Good. I was coming to that. It may be better if you do not attempt it for a time. No sense running the risk of reopening old channels of vulnerability until you have toughened your psyche a bit more."

"That sounds reasonable."

The door opened. Alec led him out into the observation lounge—a long, curved room, chairs and benches spotted about it, lit only by the stars and the great globe of the Earth beyond the transparent bubble that roofed it.

Dennis gasped and flattened himself against the wall.

"It's all right," Alec said. "Safe. There is nothing to fear."

"Give me a chance," Dennis said. "Wait and let me look. Do not talk. God! It is lovely! Up there. The world . . . I have to paint it. How will I get the colors . . . here?"

"Ms. Brant will give you paints," Alec said.

"But the light . . ."

"There are alcoves farther along which can be illuminated—" He gestured. "You never realized . . . that all this was here? That this was where you were—the moon?"

"No. I—I want to sit in one of the chairs."

"Of course. Come on."

Alec led him to a pair of chairs, reclined them, saw Dennis into one, took the other himself. For perhaps an hour they regarded the sky. Alec tried probing Dennis twice during that time, but on both occasions was met with that fierce concentration which blocked further reading.

Finally, Dennis rose.

"It is almost too much," he said. "Let us go back now."

Alec nodded.

"Want to try eating in the cafeteria? Or would that be too much excitement for one day?"

"Let us try it and find out."

As they rode the elevator down, Alec remarked, "We will probably never know what specific thing it was that set off this improvement of yours."

"Probably not."

" . . . And there are many things about it which I do not understand."

Dennis smiled.

". . . But the one that puzzles me the most is where you could have picked up an Italian accent."

"If you ever find out, tell me," Dennis said.

Dr. Timura could detect no signs of neurological dysfunction. His main remarks centered about Dennis' interest in the testing equipment and his questions concerning localizations of function within the brain. He spent half an hour more than he had intended with Dennis, going over neural anatomy charts.

"Whatever did it," he told Alec later, "it was something functional—and you are asking the wrong man when it comes to that. It is more your area than mine."

"I had figured it was," Alec said. "We actually know so little about telepaths. . . ."

"For whatever it is worth, it looks as if the idea behind his being sent here in the first place has proved valid. It got him away from the adverse stimuli, gave him a breather, he took advantage of it and now he is pulling himself together. It just took a while to have its effect."

"Yes, there is that. But to come this far from borderline sentience in one day is—remarkable. He's got paint and canvas and a box of tapes now. He is asking questions about everything—"

"Long-suppressed curiosity coming to the fore? For that matter, there is no way of knowing what his intelligence level really was. Quite high, I'd guess."

"Granted, granted. But what about the time he thought he was Condorcet?"

"He had to have picked that up through some use of his telepathic faculty. You will probably never know exactly where."

"I suppose you are right, but there is something peculiar about his present state of consciousness, also."

"What is that?"

"I can't read him. I am a pretty good telepath myself, or I would not have gone into TP therapy work. But every time I try a scan, I never get a millimeter beyond his immediate object of concern. He possesses the concentration of a tournament chess player—at all times. *That* is not normal."

"There *are* other people like that. Artists, for example, when they are wrapped up in a piece of work. And he *is* interested in art."

"True. For that matter, he is an extremely powerful telepath, and it may be some sort of unconscious block he has set up. Do you think he might be moving too fast now, heading for some sort of reaction?"

Dr. Timura shrugged.

"There will probably be a reaction of some sort. Depression . . . Fatigue certainly, if he keeps going the way that he is. On the other hand, it might be worse to try to head it off at this point, while he is trying to learn everything he can. When he gets his belly full he will quit and digest his gains. It will be after that that your real work will begin. That's just my opinion, of course."

"Thanks. I'm grateful for any advice on this case."

"You have monitors in his room, don't you?"

"Of course, ever since he came here—and a few extras since the incident when he was Condorcet."

"Good, good. Why don't you give him some more time to himself now—since he is covered on that front—and see what he makes of it?"

"You mean stop therapy and give him his head?"

"Nothing quite that radical. But you are going to want to observe him a while before you decide what course of therapy is now in order. You do not want to keep things as highly structured as when he was barely able to get around on his own, do you?"

"No. That is true. I guess I will lie low a bit and let the machines do the watching. I will just drop in on him later to see how the painting is going—and observe. I will see you."

"Take care."

Alec knocked on the door, waited.

"Yes?"

"It's me—Alec."

"Come on in."

He entered, to find Dennis seated on the bed, a portable viewer set up at his side. Across the room stood an easel bearing a completed canvas. It was the skyscape as seen from the deck, the Earth prominent within it. Alec moved to stand before it.

"You did the whole thing that fast?" he said. "It's wonderful! And this is your first painting. It is very impressive."

"Acrylics are really something," Dennis replied. "No fooling around, and they dry fast. A lot better than oils when you are in a hurry."

"When did you ever use oils?"

"Well— What I meant was that it seemed that way. I had watched people using them back in class."

"I see. You continue to amaze me. What are you doing now?"

"Learning things. I have a lot of catching up to do."

"Maybe you ought to take it a bit easy at first."

"No problem. I am not tired yet."

"Care to take another walk?"

"To tell you the truth, I would rather stay here and keep working."

"I meant to ask you about reading. . . ."

"I seem to have absorbed the basics somewhere along the line. I am working on expanding things now."

"Well, that is just great. What about dinner? You have to eat. The cafeteria is open."

"That is true. All right."

He turned off the viewer and rose, stretched.

101

"On the way over, you can tell me what things are like back on Earth," he said, "and tell me about the telepaths."

Dennis let him out, listening.

That evening, Alec made a full report to Dr. Chalmers.

". . . And I got through to him at dinnertime," he said. "He agrees that he is Dennis Guise, but he does not really believe it. He says it for our benefit. He is personally convinced that he is Leonardo da Vinci."

Dr. Chalmers snorted.

"Are you being serious?"

"Of course."

Dr. Chalmers relit his pipe.

"I don't see any harm in it," he finally said. "I do see possible harm in trying to rid him of such a delusion at this point, when it is allowing him to make such fine progress."

"I agree on leaving the da Vinci aspect alone," Alec said. "But my concern with it goes far deeper. I am not at all certain that it is a delusion."

"What do you mean?"

"I got through to him at dinnertime. He was relaxed, his thoughts drifting. I tried a probe and succeeded. He believes he is da Vinci, does not want us to know it, is doing everything he can to make us believe he is a recovering Dennis Guise. At the same time, he is trying to learn everything he can about the world in which he now finds himself."

"That does not make it anything more than a paranoid situation—one which we are fortunately able to capitalize on."

Alec raised his hand.

"It seems more than just the belief, though. With Condorcet, he picked up the man's thinking as well as the French language. Now, with da Vinci, he has acquired artistic skills, and he shifted hands—da Vinci was left-handed, I just looked it up—and an almost pathological curiosity with respect to just about everything—"

102

"Then why isn't he speaking Italian?"

"Because this time he has taken his thought patterns from one of the greatest minds that ever existed, and he has decided to play along with us, to fit himself into the situation in which he finds himself. He has therefore been learning modern English all day, at a phenomenal rate. If you listen to him, though, you will hear that he speaks it with an Italian accent, which he is already attempting to cover. He is trying to adapt himself."

"The entire notion is preposterous. But even granting it for a moment, by what possible mechanism could he be achieving it?"

"All right. I have been doing a lot of thinking. How does telepathy work? We are still not certain. Our approach has been mainly practical. All of our telepathic security guards, communication specialists, psychological therapy workers, semantic engineers, precision translators, have worked out various ways of exploiting the faculty without really advancing our understanding as to its mechanism. Oh, we have our theorists, but they've really very little substance on which to base their guesses."

"So you've another guess to add to the list?"

"Yes. This is really all that it is. A guess—or a strange feeling. The reason Dennis was sent here in the first place was the phenomenal range of his ability. He is the most powerful telepath on record. Here, he was effectively blocked from reaching the sorts of minds for which he seemed to have an affinity—a matter of distance. He simply could not reach far enough to make the contacts he seemed to require. Now, what did that leave him?"

"He had to fall back on his own resources. He finally did so, according to plan, and he has now begun the recovery we had hoped for."

"Unless I am right about the continued personality assumption."

"Alec! Condorcet, da Vinci and anyone else he might have been play-acting—they are all dead. Surely you are not suggesting something like spiritualism?"

103

"No, sir. We know even less about the nature of time than we do about telepathy. I was wondering whether, frustrated in his efforts to reach across space, he has succeeded in driving his mind back through time and actually reaching those individuals whose identities he has assumed."

Dr. Chalmers sighed.

"As in paranoia," he said, "and as in those attempted age-regressions to other lives which amateur hypnotists occasionally write books about, one significant feature is that everybody wants to be important. No one identifies himself as a skid-row bum, a serf, a common laborer. It is invariably a king, a queen, a general, a great scientist, philosopher, prophet. Does that strike you as peculiar?"

"Not really. It simply strikes me as irrelevant to Dennis' case. Granting the ability to penetrate time, those are the sorts of minds to which one would be most attracted. They were certainly the most interesting. If I would reach back, they are the ones I would attempt to scan."

"All right. This is not getting us anywhere. You say you got through to him earlier, and he is indeed convinced that he is da Vinci."

"Yes."

"Whatever the source of this new identification, it is motivating him to do things he has never attempted before. It is therefore a good thing. Let him retain his delusion. We must capitalize on it as fully as possible."

"Even if he is not really Dennis Guise?"

"Look, he answers to Dennis Guise now and he acts the way he believes Dennis Guise should act. He is suddenly showing high intelligence and the beginnings of remarkable skills. If, in his heart of hearts, he chooses to believe he is Leonardo da Vinci pulling a fast one on a world of twenty-first-century clods, what difference does it make, so long as he behaves in an acceptable fashion in all other ways? We all have our pet daydreams and fun delusions. There are certain areas where therapy ceases to be therapeutic and simply becomes meddling. Leave him with his daydream. Teach

104

the outer man to behave in an acceptable fashion in society."

"But it is more than a daydream!"

"Alec! Hands off!"

"He is my patient."

"And I am your boss, here to make sure you do a proper job. I do not see a proper job as involving your proceeding along lines dictated by so tenuous a matter as this telepathy through time notion. We must act on the basis of knowledge, not guesswork. We do possess knowledge of paranoia, and have for a long time. Some forms are quite harmless. Leave him with that part and work on the rest. You will probably notice that as he gains more experience, becomes surer of himself, that part will simply fade away."

"You do not give me much choice."

"No, I do not."

"Okay, I will do as you say."

". . . And keep me posted, informally as well as through channels."

Alec nodded, turned to go.

"One thing more . . ." Dr. Chalmers said.

"Yes?"

"I would appreciate your keeping that notion about time to yourself, at least for now."

"Why?"

"Supposing there is something to it? Just supposing, of course. It would take a lot of substantiation, a lot of research. Premature publicity would be the worst thing."

"I understand."

"Good."

Alec went out, returned to his own quarters, stretched out on his bed to think. After a time, he slept.

The following day, Alec decided to leave Dennis alone with his studies and his painting, dropping by only at mealtimes. Dennis was not particularly communicative at breakfast or at lunch. Over dinner, however,

105

he grew more animated, leaning forward, fixing him with his gaze.

"This—telepathic ability," he began. "It is a strange and wondrous thing."

"I thought that you said you were not going to fool with it for a while."

"That was yesterday. I said that I would not experiment with it for a time. Very well. Time has passed. I grew curious."

Alec made a small noise with his lips and shook his head.

"You could be making a serious mistake . . ." he began.

"As it turned out, I was not. I can control it. It is amazing. I have learned so many things, so quickly, by taking them from other minds."

"Whose minds?" Alec asked.

Dennis smiled.

"I do not know that it is proper to say. From yours, for instance, I learned that there is a certain code of courtesy which precludes wanton browsing among the thoughts of others."

"I see that it impressed you a lot."

Dennis shrugged.

"It works both ways. If it does not apply to me, why should I observe it myself?"

"You already know the answer to that. Your status here is that of a patient. I am your therapist. It is a special situation."

"Then I do not see why I should be castigated for my actions by those who do not consider me fully responsible for them."

Alec chuckled.

"Very good," he said. "You are learning fast. Obviously, things should be revised very soon. In the meantime, all I can say is that it is just not nice."

Dennis nodded.

"No argument there. I have better uses for my time than voyeurism. No. I was leading up to a discussion of two things in which I am currently interested: my own case, and the telepathic function itself."

"If you have indeed been behaving as you indicated, then you probably know as much about them both as we do."

"Hardly," he said. "I cannot plumb the depths of your mind and dredge up all your experience and skill."

"Oh? Since when? You seemed able to manage it before."

"When?"

"Let me ask you a question first. Do you remember anything of other periods of clarity, times when you felt as if you were someone else?"

"I—I do not think so. Things—like dreams—sometimes come and go, though. Idle thoughts, occasional disjointed fragments of something like memory. But I do not really have much to associate with them. Do you mean that I *have* been other people, that everything I now feel and think is just some sort of—overlay? Are you saying that there is really someone else buried within me and that the person I think I am may be subject to recall at any time?"

"No, I am not saying that."

"What, then?"

"I do not know, Dennis. You know yourself better than I do. You appear to be learning things at a fantastic pace—"

"You do not believe that I am really Dennis Guise," he said.

"Are you?"

"That is a silly question."

"You raised it."

"You think that I am still some sort of overlay, and that the real Dennis Guise is still buried within me?"

"Dennis, I do not know. You are my patient. More than anything else, I want to see you fully recovered and functioning normally in society. It was never my intention to raise these doubts in your mind. A therapist just naturally tends to speculate, to go over every possibility, no matter how farfetched. Generally, these things remain unvoiced. At this point, it seems unfortu-

107

nate that you are such a good telepath and that you chose to exercise your ability just when you did."

"Then you are saying that you now feel you were wrong in this?"

"I am saying it was just one of those guesses one sometimes makes with very little to go on. Guesses are made and discarded countless times during a course of therapy. It should not really concern you."

Dennis took a drink of juice.

"But it does, you know," he said, after a time. "I am not tremendously fond of the notion that I am keeping the rightful inhabitant of this body, this brain, from his proper existence."

"Even if he may never be so fit as yourself to do so?"

"Even so."

"Beyond the fact that this is all idle speculation, I fail to see where there is much that you can do about your tenancy."

"I suppose you are right. It is an interesting hypothetical situation, however, and coming out of the dark as I so recently have, matters of an existential nature do hold a certain fascination."

"I can see that. However, I feel that this is not the best time to consider them—coming out of the dark as you so recently have, as you put it."

"I can see why a therapist would feel that way. . . . But I may be more stable than you realize."

"Then why are you expressing all these doubts about yourself? No. I want to give you support right now, not provide a dissection of your inner landscape. Let all this pass, will you? Concentrate on perfecting your strengths. After more time has passed, these problems may not seem as important as they do now."

"I have a feeling that you are talking for Dr. Chalmers rather than yourself."

"Then consider the idea, not its source. You were ill, you are getting better. These are two things we know, two things we have to work with. The hell with theory. The hell with speculation. Curb your introspective tendencies for the time being and concentrate on matters of substance."

"Easily said. But all right, let us drop it."

"Good. You realize that it is the next thing to miraculous that we are speaking of things at this level this soon? You are an amazing person. If this is any indication of what you are to become we should both be impressed."

"Yes, I guess that you are right. I should be thankful for this flash of existence which has been granted me. Now, just for purposes of rounding out my education, tell me about this telepathy through time business that I caught a thought or two concerning, here and there. Is there anything at all on it in the literature?"

"No. I have checked recently. There is not."

"Have you ever managed it yourself?"

"No."

"Any idea how it might be done?"

"None whatsoever."

"Pity, is it not—when you consider all the things that might be learned from the past, if it could be taken more seriously?"

"One day . . . Who knows?"

"Indeed," he said, and he rose from the table.

Alec stood also.

"Walk you back?" he asked.

"Thank you, but I would rather be alone. There are many things I wish to think about."

"All right. Sure. You know where my rooms are, if you should want to talk about anything—any time."

"Yes. Thanks again."

Alec watched him go, seated himself and finished his coffee.

The next day, Dennis did not take breakfast with Alec, nor did he invite him into his room. Through the partly opened door, he told him that he was very busy and was going to skip that meal. He offered no comment on the nature of his activities. After breakfast, Alec checked the tape in the monitor for Dennis' room, from which he learned that the light had been burning

109

all night and that Dennis had alternated between long periods at his easel and sitting motionless in his armchair.

Returning at lunchtime, Alec received no answer when he knocked on the door. He called out several times, but there was no response to this either. Finally, he opened the door and entered.

Dennis lay on the bed, clutching at his side. His eyes were fixed on the ceiling and a small trickle of saliva had run back over his cheek.

Alec moved to his side.

"Dennis! What is it?" he asked. "What happened?"

"I—" he said. "I—" and his eyes filled with tears.

"I'll get you a doctor," Alec said.

"I am—" Dennis said, and his face relaxed, his hands fell away from his side.

As Alec turned to go, his eyes fell upon the canvas still resting on the easel and he stood for several moments, staring.

It bore a study of the Mona Lisa, quite complete and exquisitely rendered, he thought, because acrylics are so much better than oils. That has to be it, he thought. I remember that that was his thought, right before he hurried out.

Part IV

I am.

I remember them all. There were so many. But I do not remember myself, because I was not there. Not before that moment.

It was in that moment that I first knew myself.

That moment.

Once there was a man. His name was Gilbert Van Duyn. We watched him in the General Assembly of the United Nations. Watched him get up to say that the preservation of the Earth required some sacrifice. Watched as the world froze about him. Watched him make his way through that still landscape of flesh. Watched him go out of the hall and meet the dark man. Watched them fly to the roof of the tower and regard the city, the world. Listened to the dark man's story. Watched them return to the ground. Watched Gilbert Van Duyn return to the hall, to the lectern. Watched as there was movement once more and the bullet struck us. Watched the blue flag as the life left us, by our own choice.

And in that moment we knew, I knew.

Once there was a man. And so I am.

He who showed me these things claimed that nothing was ever done. He died at that moment also, again, that I might live. Yet he lives in me still. A man there once was.

And I fled through all I had ever been, over that bridge of ashes, the past. To each, each, as he died or was conquered. And I was there. There were men. And I am so.

Fled that final image that gave me birth, each to

each to each, and it returned, ever, to the final sight of Gilbert Van Duyn's eyes, the first sight of my own. I. I fled.

Back, back to the place where the dark man lay bleeding. Dying? Dying also, like the others? But he lived, and rose, and moved again among his children. I saw through his eyes, and I knew. Once a man there was. And a woman. And I knew. I began to understand.

All, all, all of them came clear to me now. The hundreds I had known. Or was it more? There is no count. All. I knelt atop the building and raised the .30/06, sighting in on the governor. Fallen, I watched my blood pool as the Persian army pressed the attack. There, in the sand, I strove to create the calculus, when the sword came into me. And you, my Thérèse! Where are you tonight? My words have been eaten by the wind. My vision doubles in my head and the world is twice as monstrous. I squeeze the trigger and the man falls before thunder. I shift the barrel. Here in my cell, I contemplate the Terror and think upon the future of man. My own end will be small by comparison. I sketch the elements, here at Amboise, the great forces that walk naked in the air and on the seas, the high storms with their winds, the rushing of mighty waves. I shoot again and another man falls. I wipe the .30/06 quickly but carefully, as planned, lean it against the wall beside the mark of the Children of the Earth, turn, crouching, and begin my retreat along the rooftops. There, atop the building, I follow the dark man's gesture and regard the East River, a piece of muddy glass, and the hazed and grainy sky where strands of smoke lay like bloated things on a beach. Then to the other side, where I look upon the tangled city. Driving, driving through the night, a pain in my shoulder and hoping for rain. But the land lay still and rugged. So be it. I may prefer it another way, yet still it pleases me that the grasses are dry and the animals in their burrows. The pleasure and the pride of humanity are best enjoyed against the heedlessness, the slumbering power of the Earth. Even when it moves to crush, it adds something. To isolate oneself too much from it detracts from both our achievements and our failures. We must feel the forces we live with. . . .

And the white circle on the field of blue remains for a moment as all else collapses about me. Then it, too, fades and is gone. Only I remain, a rock fresh-exposed above the beat of the surf. I am Dennis Guise.

Alec has left the room, is hurrying to fetch a doctor. The pain lessens in my side as I understand.

Alec's recent thoughts echo within me and I turn my head to regard the acrylics which dry so fast, seeing there on the easel the lady he has left me, smiling.

Once there was a man.

I ran a fever. I know that I was delirious. I slept a lot. I was in and out of the fog countless times during the next couple of days. As things finally settled, I became aware once again of the dispensary ceiling and of Alec's gentle presence at my side.

"Got any water there?" I asked him.

"Just a minute," he said, and I heard him pour it. "Here you are."

He passed me a glass with a bent straw in it. I held it with both hands and drank.

"Thanks," I said, passing it back.

"How are you—feeling?"

I managed a chuckle. I could feel his mental probing. Better not to block it entirely at this point, or to let him know that I was blocking at all—or that I was even aware of his quick survey.

"I am—myself," I said. "Ask me my name, if you wish."

"Never mind. I would give a lot to understand all the preliminaries—to this."

"Me, too. I am weak. I feel well, though."

"What do you remember of the events of the past two months?"

"Not much. Fragments. Disconnected impressions."

"You *are* a new person."

"Glad to hear you say it. I think so, too."

"Well, I have a feeling that you have just taken a major step toward recovery."

"I could use another drink."

He refilled the glass and I emptied it. I covered my mouth and yawned after I had passed it back to him.

"You seem to be right-handed."

"So I do. I am sorry, but I think that I am going back to sleep again."

"Sure. Rest easy. I will be around. You should be up and out of here in no time now, unless my guess is way off."

I nodded and let my eyelids droop.

"Good," I said. "Glad to hear it."

I closed my eyes and let my mind swim. Alec rose and departed.

I knew, even then, what I had to do, and I was scared. I had to find one man, out of the entire population of the Earth, and ask him how to go about it. Which meant that I had to convince the staff here of my cure—I suppose that is a better word than "recovery," since I had never been normal—and of my continuing stability in order to be permitted to return to Earth. Which meant I must work to assure this condition. Time was essential, or so it seemed to me then. I hoped that I had not happened too late.

I was not at all clear as to the particulars of what it was that separated me from the others I had known and been. It seemed worth seeking the information just then, especially since there was not much else I could do at the moment. With a full medical staff about, it was just a matter of locating the proper person.

I moved forth with my mind, searching.

Shortly, I found that person, a woman working in the lab two buildings over, a molecular biologist, a Dr. Holmes. The thoughts were not right there at the surface, but there were indications that she had the concepts on file. I sought more deeply.

Yes. J. B. S. Haldane had once calculated that the deaths resulting from the operation of natural selection in the substitution of a new model gene for an old one were so great that the species could only afford the establishment of a new gene every millennium or so. This view had held sway for a long while, but then a new notion of mutationism arose in 1968. The rapid growth of molecular biology around that time had had a lot to do with it. In the February issue of that year's *Nature* there had appeared a paper by the geneticist Motoo Kimura, wherein he speculated over the great differences then recently determined to exist among the hemoglobin, cytochrome c and other molecules in various species of animals. They were much commoner than had previously been supposed. Considering the large number of molecules and genes, it would seem that a mutation must be established every few years. He felt that such a high rate of molecular evolution was only feasible if most of them were neither helpful nor harmful, representing random, neutral mutations drifting through populations. This raised hell among classical evolutionaries because it indicated that evolution might be influenced by a strong element of random genetic drift, in other words a much higher chance factor, than good old natural selection. The new techniques, put to work in earnest on seeking molecular alternatives in living populations, continued to uncover them in abundance—gratuitous changes, giving rise to molecular diversity. . . .

Which meant . . .

Which meant that the sleeping masters of human evolution, of whom the dark man had informed Van Duyn, could not possibly have a *complete* say in the development of the species. They would have had more control long ago, with a smaller population, in determining the route we would take. Once established as man, however, once spread across the entire globe and breeding our way through the hundreds of millions and finally the billions, there was no way to continue this control by means of whatever primary influences they had once exercised. Nor was this necessary, since we were proceeding in the proper direction. Once we were established as a rational, toolmaking crowd, their task shifted over to one of superintendancy, to keeping a watchful eye or three on our ideas, philosophies, technological developments, pruning the undesired and encouraging its opposite. This was all that they could do, once we had passed some numerical milestones. They could not fully predict nor control the random genetic developments which must arise with statistically greater frequency with the increasing population. It was no special response in terms of natural selection for mankind to have come up with the TP gene, but we had. There was no obvious threat in it, and the sleepers had not moved against us. Now, though, I existed. I understood the situation, I had access to the past experience of the race. . . .

And I was scared, for I would now have to get a clean bill of health and go looking for the man. . . .

And I was tired. Even thinking about it was going to have to wait a little longer. . . .

In the weeks and months that followed, I learned. I attended classes, I followed programmed courses of study, I listened to tapes and watched viewscreens, I talked with Alec and let him see what I wished him to see in my mind. I participated in group therapy sessions, I exercised my special talent to learn of more things. I waited.

During this time, I felt the easing of tension about me, and I came to regard Alec more as a friend than a therapist. We talked about a great variety of subjects, played games together in the gym. A later scan of Dr. Chalmers' thinking equipment even showed me that Alec had broached the subject of my return to Earth somewhat ahead of schedule.

"You really ought to be doing more calisthenics," Alec had said. "Knee bends with weights would be useful."

"Sounds awful," I replied.

"Can't let yourself waste away," he said. "Supposing they recommended a trial visit down yonder and you were in no shape to go?"

"Are they thinking about it?"

"I couldn't say. But if they were to, would you want to hang back for a month or so, just because you had not been paying attention to the physical preliminaries?"

"Now that you mention it," I said, "no. But the whole idea raises a matter I have not really spent any time thinking about."

"What is that?"

"My parents. I have already gathered that their separation is probably a permanent thing. When the time does come for me to go back, where do I go?"

Alec moistened his lips and looked away.

"Do not worry about all that anxiety business," I said. "It is a pretty neutral matter to me after all the sessions I have had with Dr. McGinley. I just want to know where I go when I do go."

"Dennis, the matter has not really been discussed yet. I do not know whether your parents will fight over your custody. Do you have a preference?"

"As I said, I have not really given the matter much thought. Would my choice count for much?"

"From all reports I have received, your parents are both reasonable people. They have been very pleased with your progress here. They both want to see you again. You have had letters from both of them. Was there anything in them that might influence your preference?"

"No."

"Then I can only suggest that you spend some time thinking about which one you would rather be with. There is still plenty of time. When the day does come that you have to make a choice, I can add a suggestion that it would be best for your adjustment to honor your preference—for whatever that may be worth."

"Thanks, Alec. Show me some of the exercises I should be doing, huh?"

. . . And this was what caused me to go rummaging in Dr. Chalmers' head. I had found myself loathe to probe Alec since we had become friends.

Later, I thought about the matters he had raised. My father had money, power, connections—all of which could be useful in my quest—and he was now living in Washington, near to so many other things and places which might benefit me in the search. My mother was still in northern New Mexico, tending her flowers, isolated. But my father would not have much time for me—a good thing, if that was all there would be to it. Only, with full access to my own impressions past, I could now form a picture of the man. It was my guess that he would enroll me in a fancy private school, someplace where they would make a fuss about nonattendance, would keep a tight rein on me. On the other hand, I was certain that I could persuade my mother to let me stay at home, coming and going pretty much as I chose, continuing my education in programmed units via a rented machine similar to the one I was using here. At least, I would have a better chance of working things that way with her than I would with him.

Then I asked myself another: Aside from these considerations, if everything else were simple and uncomplicated, who would I really want to go to?

I could not make up my mind. I almost welcomed the external factors, terrible as they were, which relieved me of the necessity of making a real choice.

And so I prepared myself, physically and mentally, for my return. A month later, the matter was mentioned officially. Dr. Chalmers came around to see me, commended my progress, told me he felt that perhaps another month of preparation and observation was in order and if everything continued as was expected I could go home and see how things worked out. It was then that he asked me which home I might prefer. Keeping in tune with the therapeutic note I had sounded, I told him that I felt the simpler the environment the more comfortable I might feel. He seemed to think that was a good choice, and I saw in his mind that I would have his recommendation, also.

Which is how things worked out. I was given a provisionally clean bill the following month and a date was set. I realized during that time that I was growing increasingly anxious, not so much over the task I had set myself, but simply at the thought of heading for that place in the sky, so full of people and things. I visited the observation deck on numerous occasions, assumed my old chair and watched the world, glowing, mysterious, attracting and frightening by turns, far and yet near. I fancied a summons, I assumed a threat.

Despite the exposure involved in all my vicarious existences and the sum of my salvaged personal impressions, I had never been there before, as a rational, individual being. I talked about it with Alec and he told me that it was a natural feeling, a thing to be expected, a thing that would vanish not too long after I got back. I had already thought these thoughts myself, but as with so many other conclusions, it was nevertheless comforting to hear them from another.

In my room, I paced, stared at the paintings, paced some more, thumbed through the sketches, again and again. The lady smiled.

Finally, I packed them all carefully and went to sit by the fountain. I walked among the flowerbeds.

I began taking all my meals in the cafeteria, and for the first time I began talking with the other patients. There was one old man whose eyes misted over when he learned that I was going back.

"Go to New Jersey," he said.

"New Jersey?"

"Not the cities. The pinelands. They still stand as they did when I was a boy. Go there one day and look at the trees. Get out and walk among them. If you ever do that, think of me then," he said. "Promise."

He reached out and laid a hand on my arm, veins like blue worms crawling across the back of his hand. He leaned forward and his breath was bad.

"Promise."

I nodded. I could not speak, for his tremor, his faded eyes, his odor, were lost in the barrage of thoughts that fell upon me: cranberries, huckleberries, blueberries, sweet fern, sheep laurel, dewy mornings, sunshot days, foggy evenings, bogs, the smell of pine, a gentle rainfall, autumn smoke, winter's chill, homemade whisky ... Pieces, textures ... Memories. His vanished youth. A place to which he literally could not go home. With difficulty, I raised a shield against these things.

"I will remember," I said finally; and thereafter I maintained a tight shield when speaking with my fellow patients.

When the time came, most of the staff and some of the patients turned out to see me off. I said my good-byes, to Alec, to Dr. Chalmers, to the others, then boarded the monorail that was to take me to Luna Station. I tried to hide my emotions with a forced casualness, not wanting them to think I was anything less than stable at this point. However, my voice broke and I embraced Alec before I boarded. This was, after all, the only real home I had known, as myself, Dennis Guise. I paid little heed to the rocks, the craters, the inky shadows I raced past. I thought only of what I was leaving and where I was going.

I was landed at the field in Texas, and my mother met me there. My first impressions of Earth were mainly of the countless thoughts which swirled about. It was easy to see how they had unbalanced me as a child. Now, though, I was able to put them aside, ignore them, force them into the background, turn them off.

"Dennis . . ." she said, and there were tears in her eyes. She kissed me. "You—you understand things now?"

"Yes," I said. "I'm all right."

. . . And all this does not bother you?

There was an initial shock. It has already passed. I can handle the thoughts now.

You will never know what it was like.

I remember some things.

It is so good to see you well, to finally know you. . . .

I nodded and tried to smile.

We are going home now. Come this way.

She took my arm and led me from the terminal.

How to begin?

It was strange, settling into my old room. I had

122

memories of the place, but it was almost as if they belonged to someone else, a phenomenon with which I was not entirely unfamiliar. I spent days of introspection, sifting through my old recollections of the place. This was less an exercise in morbidity than a search for things of value.

The teaching machine arrived and was installed. My father was footing the bill for it. I spoke with him on a number of occasions. He wanted me to come see him as soon as I felt able. He promised to come see me as soon as he could get away. I began using the machine.

Established now, with some of my feelings and thoughts sorted out, I commenced the efforts I had been contemplating since my arousal in the dispensary on Luna.

Each day, I undertook a telepathic search, swinging and skimming about the world, seeking one mind or some sign of its existence. The act was not as hopeless as it sounds, for I was certain that the one I sought would stand out like a beacon on a dark night. Even as the days passed without the slightest intimation of his existence, I did not grow discouraged. The world is a large place. I was learning things, I was refining my skills.

But the weeks passed and there was nothing. It had of course occurred to me that the man I sought might well be dead. It had been a long time since his last appearance. His enemies might finally have caught up with him. I redoubled my efforts. I could do nothing but keep looking.

It was on a Friday evening that I came across something peculiar. I had climbed a nearby hill, a concession to my mother's complaint that I was not getting enough exercise, and seated on a rock out of sight of the house I had set forth with my mind once again, casting first at places nearer to home. After a quarter of an hour of wandering, I encountered familiar thought-patterns. When I closed with them, I determined that they originated in Albuquerque, and I became aware of the thinker's plans for the following day. He would be heading north, and passing on the highway, not too far to the east. I was filled with excitement. He was not my quarry, but he was someone I greatly desired to meet.

When I returned to the house, my mother saw my face, felt my mood and smiled.

"I told you," she said. "Exercise. This is the best I've seen you look."

"Yes, Mother," I said.

"You will be in good condition for your surprise tomorrow."

"Surprise? What is it?"

"If I told you . . ." she began.

"It isn't Dad, is it? Is he coming?"

She looked away.

"No," she said, "not your father. You will just have to wait and see."

I thought of trying a probe, but she would have caught it and blocked it, I am certain. And she wanted it to be a surprise. I left it at that. I had more important matters to consider, anyhow.

I yawned.

"All this fresh air and altitude . . . I am going to turn in early."

"Good idea," she said, and kissed me.

I was up early the next morning. Before I even got out of bed, I reached out with my mind and found my man. Then I left a note saying that I had gone for a walk, and I made my way to a bluff above the highway. I seated myself and waited, listening to his thoughts as he drove on.

After a long while, the car came into view. I climbed down and waited at the side of the road.

When the vehicle drew near, I stepped out into the road and raised my hands. I was in his mind at the time and saw that he had noticed me and was going to stop. Else I would have gotten out of the way.

He braked to a halt and called out, "What's the matter, kid?"

I walked up beside the machine, studying the face of the man I had once been.

"Hello, Quick," I said. "It's been a while."

He stared at me, then shook his head.

"I'm sorry, he said. "I don't remember where . . ."

"I remember the shootout when they got Leishman," I said. "You got the last cop and made it away. They never did figure out who the other man was."

His eyes widened, then narrowed.

"Who the hell are you, anyway?"

"I have to talk with you. It's important."

"All right. Get in," he said.

"No, thanks. Why don't you pull off to the side and get out? We can climb up in those rocks across the way."

"Why?"

"It's a place to sit down."

"Is anyone else there?"

"No."

He pulled over, opened the door and stepped out.

"I want you to know something—" he began.

"—that you are carrying a loaded .32 automatic in the right-hand pocket of your jacket," I said, "and you intend to shoot anyone else you encounter the moment you see him. But I am not lying to you. There is no one else. I just want to talk."

"How did you—? Are you a telepath?"

"Yes."

"Okay. Anyplace special?"

"No. Just up."

"Lead on."

He followed me to the top, found himself a perch and lit a cigarette.

"What do you want?" he asked.

"First," I said, "I wanted to meet you. You see, once I was you."

"Come again?"

"I will have to tell you something about myself . . ." I began. And I did. I told him of my condition, of how I had become Leishman and been used to trace him, of how I had later, briefly, been Quick Smith. The sun was higher when I finished.

He had remained silent as I had spoken, nodding oc-

125

casionally. Now he sat, staring off toward the horizon, as if listening to some faraway voice. I waited for him to say something, but he did not.

I cleared my throat.

"That is—my story," I said, finally. "I wanted you to know that much before—"

"Yes, it is—quite interesting," he said then. "You certainly are a different sort of person. Now what?"

"Now? Now I was going to ask you, as the only COE member handy, whether you really believe that our rural past possessed all the virtues, whether all the clichés about cities might not make that past seem like something it never was, whether exploitation of the land and the people—like child labor—might not have been far worse in the old days, as it still is in agrarian countries today, whether the cities might not really offer more than they have taken when contrasted with that past."

"That was not what I meant when I said 'Now what?' and that is a string of loaded questions," he said. "But I will give you an answer anyway, before I go back to it. I am hardly a spokesman for the COE. I am just a dirtywork specialist. It is true that a lot of us might romanticize the simpler life, turn it into a pastoral. I am not one of them. I grew up on a farm. I was child labor myself. I do not have it in for the cities. In fact, they represented something I wanted to get away to as soon as I could swing it. They may well offer more than they have taken. I think that they probably do. I am just a dirty, mean little guy who was probably simply a troublemaker to begin with. If it had not been the COE it would have been something else—then. Your asking me these things makes me think back over it, though. Now, it is a bit different. But okay ... For all that, when I look back at my childhood, I see that I always loved the land. I can't romanticize it, I was too close to it. I am a conservationist, an environmentalist, an ecological activist—whatever term is currently fashionable—because I am pro-land, not anti-city. You set up a false dichotomy when you reeled off those questions. Being for the land does not mean being against the city. We cannot junk them all and turn back the clock. Not now. When we blow up a dam or screw up a source of pollution, we are not telling them to turn off all the technology in the world. We are telling them to be more judicious in its disposition, we are encouraging the consideration, the development, of alternatives. There are men who see no more in public lands than lumber, minerals, grazing and the building of dams, men who claim they are benefiting the people in this and are really only out for a fast buck. Rod told me the history of the national parks, for example. They faced this kind of invasion and destruction, with the same excuses offered, long before our present problems existed. I want to protect what remains of the natural world, that's all. Now you tell me something. I had asked you, 'Now what?' What I meant was, you have this powerful ability no other telepath seems to have developed yet. What are you going to do with it?"

"What do you mean?"

"Your interest in these matters seems more than simple curiosity. I could not help but wonder—"

His eyes flicked upward, past my shoulder.

I had not heard anyone approach, nor felt them with my mind, and I was not in Quick's mind at the moment. I turned.

She had come up the easy grade on the far side of the bluff. She seemed taller than I remembered, and a trifle thinner.

"Lydia!" I said, rising. "Mother spoke of a surprise. . . ."

She smiled.

"Hello, Dennis," she said. "Hello, Quick."

"You know each other?" I asked.

Quick nodded.

"Oh yes," he said. "We've met. A long time ago. How've you been?"

"Fine," she said, drawing nearer.

"Lydia is the therapist I mentioned," I said, "who took care of me. Before."

"Quick, you have changed," she said.

He nodded.

"Everyone does, I guess," he said.

She looked at me again.

Dennis, let me see you.

I nodded and felt her move further into my mind.

After a time, *Congratulations. We have succeeded,* she told me. *You exist. You have followed the leads that I left you. You are seeking . . . What?*

A man. The man who spoke with Van Duyn, years back.

Why?

To ask how I can help him with his efforts.

What makes you feel you have anything to offer?

You know that I am special.

You feel that is enough—being special?

I guess that is for him to decide.

It is good that you wish to help. Supposing he asked of you what he asked of Van Duyn?

I do not know. It would be a waste.

Perhaps. Whatever, I will help you in your search. So will this man.

How?

Later, Dennis. Later. All in good time. We had best get to your home now.

"You are heading north, Quick?" she asked.

"Denver, to spend a few days with some friends."

"Let me know where I can get in touch with you, all right? There is an enterprise in which you may be useful."

"Sure," he said, and he fished a piece of paper from his pocket, scrawled something on it, passed it to her. "I'll be at the first one till Tuesday, the next one afterward."

"Very good. Thank you. You may hear from me before too long. Have a nice trip."

"Thanks. So long."

"Goodbye."

He headed back down toward the road. We went the other way.

We walked back to where Lydia's car was parked on a side road. From there we drove on home, announcing that Lydia had encountered me on my morning hike. My mother prepared breakfast, and the morning was spent in conversation. After lunch, Lydia examined me at some length. I tried blocking in some areas, just to see what the result would be. She caught me on all of them.

Excellent, she told me after a long while. *You have exceeded my expectations.*

In what way?

I mean that you have pulled through beautifully.

That is not what you mean. You are masking something.

You are *good. Congratulations.*

That is not an answer.

Let us say then that it was really a form of directive therapy in which we engaged.

There was not really that much of me to direct.

I did not say that it was easy.

Did you influence the development of my temporo-pathic ability?

No, but I might have influenced the kinds of choices you would make if you did succeed in reaching back after other minds in times gone by.

Why?

I only said "might."

You did not come back just to play games with me, did you?

No. You will have your answers in good time.

Where does Quick figure in all this?

He did some work for me once.

Is there anything at all that you feel like telling me?

Yes, but you are not letting me. You are asking all the wrong questions.

What are the right ones?

I said that I would help you in your search. You said that you want to find the dark man. Had you asked me, I could have told you that he is still living. Had you asked me where, I could have told you that you will find him in East Africa.

You know him?

Yes, I know him.

I have searched, but I found no trace. . . .

You will not find him unless he chooses to be found.

Why is this?

His is a cautious way of life.

Yes, I gathered that they seek him in particular.

They may seek you now, also.

Why?

You have been broadcasting your presence ever since your return. They are suspicious of concentrations of power in the hands of a single individual. They must convince themselves it is harmless, tame it, turn it or destroy it.

Then I am in danger, even now?

It is possible. This is the reason I came so soon. You are firm in your decision?

I am.

Then we must leave as soon as possible. The longer we delay the less your chance of reaching your goal. They have human agents as well as mechanical devices.

Are the enemies TP, also?

That, or something like it. They have their ways of knowing things.

How shall we go about the whole business?

I have already obtained travel papers in your name. This evening we shall discuss with you mother your desire to see more of the world now that you are adjusted to this much of it. I will second the idea as a therapeutically sound thing. I believe that I can persuade her.

Supposing she wants to come along?

This possibility has been considered. Fortunately, her contacts with your father since your return seem to be leading them toward a reconciliation. I believe they are going to discuss the matter this evening. Should this come to pass, they might well appreciate your absence on a short trip.

How can you know all these things?

As a TP and a personal friend—

No! That is too much to ask me to believe.

What, then, would you believe?

The only alternative that presents itself. You are

130

devious, Lydia. I know that now, from my own case, from your plans for handling these things, from your acquaintanceship with a COE troubleshooter. I am forced to entertain the possibility that you possess considerable means for manipulating people and situations, that you are somehow responsible for my parents' breakup and their coming reconciliation, for my transfer to the moon—for the entire course my condition has taken. I suddenly look upon you as the architect of my existence.

Ridiculous!

Call it whatever you want. That is how I feel about it.

Then believe whatever you want. Does it affect your plans?

No. I am still going. I have to.

Good. Then the rest does not matter.

But it does. You see, I am not going to forget. If I live a few more years I am going to be even stronger than I am now. If I ever discover that you caused my parents needless pain, I want you to know that I am not going to forget.

She lowered her head.

So be it then.

And things worked out pretty much as Lydia had said. Dad called and wanted to come out. To see me, he said. Mother said okay, and he arrived the next day. I quickly saw that Lydia had been right. They hit things off and were talking friendly again right from the start. He was happy enough to see me, very happy. We had several long talks and even went walking together a few times. But it was plain that he had come back for more than that.

It began to occur to me about then that perhaps I had been too hard on Lydia. Common decency forbade my trying to probe my parents' thoughts at that time, but I suddenly realized that the strain of my prolonged condition must have been pretty hard on them, particularly on Dad. I may well have contributed to the initial breakup, just as my recovery might have served as catalyst to the reconciliation. It had been insensitive of me not to have realized this earlier. It began to seem possible that, though I still felt Lydia to be a manipulator, she had in this one respect merely capitalized on something already present, rather than creating the entire situation. It left her no less culpable, if she had somehow provided the necessary pushes at various points, but it softened the picture somewhat, if only through the mitigating agency of my own newfound guilt feelings.

And these feelings made me anxious to be under way, as anxious perhaps as my parents were for some time alone together. At least, they bought Lydia's endorsement of my request for a vacation, seeing that I would be accompanied by herself and a male nurse of her acquaintance.

"It's good to have you back, son."

It did not seem so ironic later that these were the last words my father said to me as Lydia and I boarded the flier that was to take us to Albuquerque. After the talks we had had I came to realize that my recovery was a source of pride to him—the fact that I had made it through a rough piece of existence— possibly even greater than his pleasure in knowing that my ability transcended any other on record. Mine was a sadder feeling than I had thought it would be, at another leave-taking this soon after my return. I waved to them as we rose and did not let down my shield till we reached the town.

The flight out of Albuquerque was uneventful. Lydia had warned me of the possibility of danger from that point on. But I scanned all my fellow passengers and found nothing alarming. In fact, it grew boring after a time, and I read most of the way to Libreville, in Gabon. Only Quick seemed constantly alert.

Shortly after our arrival, a man appeared at our hotel with a case full of pistols. Quick selected one—a revolver—and a box of cartridges. No money changed hands. Lydia shielded the man's mind, but I was still able to skim a few surface thoughts indicating his connection with a local COE-type group.

"With this," Lydia said to Quick, "you are in a position to take over my function as bodyguard. I have to go on ahead now to make arrangements, which gives you a little time to spend." She passed him a slip of paper. "Be at this field in Moanda at 1800 hours, tomorrow. You will be met there and transported east."

It was not clear to me how she could have been acting as a bodyguard, but then Quick had never seemed much like a male nurse either. I refrained from commenting.

"What is there to do in this town?" Quick asked her.

"For one thing, you can get out of it in a hurry," she replied, smiling. "There are more instructions on the back of the page. Take the shuttle down to Moanda tonight and go visit that place tomorrow."

Quick turned the sheet, read there, looked up.

"What do we do when we get there?"

"Sightsee. That is all. Look at that thing and think about it. Nothing more. An amusement perhaps. A way of passing the time."

"All right. Shall we get something to eat now?"

"Let's."

Lydia departed after dinner, and Quick and I returned to the hotel and checked out. We caught the shuttle and leaned back to watch the country pass. After a time, I dozed and did not awaken until we had reached our destination. It was quite late when we checked into the local hostel, and we turned in immediately.

I was awakened.

I had come around suddenly from a very deep sleep, a strong feeling of pursuit filling my mind. For several moments, I was Leishman again, wondering at the enemy's identity, assessing the unfamiliar surroundings, dim in the darkened room. Then I knew a sense of wrongness. This was someone else's game.

Look up, old man! We must answer! The blade comes out of the scabbard. . . .

I grew with the shudder which followed, and Leishman faded to something more than memory, less than controller.

I was in a better position than Leishman to understand the situation.

Some TP was attempting to scan us. I set up a partial block, covering my main thinking, leaving a jumble of reverie for his consideration: moonlight, shadow, the texture of the bedclothes, a small thirst, bladder pressure, the various night sounds from beyond the window. Within this fortress, I was troubled that he had already had a look at the Leishman persona.

I slid out of bed, crossed to the window, stood beside it and looked out.

The night was warm and a dank breeze was blowing from the direction of an irrigation ditch we had crossed earlier. The nearest streetlight was on a corner far to my right. Carefully, with thoughts and eyes, I sought the mental eavesdropper.

I became aware of a figure in a shadowed doorway up the street.

Still blocking, I retreated, moved to Quick's bedside. I placed a hand on his shoulder.

He gave no physical sign of having come awake, but said softly, "What is it?"

I moved to cover his thoughts, also. I said, "There is a TP trying to read us. I am preventing it. He is across the street, in a doorway to the right. What should we do?"

He did not answer, but sat up, reached for his trousers, pulled them on. He stuck his feet into his boots and rose, running both hands through his hair.

"Keep preventing him," he said, drawing on his shirt and crossing to the door, buttoning it as he went. "Lock the door after me."

"The gun is still under your pillow."

"That's a good place for it."

I locked the door and followed him with my mind, holding a total shield about his thoughts. I found it easier than I thought it would be to maintain my own partial shield while doing this—slow stream of consciousness, surface thoughts leaking. I returned to my bed and lay down.

As the minutes passed, I realized that the observer was not merely observing. A gentle but definite pressure began to occur as he tried to influence my exposed train of reverie. It was something I had never attempted myself: taking control of another mind. I permitted him to gain his simple objectives, wondering the while whether I should make an effort to try the same maneuver on him.

Before I could make the decision, however, the pressure was off and the sounds of a scuffle occurred beyond the window. I dropped my shields and raced across the room. I could make out little beyond the movement of shadows within a courtyard to the left of the doorway our observer had occupied. I moved into Quick's mind and was swept up by a sequence of motor activity.

. . . We were blocking a knife thrust, then chopping with the edge of our hand. We kicked then and closed for a succession of blows. There was a brief pause, then a final, calculated chop. . . .

I broke off contact immediately. I lay quietly and attempted to still my mind.

Later, when I let Quick in, I asked him, "What did you do with the body?"

"Irrigation ditch," he said.

"I suppose it was necessary . . . ?"

"He didn't give me much choice."

"And if he had?"

"I hate hypothetical questions."

He returned to his bed, got in. I went back to mine.

"How much do you know about where we are going, what we are going to find there?" I asked him.

"Absolutely nothing. Lydia says it is important. That is enough."

"How is it that you know her?"

He coughed. Then, "I'd supposed you had found that in my mind."

"I don't go poking around in my friends' heads."

"Good to hear," he said.

135

"So how did you meet her?"

"She saved me once when I was running from the police. Came up to me on the street in Omaha, called me by name and told me I had better go with her if I wanted to be safe. So I did. She put me up for a couple of days and got me out of town. She got me fake papers and a legitimate job while I was lying low. Later, I did some work for her."

"What sort of work?"

"Oh, you might say courier, guard, delivery boy."

"I don't quite follow you."

"That's all right. Go to sleep."

"Is she COE?"

He was silent for a time. Then, "I don't really know," he said. "Sometimes I think so. But I have never been certain. She is certainly sympathetic."

"I see."

"Probably not. G'night."

" 'Night."

In the morning we had a bad breakfast and found transportation out to the site. I did some probing but was unable to discover any sign that a body had been found in the ditch. Perhaps it had not yet been located. Or perhaps it was a common occurrence and excited no special interest.

It took over an hour to get out to the mine and the temperature was already beginning to rise out of the comfort range when we arrived. A number of our fellow passengers proved to be part of a tour. We stayed near them to benefit from their guide's explanations.

Following, we approached an abandoned open pit mine, taking a trail that led around to its far side. We drew up beside a railed-in area. As we walked, the guide had explained that it once was a uranium mine, from which over 800 tons of the metal had been extracted annually in the late twentieth century, until it finally gave out. Most of it had gone to France.

". . . And here," he said, leaning on the rail and gesturing, "is the truly interesting area. It was here that, back in the last century, the miners suddenly came upon strata bearing abnormally rich ore. It was about 10 percent per weight of the soil, as opposed to 0.4 percent elsewhere in the area. The deposit was also unusual in that the uranium 235 isotope which normally occurs in natural uranium was almost entirely absent. This discovery, of course, led to considerable interest and study, resulting in the conclusion that you are looking at the remains of a natural nuclear reactor."

There were appreciative mumblings from the dozen or so persons before us. I moved nearer to the rail for a better look. It was not especially impressive—a big, rocky pit, scarred, gouged, gravelly at the bottom.

Fitting. A place like this perhaps, where the Galilean went to be tempted. . . . Is this irony necessary, new Lord? You have wrested the earth from its keepers to throw it away. . . . It is another world you claim to lead them to. . . . You care no more for the green, the brown, the gold, the glades, the glens, than this dry, hot place of rock and sand . . . and of death. What is death to you? A gateway . . .

". . . It was a spontaneous fission process which ran for over a million years," the guide went on. "We still have no idea as to what set it off in the first place. Nor can we say what genetic effect it may have had on local life forms. It could well have been quite spectacular. The resultant mutants could have spread themselves throughout the world in those millions of years since it burned itself out. Who knows what plant or animal, common today, owes its origin to the atomic pile which once smoldered here? Makes you stop and think." He paused to grin. "The world might be an entirely different place than it is today, were it not for the rocks from this strange hole in the ground—the only natural atomic pile of which we have ever found evidence."

"Didn't mankind originate in Africa?" one of the tourists asked.

"Many researchers believe so," answered the guide.

"Then could it be possible that this place had something to do with it?"

The guide smiled again. I could see in his mind that

he had heard the same question countless times before. He began a measured reply.

"Of course no one can say for certain. But it is curious that . . ."

I tapped Quick's shoulder.

"I get the idea," I said. "Let's go."

He nodded, and we turned away and made our way back to the transportation stand.

"It was very interesting," he said. "But I wonder why she wanted us to see it?"

"My benefit," I said. "I had never heard of it."

"Really? I thought everyone had."

"My education is still pretty limited. She wanted to prove something to me."

"What?"

"That something I was already positive I had experienced was not just some sort of psychic plant, from back when she was my therapist—and that the story I heard under those circumstances had something like a factual basis. All this, in case I started to wonder. All right. I believe her. Damn it!"

"I am afraid I do not understand."

"That's okay. I guess I am really talking to myself. Quick, I'm scared."

"Of what?"

"That guy last night. They have human agents. I had not known about that until just recently. I should have guessed as much, but I didn't."

"Who has human agents? What are you talking about? You are going too fast for me."

"She never told you about the enemy?"

"No."

"She must know, if she knows the man I am looking for, knows as much else as she does. . . ."

"Then I guess she just did not see fit to tell me."

"Well, I do. I've got to tell someone."

I did not finish till we were back in town, back at the hotel. When I had, he shook his head. He lit a cigarette.

"Damnedest story I ever heard," he said.

"You don't believe it?"

138

"I do believe it. Wish I didn't. It makes a kind of ghastly sense. I do not understand what you are going to do to help the situation, though."

"Neither do I."

"Let's get packed and go eat. Then we had better find that airfield."

I nodded, and we did.

Night. Crossing the Congo in a small flier. Quick, me, a nameless pilot. The only light in our small box in the sky came from the dim dials of the instrument board and the glow of Quick's cigarette. We flew low. I watched the night sky and communed with my other selves. Slowly, I began to appreciate what might lie ahead.

"Something out there," Quick said.

He was looking to the left, his head tilted slightly downward. I unfastened my belt and rose partway from my seat to follow his gaze.

Sixteen or seventeen meters off and three down, a dark shape paced us. Its form was birdlike, but its wings did not move. It was perhaps a meter in length, and half again that from wingtip to still wingtip. I probed, but no infrahuman awareness met my scrutiny.

"That is no bird," Quick said, "at this speed, gliding that way."

"You are right," I told him.

He swung his side window farther open and rested his left forearm on the frame. He lay his right wrist atop it, and I saw that he had the pistol in his hand. I raised my voice to be heard over the wind.

"I do not think that is going to do any good."

"Let's find out."

He fired. There came a bell-like tone.

... *And I remembered the beast, driving in among the rocks, its horns slashing toward my belly. Inches short, it began to throw its weight from side to side, spatulate legs continuing their paddlelike movement, body ringing like a great bell each time that it struck against the stone. I could smell the dried brine....*

"Didn't faze it," he said.

The pilot shouted a query, and Quick yelled, "Take it up."

We began to climb.

"No good," he muttered half a minute later.

"Quick, I do not think we are going to get rid of it," I said, "and it has not made any hostile moves."

He nodded and put the pistol away. He adjusted the window.

"Just an observer, huh?"

"I think so."

"Ours or theirs?"

"Theirs."

"What makes you think so?"

"It reminds me of something else—from long ago."

"And we should just let it be?"

"I think we have no choice."

He sighed. He lit another cigarette.

It followed us that entire night, all across the Congo. The first time we landed—a fueling stop at a primitive field, used mainly by smugglers, according to our pilot's thinking—the bird-thing simply circled overhead.

Aloft again, it took up its position once more. I slept for a time, and when I awoke we were over Uganda and a pale light was infusing the sky before us. I was still feeling fatigued but was unable to return to sleep. Our escort was a piece of the night, reflecting nothing of the morning's illumination. Each time we fueled it waited, joining us again when we resumed flight.

The full light of day flashed upon Lake Victoria. I searched ahead with my mind. Something. For a moment, I detected something bright and powerful, and then it was gone. I ate a sandwich and drank some tea. We crossed into Kenya, kept going. I thought back to whatever it was I had touched upon, and I began to grow nervous. Toward what were we rushing and what would be expected of me? In myself I was nothing, possessed of no special skills beyond my TP abilities. Was this the desired quantity? Or would it be better to confront whatever lay ahead in the person of some greater individual I had been? I could reach out so eas-

140

ily to touch once again those minds. . . . But then, I had no way of knowing which to choose. I watched the land pass beneath us—green, brown, yellow. Quick had finally nodded and was breathing gently. The pilot's mind indicated that our next stop would be at the Somali coast, our destination.

The bird-thing left us when we disembarked at that final landing, streaking eastward, dwindling, gone. I was feeling faintly feverish, a combination of the fatigue and the tension, I supposed. It was a sunny afternoon, and we were near the center of a freshly cleared area. A new-looking hut stood across from us. Both the hut and a stack of fuel drums were concealed beneath thatched canopies. I sensed two presences within the structure—a mechanic and his assistant, who would shortly be checking over the flier and fueling it. Our pilot entered and spoke with them in Swahili. Neither knew what we were to do next.

"Quick, I don't feel so good," I said.

"I'd imagine. You don't look so good. How about a drink?"

"Okay."

I thought he meant water, but he produced a small flask from one of the many pockets in his bush trousers and passed it to me.

I took a long swallow of brandy, coughed, thanked him and passed it back.

"Have you any idea what we do now?" he asked.

I realized suddenly that I did. My tension, my physical distress, my anxiety, my curiosity and my desire were instantly fused into an aching from which I reached out, moving in the direction of the vanished shadowbird. I felt once again the presence I had touched upon earlier, and in that moment realized that it now lay upon me to make my own way. I turned east and began walking toward the sea, of which we had had a glimpse on the way down. Yes, it felt right to be doing that. There was some sort of easing of pressure as I moved.

Quick was beside me, reaching toward my shoulder.

"Hey! Where you going?"

"This way," I said, avoiding his hand. "Stay here. There is nothing more for you to do."

"The hell you say! I am your bodyguard till Lydia discharges me." He fell into step beside me. "Now, what happened?"

"I know where I must go."

"Great. You could have told me, though."

"It may be better if you do not accompany me."

"Why?"

"You could be injured."

"I'll take my chances. I have to be certain you get where you are going—all the way."

"Come on, then. I have warned you."

There was a trail through the brush. I followed it. When it turned right, I did not. By then the brush had thinned, however, and we were able to make steady progress. The way slanted gently downward for a time.

"Heading toward the water?" Quick asked.

"I think so."

"You said I could be injured. Can you be more particular as to the nature of the threat?"

"No. I do not know what it is. It is just a feeling that I have. They really only want me."

"Who are 'they'?"

"I haven't any idea now."

Walking. The way grew steeper. I continued to feel feverish, but I now regarded myself in an almost abstract fashion. It was as if, having hosted so many minds, my body might be something of a way station, a place where I, too, was but a passing fragment of the humanity come to temporarily inhabit it, ready to abandon it to another when my stay was done. I steered it over outcrops of shale, occasionally using my hands in steeper spots.

"Dennis, I think we ought to stop to rest," Quick said after a time.

"No. I have to go on."

"You are breathing hard and you've cut your hand. Sit down. There!" He indicated a flat-topped stone.

"No."

He seized me by the shoulders. I found myself seated on the flat-topped stone.

"Drink some water." He passed me a canteen. "Now let me see that hand."

He dressed my right hand as I drank. Then he lit a cigarette and readjusted his belt holster to place the pistol in a more accessible position.

"I cannot believe that Lydia wants you to get there in less than good shape."

"It doesn't matter, Quick. Something is drawing me toward it now, making me regret every moment I waste like this. It does not matter if I get there tired. It is my mind that is important."

"Never slight your body, Dennis. You might be capable of all manner of mental gymnastics—but these days everybody talks so much about psychosomatics that I think they sometimes forget it works the other way around. If you want that mind of yours in good shape for whatever lies ahead you will be a little kinder to the anatomy and psysiology that go along with it."

"I cannot look at it that way just now."

"Then it's a good thing I came along."

We rested for several more minutes. Then Quick ground out his cigarette and nodded to me. I got to my feet and continued down the slope. I decided against further thinking. My emotions were numb and I no longer trusted my intellect. I concentrated on moving in the direction which summoned me with greater authority with each step that I took. I felt that I was no longer in a position to judge anything, but that I could only respond to what was presented to me. Whether this feeling itself was a response planted in my mind long ago by Lydia, or whether it was a totally appropriate reaction dictated by the physiology of survival I would probably never know.

The man hurries toward the meadow his party had crossed earlier. There had been a rocky knoll in its midst. . . .

He breaks into the open, running toward the hillock. From the thunder at his back, he is already aware that

*he will be unable to attain a sufficient vantage in time
to roll rocks down upon his pursuer.*

*He races toward a stony cleft, slips within it and
turns, crouching.*

The ground leveled off and we entered an area of
heavier brush. I located a trail, though, and we continued to make good progress. Perhaps twenty minutes
later, the foliage began to thin. At the same time, the
trail took a downward turn. We moved along until it
lost itself in the place where the brush dwindled to low
shrubbery and dry grasses. I still knew the way—better
than ever, for the strength of the summons continued
to grow—and I bore toward my left through an area of
sandier soil.

At length, we came to a hill and climbed it. From its
top, the sea was now visible, perhaps two miles distant,
green, sparkling.

Old.

The sea and this land, both.

I halted for a moment. It was the first time in my
life that the concept of vast ages struck me in just that
fashion. I suppose that my youth had something to do
with it. I had not existed long enough for the accumu-
lation of much personal history; consequently, I had
never reflected on the nature of duration as it applied
to me. As for those other lives I had touched during
my stay on the moon, the time spans which separated
us meant nothing when I could simply reach them as I
would call to a friend across a room. But this, this
prospect of rock and water, told me of geological chro-
nology in a way that even the view from the moon had
not. There, though I had seen the world *in toto*, bright
and lovely, I was too removed, too distant—too new to
the fact of seeing, perhaps—to look upon it as more
than a celestial artifact, cunningly wrought, existing in
the moment. And the moon itself, about/above me . . .
The static character of its airless surface, its mo-
tionlessness . . . It was a place where time was frozen,
process outlawed. . . .

And so the present vista made me think for the first
time, as my own thoughts, of the age of the world, of

its—lifetime. It made me think of all the tamperings with its life systems. And suddenly, in the play of the afternoon light upon water and this small corner of Africa's old estate, I saw my movement as something more than a compulsion. More, even, than a duty; though this, too, was of it. There rose in me the desire to do anything to preserve the ancient land and waters of my world against the planned obsolesence which had pursued them across countless afternoons—perhaps since the stoking of the now-dead reactor in Moanda. I realized, too, that I might not be what I am but for that ancient device. Yet, I had to be more than a windup toy. We all did, or life was meaningless. The dark man had told Van Duyn that the one answer to the course of human affairs, the answer no longer taken seriously—the teleological one—was correct. We had had a rule of determinism forced upon us. Only by breaking it, somehow, could we save our home, our lives. . . .

Whatever was asked of me, that now was my desire.

But tell me . . . Is anything ever done?

I headed down the hill, my eyes on the coastline. The beach was dun, rock-strewn; the sea drew creamy curves along its length. I smelled it now in the racing wind. Dark birds circled, slid above its waves. A finger of land almost touched the water below and to my left. I could not see beyond it, to where my course led me.

Fifteen minutes later, we trod the sand and the pebbles, moving to round that prominence. I could hear the calls of the birds, the splash of the waves, feel the cold force of the winds. . . .

The wind blows on, the world goes as it will, coursing the same route it would have taken had I never been at all. . . .

The force that was drawing me grew into vision, so that I saw the dark man standing facing the sea before we passed the rocky hill and beheld him with our eyes.

He knew that I was there, though he did not look in my direction. I could sense this awareness within his consciousness. Most of his attention, however, was focused on something farther east, beneath the waters.

Quick halted, his hand upon the butt of his weapon.

"Who is it?" he asked.

"The dark man," I said, "who spoke with Van Duyn. The ancient enemy of our ancient enemies. He who was gored."

The man turned and regarded us. He was of medium height. He had on shorts and unlaced tennis shoes. He wore a medallion about his neck. He leaned upon a lance of dull metal. I felt the full force of his attention shift toward me.

Dennis Guise. This is the time and the place. Things are ready. Are you?

Yes. But I do not understand.

He smiled across the ten or twelve meters that separated us. Neither of us moved to draw nearer.

. . . The vision of Van Duyn as he looked at the East River, as he looked out across the silent city . . .

I have seen. I remember. It is not this which I do not understand.

Quick caught my eye.

"What is happening?" he asked.

I raised my hand.

Quick nodded.

"I hear him," he breathed.

They dwell out there, the man indicated, gesturing with his spear, *beneath the waters. I come to this place periodically, to speak with them. As always, I have been attempting to convince them that their plan is failing, that mankind is more complex, has become less responsive to their promptings than they had anticipated, that sufficient remedial action has been taken to thwart them, that something has been learned from all man's missteps, that it is time for them to concede the game and depart.*

Do they answer you? I asked.

Yes. They maintain the opposite.

How can such a matter be resolved?

By means of an example.

What am I to do?

You must go to them and let them examine you.

146

How will that win your case? I asked. *What can I show them?*

But even as I asked it, realization after realization swept over me. It was as if this dark stranger, rather than Lydia, were my only begetter, and that he had treated me as the enemy had treated the entire race, shaping my life—my illness, my recovery, the precise nature of each of my experiences—manipulating me to the extent necessary to produce just such a being as myself at this moment, in this place, so that he might give me to the enemy to examine in any way they saw fit, hopefully demonstrating that mankind had changed from the being of their original specifications, and that—as I now knew from my experience of history— the past is not lost to us, is not a bridge that has been burned leaving only ashes, but rather is an open way, that all of history is there to be explored, learned from, and even if they destroy me, more such as myself may arise at any time. He would offer me as a symbol, an example, showing that the race has learned and continues to learn from its mistakes.

You gave Van Duyn a choice, I told him.

How can I do it for you when I already know your answer?

I lowered my head.

The dice were loaded then, too.

There was no other way. There still is not.

I looked out at the waters, up at the sky, down at the beach. I might never see them again, I realized.

Where are they? I finally asked.

I will call them.

He turned away, facing the waters.

"And now?" Quick asked. "What is he doing?"

"Summoning my judges."

He placed his hand on his pistol.

"I don't like the sound of that."

"It must be."

"All right. Then what I do must be also, if they try to harm you."

"You must not interfere. You know what is at stake."

147

He did not answer, but jerked his eyes from mine and stared out over the waters. Even before I turned and looked I saw it in his mind.

A sphere with a mirror finish had broken the surface of the sea. As I watched, it advanced. I could not judge its size or distance accurately. Reaching out, I detected living presences within, of some order of thought which I could not approach. They were aware of my scrutiny and they gave me no more than this glimpse.

It came rolling in, gleaming, circular, enormous. It struck a sandbar or some obstruction, perhaps forty meters offshore, and maybe a quarter-mile north of where I stood. There it rested.

The entire affair was managed without a sound interposed among the wind and the waves, the cries of the birds. As I watched, an opening appeared on the shoreward surface of the globe and a ramp was slowly extruded, slanting down into the water, just as soundlessly as the vessel's arrival.

They have come. The rest is up to you.

I licked my lips, tasted salt, nodded. I took a step forward. Quick moved with me.

No, said the dark man, and Quick froze in his tracks, reminiscent of the audience we— I had seen at the General Assembly meeting, that day, both long ago and yesterday.

I continued on. I approached the dark man, passed him on the seaward side. He was as expressionless as I knew myself to be at that moment. He clasped my shoulder as I went by. That was all.

As I paced beside the lapping waves, I thought of Quick, immobile. It had to be that way. He would have taken a shot at anything that tried to touch me. We could appreciate that. It was so simple. . . . We . . . For suddenly it seemed that I was no longer alone. My mind had played some trick, reaching out unconsciously perhaps, in some peculiar fashion, so that it was as if I were simultaneously myself and one other. Somehow, Roderick Leishman was with me. I felt that if I turned around I would see him walking at my back.

I did not turn around. I continued, my eyes fixed on the globe, far ahead, wave-washed, spray-swept, laced by the flight of dipping, pivoting birds.

The birds ... Their flight ... I saw them as through a stroboscope, slowing, the details of each movement clearly recorded in my brain, ready at a moment's notice to be transferred to my sketchpad.

... And it was as if Leonardo da Vinci walked beside Leishman at my back.

We passed on, scuffing sand, seeing where the surf drew its lines ... as it had that day, aye, near Syracuse, where we almost captured the calculus ages early.

Archimedes joined da Vinci and Leishman, as we moved on in this ancient place, this land still virtually untouched, still throbbing with the pulse of the clean elements, oh gods, and might it be that man could live in greater harmony with your bounty.... And Julian, Flavius Claudius Julianus, last of the old defenders, was with me, to be joined moments later by Jean Jacques Rousseau, staggering.

And as I walked, as at the head of an army, the others came, and I reached out across the bridge, no longer ashes, touching one by one, two by two, then dozens of the men I had been, filling myself with their presences—all of those who had been defeated in the name of man, great failures and small, suppressed men of learning, broken geniuses, talents cut short, twisted, destroyed—I was immersed within their number, but I was one of them: the switchboard, the contact, the point man. There was Leonardo; there, Condorcet; there, Van Duyn ...

As I waded out into the surf, approaching the downshot ramp, I made the final leap back, to become the dying god-king who will be resurrected to a sweet-smelling springtime, he whose sons and sons' sons have hunted the land since before the hills were made, he who had spoken with the powers beneath the sea, he who had summoned them here, he who stood now

149

upon the beach with his spear upraised. I was the dark man, who bore all names.

Walking up the ramp, as in slow motion, we entered the darkened interior of the vessel, seeing nothing. But we could feel their presences, cold and powerful, scrutinizing the thing man had become. . . .

Walk. This way.

And we were guided. We felt them. We saw nothing.

Around the vessel, slowly, counterclockwise, we stepped, moving beneath the pitiless gaze of our makers. . . .

Time, somehow, meant nothing. We paraded before them. All of us they had thought destroyed. Back again. Moving through the darkness of their judgment.

And then there was light. Far ahead. We hesitated.

Keep walking, man.

We continued on in the direction of the light. As we drew near, we saw that it was a port, not unlike the one by which we had come in. Only . . . the day was waning now, the sun falling behind the rocky shoreline bluff to the west. I halted.

Keep going, man.

Is that all you have to say to me? After all this time? After all that has been done?

Goodbye.

I found myself moving once more, down the ramp, into the water, shoreward. I did not look back until I had reached the beach. When I did, the vessel was gone.

I found that I was shaking as I headed back to the spot where the dark man still stood. Somewhere along the way I lost my companions. Quick lay, apparently asleep, on the sand. He stretched and yawned as I approached.

"Come this way," the dark man said. "The moon is up. The tide is rising."

Quick and I followed him down the beach and retreated back along it. He moved a stone and dug beneath it with his spear. He uncovered a cache of supplies and proceeded to build a brushwood fire.

"What now?" Quick asked.

"Eat with me and wait with me," he said.

We did. The sun had gone away and the stars come out. The fire warmed us against a chill wind. A heavy moon silvered the waters.

Long into that night we waited. It was Quick who suddenly stood and pointed out over the ocean.

The moon, now westering, turned their surfaces to pale fire.

Like bubbles they rose from the sea and lifted into the air, climbing the night. I watched, losing count quickly, as they rose, climbed, vanished, rose, climbed, vanished, like strings of pearls losing themselves among stars.

"They are going!" Quick said.

"Yes," answered our companion.

"Will they try the same thing somewhere else?" Quick asked.

"Of course."

"But we have won? The world is ours once more?"

"So it seems, with no one to blame but ourselves for whatever follows."

For perhaps another hour we watched, until the sky was empty of them once again. Our companion was smiling in the firelight, when suddenly his expression changed and he clutched at the medallion he wore.

He was on his feet in an instant.

"What is it?" Quick asked.

"Get out of here! Now!" he shouted.

He scrambled to where his spear stood upright in the sand.

Then I heard it, a deep, hooting sound, rolling in over the waves, rising, becoming a whistle, vanishing somewhere above the audible. I was stricken, unable to move with the sudden clutch of fear that took me then. Reflexively, I reached out with my mind, but there was nothing there.

"Go! Get out!" he shouted again. "Hurry!"

At that moment, the sound came once again, much nearer, and some dark form rose from the waters and advanced toward us across the wide expanse of the beach. Quick dragged me to my feet and pushed me in the direction of the foothills. I stumbled forward, broke into a run.

Our companion was retreating also. When I glanced back, I saw streaks of moonlight upon a moving shape. It was long and supple; it appeared to be scaled. We departed the beach and began to climb. Behind us, the sound bellowed forth once more. It was coming at an extremely rapid pace, and in the moments of silence following its challenge I could hear a metallic clicking as it passed over stones, pebbles. Shortly, I felt a vibration within the ground.

We climbed. Our ancient oppressors had departed, but they had left this final doom for their greatest enemy. I saw this within the dark man's mind.

We reached the place where the grasses began, and then low shrubbery. I hoped that the slope might slow something of such obvious bulk as our pursuer. But its next blast was even louder than the previous. The ground was definitely shaking now. When I looked again, moonlight glinted on a great horned head and unnaturally crooked legs, splayed almost sideways, digging into the ground, propelling it through all obstacles. It was almost upon us.

The dark man swerved, moving away from us. It followed him, knocking down trees, dislodging rocks. Quick turned and pursued it across the slope. I heard his pistol firing. It rang like a bell with each shot as the rounds ricocheted from it.

The dark man turned to face it, bracing his lance against the slope. The beast rushed upon it, and I heard a grinding, rasping noise. The entire scene was, for a moment, frozen in the moonlight, like some awful statue: the beast had halted, the lance half-buried within it somewhere beneath the head, the dark man straining to hold it.

Then the head swung, once, and a horn caught the dark man somewhere low, throwing him far to the side. At that moment, it rang once more as Quick struck the back of that head with a large rock. It slumped then

152

and lay still. Whether Quick's blow had done it or whether it was already finished, we would never know.

I rushed to the dark man's side. Moments later, Quick joined me, breathing heavily. Our companion was still alive, but he was unconscious. His side was very wet.

"Good God!" said Quick, tearing off his shirt, folding it, pressing it against the wound. "I think he's had it! There is no hospital anywhere near—"

"Leave him. Go. Get back to your flier. Never speak of this," came a familiar voice which I could not for the moment recognize.

When I turned, I saw that it was Lydia, coming down the slope.

"Your job is finished," she said. "Take the boy home, Quick."

"Lydia," he said, "we can't just go."

"There is nothing more for you to do here. Leave him to me. Go!"

I reached out with my mind. There was still life within the dark man, but it continued to wane.

"But—"

"Now!"

She gestured up the slope, and something about the way she did it made us turn that way.

"Come on, kid," Quick said. "Don't say anything else."

I went with him. He was right about not saying anything else. I could not have, even if there had been something to say. We walked, and I wanted to look back, but I was unable to do that either.

After a time, when we were higher and moving through heavier brush, passing among trees once more, I heard a sound like singing, from far away. I could not fully hear nor understand the words and I tried to listen with my mind.

. . . *Trees and mountains, streams and plains, how can this thing be?* I seemed to hear. *Rend yourselves, hide yourselves, spill yourselves over, weep* . . .

I— I staggered. For a moment, I seemed to be lying

there, bleeding, my head in her lap. Then the song was lost to me, there among the trees.

We hurried on, through the faded remains of the night.

ABOUT THE AUTHOR

ROGER ZELAZNY is an expatriate Ohioan who now resides on a mountaintop in New Mexico with his wife, Judy; sons Devin and Trent; daughter, Shannon; assorted typewriters, oriental rugs, unanswered letters, and science fiction awards. The awards, which he keeps close on hand in his office— "Never can tell when you might need one in a hurry" —consist of three Hugos, three Nebulas, a Balrog, and the mystical presence of the Prix Apollo. He has had 26 books published, and his works have been translated into 14 foreign languages, transcribed in Braille, and done as Talking Books. One of his novels was made into a movie, and another has been sold for the same purpose. He is currently working on a new novel. Available in a Signet edition is Roger Zelazny's fine novel, JACK OF SHADOWS.

More SIGNET Books by Robert A. Heinlein

- [ ] **ASSIGNMENT IN ETERNITY** (#J9360—$1.95)
- [ ] **BEYOND THIS HORIZON** (#J9833—$1.95)
- [ ] **THE DAY AFTER TOMORROW** (#W7766—$1.50)
- [ ] **THE DOOR INTO SUMMER** (#J9628—$1.95)
- [ ] **DOUBLE STAR** (#W8188—$1.50)
- [ ] **THE GREEN HILLS OF EARTH** (#J9952—$1.95)
- [ ] **THE MAN WHO SOLD THE MOON** (#J8717—$1.95)
- [ ] **THE MENACE FROM EARTH** (#E9870—$2.25)
- [ ] **METHUSELAH'S CHILDREN** (#E9875—$2.25)
- [ ] **THE PUPPET MASTERS** (#E8538—$1.75)
- [ ] **WALDO & MAGIC, INC.** (#J9754—$1.95)

Buy them at your local bookstore or use this convenient coupon for ordering.

THE NEW AMERICAN LIBRARY, INC.
P.O. Box 999, Bergenfield, New Jersey 07621

Please send me the SIGNET BOOKS I have checked above. I am enclosing
$_____(please add 50¢ to this order to cover postage and
handling). Send check or money order—no cash or C.O.D.'s. Prices and numbers
are subject to change without notice.

Name _____

Address _____

City_____ State_____ Zip Code_____
Allow 4-6 weeks for delivery.
This offer is subject to withdrawal without notice.

More MENTOR and SIGNET Reference Books

☐ **ALL ABOUT WORDS by Maxwell Numberg and Morris Rosenblum.** Two language experts call on history, folklore, and anecdotes to explain the origin, development, and meaning of words. (#ME1879—$2.25)

☐ **HOW DOES IT WORK? by Richard Koff.** A practical and entertaining guide to the workings of everyday things—from air conditioners to zippers. Illustrated. (#W6920—$1.50)

☐ **BEGIN CHESS by D. B. Pritchard.** An introduction to the game and to the basics of tactics and strategy. Foreword by Samuel Reshevesky, International Grand Master and former American chess champion. (#W9516—$1.50)

☐ **WORDS OF SCIENCE and the History Behind Them by Isaac Asimov.** A famous author makes the language of science accessible to all. Some 1500 terms are traced through history, from their simple roots in the language of bygone times—to their complicated usages today. (#MJ1799—$1.95)

☐ **WORDS FROM THE MYTHS by Isaac Asimov.** A fascinating exploration of our living heritage from the ancient world. Isaac Asimov retells the ancient stories—from Chaos to the siege of Troy—and describes their influence on modern language . . . and modern life. (#W9362—$1.50)

Buy them at your local bookstore or use this convenient coupon for ordering.

THE NEW AMERICAN LIBRARY, INC.
P.O. Box 999, Bergenfield, New Jersey 07621

Please send me the SIGNET and MENTOR BOOKS I have checked above. I am enclosing $_____ (please add 50¢ to this order to cover postage and handling). Send check or money order—no cash or C.O.D.'s. Prices and numbers are subject to change without notice.

Name _____

Address _____

City _____ State _____ Zip Code _____

Allow 4-6 weeks for delivery.
This offer is subject to withdrawal without notice.

SIGNET Books You'll Enjoy

☐ **TRIPLE** by Ken Follett. (#E9447—$3.50)

☐ **EYE OF THE NEEDLE** by Ken Follett. (#E9550—$3.50)

☐ **THE REVENANT** by Brana Lobel. (#E9451—$2.25)*

☐ **THE BLACK HORDE** by Richard Lewis. (#E9454—$1.75)

☐ **A FEAST FOR SPIDERS** by Kenneth L. Evans. (#J9484—$1.95)*

☐ **THE DARK** by James Herbert. (#E9403—$2.95)

☐ **THE DEATH MECHANIC** by A. D. Hutter. (#J9410—$1.95)*

☐ **THE MAGNATE** by Jack Mayfield. (#E9411—$2.25)*

☐ **THE SURROGATE** by Nick Sharman. (#E9293—$2.50)*

☐ **THE SCOURGE** by Nick Sharman. (#E9114—$2.25)*

☐ **INTENSIVE FEAR** by Nick Christian. (#E9341—$2.25)*

☐ **AUCTION!** by Tom Murphy. (#E9478—$2.95)

☐ **ELISE** by Sara Reavin. (#E9483—$2.95)

☐ **HAWK OF MAY** by Gillian Bradshaw. (#E9765—$2.75)*

☐ **GAMEMAKER** by David Cohter. (#E9766—$2.50)*

☐ **CUBAN DEATH-LIFT** (3rd in the MacMorgan series) by Randy Striker. (#J9768—$1.95)*

* Price slightly higher in Canada

Buy them at your local bookstore or use this convenient coupon for ordering.

THE NEW AMERICAN LIBRARY, INC.,
P.O. Box 999, Bergenfield, New Jersey 07621

Please send me the SIGNET BOOKS I have checked above. I am enclosing $_____ (please add 50¢ to this order to cover postage and handling). Send check or money order—no cash or C.O.D.'s. Prices and numbers are subject to change without notice.

Name _____

Address _____

City_____ State_____ Zip Code_____

Allow 4-6 weeks for delivery.
This offer is subject to withdrawal without notice.